To Peter

wr

C000153959

L James

25 - 11 - 17.

A Rough Kind of Magic

Louise James

authorHOUSE®

AuthorHouse™ UK
1663 Liberty Drive
Bloomington, IN 47403 USA
www.authorhouse.co.uk
Phone: 0800.197.4150

Published by AuthorHouse 04/22/2017

ISBN: 978-1-5246-8049-7 (sc)
ISBN: 978-1-5246-8050-3 (e)

Print information available on the last page.

For Bryan and our children
Phillip Christopher Lester Julie Linzi Gareth
And in loving memory of 'Pops' Arthur Thomas James
Who wanted to see this book in print.

Acknowledgements

I wish to thank all the team at AuthorHouse for publishing my books.

Thank you Jude Cure and her team for talking me into this one I did have doubts. Thanks to the graphic team who I know will sort out my illustrations as usual.

To Bob and Chrissie Thompson for their work on the electronics which enabled me to send my work so quickly.

As ever I am grateful for the help and advice from all of you. Thank you.

Chapter 1

'Put your head down a moment lad' The words barely penetrated but Greg felt the firm pressure urging his head down to his knees. As the swirling mists cleared he looked up to the sympathetic face of the nurse bending over him. He shuddered, pulling himself together with a tremendous effort out of the void which threatened to engulf him; bile rose in his throat gagging him, the nurse moved swiftly to bring a bowl and tissues. The keen grey eyes of the consultant met his with compassion. He sat up straight meeting those eyes with a great effort, His head swimming.

'How long do I have?' he demanded.

Mr McLaughlin spread his hands eyeing the young man appraisingly. He recognised the type only straight talking would suit this one. Greg Morgan stood before him, six foot two in his socks, his body deeply tanned from sailing and his work on the oil rig, muscles honed to perfection with physical work and exercise routines. His hair dark and curling, eyes that could turn to steel with anger or lighten to deep sparkling green with laughter, a wide sensitive moth and dimpled chin, he was a hit with the girls, one describing him as "Sex on legs and lovely with it". At the moment he didn't feel like either.

Mr Mcloughlin looked him over thinking it was so unfair that such a young specimen of manhood should have this burden; no one looking at him could begin to guess at the closing heart that could not be repaired. A transplant the only answer but Greg's blood contained rare antibodies which made finding a donor more difficult. The failure to find one in time was a grim possibility.

'We didn't want to find this Greg.' The Consultant placed a hand on his shoulder.

'I am not going to hide the truth from you. We don't have a lot of time to spare. You are young and very fit but without that replacement all I can estimate is a year to eighteen months but keep your courage, an urgent call will be on its way. You will have a bleeper which will alert you day or night once a donor is found and we will be waiting. You have a repeat prescription which you can pick up anywhere and we will keep a close eye on you. You must give up your job at once, rest, just laze about, no more keep fit routines. Do you have anyone you can stay with rather than live alone?'

'My parents, they live in Swansea.' Greg turned away and began to dress. 'Just tell me how I can look after myself. I must get my life in order.'

'It will take time for you to accept and I know you haven't taken it in yet. Take care of yourself, avoid smoking or smoky atmospheres, take a little alcohol but not to excess. Plenty of rest out where the air is clean and pure, mountains or sea preferably (looking no climbing) plain food, no fats, no sugars, no stress, don't get overtired, sleep with windows open but keep warm and dry. If you get problems come back and we'll sort you out. Think positive, any day we may receive the message. It's all in the hands of God. I cannot do more for you at present, you know the score. I have been as straight as I can because I know you wouldn't want anything less

Greg held out his hand. 'Thank you for that. I have to cope with this in my own way although I don't know how.' Mr McLoughlin shook his hand firmly.

'I know you will. Don't forget that bleeper can go off any time. Keep faith in that.

As the door closed behind him, Nurse Romsey busied herself clearing up the consultation room. She glanced at the consultant who was standing at the window looking out at the Plane tree overhanging the courtyard, a green film beginning to spread over its branches where sparrows squabbled as they picked at minute insects in the bark, spring was on its way. Mr Mcloughlin was a tall grey haired man liked by his patients and a situation like this was not uncommon to him but his face at the moment was grim. He murmured to himself 'Sometimes I think we are here to work miracles and we do, other times I feel completely useless'

Nurse Romsey softly closed the door behind her. Her throat was full of tears she was seldom affected by patients but today had tugged her heartstrings and if she didn't leave quickly she would sob her heart out. She too had a grown-up son of about the same age; her heart bled for his parents.

Greg found himself in his car without any recollection of how he got there. He sat keys in hand feeling nothing. The nausea and fainting he had experienced earlier was replaced by numbness, all thoughts and feelings were suspended, although he was dimly aware perhaps he should not be driving, no one had told him so he sat completely lost. His first impulse was that of a small child, he wanted to run to his mother's arms, sob his heart out, have her hold him and tell him it would be alright. 'Mam, make it right' he whispered but his parents were far away, he'd have to keep this to himself for a while; it couldn't be told over the phone, he would have to go to them and tell them that their son was ill. How could he tell them already in their sixties that their only child was almost certain to die before they did. He was alone very frightened. How he needed their strength at the moment. He sat back in the driving seat looking at his hands on the steering wheel, broad well shaped hands with artistic tapering fingers. He held his hand up to the sunlight seeing the transparency of skin almost seeing the pink glow of blood flowing through; for how long?

He suddenly found himself wanting Stephanie his ex-fiancée wishing that she wasn't ex. He had always been able to talk to her but in reality he was glad that particular entanglement was over because that is what it had become more than a relationship. They had lived together for almost six years, their intention to marry postponed time and time again. First they had planned to go into the hotel business together, then realising that Greg was happy in his career, they planned a large fashionable wedding (Steph's parents were expecting it and more than happy to pay for it themselves) this was postponed yet again as Stephanie headed for promotion in the well-known fashion house where she was head buyer. Greg himself was away for weeks at a time, plans for home and family drifting further and further away.

Greg coming home late one night finding Stephanie out sat for a long time deep in thought. She was obviously dining yet again with bosses or clients he didn't know which suddenly realising he really didn't care. He knew they had grown worlds apart and it had become pointless at least for him. He waited until she returned towards dawn, not missing her; not particularly caring where she was or who with, realising how long it had been since they had shared time and friends, talked about their future. It had been a long time since they had made love as lovers only taking each other out of need and habit.

Steph had crept in at five startled to find him waiting more startled when a cold, calm Greg told her that it was over. She had cried, stormed, shouted and raged but Greg sensing through her tears a savagely wounded pride greater than the loss of their love, stood firm. They had argued for a week before she moved out to stay with a friend, he had loved her once but it was over, only now in this dark place did he have a regret that now he had no one to hold on to, an only child he was used to being alone. After his break –up with Stephanie he spent most of his time on the rig where he had several good friends, united in their work and the confined off shore life they led. On leave he'd missed Steph for a while but his good looks and humorous charm always bought him a date if he needed one. His biggest problem was keeping his flat empty and his life unencumbered; here his best mate Ray Bower was the expert at loving and leaving the girls so Greg took a few tips off Ray and was happy however in this awful moment of truth, he missed Steph, her cool practicality and common sense might have kept his mind balanced. He felt at the moment it might soon snap. It was too late now, Steph must not come back, not only unfair to her but she was an organiser and Greg hated to be organised. He started the car, aware that the impact of what he had just learned had not yet hit him and a storm was yet to come. He swung the Jaguar into the traffic. He needed to be at the place he called home although he felt more at home in his cabin on the rig.

As the car idled at the lights, he realised to all intents and purposes his life didn't amount to much in the face of what he had just learned. The flat was his, no mortgage and he had savings, and financially he was well off not that he would be for long if he couldn't work. His pride and joy was his car, his heart always lifted when he could drive her around. The bright red Jaguar Mark 11 had been acquired through a friend of a friend when he was looking for something special. He and Ray had worked hard to bring her to concourse condition he had probably given her more tender care than he had Steph; perhaps that had been part of the problem. The lights changed and momentarily he felt the usual deep thrill he always felt as the car leapt forward. How long would he be able to drive? Not long, the pain and fatigue would make it impossible even before the doctors stopped him; he was surprised that Mcloughlin hadn't already done it. At the top of the hill, Greg slammed into top gear swooping down to the seafront where he turned left continuing a further couple of miles then turning into a side road where he came to a stop in front of double garage doors. The instinct to go to ground was now overpowering.

He slammed the car doors locking them and made for the stairs ignoring the lift although he knew that he shouldn't; he let himself panting into the long quiet room, flinging himself onto the wide couch, he wept.

The day moved into night and the room darkened but the man never stirred. From deep uncontrolled sobbing had come exhausted sleep, sounds from the street drifting into silence.

Chapter 2

The cold light of dawn slid through the undrawn curtains, its fingers crept over the thick blue carpet, trailed across the misty prints on the walls, caught the gleam of the Egyptian figurines on the cabinet, finally touching almost as a caress the dark head hanging over the edge of the couch showing harshly the ravages of the night. Exhaustion had sent Greg into a deep sleep an hour before dawn but even as the window lightened he lifted a haggard face staring about him. Within seconds came remembrance and he groaned aloud, pulling himself up, he sat head in hands until the clock on the wall chimed the hour of six.

He rose staggering into the little kitchen, the need for coffee and painkillers keeping him busy for a moment then he was back on the window seat looking out where a triangle of sea spread like a silver hand between the buildings. Exhaustion and tension had brought back the nagging ache that gripped spasmodically though his chest and back; the strange pains that he had ignored as indigestion for weeks until their increased severity had sent him to the medical officer on the rig who after some tests had sent him to the mainland hospital for more until the final confrontation with the consultant. Now he knew.

When the phone rang sharp in the silence, glancing at the clock he saw with surprise it was a quarter to eight, early for a call. He let it ring, he was the only emergency now, he thought savagely. 'It's my time." The phone rang and rang with monotonous regularity when it stopped the silence flowed back almost tangibly. An hour later it rang again, Greg cowered on the window seat wrapped in himself like a whipped dog. Time passed unnoticed, he sat unmoving, not thinking numb.

The phone shrilled again midday, cutting into Greg's frozen state like a knife. He picked it up instinctively, his arm pins and needles. A cheerful voice the other end shouted down at him.

"Hey you, what time do you call this? The day's half over, called you at eight I've tried several times and your mobiles off. Thought you were coming on the boat today? We've missed the tide now!"

Greg tried to get his voice to work it came out gruff and strange. 'Sorry Ray, I forgot must have caught a bug or something- sleeping it off with a dose of whisky'

'The hell you are' answered his long-time friend. "Come on man and have lunch with Sheena and me. I'll give Mandy a ring she'll come if you do, like a shot."

"Sorry, Ray no." Greg took command of his senses. "Some other time mate, honestly I'm bushed."

"You ok, really? Want me to come over? Hey, you were going to see the doc yesterday, weren't you; you alright kid?"

"I'm eighteen today, honestly I'm fine, can't tell you anything yet though, will as soon as I can. Catch you. Ok. Going back to bed now, see yer."

As he put the phone down a tight knot of anger began to build deep in his being, it grew until he didn't know if he would explode or go mad. A great rage filled him, choking, hot, filling his throat, searing across his brain. 'Why? In God's name why? He had a right to life. Who dared cheat him out of it at only thirty-five?' A deep hatred of himself for housing the monstrosity, the doctors for not having a cure, God for allowing it to happen, the consultant for telling him, anybody, everybody, his mother for giving him birth. His rage filled his mouth with bile, his head with pain, a tight band growing ever tighter, red mist blurred his vision, and loud roaring filled his ears. With a howl like a wounded animal he swept the collection of statuettes, that Steph had bought him, from the cupboard, the clock he hurled against the wall. The lust for destruction sent him crazy, he swept the shelves bare, hurled pictures from the walls, tore at cushions, kicking over tables he threw lamps wrenching the sockets from the walls whimpering like an animal red mist clouding his vision. For what seemed an eternity he tore, smashed and destroyed. When the storm finally burned itself out, he lay in a heap on the floor with no sense of time or feeling, complete darkness.

He came to slowly aware of cold and wet, the room dark. He lay contemplating the fact. Something cold and sticky was annoying him, it could be blood, his blood, he wondered if it mattered, finding to his surprise it did. Perhaps he had better have a look, gingerly levering himself up with the arm of the chair he was leaning against, he found he was light headed strangely without pain but disorientated. He realised that he hadn't eaten, couldn't remember when he had last eaten. He thought he must have some kind of injury but was quiet definitely hungry. Pulling himself to his feet he moved to find the light switch crunching china and glass beneath his feet. 'Hell!' he exclaimed as he slid in something in something soft and squishy. The room leaped into light. He stood staring in disbelief. The mess was appalling, china, glass, tapes lay broken everywhere. Earth and plants, fillings from cushions and papers from the desk lay scattered over the carpet. His computer thankfully remained untouched but the pool he had been lying in proved to be the remains of weed and dead fish from the aquarium which now lay on its side seeping water, a few fish still flopping in the small amount of water remaining. Splashes of blood were everywhere, looking down he saw it dripping steadily from a deep cut in his hand; for a moment the madness came back. Why not take a piece of glass and cut his wrists or his throat? It would soon be over Why not put an end to it now?

His stomach growled loudly and he burst into almost uncontrollable laughter, 'I'll do it later but I had better eat something first, damn and blast it all, I'm bloody hungry'. The irony of this struck him and he laughed until he cried again heartbroken. His sobs gradually died away, in their place grew slowly a great calm; watching the blood from his hand dripping onto a broken plate at his feet; a sense of peace entered his heart and held him as gently as a child rocked in safe arms, a strange feeling of almost contentment eased his tired brain, he was aware of sanity returning. He crouched down again on the floor, absorbed in wonder something had entered his soul out of the pit, the sensation of strong arms lifting him gently and firmly driving away the madness, pain and fear.

A car backfiring in the street roused him and a deep growl from his empty stomach forced him into action. The cut in his hand was still bleeding though more slowly; crunching his way to the bathroom he washed it clean and bound it as best he could. It didn't appear to need stitches. He looked at himself in the mirror, a haggard face with bloodshot eyes looked back, and a few strange lines around the eyes had not been there before. His clothes were creased, smelling of stale sweat and vomit. His natural fastidiousness sent him into the shower where he stood a long time under the hot before switching to cold. With a shaking hand but a calm eye he shaved and dressed in fresh jeans and a dark blue shirt. He drank a bottle of milk from the fridge, his stomach churned then settled. 'Thank God I didn't turn myself lose in the kitchen' he thought wryly.

He scrambled eggs, making toast and coffee, eating hungrily before arming himself with black bags, dustpan and brush. Two hours later his room although with deleted possessions was somehow back to a semblance of normality except for the ruined carpet, tired out he crawled into bed and into a deep sleep.

Next morning he carried the remaining fish in their bowl to a house down the street where he knocked firmly. The door flew open and a very small person with a tousled head of dark curls appeared around it. There was a shriek of delight. 'Uncle Greg's here. Mummy, Mummy, it Uncle Greg and he's got fishes!"

A tall slim woman came running down the stairs. "Hi Greg haven't seen you in a long while, you want to come in?" Her American accent softened after years of travelling with her nomadic husband Lee Ross, Patsy was good to look at even first thing in the morning. Huge pansy brown eyes and a riot of curls like her daughter Patsy drew attention wherever she went. An army family, friends of Stephanie, it had been difficult to remain so after the breakup though Lee and Greg sometimes met at the social club Samantha their adorable four year old adored Uncle Greg and he often brought her small gifts. Now Sammy stood at the door finger on lips her sparkling violet eyes questioningly on the bowl of pretty coloured fish.

"Not at the moment thanks, Patsy. Hey Sammy, do you think Daddy would like some more fish for his tank?"

"My tank" stated Sammy emphatically. "My fish, Daddy only cleans them for me."

Patsy and Greg laughed.

"Well! Here are a few more for you," smiled Greg handing the bowl to her mother. "I had an accident with my tank and I don't have time to set it up again at present, I thought Sammy might like them?"

"Course I do." Sammy held up her arms for a kiss. Greg crouched to her level and felt warm arms around his neck. "Thank you Uncle Greg. I'll go tell the others they are coming." She ran off down the passage.

"Thank you Greg." Patsy noticed his hand. Why, you've hurt yourself." He put his bandaged hand into his pocket. Patsy was staring at him.

"You alright Honey? You look kind of sick since I last saw you. Won't you come in and visit for a while? I was so upset about you and Steph, she babysits sometimes. She's alright now but you look awful. Anything I can do you just say. Come on in."

"No, I can't just now but thank you. Can I ask a favour? I am going to see my parents for a while I may move down there, I'm selling my flat but I don't yet know my plans. There is a lot of food in my freezer and I have plants, you know the sort of things. Could I unload them on you? Sorry to be a nuisance, say if you'd rather not and I'll dump them."

"Sure you can, glad to help but we don't want to say goodbye Greg. Do you have to go?"

"I think it will be for the best, I will know more when I get back. I'll pop the perishables around in the morning. Thank you."

"Anytime Honey, I'll make room in the big icebox today. Hope you come back soon. Greg, should I say anything to Stephanie?"

'Lord, no It's all over and she knows that, better not to mention it at all. Say goodbye to Lee if I don't see him before I go." She kissed him briefly before closing the door. Greg decided he would leave the goods in the porch early in the morning rather than face further questions. He sat in thought that evening. His new found calm still with him, his mind clear. The storm had passed, cleansed him, throwing him like flotsam on the beach, high above the tide of his agony and anger. Rebellion still burned within him but the fire was taking a more positive role, almost forcing him to make decisions. He took mental stock. He would have liked to throw himself into his work, he loved it and was good at it, work until the pain and illness forced him to stop but he knew the firm he was contracted to would not allow it. Mr McLaughlin would make his report, he would be granted indefinite sick leave but after a reasonable time they would pressurise for a replacement far better to retire gracefully. He was damned if he would go into any rest home to lie waiting for a donor to be found, he would rather go out in Ray's boat and end it there. That thought struck him for a moment then Mr McLoughlin's last words to him were. 'While there is life there is hope and hope springs eternal' No he was no coward. The madness had passed in the night along with his anger and fear. He would see it through to the end, whatever it was but where and with whom? He had better find an answer soon. He thought of his parents. John and Sally Morgan were people rather set in middle-age. The blow he was about to give them would be devastating. He hadn't lived with them for years there was no way he could live with them now. He loved them dearly but couldn't stand his mother's protective attentions His heart bled for them, telling them would have to be a gradual process. He could say that he was exhausted and came home to have a break and rest, blood condition maybe. They would have to know the truth sooner or later but he would play it cool until he decided what he wanted to do. Thoughts whirled through his head like leaves. His mother had been upset over his break up with Steph and might think this a good time to get them back together. No way, the one thing he was going to do in the time that he had was to please himself as much as possible. He didn't know how much mobility time he had the time would come surely when he would have to be nursed so he would make sure of this precious time and presume that a donor would be found. As he sat pondering a thought struck him. He had always wanted to take a holiday in Wales. Grandfather had been born on the borders near the Black mountains. He remembered visiting the little farm as a child; he had wanted to go back but something always prevented him. Suddenly he knew what he wanted to do; go and look for his roots return to the land of his fathers. Perhaps in finding his past he might find acceptance of his future.

Chapter 3

The rain that had been threatening all morning unleashed its fury as Greg left Swansea heading for the heads of the valley road over Merthyr Tydfil. He soon had to put wipers and headlights on full as visibility decreased over the mountains. He was later leaving his parents then he intended, they were reluctant to see him go cooking him breakfast then persuading him to brunch. The week he had stayed with them had been a strain as he tried to keep his secret but his father had soon realised there was something wrong and on one of their evening rambles Greg had to tell him. His father aged before his eyes, they both sat for a while on an old stone trough in a lonely lane while he fought for control.

He very reluctantly agreed that Sally should not be told yet as she wouldn't have let Greg leave and his father realised when they were able to discuss it without tears that he should live out his life as he chose, it would be the only way he could cope as his mother would wrap him in cotton wool and never let him out of her sight. John being an independent person himself understood his son's need for solitude and space.

"Only a short while until you get things sorted in your mind. Your mother must be told soon" Even so he was hesitant to agree as Sally's anger and grief would be devastating. Greg's eyes filled as he recalled his father's anguish and the desperate clinging of his arms. He was a lay preacher and Greg knew his faith would sustain him. The situation with his mother was made a lot easier as she was excited and preoccupied with a cousin's wedding taking place the following week. She had made the bridesmaids dresses and was helping with the catering and was so delighted to have her son home and show him off among her friends and neighbours. Greg told her he was on sick leave but made time to drive her around suffering heartache at her pride in him. When he told them he was heading for the Black mountains to find his grandfather's farm, she was delighted and thought it would do him good. "You are looking peaky dear. The holiday will do you good."

He hated leaving his father with his awful burden although Greg knew that he would cope. John had been a miner and school governor as well as a lay preacher during his life around Swansea, all his troubles would be firmly left in the hands of God and if prayers were answered Greg would live. Maybe from this background Greg inherited a strong upper lip and strength of character that was now coming to his aid. He had always hero worshipped his father. John Morgan was a good and brave man, on two occasions in the pit he had saved men's lives, once during an explosion and again pulling a young lad from the path of a tram; each time the deed had been done and little said but the men had known and told many more. John was loved and respected practising what he preached; many a child had been helped through college with a word here or a pound there. Few of his neighbour's lives had not been touched in some way with a timely word or a helping hand. Greg remembered that he always had time to spare and if money was needed he reached into his own pocket or raised funds elsewhere being a great fund raiser he always gave generously of his time and energy.

Greg inherited many of his qualities while from his mother came his exceptional good looks, the large grey-green eyes, her wit and charm. Sally sang in the choir was always good for babysitting, cake making and with her flair for dressmaking was kept busy with weddings and other functions. It was she who had formed the local craft group and their exhibitions were well known. Her eyes were merry and her wit sharp, tea and gossip were the breath of life to her, matchmaking and practical jokes were often traced back to Sally, never hurtful or unkind or doing harm she nevertheless often tried her more serious husband's patience but he adored her and her puckish nature did not diminish with age.

Greg was the centre of their world and they had been good parents. His father had made sure that he had a good education and his mother had played with him as a child so he had never missed out on siblings. He had grown up loved and secure, well balanced and self-confident from a happy and disciplined home. All these memories and more flitted through Greg's mind as he drove down the valley to the little town of Abergavenny. Only last night Greg and his father had poured over maps of the Black mountains, John recalling incidents of life on the farm.

"I left at seventeen to go in the army, returning on leave and later with Sally" he recalled. "Then when we married we came to live in Swansea then later when your grandad died, granny sold the farm and came to live with us. You remember her don't you?"

"I remember her stories of the house under the great rock and of all the animals; Briar the shire mare who worked the small fields. She told me about the sheep up on the hill but best of all I liked the stories about Rocky the black and white sheep dog who brought them all down when the snow came."

"After she died I had to tell them all over again"

Greg laughed "I knew them all by heart and wouldn't let you leave anything out. I only went there a few times when grandad was alive and I can only dimly remember it."

They had enjoyed reminiscing and both felt sad the farm had gone from the family.

"I am looking forward to seeing it again. Maybe whoever owns it now may let me look around."

"Yes his father said sadly. "It should never have been sold. It had been in the family for over a hundred years but I was no farmer and there was no one else to take it on. Let us know how you find it and take some photos"

"Of course I will." They returned to the maps and it gave Greg a thrill to pin point where Greg-y-Dorth was and trace the lanes he would take. Now he was on his way. He needed to get to the area before dark and find somewhere to stay. He was still very disturbed himself and the strain of being with his parents and not being able to talk was getting to him. Following the map his father had marked he turned onto the Hereford road. He felt very guilty at driving himself but until told otherwise he would just take care, it wouldn't be long until he had a letter wanting to know why he hadn't notified them. The rain was easing now but the light fading and there seemed many lanes turning off into the hills, he worried that his father may have forgotten the way. Turning at the first pub he came to he headed up the valley. The road soon became a lane and he needed all his concentration as there were many bends and the hedges grew high, the lane became muddy, twisting and turning for what seemed miles. The sweep of the headlights on a particularly bad bend caught the grey bulk of ruins on the right. His heart sank his father had made no mention of any ruins he must be on the wrong road. "Damn! I will have to go back when I can turn around" As he slowed the car lights appeared on his left and to his great relief a sign swung to and fro 'Old Abbey Inn' B/B.

'Thank God' he sighed with relief, noticing with surprise that an unlit car park at the side of the building was full of vehicles. He had some difficulty in parking the car and finally entered to find a crowded bar. The room was full of loud talk and laughter, the smell of smoke, wet macs and three big dogs who were occupying all the space in front of a large open fire, giving off an odour more pungent than all besides keeping the heat off everyone else. Greg's dream of a cosy pub supper vanished rapidly, if it wasn't for the weather and the fact he was totally lost he would have driven off.

"Evening Sir. What can I get you?" The young man behind the bar shook back his long black hair and reached for a glass.

'I'm looking for a room for the night if you have one vacant"

'Carol, Here a minuet' The lad yelled over his shoulder. He turned back to Greg "Drink?' 'Half of Cider Please." Greg nodded at the pump he was surprised at being so quickly served as people were standing elbow to elbow and two deep at the bar until he noticed that the focus of attention was an extremely attractive brunette at the far end of the room who was serving at least three people at the same time. There seemed to be a lot of talk about rallying and cars. A soft welsh voice spoke behind him.

"Would you like to come through? It's a bit quieter out here"

Greg turned to see a pretty plump woman beckoning him into a back room, he assumed her to be the Landlady. He followed her into the haven of a small reception room where she moved behind a large desk, where a stand with leaflets of places to visit was almost obscured by a large potted palm. The room felt chilly and was poorly lit, two green leather settees stood against one wall while a huge painting of a snow covered mountain almost filled the other.

"It was a room you were wanting, just one night was it? Single perhaps."

"Yes Please." Greg replied. "You seem very busy tonight?"

"Oh! It gets like this at times, there's been a rally tonight, you see, up the valley. Mind you there is always something on, a dance maybe or we get hikers and pony trekkers according to the time of the year and the food is good here although I says it myself. Sometimes it's a sheep sale all sorts of things really. On your own are you? Now will you want a single or a double?"

Greg hesitated. He had been caught by the word single, a box room and a narrow bed?

22

"You'll find a double in all the rooms but we don't charge if you're a single if you know what I mean. New to the area are you? Visiting perhaps or were you in the rally? Haven't seen you before, have I?"

Greg's sense of humour stirred, he was dying to say. "Oh! I've been coming here for weeks now. Haven't you noticed me at the back of the crowd?' A smile curved his lips, he firmly quenched the remark, she might take it as sarcasm and he would need her directions in the morning.

"No I'm afraid I got lost. I was looking for the road to Graigwen but all this seems different to the directions I was given and not at all like the map."

"Oh! You are in the wrong valley entirely. Stranger you are to be sure. Never mind we'll set you straight in the morning. Now breakfast! What time and do you need a call?'

"About eight and I'm always awake early. Thank you?' Greg was suddenly very tired, his chest ached and his legs felt weak.

"Could I have some sandwiches and another half of cider in my room? Please."

Carol Evans had been admiring the good-looking young man and would have enjoyed extracting more information but his sudden pallor and the strain in his face stopped her. She felt sympathy so with great difficulty controlled her curiosity.

"You must be tired. I'll show you to your room and George will bring it up to you. What do you like ham, tongue, beef, you just say."

"I honestly don't mind." Greg was too tired to care.

"Right you are follow me then." She led the way down a dark passage and up a wide polished oak stairs at the top

23

of which she opened a door on the left. Greg stepped into a
room softly lit with side lamps. He took in the charm of old
beams and tapestry hangings. It was warm and welcoming.
The bathroom she showed him was tiled in blue and white
with big fluffy towels on a heated rail.

"There's plenty of hot water, Mr Morgan. You just
relax now. George will be up directly. Have you any other
luggage?" Carol nodded towards his single holdall.

"No I haven't but thanks." Greg looked around
appreciatively. "This is fine."

"No trouble at all. Goodnight!" The door closed softly.
Greg collapsed onto the bed, sounds from the bar, muted
sliding further and further away as he dropped into a sudden
deep sleep. He was startled awake by a rapping on his door,
on his call a portly man in a white apron edged his way in
bearing a covered tray.

"I've brought your sandwiches Sir. Is everything alright
for you?' Greg struggled to concentrate. 'Perfect, thank you'

"Thank you Sir. Anything you need just give a shout for
Carol or me. I'm George.'

"I certainly will. Thank you again.'

"Goodnight Sir, sleep well.'

As the door closed behind him Greg gave a sigh of relief,
shrugged of his jacket, kicked off his boots and ate the thick
beef sandwiches realising he was hungry and they were very
good. Later he relaxed in a hot bath then climbing into
bed within minutes he was soundly asleep only waking as
early morning sun peeped through a gap in the curtains.
His watch told him it was only six o'clock but he knew he
wouldn't be able to sleep any more, swinging his legs over the
side of the bed he fully awoke to the sick realisation that what

he thought had been a nightmare was harsh reality and he realised it anew. It was not going away. Once again he faced his adversary. He was never going to get used to the awful knowledge that his tide was running, that each day brought him nearer to an untimely end. Why was he fooling himself and what was he doing here? He might as well go back and die in his flat instead of pretending he had time to go on a wild goose-chase. Depression, fear and panic momentarily held him paralysed. Since his breakdown when he trashed his flat, he had been relatively calm. The night he told his father had been a bad one but they had been together giving each other strength. For a moment now Greg was fighting his demons again until a realisation of his surroundings reminded him of his quest. A touch of excitement caught him and he moved across to the window hooking back the curtains. He was immediately gripped with awe and wonder.

An early sun was replacing the night clouds of rain that were rolling like a carpet away to the west. Long fingers of pink and rose streaked the sky above broad bands of pale turquoise while deeper bands of violet and blue streamed out pushing the dark grey of night from the sky over the edge of the world. Silhouetted black against the bright tapestry were the ruins of an old priory or abbey, half hidden in trees of deep grey each branch and tiny twig etched onto the background of a great mountain that stretched from the valley floor to meet the pink band of sky. A great chorus of birdsong burst upon his ears as he lifted the window, as if every bird in the world had gone mad with praise for their creator. It vibrated, echoed and repeated throughout the valley; the joyous outpouring of a blackbird singing as if his tiny heart would burst was repeated in fifty blackbirds' throats. Thrushes asking questions about the weather and other matters of the day were answered by cousins across the hill. Robins sang creamy songs in the heavily scented lilac bushes in the garden below and great drops of water fell each time a tiny wren hopped in and out with a piping little tune. Cuckoos called over the hill to be answered by doves cooing on the ridge top and lambs on the mountain called to their mothers as if they too would sing if they could.

The great cacophony of sound and the huge sky painting took Greg's breath away. He was transported, pure delight caught him by the throat and he felt as if he dare not let go of the window or he would join the larks and whatever else he could see high in the golden light that grew brighter by the minute. The heady perfume of lilacs and wallflowers growing beneath his window filled his nostrils so that nose, eyes and ears were completely filled. The whole heady mixture made him feel small as an ant and as powerful as an angel, his troubles dropped from his back like a stone, love beauty and pure worship filled him from head to toe. The air was like wine and he reeled from its potency, just when he could bear it all no longer and must fly out of the window, a voice spoke below him.

"Morning Mr Morgan. It's a lovely morning after the rain. Sleep well did you?"

So far had Greg travelled in the last hour, he would not have been surprised to see an angel complete with wings standing in the garden below him but after blinking rapidly a few times he could see it was Carol in a blue and white dress looking up at him, a large box of salad in her arms.

"Hope we didn't wake you. We start a bit early around here especially when there's Trekkers coming over for lunch, got to get the cleaning done early see. Breakfast in half an hour suit you?"

Greg finally found his voice. "Ok, thanks, I'll be down directly."

He managed to ignore the glory around him and get back from the window in one piece but the passion stayed and he found himself for the first time since learning of his illness, whistling while he showered and dressed in jeans and a dark blue sweatshirt. He was the only person in the old fashioned dining room facing a table laden with cereal, bacon, eggs mushrooms and tomatoes before he could cope with this, a young girl entered with toast, marmalade, honey and a large pot of coffee. Greg who had been in terrible trouble with his mother for not eating did manage to eat enough not to cause comment this morning his head and heart still full of his introduction to the dawn chorus and the Welsh mountains in spring. He now couldn't wait to be on his way. He would like to have been able to explore the ruins but promised him another time. The early morning joy was driving him on he knew he would find Graig-y-dorth this morning.

After a consultation with George and his map, Greg found that he had to retrace his steps almost to the main road. Settling his surprisingly modest bill and promising to come back soon, he headed down the lane, a far different picture than that of the night before; either the euphoria of the morning had coloured his vision or because the sun was shining, the way seemed shorter and although a bit of sharp braking was needed now and then the distance was covered in a relatively short time. As Greg turned back into the hills, a strange sense of Deja vu came upon him almost as if he were heading for a well-loved home. He took the lanes slowly enjoying the feel of the day. It was bright and sunny now with the promise that spring often gives but does not always fulfil. The road was good until he reached a hump-backed bridge when it narrowed dramatically as he spotted the sign for Graigwen and dropped almost immediately into the village. It began with a pub 'The Green Man, passed a general store, several houses which had notices over their doors declaring the butcher and a gift shop among them. A large house standing on its own with the word Surgery over the wide gateway, then a garage and another shop of some kind, further on another pub 'The Lion'. At the top of the hill a cluster of council houses, bungalows clustered around the church with a Norman tower peeping over the trees. A school stood at the crossroads near a small chapel where he had to consult the map again as several lanes led into the mountains which ran behind the village on both sides. He finally left the village with its bright flowers. So far he hadn't seen many people, a woman coming from the butchers, a couple walking, a man with his dog and several children going to school. He was going to enjoy exploring later, the map mentioned an old castle hereabouts but at the moment his whole being was geared to finding the farm. The lanes were very green and bright with young leaves, daffodils and tulips filled cottage gardens, lilac and golden forsythia hung in the hedges, dandelions edged the roadside with gold and birdsong filled the air rather muted now the business of the day was on, nesting and feeding darting in front of him in a fluttering of wings.

Greg had spent so much time on the Rig or in his town flat he had never experienced the full force of country springtime since a boy and then had not taken it in. His elation and delight grew as the road climbed higher. The lane seemed to go on for ever until he came to a shallow ford where water crossed the road then gurgled its way into a brook which ran through fields bright with buttercups and daisies. A little further he had to stop. A stony track looked as if it led to a house and he dared not take the car down it to look. Water from last night's rain lay in ruts among the stones; locking the car realised this might be the end of his journey. He had no idea what might happen next, there could be people living here who might not like strangers, it was very quiet and lonely only the sound of the brook and some sheep on the hillside broke the silence, maybe he should have stopped in the village and asked about the farm, there didn't appear to be any neighbours, he had passed a couple of farms and a ruined cottage a mile or two back perhaps he should go back and get some information. Greg realised he was only putting off the moment so slipping on his jacket and wishing he had brought wellies he picked his way between banks thick with primroses and violets down as far as a gate tied up with string. He stood looking over at a cobbled yard. To the left he could see part of a stone built stable, further on the corner of a cottage or house, to the right of his vision trees overhung a brook which was diverted out of its course with branches and debris partly flooding the yard further down. High above him a great mountain reached great arms around the little farm protecting it on two sides so that snow or high winds was safe from the worst of the weather. It rose softened now with the green of young fern pushing through last year's bracken. Huge stones reared above the waving green as if they too would answer the call of spring. Above them the granddaddy of them all; the rock the house was named for, the one Greg had heard stories of as a boy. The great rock, even as he stood below he could feel the sense of timelessness, the everlasting endurance, a feeling of security and peace. Silence flowed, broken only by larks high above out of sight, their notes falling like silver droplets from some heavenly fountain, the sound of lambs calling from the hill; nearer the soothing babble of the little brook chuckling it's way to the fields even as he stood his hand resting on the gate, his other hand moved the ivy which had crept up the post. He felt the edge of a board. He knew even as his fingers traced the almost illegible lettering what it said. 'Graig-y –Dorth'. Here at last were his roots.

Chapter 4

The gate stuck on the uneven stones because a rail which had been attached to the bottom of it at some time to keep lambs on the yard. Caught in big tussocks of grass, in fact there were so many weeds growing around the yard Greg had doubts anyone lived here. He passed a stable, divided into two, the inner door hanging off its hinges, the outer falling inwards. He approached the house cautiously half expecting a dog to come hurting around the corner or someone to open the door and ask his business. The house was strongly built of stone, facing south and overlooking a walled overgrown garden. A door set in a porch under a tangle of bushes had obviously not been used in a long time, further around the house another was more accessible, here Greg knocked almost certain that no one was going to answer. A dirty net curtain covered the little window set in the door preventing him from seeing in. He knocked louder finally hammering on the door but all remained silent. Stepping back he looked up; to his dismay he now saw that the entire roof which should have been slate or stone tile was instead corrugated sheets painted black, surely no one lived here now.

He walked to the back of the building where an upper window faced the mountain and two lower ones overlooked the garden. He peered in at the first, inside was dark and gloomy he could just make out a stone sink under the window, some shelving, a huge dresser filling one wall and an old coat hanging behind the closed door opposite.

"Certainly looks abandoned." He muttered.

Walking with great difficulty through nettles knee high to the far window, he could see even less except for a huge beam which seemed to be crossing the centre of the room until he realised he was standing in a dip much lower than the kitchen window. There were no curtains on these windows and he was now certain that the house was empty. Some distance behind him stood an old apple orchard, the trees gnarled and twisted although they were coming into full leaf with fat buds.

"It will be pretty in a month's time." He muttered to himself. The ground where he stood was rank with docks and nettles. Someone had laid an ash path from the house to the orchard through a wicker gate also tied up with string. To his left trees blocked his way while to the right stood a large shed of bricks and wood, the bricks rosy and mellow, the upper wood weathered to a silver grey. It was in quite good condition except for the far end where a tree had come down in some storm and actually crashed through the roof. The double doors were padlocked but through a knothole Greg could just make out the shape of some machinery, he managed to push his way through some brambles to a side window where with a toe on a stone, he could just make out a tractor and behind it some kind of jeep or Land rover he just couldn't see. The tree had come through the roof at that point and had been there some time. There appeared to be other pieces of machinery but as there was no way of getting in or seeing properly, Greg reluctantly abandoned the idea.

To his right a small waterfall fell three feet into a pool which in turn fed the stream running through the yard where it was supposed to drain away under hedge and across the road into the brook which ran down the fields but as the stream was full of debris it overflowed and flooded the yard. He stood looking about him. The farm nestled like a small animal in the curve of the mountains, its fields running along the roadside and towards the mountain behind the house. High above him stood the great rock, a sentinel guarding the way into the hills.

He spoke aloud. "This is a special place no wonder Gran loved it so much. It must be magic to own this, live here all your life; have your children born here and know that it's yours and theirs forever. I wish she had never sold it."

The walled garden was a riot of spring flowers and flowering shrubs flanked by the house on one side and stables on the other the remaining walls were mossy stone making an oasis of warmth and growth. Daffodils, tulips and narcissi had grown undisturbed for many years so huge beds of colour glowed through the weeds. Blocking the way to the door and windows and over the porch at the front of the house rambled a mass of early clematis and roses, they scrambled where they wished and from the size there were many more to come. Many more plants were waiting their turn as the season moved on, soft fruit trees would feed the birds later, rhubarb poked spears through the grass and an old pear tree leaned over the wall to whisper to the raspberry canes below. The garden was alive with birds, early bees and butterflies, wild and very beautiful.

It filled Greg with another wave of the joy he had experienced that morning, a sense of home coming as he stood in the warm spring sunshine. Shades of his grandparents moved about the garden, grandfather digging his vegetable plot and grandmother picking her herbs. He felt as if he had lived here as long as they, mentally he shook himself back to reality and tried once more to see in the windows of the house but curtains were drawn in the one nearest one to him and roses and brambles refused to let him even try to stamp them down. A branch caught and held him cutting his cheek drawing blood and an oath. As he turned away a blackbird dived out of the bushes screaming a warning so close he felt the brush of wings.

"Damn and blast, serves me right for being so nosy." Greg dabbed at his face with his sleeve. "Hell I want to know about this place. Who owns it? Is it for sale or let? I must find out."

He made his way back to the car where he had a flask and a sandwich, checking his watch he saw he must take his tablets and have a rest. 'Strange' he thought that while he was poking around he had felt no pain, now his heart dropped as he remembered why he was here. He was roused from sleep by the sound of footsteps, opening his eyes he watched a woman walking up the road towards him, he idly wondered where she came from as it was a long way back to the last farm or cottage. As she drew nearer he noticed that she was exceptionally tall, her height more pronounced by the crown of white hair she wore piled on her head. Her bearing was regal, although big boned she walked with grace and lightness, an air about her of someone much younger. As she became closer Greg could see she was weather- brown and wrinkled, her head held high and chin jutting as if in defiance of some unspoken criticism. She wore brown cord trousers, a high necked jumper of indiscriminating colour an open barber jacket and knee high boots. She carried a large basket on her arm. As she drew longside Greg suddenly thought she might be able to tell him about the farm.

Good day" he called. "I wonder if you could help me?"

She stopped and turned towards him, Greg caught his breath, startling in her tanned face were eyes of the lightest blue he had ever seen, very large, the gaze penetrating, as they met his the urge to drop his own overwhelming; he held steady with difficulty.

"Good day to you."

Her voice was clipped somewhat abrupt but deep and attractive. 'Are you another lost motorist? It's becoming the season for them.'

Greg smiled. "Not exactly, no, I rather wanted to know about Grag-y-Dorth, who owns it or if it's for sale?"

"And why would you want to know these things?" Greg was taken back at the barely veiled rudeness.

'I had relations living here many years ago.'

"Well I didn't live here many years ago.' She hitched her basket higher on her arm. "So I don't know who it belongs to now but I can tell you it's for sale, there is a board in the hedge somewhere, it will tell you who by but for whom I can't tell you that either.' She turned to continue up the lane.

"Can I give you a lift anywhere? The basket looks heavy.'

"No thanks, used to it.' She didn't turn around and he watched her walk over the ford and out of sight.

'That's a weird one' he thought. 'I hope that's not a sample of the neighbourhood'. The realisation of what she said suddenly struck him. He shouted aloud "It's for sale." He jumped from the car and began searching first one side of the road then the other but found nothing.

"Damn that woman she must have seen that sign sometime and must know who the agent is.' About to give up and go to find someone more helpful, his eye caught sight of a green board down in the ditch. He tugged it free to read.

FOR SALE BY BROWN TURNER AND CO.
AUCTIONEERS AND ESTATE AGENTS.
ABERGAVENNY 01843 6874286 and 01843 687544

Greg held it a moment in deep thought. "Is this meant for me? Why should I come here? Father would probably say that God moves in mysterious ways. Some would call it destiny but is it what I want and can I afford it? I don't have a job or much time either" Greg slowly stood the sign back up in the hedge.

"First things first I suppose, go and see how much they want. I could get a key and have a good look around again. I'd like to do that anyway. I must follow where I am led it's all I have to hang on to.'

He started the car driving slowly down to the ford suddenly slamming into reverse gear he fled back up the road to where the sign now stood upright. With a wicked grin he pulled it out and thrust it deep where he had found it upside down. 'There's no harm in giving fate a helping hand.'

It took him fifteen minutes to the Auctioneer's office in town.

He decided to spend the night in Abergavenny. There were several things he had to do and it was a very interesting market town. First he booked into an attractive looking guest house on the outskirts then made his way into the old market place to do some shopping. He needed wellington boots and a pair of gloves for the nettles. An ordinance survey map and a good torch completed his purchases.

Arriving back at the guest house, his landlady greeted him with warmth until her husband jealous of Greg' good looks banished her back to the kitchen where she contented herself preparing him a culinary masterpiece instead. Mr Williams was a born host and knew how to treat his guests. Two other men were also staying and Greg enjoyed the chat. Afterwards he sat in the small annex and phoned Tom his boss giving him an update. He and Tom worked well together and after five years were more friends than employer and employee. Greg and Stephanie had enjoyed their hospitality on more than one occasion and had wined and dined them in return. Strangely Tom had never cared for Stephanie, although his charm and good manners never let it show but he had once said to Greg. "She is not the girl for you Greg." The words had stayed at the back of his mind. Now Tom was at a complete loss on what to say. He was devastated at Greg's words, to be losing him as a colleague and a workmate. He had received the report from James Riley the medic aboard the rig and could find no words to express his grief. He had hoped that Mr McLaughlin's had come through with a different verdict or at least with news of some kind of cure. This was dreadful and he was almost unable to speak. Greg promised to meet him on his return, accepting an invitation to meet him and his wife Betty in the privacy of their home.

His next call was to Ray Bower, unable to tell him the truth he only told him a little of what he was up to. Ray complained down the phone.

"Wish I was there with you, I could do with prowling around the mountains for a while"

Greg smiled to himself, Ray would enjoy that and the current girlfriend would have to come too or be packed off home for the weekend.

"Nothing is stopping you if I should decide to stay here for a while. I'll let you know my plans soon. Anyway I'll be back next week so catch you then. See you Saturday"

Greg mulled things for a while before he rang his father. He was pleased Greg had found Graig-y- dorth. "What do you intend to do?"

"I'm going to take a good look tomorrow and if it feels good I'll put in an offer. It's a realistic price but in bad state. I have enough for a deposit but I'll sell the flat only hope it shifts quickly but it would be stupid to look at a mortgage in my condition"

There was a deep silence as John blew his nose sharply. "We have a little put by, Greg." His voice was gruff and Greg quickly interrupted. 'Dad I don't want to do that let me handle it in my own way

Thanks anyway. Maybe I could get a loan until the flat sells. I'll talk to you tomorrow. If I do go for it will you come and see it first?"

"Of course I will." his father replied. "Take a good look, see what you think and we will join you on Sunday and have another look around. You had better have a word with your mother she is pacing around the floor here."

"Thanks Dad." Greg had to school himself to sound normal to his mother. In one way he would be glad when she knew but couldn't bear the thought of her pain when she did. Luckily for him she was still full of the wedding next day, entreating him to at least to come to the evening do to which he had been invited, barely stopping to enquire how his digs were before she was gone. He went back to the bar for a nightcap.

Greg read the brochure for the third time. "Twenty acres of land and hill rights, not really suitable for an invalid" he muttered aloud stuffing the papers in his pocket. It was still early as he headed out to the little farm that drew him like a magnet. The morning was chilly and damp with clouds lowering over the mountains as different from the previous day as autumn is from spring. He splashed his way through the puddles into the yard. He realised that he must be very careful and disciplined in his inspections otherwise his emotions might lead him into doing something silly. He still wasn't in a good place yet; with this in mind he shut off his emotions and went to work as if this was one of his lab security checks.

The key was stiff in the lock and took some jiggling until he was in the porch. Here a pair of cracked wellies stood on a stone bench to the side underneath which stood an old bucket containing a few pieces of coal and some kindling. The inner door opened easily enough and he went up a step into a large room. It was dark and smelt of mice and soot. The curtains were closed and the pressure of bushes closed the other. He pulled at the curtains that hung drunkenly from overstretched wires, spiders fled down the walls. The light streamed in and he saw with relief the general condition was good so far. Patches of damp showed on one wall, paper had fallen away and some plaster had fallen on the flagstone floor otherwise the room was surprisingly in fair shape. Greg was relieved to see the huge beams that ran through the ceiling were sound. 'Definitely oak' he decided after proving them with his penknife, pegs protruded but no hooks or nails. The windows were small but well made with deep panel lined seats. The doors oak with peg latches and the outer walls at least six foot thick. He examined the old range, once black and shiny; it now stood rusty, its tripod bent, oven door hanging off its hinges. Fire dogs and fender were black with neglect and soot lay deep out on the floor. Shining his torch up the chimney it was as he thought full of old nests.

A huge welsh dresser filled one wall, an old settee gave him the shudders but a small corner cupboard although filthy he could see at once was of value. Stephanie had taught him well it had been her hobby going to auctions buying small cabinets and tables and never far out in her judgements had made herself a few pounds. "Why did they leave it behind?" he wondered aloud. "Its amazing the place hasn't been broken into." He smiled to himself, if the lady he had met yesterday was a sample of the neighbourhood, it wasn't surprising at all. The kitchen beyond was slightly bigger, the deep stone sink had been fitted with double draining boards, large new looking brass taps and was quite clean. One wall held cupboards and shelves, every shelf carrying about twenty cup hooks. The cupboards smelt of mice but were otherwise sound. Greg tried the taps, muddy brown water gushed out then abruptly stopped. A single light bulb hanging from the ceiling reminded him to look at the fuse box which was hidden above the porch. The resulting feeble light did little to dispel the gloom of a house abandoned.

Slightly daunted he opened the remaining door. The whole area was an intended extension that had never been completed crossed with supporting beams and open to the tin roof above, stone walls awaiting plaster with a window not fixed which looked out over the orchard and the hill behind the house. The whole was amateur; no qualified builder had any hand in it. A new staircase rose on the right hand side of the room, Greg wondered what awaited him at the top. He was pleasantly surprised. The landing ran the length of the house with doors opening off it down the right hand side; the left wall had been fitted with a huge picture window where Greg stood a moment enchanted. The whole panorama of the mountain with the great rock rising in the centre spread before him the top reaching the skyline above. Sheep were tiny models seemingly without movement. Clouds hung across the mountains brow like hair rolling away as the rain passed allowing glimpses of sunlight wander over scenes of green and brown. Birds swung in the air against the background of rock as if the sky was too high for them. Greg would have liked to have sat there all day watching the changing tones of light and dark ebbed and flowed with the sun picking up and highlighting different points of trees and rock. 'This must be a fantasy when snowstorms or thunder is coming in. A view like this should be in the main bedroom' reluctantly he tore himself away to look at the rest of the house.

The three bedrooms were similar in size with wide oak floors which would have once gleamed with polish now thick with dust, good condition with built in wardrobes and wonderful views of garden, orchard or mountains. A bathroom of sorts was squeezed between the first bedroom and the top of the stairs.

Keys jingling in his pocket reminded him of the shed and the land rover, locking the house Greg made his way to the shed glad of the wellington boots he had bought. The weeds grew tall wet clinging to the door for although the padlock opened easily enough he had to pull at clumps to get the door open enough to slip inside. It was dark and he couldn't find a light switch without doing himself a mischief on the rubbish piled inside the door. He waited a while until his eyes were accustomed to the light. His gaze sharpened as he made out some of the objects around him. Greg loved old engines, he and Ray had restored several cars, boats and motorbikes and there appeared to be an couple of engines lying here including a old Fordson tractor, he could just make out, batteries, a mower and a load of garden tools. He wanted to make his way to the back of the shed where the ash tree rested on outer walls but branches and rubbish blocked his way. The tree would have to be moved before he could even see the Land rover and he was beginning to feel unwell and could walk no more. He locked the shed and went to have his packed lunch in the car.

As he ate he thought of the sad story the agent had told him about the previous owners. A widow and her son had lived here for about fifteen years until the son had been killed when his tractor had overturned on a neighbour's farm down the valley about four years ago. His mother had stayed on keeping very much to herself and no one knew when a bad storm had damaged the roof or when she had it galvanised or who had done it for her. (The agent guessed that the son had started the extension and run out of money) The old lady had been found one winter's day collapsed on the road. She had been taken to hospital and later to a nursing home where she had died about a year ago. It had taken until now for a distant relative to be found who had ordered the farm to be sold without ever seeing it but obviously someone had come and removed all the furniture and the old lady's possessions. No one had seen them according to the agent but the letter came through to sell. Reading again through the brochure, he noted there were two small fields of about four or five acres each. They were protected by an order which prevented them being ploughed or grazed at a certain time of the year because of wild flowers the rare meadow saffron and several types of orchid. There was an address and telephone number of a Mr T Davis of the local Conservation Society whom the new owner would have to contact.

Besides these fields there was a larger one of twelve acres and a strip of about two and a half between these and the mountain, the rest of the acreage was made up of the orchard and the wooded area where the stream came through. The original acreage had been sold many years ago.

'Neat little parcel.' Greg mused. 'Dad thought it was about seventy acres when he was a boy and that Grandad had rented more as well.'

He decided that he felt well enough to have a gentle stroll around the little fields, he found hedges and ditches needed attention, there was a lot of work to be done and he wouldn't be able to do it that was for sure. He noticed there were some good trees in some of the hedges and in the little wood, some fine sycamores, oaks, ash, birch and a few beech trees; someone must have loved trees to plant such a choice. He realised with a start it must have been his great grandfather, he had been born here and some of the trees weren't that old. A feeling of belonging crept over Greg again, he pulled some leaves from an elder tree as he walked and remembered his grandmother giving him a cordial when he had tummy ache as a child. 'Maybe I could make some wine.' He thought. 'I must get a book.' He could go no further the long strip edging the other field was rough filled with nettles, docks, fern and briars. 'Take some cleaning." he pondered, "It's too small to crop and too rough to graze?"

The light was beginning to fade and it started to rain. Greg headed for the car. He sighed heavily as he dragged the gate shut retying the string around the post.

"Found the answers to your questions then?"

He turned quickly; the woman he had met yesterday stood on the lane, dressed as before, hands deep in her pockets. He had the feeling that she wouldn't have spoken if he hadn't almost bumped into her.

"Yes I did." (no thanks to you) he added mentally.

She turned to walk on up the road giving a funny shrill whistle. Out of the hedge beside him jumped the strangest dog he had ever seen, built like a collie but he was blue-grey in colour with a heavy curly coat and a silky plumed tail. As he saw Greg he ran towards him sniffing at his jeans. Greg caught his breath for the eyes of the dog were odd, one dark brown and the other the same strange light blue as the woman's.

'What a strange dog." he exclaimed. "Am I seeing things or is he blue?"

The woman turned back. "Of course he is; he's a Blue Merle. They are usually wall-eyed. Don't stare at the blue one it's the brown one you need to watch"

"What's his name?"

"Samuel Peeps'

He burst out laughing. 'Samuel Pepys? I'm sorry." he spluttered. "I'm not always so rude. I had better introduce myself. I'm Greg Morgan.'

As he held out his hand, he thought for a moment that she wasn't going to take it but she moved forward gripping his hand firmly.

'Bronwyn Rys' The strange light eyes met his, again Greg was unnerved by the colour and the intensity of her gaze, he felt as if she was looking into his very soul indeed she may have been for as she released his hand she said.

"You are a fine strong lad, well favoured but you have a problem; heavy to bear. The mountains will help one way or another. Going to buy?" she nodded at the house.

"Don't know yet." Greg was disconcerted at her perception. 'It needs a lot of thought and hard work.'

"You'll have enough time on your hands for that no doubt but you won't want that fancy car, rip the guts out of it on these roads, good thing too if you ask me it's no good for passengers or goods; place for that is on a race track. Too many think these mountain roads are just that in the summertime, good job when it snows and stops them coming."

She turned on her heel abruptly then suddenly stopped without turning back

"Don't think too much, young man. You'll need to do something with the time you have." She whistled the dog and was gone.

Greg stood looking after her in the deepening light. Was she weird or what? He shivered suddenly, perhaps she was a witch, and they lived in the hills in lonely places didn't they? Though she did have an educated voice and was obviously once a very attractive woman. He could almost believe it though even though she had gone he could still feel her presence- and that strange dog! He remembered that it was Samuel Peeps not Samuel Pepys and was still chuckling as he headed for town.

Chapter 5

Sally put her foot down as the big car ate up the miles from Swansea. She preferred to drive when she was excited as she was today. She felt guilty as she knew that she hadn't given Greg much attention since he had come home and she had been so busy with the wedding. Now she was going to revisit the place where she and John had married and Greg was going to live. Of course it would only be a holiday home as his work was in Hull but it would be nice if he was nearer some of the time and they could visit.

John was deep in miserable thoughts. Sally still hadn't been told of Greg's illness and that had to happen soon and should he encourage him to buy this hard little mountain farm miles from anywhere? He hardly noticed the speed Sally was doing and only answered her chatter in monosyllables. She wondered what was wrong with him. They pulled into the Green Man carpark as Greg arrived. His father was pleased to see he was relatively cheerful although giving his mother guilty glances.

The food was excellent and Sally enjoyed it chattering happily not noticing the men picking at theirs. They were on their way to Graig-y-dorth when the little church on the hill came into view.

"Oh! John! We must stop. This is where we were married, Greg you must see inside"

The church was old and mellow with a small spire and bell tower; small inside with a simple wooden alter that had two brass candlesticks and a plain cross standing on snowy white lace. Someone kept it beautiful with masses of spring flowers and tall white candles. Greg not as religious as his father nevertheless felt compelled to kneel with him a moment at the alter rail while Sally sat at the back of the church admiring the tapestry kneelers and reading leaflets on the church's activities. Greg rose knowing that his mother must not be deceived any longer. As they followed her back to the car his father touched his arm.

"I'll tell her tonight son. It must be done, it's not fair. God help me.'

"Thank you." murmured Greg, "I can't do it.' John brushed tears from his eyes and hurried to unlock the door for his wife.

His parents were horrified at the state of the farmhouse agreeing with Greg about the amount of work and money to put it right although John was unable to voice his real opinion. He was however fascinated by the machinery in the shed while Sally fell in love with the wild garden. They nostalgically remembered John's parents and remembered friends, reliving John's childhood when all the tumbledown cottages down the lane housed big families. Sally loved it all and it seemed to the two sad men that she had never been so happy and bright, their hearts growing heavier as they realised it may be the last time that she would laugh and joke so freely. Later that afternoon they explored the little market town of Abergavenny, reliving their courtship when there had been two cinemas in the town besides four fish and chip shops and about seven or eight pubs. It hadn't changed a lot but they were relieved to find the poorer area had disappeared and been taken over by a large car park, they found the Post Office now re located in a tree lined avenue surrounded with big beds of spring bulbs. They went for tea in The Appleyard tearooms to discuss the farm in detail. His mother couldn't believe Greg would want to buy it in the state it was in although she agreed the Greg and Ray would have a lot of fun doing it up in their holidays except it could be rather a long way to come for short breaks.

Greg sadly waved them off promising to phone later, he would keep them in touch with any developments; after they had driven off, he remembered that he hadn't told them about the witch and her impression on him, he'd intended to but somehow the time had never been right so he'd remained silent.

His mobile rang at ten o'clock. Greg was just going to bed after a nightcap at the bar. He hadn't been able to give his mind to the chat around him as he was worried about his parents. He couldn't ring them as he didn't know when his father would have spoken. At ten his mobile rang, his father's voice barely recognisable "Your mother has collapsed and the doctor's with her now but she is asking for you, are you able to come, Greg?"

"Tell her I'm on my way. See you soon. Stay tight.'

There were murmurs of sympathy from the bar as he paid his bill barely stopping to explain that his mother was ill, within minutes he had cleared the town and was on the Heads of the valley road. Mercifully the roads were clear and he made good time. He barely registered the journey or remembered his thoughts. His father came to meet him as he quietly let himself into his parent's house, leading him immediately upstairs where his mother lay in a drugged sleep, the doctor had sedated her fairly heavily and it would be morning before she awoke.

"She took it far worse than even I anticipated Greg. She just wouldn't believe me at first, accused me of making it up for some strange reason. Then she called me all the names under the sun for keeping it from her, demanding to see the doctor who had told you such stuff then she screamed pulling her hair out. I just didn't know what to do when suddenly she fainted." His eyes filled with tears. "I rang the doctor and he came straight round. I don't know how she will be tomorrow'

"Is the he coming back?" Greg asked. "I feel ashamed that I left you to tell her I should have been here.'

"Perhaps it was a good job you weren't, she didn't know what she was doing but I am glad you're here now. Perhaps between us we can help her handle the situation but I don't know what you are going to do; she won't let you go from here now."

"I may be able to talk to her about that." replied Greg, somewhat doubtfully. "If only we can keep her calm. I'm going up to sit with her for a while. You get some sleep Dad. I'll manage on the chair upstairs for a while I'll call you if she should wake."

John ran his fingers through his sparse grey hair. "The doctor said he would come if we need him, he wants to talk to you tomorrow anyway. He could explain things better to her than we can too."

Later when John took over from Greg at Sally's bedside; Greg made his way to his old room but knew that he wouldn't sleep. He paced the floor and looked through the window at the lights in the valley below. All those tiny lights each in different boxes where people lived, loved, were born and died. Behind each tiny glow a million mighty emotions were being experienced, love fear, hatred, laughter, anger, remorse, all re-enacted over and over again in ever repeating patterns. A person died and a child was born, a couple made love, a child was conceived. Anger spilled into hate, relationships ended or just began with new hopes, plans and ideals. 'What a complex world.' He thought. 'to think that it's happening all over the world makes me feel very small and insignificant, yet it is to each as it is in this house, the whole world within four walls'.

Greg began to realise that he wasn't alone in his troubles others were suffering in different ways and each needed some kind of faith to be able to carry on. His father had faith in God and Greg now suddenly felt that religion, grown up with and casually taught in churches was not as random as it had always appeared to him. He suddenly remembered words he had heard many times and paid no heed to. 'if you only have faith like a grain of mustard seed' and again 'Except ye become as a little child'. It had all seemed meaningless but he realised with new insight how easy it really was. Faith took away pain and fear like placing your hand in an outstretched one that folded around yours warm and safe. Greg in the early hours of dawn was comforted, much of his fear left him and a new kind of strength was born. The morning found him asleep with a smile on his lips and recent lines of strain eased from his face.

Greg woke with a start and lay for a moment remembering the feelings of hope which had eased his mind the night before. His face clouded as he thought of the pain this day would bring to his mother but felt better equipped to help her than he had been before. He showered and changed his clothes before making a cup of tea for his father who was asleep in the chair. Sally was beginning to stir, moaning softly as she surfaced from the deep drug induced sleep; rousing, slipping in and out of consciousness, Sally finally awoke as Greg put his arms around her, tears of pity in his eyes.

"Greg" she screamed his name. "Darling, tell me it's not true, I've had a dreadful, dreadful dream."

Greg knelt beside the bed drawing her into his arms and rocking her gently. "I am sorry Sweetheart; it is true but not yet, not for a while. I have things to do and I need both your strengths to help me."

"I can't bear it." His mother sobbed. "We must get more specialists we will sell the house, pay anything."

"No Mother you won't. No one can do any more than they are doing and there is no one to tell us any different. I have had all the tests and Mr Mcloughlin is one of the country's top men. I have known there was something wrong for a while and it is better to know what we must face."

"Why? Why should it be you, young fit and strong? We need you. You have a whole life in front of you, a whole life Greg."

"I know but if a donor is found I stand a chance if not then my time is up, we have to accept that, and father does now." He glanced at the chair where his father exhausted slept on"

"Don't talk to me about your father." Sally's voice rose hysterically. "he never told me, he deceived me letting me believe everything was alright. All that day out at the farm, talk about believing in make belief."

"Mother stop, listen to me. It's not his fault, I'm the coward here. I'm the one who couldn't handle it and asked him to wait a while until I knew what was happening. He's suffering too. He had to adjust to what I told him and learn to accept it. He couldn't tell you until he could handle himself. How could he?

I'm the one who should have come and talked to you, helped you both but I couldn't."

Here Greg's voice broke and putting his head down in his mother's arms, he cried. Sally gathered him close comforting him she found some comfort of her own. She still felt resentment towards her husband but couldn't find it in her heart to blame Greg, looking back at the time he spent with them, she was amazed at the strength he must have had to handle himself and talk as if nothing was wrong.

John waking found them both relatively calm. "I'm sorry, Sally." He stumbled over to the bed. "I tried to act for the best, forgive me but I found it hard to hurt you so much. I knew you had to face it and I could not go on any longer."

Sally put up her arm and drew him close so that she held them both tightly to her. "I am finding it hard to forgive you but now I know. What are we going to do?" Her voice breaking they clung together in grief and despair.

After a while Greg gently detached himself. "let me tell you what I want to do, I am going to buy Graig-y-dorth. I shall ring in with an offer this morning.

Sally pulled herself together. "No Greg no, I will not allow it. You must stay here where you will be looked after. You are not shutting yourself up there in that coal-shed of a place. You shall have the best care that money can buy right here until a donor is found. That is final." She lay back on her pillows.

"Hold on Sally." John was struggling for composure. "I agree that is what we would want but Greg is not a child anymore. He knows what he wants to do and he must do it. This may be all the time he has left but it is his not ours. It is Greg's and if it's all he has he must enjoy it"

This brought on such a paroxysm of weeping that John reached for the phone but Greg put out his hand. "Let her be Dad, we can't keep drugging her, leave it for a while and we will talk to the doctor later and get some sleeping pills for tonight. He turned to his mother.

"Look Mum, I'm still here. Mr Mcloughlin's favourite saying is 'Where there is life, there is hope, miracles still happen. Please don't condemn me yet. Help me to face what is coming in a positive way. I would love you to look after me if the time comes but I am not an invalid yet. I want to work at something that will go on after me and show that I lived for some purpose. I don't know what yet and I may not have much time to do it in. I have a strong feeling that it is something to do with Graig-y-dorth so I am going to try to buy it. Don't even know how I am going to do that yet but I am certainly going to try--

His father interrupted. "We have some money put by if that will help you --"

"No thanks Dad, I told you before, I want to do it my way. I'm going back to sell my flat and a lot of the furniture. If I should need help I will come to you I promise. Mum I need you to be the brave smiling girl you always were. You can mend my clothes and fill my freezer any time that you come to see me and make everything as normal as possible for as long as possible. Please both of you try to understand." His father gripped his shoulders "We do lad, we do

It was late afternoon before Greg was on his way home. He had put his offer in at the estate agents, now he had to do his homework. He had shares in the oil company, some of them would have to be sold but some of them he must keep back until his operation. It could be sometime until he could work again. He put a call through to his broker who urged him not to sell at the moment as shares were rising. Greg told him to sell half immediately and notify him as soon as the money was through. ………still doing his calculations he estimated that he had more than three quarters of what he needed. How in the world could he raise the rest in the time? It had to be cash in the circumstances, no time for loans. He would sell the flat of course but how long would that take? There was some furniture which would fetch very little and with no income he could very soon be in trouble. He had no intention of taking his parents savings, that was out of the question. The problem of raising the rest of the money gave him a sleepless night.

Next morning he rang two estate agents to call with the emphasis on urgent, with Graig –y Dorth in mind he set about sorting his possessions even if he lost the house he would have to downsize anyway; if he had to move to his parents he wouldn't need a lot and he didn't want to leave them with a load of things to sort if he didn't make it. This needed a great deal of careful thought. He felt very alone.

Chapter 6

Olwen Jameston slammed the door behind her as she made for the stairs. Two minutes later a little red jeep left the carpark with screaming tyres. She drove too fast, her foot almost to the floor, her mouth set thin and grim. It was normally a very pretty mouth wide and generous given to smiles but not today, her large grey eyes blazed with anger and her mass of red hair almost alight with static. She knew she was in no fit state to drive, she shouldn't be driving but so keen was she to get away from the furious row that she had just had with Aiden Camborn her partner of almost two years that she didn't care.

'He's arrogant, egotistical, selfish and stupid." She screamed at the windscreen as she took a bend too fast wrenching the wheel as the jeep mounted the bank pulling it back onto the road. The drizzle that had started in the afternoon grew heavier and the wipers began slapping against the windscreen matching her mood. This row had been building for some time and tonight was the match that lit the fire.

"Always digging up something else to do just when I've arranged to go to Granny and what else would I be doing on a night like this? He'll be away to his talks and things or something else and I'm not going to sit in wondering where he is, bored out of my skull. Never ever again will I be doing that."

"You're not going to see your Granny at all.' He had shouted at her. You've some fella down there your after seeing. The old witch is as fit as a flea and doesn't need your nursing all the time.'

"I am not nursing her and if I was she is all I've got since Mother went away.'

"She's a waste of space that one." Aiden flung his brief case on to the table.

"Thanks a bunch. It's sick of you I am, you don't care about anyone bar yourself and haven't for a long while, maybe someone else has taken your mind.'

"You're talking rubbish as usual." He scowled kicking a chair out of his way as he made for the shower. Olwen followed him shouting.

"I've told you before; it's the same argument every time I go to see Granny. I've no one else, I've always been faithful to you and a waste of time that is.'

She glared at him; she had never seen him so angry although the row was the same as many they'd had over and over. The feelings of contentment and the idea they were soulmates had begun to falter after their first year together. She knew he would never hurt her. He had never shown any violent tendencies but he became so irate that she dreaded the arguments starting and unless she became subservient to him it was never going to stop. Olwen didn't do subservient and rebelled all the more. This had gone on long enough, talking didn't work neither did arguing. Olwen wanted out of the relationship. She hoped that secretly Aiden did too.

Aiden was a teacher and lecturer of music in the Academy where Olwen was working with art and design advanced studies. His good looks and Irish charm always attracted large classes mainly female. When he and Olwen met the attraction was immediate and passionate. They enjoyed each other's company so much so within two months Aiden had moved into Olwen's flat. The first year passed quickly as they explored each other's bodies and minds finding they were both lovers of sex, art and music. In the second year of their relationship Olwen began to find another side to Aidens character, at first she felt it might be caring and protective but as time went on it revealed him to be jealous and possessive. As long as they did what he wanted to do or went places he wanted to go he was loving and generous but if Olwen wanted something different he could change in an instant usually causing a row in the process. Olwen was unable to convince him there was no one else on her mind and often begged him to come to Graigwen where her granny lived but he wouldn't go with her after the first couple of times. He didn't like granny and she didn't like him. He met her mother Anwen once and didn't like her either although she was flirty and flattering with him. Afterwards she told Olwen he was an 'idjit' only good for one thing ;as to what that was she didn't enlighten her daughter so Olwen went alone to visit, it always caused the inevitable row.

Aiden wanted to get married. At thirty he'd had relationships that he was completely honest about but they had all come to nothing. Olwen thought this time it might be different; she had been quite ready to accept if he proposed but the longer they lived together the more possessive he had become, now she hoped he would never ask because she was certain it was the last thing she wanted to do. She was sure that if they did marry he would take full control of the relationship but wouldn't stay faithful for long; he was too attractive to women and knew it. His thick black curls, startlingly blue eyes and lilting Irish charm he laid before every female he met. The girls flocked to his classes to listen and sigh over the exquisite music of his violin and begged that he would sing to them at the end of his lecture. All this had attracted Olwen at first but she soon found that he was a different character behind closed doors. At first she had loved his possession of her but gradually she felt stifled and began to dread him coming home unless they were going out somewhere that he enjoyed or had friends in to flirt and drink with.

Olwen herself had a fiery temper, hated being manipulated defying him at every opportunity, the time they spent together spoilt with endless wrangling and petty arguments. She knew that she was no longer in love with him; if he bothered to read her note or remembered her final words as she left he would realise it was all over and would be gone by the time she got back. She loved her job and was good at it bringing her students to high standards holding exhibitions where they could sell their work, teaching them to design and display for maximum affect. She sold her work receiving commissions for portraits which were her speciality. She also designed fabrics and involved her class in that too. She planned to develop further ideas but the situation with Aiden held her back. To be fair he had encouraged her at first but later as her popularity grew he began to put her down while exaggerating her talent.

"I have to keep chasing her along." he smugly told their friends at dinner or the pub. 'She has a lazy streak so she has and it's myself has to keep on at her then she turns out some brilliant work. The best in the business when you keep after her." This was such a blatant lie Olwen could have strangled him with his own tie. She worked her best away from him thus causing more complaints She had left a note as well as telling him it was over she knew either he'd be furious or ignore the situation later coaxing and promising all sorts until she either lost her temper and threw things or gave in then he would laugh, ducking out of the door returning late with an unsuitable present or a take away pretending it had never happened.

There would probably be a shouting match when she returned anyway, she couldn't see him leaving quietly it would probably mean waiting for him to leave the flat and changing the locks. She could only hope that he was as unhappy as she was and just leave.

As she approached Hereford she had to slow down as the traffic was heavy, no point in killing herself or anyone else. Her anger was fading now leaving a strong urge to cry, slowly leaving the city she tried to look forward to a peaceful weekend. It was always restful at granny's house with her dog Samuel Peeps, who had funny eyes, she smiled at the thought of him, she would love a dog one day. She pulled into the drive switching off the engine with a sigh of thankfulness feeling drained. It was getting dark and soft lights from the cottage glowed welcome, the door opened Bronwyn stood wearing a flowered apron a huge cat in her arms. As the security light came on Olwen lifted her holdall and briefcase before giving her a hug, cat and all. Samuel Peepes came rushing through barking as he just realised someone had come and he hadn't noticed only subsiding after he had done his greeting bit which involved licking Olwen's hands and face as she bent to give him a cuddle.

"Come on in, Girl. He doesn't feel the cold like we do, it's heading for a cold wet night. There is a stew on, your favourite and a hot cup of tea waiting. Go and sit by the fire and take Marmaduke with you, Lisa is hogging the best chair as usual you will have to move her."

Olwen entered the warm cottage the dog bounding around her his wall eyes shining a welcome as he pestered for attention. Olwen immediately felt herself relaxing as the smell of beef stew and rosemary filled the little kitchen.

"Granny, you don't know how good this is. I needed a bit of loving care."

"Not going well? Haven't you got rid of him yet? By the look of you it's about time that you did."

"Almost did Granny. Tonight was the last row I hope." She told what had happened that morning. Bronwyn was more than indignant.

"I told you bed before marriage was a mistake and marriage before proper courtship no use at all. You don't know the man; thank God you didn't get married to him. He's not going to change, you should have put him out a year ago or not had him in the first place would have been better. If you don't you'll lose your looks, your talent and then you'll lose him anyway"

"Oh! Granny that's a bit strong"

"It's the truth and you know it. Now sit and eat before you fade away."

The stew was delicious, that and the warm fire almost had Olwen asleep before she'd finished. The cats lay watching her with dreamy eyes.

Bronwyn gathered up the dishes moving into the kitchen closely followed by a hopeful Samuel Peeps, "Not strong enough" she called back over her shoulder "Quit while you're ahead. He's not going to leave until he finds himself a yes girl whom he can manipulate. He should have a couple of dogs; train them to obedience. I don't understand him he's a talented educated man who should know better." At the word dogs Samuel Peepes gave a sharp bark. Olwen laughed.

"Changing the subject, any gossip going?"

"A new neighbour at Graig-y-dorth."

"Oh! Have you met them yet?

"A single young man by all accounts but he's not well by the looks of him, drives too fast in one of those low slung types that won't last two minutes on that road."

Olwen stretched and yawned; an indignant cat fell off her lap giving her a nasty look before leaping onto another chair. "Are you seeing things again, Granny? How do you know he's ill"

"He looks sort of haunted. Good looking chap for all that, the village girls will be after him"

"What did he tell you? When is he moving in? Is he on his own? Surly that place has gone too far to save?"

Bronwyn refilled their cups placing a plate of flapjacks on the coffee table.

"My! We do want to know a lot don't we? I think we should get rid of the other one first.' Olwen laughed. I think it's sort of exciting reclaiming an old place like that.'

"How do you know? He may be going to pull it down and rebuild."

"I hope not, I think it's a quaint sort of cottage what I have seen of it. Maybe we'll take a walk up there tomorrow have a look around.' Bronwyn gave her an odd look. "Won't be anybody there, it hasn't happened yet.'

Olwen pulled the band from her hair letting the shawl of red gold flow down her back. "All the more reason for taking a look. I'm off to bed Gran. See you in the morning."

"Good night Lass, sleep tight and no dreams about strange young men."

Laughing, Olwen kissed her, hugged Samuel Peepes then taking a handful of flapjacks ran up the stairs. The little bedroom was warm and lit with a full moon. She stood a while looking out to the mountains bathed in bright moonlight. The stars were appearing one by one in the blue velvet sky. She caught her breath; how peaceful it all looked, she didn't want to go back to Worcester. She loved her job but would give anything to stay in the mountains that loomed silent and silver but her work was there and here was a dream she could only indulge in when she could make time. One day she would live here she promised herself. 'When I retire and am old and grey.' She smiled turning to her bed where a large white cat lay in the centre.

"Liza Dolittle! I didn't see you sneak up the stairs. I think you had better go back down or we'll both be in trouble" picking her up for a cuddle Olwen pushed her gently out before closing the door and climbing into bed where she soon fell asleep with the moon on her face.

Chapter 7

Greg spent the next few days sorting his possessions. Stephanie and he had furnished the flat with care. Everything designed for comfort and luxury. The huge cream suite would be no use at the cottage and would be better sold at auction as would the smoked glass dining suite, mahogany bookcases and display cabinets. The aquarium could go. He still had several tall lamps left intact from his onslaught, his television, music centre and huge music collection; these he would keep along with his small bedside television, books, bedding and linen. Everything else he must sell; he needed every penny he could get. The huge velvet drapes and carpets would go with the flat. By the evening he had two lists; one of things to keep and one for the auctioneer. That evening although tired and in some pain he sorted draws and papers and phoned his parents. Later he rang Ray and warned him he would have a guest over the weekend. Ray whooped the other end of the phone.

"I'll ring a couple of the girls we'll have a night out."

"No thanks Ray save it. I want to talk. You can get some beers in though."

'Sounds good to me'

Greg was determined he was going to tell Ray tonight. Dreading it as he knew his lifelong friend would be very upset but it could not go on any longer

The next two days found Greg unwell, overdone with travelling, the emotional scenes with his parents and his own excitement over the farm. He lay on the settee in pain and fatigue praying he wasn't going to die yet. Another day and he felt well enough for telly and a book. He ate little but began to feel better and able to continue with his plans. He kept his appointment with Mr Mcloughlin, informing of a possible move but not of his plans, visited his dentist and barber, made an appointment with his solicitor about his will and went shopping for boots and country shoes also a heavy anorak and a couple of pairs of jeans.

He bought presents for Lee, Patsy and Samantha spending an evening having dinner with them managing to make his move sound like a career change. He hated saying goodbye to little Sammy but he presented her with a huge fluffy cat which she kept in her arms until bedtime when she climbed on his knee to kiss goodnight.

"Come back soon, Uncle Greg." His eyes filled with tears as he hugged her tight.

"I'll try hard." he promised.

Lee suggested a game of whist which they played until midnight with banter and laughter, parting with promises of holidays and visits.

The next day Greg met with Tom and his wife for lunch. Tom was delighted to see him but a little embarrassed to tell him that a new technician had already been invited to look over the laboratories as Greg's notice had been accepted there was every chance the post would be offered to him; Greg determined not to cause any problems for Tom offered his services for a day or two to ease the new man into the project that he had been involved in. Tom greatly relieved accepted gladly inviting Greg to fly out to the rig with him the following week. Greg accepting arranged to stay out until the following weekend, wanting to say farewell to his colleagues but depressed at having to give up a job he enjoyed so much.

By the weekend Greg felt that he had lived a lifetime. Most of his bigger decisions had been made so it came as a fitting closure to receive in the afternoon post a letter from the agents in Abergavenny. He sat holding it looking at the postmark.

"You have really burned your boats now old son" If this is a no thank you, you have a problem with one behind it. You have finished here so what would you do? If it's yes you have a bigger problem. Am I really up for all this?"

He tore open the envelope. The words leapt out at him, his offer had been accepted. He shrunk back in his chair. What had he done? The reality hit him suddenly. How was he going to cope? What a stupid thing to have done; to buy a farmhouse miles from anywhere that he couldn't work or rebuild, no one around, no income, no one with him and likely to fall ill at any time. Very soon he must give up his vehicle, he would be stuck in the wilds with no hope of getting anywhere ;maybe too ill to even phone, if there was a signal anyway. He must cancel the deal and go home to his parents that would be the sensible thing to do. He was suddenly frightened. All that evening he knew what he had to do, he tossed and turned all night only falling into a deep sleep around dawn.

The morning was bright and sunny. Greg felt his spirits rise when he awoke and felt well. Over breakfast he read the letter from the agents again. As he did so he felt strongly that something was pulling him towards the little farm. So what if it didn't work out? He could always sell it and then go to his parents or they would come to him. He wanted to give it a go. Intense excitement gripped him again, hurriedly throwing a few things in a grip he locked up and drove around to the estate agents dropped the keys through their door and drove out of town. Eight miles out he pulled up in front of a well-kept garage. Loud music led him into the interior, seeing no one around he went back to the forecourt filled his car then stuck his head around the door of the cash office where Dave Stone, Ray's business partner was staring blankly at a pile of forms.

"Hi Dave, Ray about?"

"Hello Greg, no he left about ten minutes ago. How are you doing? How was Wales? Ray said you had been down, think he was jealous." Dave's face creased which meant he was smiling. "Want a cuppa."

"No thanks, Dave, I'd better get after him before he meets some girl and I lose him altogether."

"Don't think so Greg, by what he was saying he was looking forward to you coming"

"Well, I'll just go and nail him down. How's trade?"

"Not bad, not bad at all. Want to join us?"

"Come on Dave. How many times have you asked me that? Here you had better have my card seeing I've just filled up or is it on the house as your doing so well?"

Dave's face creased again. "Not that well, Hey! Before you go back, let's have a few beers one night. Come over to the house, Liz will cook us a meal. Make it soon. When are you going back to the rig?"

"I'm not Dave. I've bought a little farm in the hills, going to retire."

"Good God alive! Greg, you're only thirty something? You come into money or what?"

"Or what" Greg grinned. "I'll have to tell Ray first or he'll never forgive me, get him to tell you about it Monday morning and yes to the invite. I'll give you a bell real soon. See you."

"So long Greg, soon mind."

Greg waved and flashed his lights, he liked Dave and his family; Ray had been in partnership with him ever since his Grandmother died five years ago leaving Ray her house and sharing her money between him and his married sister Jenny.

The mock Georgian residence was the most unlikely place you'd expect to find Ray living but live here he did and was doing well. he lived between the garage and his side line restoring old cars, not rich but able to enjoy a few luxuries like the boat that he and Greg often had fun with.

Ray was a golden, curly haired charmer, five foot ten, merry blue eyes and a pick –up truck his many girlfriends all had one thing in common, each hoping to win Ray and his house. There was always someone waiting to do his washing, cooking or cleaning trying her best to impress him with her housewifely skills. He however played the field never short of a partner on his arm or waiting in the wings, not one had won his heart for long and although he was never hurtful or unkind he made sure they knew where they stood backing off eventually disappointed or heartbroken as they realised they were only one of many. For years Greg had laughed and teased him.

"One day, my boy you are going to meet your waterloo and I will be best man at your wedding or you'll end up heartbroken. I'll say serve you right, no sympathy at all"

Ray merely chuckled waving his little black book at him. "Your only jealous,' love em and leave' that's me. I don't know if it's me or the house they are after do I or maybe it's the boat they 're after?"

"You don't wait long enough to find out." Greg retorted. "How are you going to find out whose genuine? You wait and see you'll let the wrong one go one day." Ray made a rude remark. A few days later he would introduce another girl with a wicked glint in his eye. For all that Ray was a great mate and a loyal one. Their friendship dated from their teens when they had an accident, both their motorbikes meeting on a bend in a head on collision. Ray suffered a broken arm and ribs, Greg had a broken leg, both bikes a write off. They visited each other, blamed each other and had been fast friends ever since. They shared hobbies of fishing, boating and restoring old cars. Greg's sense of humour matched by Ray's light hearted approach to life had led them into much mischief over the years. Greg felt that telling Ray about his illness was going to be as bad if not worse than telling his parents. He dreaded it.

As soon as he arrived at Ray's house against his better judgement they hit the town. A few drinks, a meal, some pool more drinks. Two thirty they fell into bed and slept until ten. Greg was woken by Ray plonking coffee down by the bed and uttering one word 'boat' Greg came down the stairs to hear Ray on the phone to his girlfriend Sheena. "It's the boat today Girlie. Greg's here, ring Mandy. Pick you up in fifteen minutes.' They picked up some beer, picnic and headed out for the day.

In spite of himself Greg enjoyed it, a light breeze, clear skies, good company. He took his turn at the wheel; the usual banter kept them laughing and the beer from the cooler was good. He liked Mandy, a buxom friendly girl that he had been out with a few times. She had always made it clear that she would like more than a casual friendship but Greg had kept it light. They stayed out till six coming in with the tide. As they moored in the harbour Sheena was coaxing Ray.

"Come on Ray, don't be a spoilsport, let's get changed and go up the club." Greg's heart sank he knew what sort of night it would be and knew that he wasn't up to it but to his surprise Ray stood firm.

"Not tonight, girls sorry but Greg's only here for one more night and that's boys night"

"Don't be rotten Ray. You were both out last night, come on its early yet." Sheena protested. "It's been a smashing day, let's end it properly."

"Sorry love no you and Mandy go and see some film or something."

"Perhaps Greg wants to take Mandy out she hasn't seen him for a while. Don't be so selfish Ray it's not all about you" Ray put an arm around Sheena and led her aside. Mandy turned her brown eyes on Greg lifting her shapely eyebrows.

"While they are sorting themselves out, let's make our own arrangements, shall we? Let's go back to my place and

I'll fix us some supper. My flat is just down town and you haven't seen it yet."

Greg looked at her appreciatively, she was certainly a cutie, a mass of dark girls framed a pretty heart-shaped face tumbled over her shoulders and around tiny ears; big brown eyes and a sweet smile almost shook his plans. He liked her a great deal but a night with her was not in his plans; besides he was Ray's guest and he needed to talk to him and so far there had been no chance. Ray and Sheena came back her head held high, her eyes bright.

"Come on Mandy, let's go, we know when we're not wanted." She turned back to Ray "You can go to hell, Ray Bower; you play these games too often. You ring me up expecting me to drop everything and come out with you but when it's something I want to do it's not convenient. Well! We'll see about that; Greg, enjoy your evening won't you? We sure are going to. Come on Mandy, there's a dance at Whitegrove and I know who will take us. See you around sometime, boys."

She walked off followed by a reluctant Mandy who gave a small bye-bye wave.

"Phew!" breathed Ray. "She doesn't like the word no that one. Perhaps it's time she moved on. If we had stuck with them it would have been an all-night job."

Greg was glad things had sorted themselves. He was not feeling that well and he still had to steel himself to tell Ray the truth; he was dreading that more than anything he had ever done. He only hoped after the initial shock Ray would accept the situation and help him get through it all or would Ray prove faint –hearted and gradually fade away from their friendship. Of course not he knew Ray wouldn't do that he knew him too well, but telling him would change their friendship in some way it was bound to. Ray was chuckling "We must be getting old or something when have we ever passed up the chance to nightclub with two dishy girls? Times are a changing for sure, but to be honest I couldn't cope with them tonight and you don't look so good either". He slapped on Greg the shoulder.

"It's time we talked, really talked, something to eat then I want to know what you've been up to. I want the truth, old son, all of it. It's time beans were spilled. What's all this about Wales? Come on let's go." He picked up the gear and headed for the truck.

Chapter 8

The evening had become wet and chilly so Ray had lit the fire as soon as they had eaten. The room was warm the sounds of traffic outside muted by the heavy curtains drawn against the night. Greg had always felt at home here. To everybody's surprise Ray had kept most of his grandmother's old fashioned furniture and except for modernising the kitchen and bathroom had changed very little. Greg tried to relax in the deep armchair and enjoy the brandy Ray passed him before throwing himself on the opposite settee.

The warmth of the spirit steadied him but his nerves tensed as he wondered about the remarks Ray had made at the boat. He couldn't possible know anything. Christ! This was hard and going to get harder. There was no way he could tell Ray that his best friend was going to die. He knew from experience it was very hard to hide anything from him but he couldn't possibly have guessed. For all his light-hearted fooling, Ray was shrewd and perceptive, had a nasty habit of suddenly coming out with the secret you had tried so hard to keep.

"Come on, Greg, what gives?" Ray settled himself and lit a cigarette.

"Well I'm getting off the rig. Doc found a spot on the lung; not serious but got to take it easy for a time, rest up, eat well and rest a lot; you know the sort of thing. Don't get the idea……. He interrupted as Ray started to speak." I'm not off to a sanatorium or anything like that but you know what life can be like on the rig, forgetting to eat or even sleep when hot on a project. I only get back to normal when I'm ashore. If I take too long on the sick it's a strain on everyone else. Tom would have to get a temporary replacement and that is next to impossible, like asking for gold there are just not enough trained bodies out there. Tom has to have commitment though I know he would bend the rules a little for me. Tom's good, not like some of the bastards out there like Forbes when Barney went sick with meningitis last year. I told you about that; I could tell a lot more tales about him and a couple of others out there that would make you sick, the conditions some of them have to work under. I'm lucky and Tom deserves the best so I did a lot of thinking and decided I would try something else in my life. I want to be nearer my folks for one thing they have aged a lot recently, I noticed that last week when I was there. It will only get worse and I am all they have."

"So!" Ray finally got his oar in. "Where does this farm and mountain lark come in?" He sat up." You've got it haven't you? Thought you were out of your tree. Sure there isn't a girl in it somewhere?

"No such luck." Greg laughed more easily now, Ray hadn't noticed his tension and had taken his explanation without more than a quick intake of breath and a muttered oath.

"Made an offer, heard yesterday that it had been accepted but I'm damned if I know how I'm going to make it."

"Why? You've savings I know, take the rest on mortgage." He rose to pour another drink Greg winced; he wasn't prepared for that one.

"Of course I can." He replied shakily. But I am trying to be clever here and pay for it outright."

"Good God! Man, how much have you got for Pete's sake?" (dodgy this)

"Not a lot, sold some shares, raided the bank, selling most of the furniture, still be a shortfall until the flat sells. A bridging loan is a swine if you don't know how long you are going to need it for. The flat should go; I've two agents on it."

"I agree, it's a great flat." Ray threw another log on the fire. "How much are you asking?" When Greg told him he whistled. "That's giving it away.'

"I know but it must sell quickly or I could be in trouble. Some of it's going to have to keep me until I know what I'm going to do with my life: I don't know that yet either."

Ray studied him closely. "You know Greg, I would never have said you were impulsive or unpredictable, in fact that's the last thing I would have said about you but in the last year you have really shaken the shit out of me. First goes Stephanie, great looking brilliant cook, made your pad posh, you've been with her; what was it six years? I did expect to be hiring the morning suit sometime soon but out she goes, no messing never to be seen again. Now shocks two and three. job gone, shares gone, a wage packet (not to be sneezed at –seven years training to even get your nose in the door) just like Steph out. Now farming! Greg, for God's sake what's happened to you? I know what you're saying;

you're not well; you being ill is a worry because you look like a stand-in for Tarzan. I don't believe your problem is as serious as all that. Take sick leave, Tom will wait for you when he wouldn't for anyone else and you know it. Take the share money, go six months in Switzerland then come back and start again.'

Ray rose and agitatedly paced the room running his hands wildly through his hair before reaching for his cigarettes.

"Don't waste it all, Greg. If there are other problems, I'll help you get it sorted just talk to me.'

'Now is the time.'Greg decided." Go for it, moron, tell him."

"Look Ray, there is something else…." The phone shilled sharply into the room as if on cue. Ray grabbed it with an oath. "Hi Dave, yes sure we will. How about next Saturday—hang on." He covered the mouthpiece turning to Greg." How about we have supper with Dave and Liz next week?"

Greg nodded assent, his mouth drying palms sweaty. God! Why did the phone have to ring now of all times. Ray was still talking. "Okay, tell Liz thanks. Hey! Did that guy come in for the Sierra? Sold a pup there, bet he thinks twice before going there next time. Tell you what I found out…" The conversation slid into work-a-day world. 'For Christ's sake come off the phone Ray 'Greg willed him to put the phone down. 'I'm not going to be able to tell you anything now'

Fifteen minutes later Ray put the phone down. "Sorry about that, Dave can never come off the subject of work. It'll be the same next weekend but they are nice people. Coffee?"

Ray came back from the kitchen putting the mugs on the floor. "Come on then, what's this place really like?" Greg led into the details almost with relief. The time had passed for confessions of that nature, by the time he had reached the machinery shed in his narrative, Ray was on the edge of his seat. He still thought Greg was mad but he was firing on all four cylinders when he heard about the Land Rover. If Greg was buying the place he was already planning a holiday to suss it out. Against his better judgement Greg told him about his meeting with Bronwyn Rhys referring to her as a white witch. Ray had an immediate desire to meet her. "She's sure to be a clairvoyant." Ray was a great believer in the occult his weakness the reading of all horoscopes and a dash into the fortune telling tent at the fair. As most predictions consisted of telling him he was going to make a reasonable amount of money (which he did) and about to meet the girl in his life which he also did (quite regularly) he believed in them implicitly They talked far into the night until Greg stretched and thought longingly of bed, Ray leapt to his feet. "Hang on a minute I've had a thought---He hurried into the kitchen returning with two steaming mugs, the aroma of brandy wafting from them. Putting them carefully on the floor and sitting cross legged beside them he lit a cigarette.

"Got an idea, bet you won't go for it though." He paused, looking intently at Greg.

"What?" Greg yawned. Ray narrowed his eyes pulling his wallet from the back pocket of his jeans. "Here's a tenner says you won't do it."

"Come on Ray, its sleep time, do what?"

"Sell me the Jag.' Greg's eyes flew open. 'What?'

Ray leant forward. "Listen, I think you crazy but I've always believed that a man should do his own thing but have a bit of adventure in his life if he can. Although I might tear a strip off you I'm not your typical nine to five man; if something came up that I really wanted to do more than what I'm doing now I'd go for it. I still think you are wrong; you're losing too much but---- he shrugged. "If that's what you want - go for it. I'm seeing it like this, no loans but you don't know when the flat will sell and you've raised all you can bar the odds and sods of furniture etc. You are still short by how much? Greg told him roughly "I have to allow for living expenses until I can find some way of earning "Again the temptation to tell him was on his tongue. Ray was quickly writing on a scrap of paper.

"Hell! the Jag is worth more than that. Sell her to me. I've a bit put by and business is good; in fact we are doing well."

"I can't do that. That car is my life and we worked damned hard on her didn't we? Anyway it wouldn't be practical I need a car where I'm going."

"Not that one you don't; not if I know anything at all about Welsh mountains which I admit is very little but you said yourself you had to leave it at the end of the drive. Are you going to keep it there summer and winter? Where else are you going to get the money from quickly without borrowing? I have the business, this house with no mortgage. I can afford it lend it you if you'd rather. Come on Greg, you need the money and I've always envied you that one. Wouldn't that pull the birds?'

'As if you need it for that.' Greg scoffed. "You and that pick-up are Hulls answer to the guided missile.'

'Yes but with the Jaguar a better class of bird could come my way, someone like Steph not these fur coat-no draws types that any Pratt in a pick-up can pick up.'

"You said that not Me." laughed Greg. "Give me time to think about it. I appreciate your offer and I guess far from helping me, you have an ulterior motive." He dodged Ray's quick punch and made for the stairs. "I'll sleep on it, let you know tomorrow.'

"Okay but I want your tenner on the table if you don't. Ray shouted after him slamming the bathroom door.

Greg sat at the window for a long while. The thought of selling his car had never entered his head. He had found her through a friend of a friend and she had been a mess when he bought her but evenings and weekends,(much to Stephanie's annoyance); he had spent time and money on her. Ray had helped him although he had lost a girlfriend over it while Greg and Steph had several rows about it but they had returned time after time to the business of bringing her to perfection. She was part of his life and he couldn't imagine not having her. Of course she was worth a lot more money but he would feel happier for Ray to have her than anyone else. He would have to accept if he wanted to bring his plans to fruition. Hell! There had been some rough moments when he had almost told him. Of course he would tell him as soon as he had a chance.

Church bells ringing for morning service roused Greg from a deep sleep. He lay a while feeling well and relaxed thinking of Ray's offer of the night before; sell the Jag? He didn't want to; he had intended to keep it until the doc said no more driving that could be anytime, strange that it hadn't happened already. If a transplant came though how soon before he could drive again? Suddenly he remembered the Witches words 'you want to sell that fancy car.....it will rip the guts out of it.' She was right the car was far too low for those mountain roads and to leave it at the end of the drive, even if he built a shelter was unthinkable, perhaps the time had come to start making some sacrifices. He would only be leaving it for his parents to sell. It would be hard to see Ray driving it but after all he had worked on it almost as much and I would have the farm. The familiar thrill of excitement stirred his blood and he knew there was no going back, job, flat, furniture and car, it all had to go and that was that.

Ray was already up. "Eggs alright? Toast and marmalade are on the table. Sleep alright?

"Fine thanks. Look Ray, you can have the car but only what you can afford mind after all you did almost as much work on her.'

"Yippee!" Ray threw an egg in the air and deftly caught it. "Don't be an idiot, I know the value of that car and what it means to you, besides you need that money'

"Just be good to her and I will be glad that she's going to you that's all'

"Hey! I just had another brilliant idea." Greg groaned aloud. "What now?"

"You're going to want wheels anyway but you also need to keep the dosh right? Guess what? At the back of the garage is a Subaru pick –up, needs some bits doing and a new set of tyres would just do for you though. I'll do it up whatever it needs. Tested, on the road add it onto the cash and you won't lose out. Fit for the Black mountains. I'll talk to Dave and have her on the road. Do we have a deal?"

"I'll trust you, thousands wouldn't" grinned Greg holding out his hand. "I was just thinking that I would have to find an old banger."

"Actually this isn't an old banger, she's only three years old but not been treated right; some eighteen year old thrashed the shit out of her until he spotted something better but she's all right you'll see." "Done" They shook hands.

"Come on let's get some air. It's going to tip down this afternoon."

They walked down to Ray's parents where they were fed at lunch time on roast pork and apple pie, walking back in the late afternoon when the rain began in earnest.

The next few weeks found Greg with a hundred and one things to do, luckily his spell of feeling good continued unless he over exerted when pain and shortness of breath warned him to slow down. He kept dates with his bank manager and solicitor, changed his will, sorted funds, visited friends and saw to the sale of his belongings. People came and went at the flat but he left that to his agent staying with Ray until the Tuesday when he lunched with Tom and Betty Gregson later flying with Tom out to the rig where he met Geoff Godard his replacement. It wasn't possible to spend the time he would have liked to ease Geoff in to the team as he was his sort of guy and they would have worked well together; he was a talented man delighted to slot into the new program. Greg felt upset when the week came to an end and very emotional when his colleagues arranged farewell drinks, surprised and delighted when they presented him with a miniature oil rig in bronze with a scroll signed by all on board. After speeches of commiseration (Tom had been a true friend only telling the men that Greg was changing careers) there was much hand shaking and good luck wishes. Greg returned their toasts, welcoming Geoff on their behalf this was followed by speeches from contractors and managers. He had made many friends and all were sorry to see him go and wished him luck with his farming although that had brought many a jest and good natured laugh from his colleagues.

Greg came ashore for the last time the following Wednesday, making an excuse to Ray that he had lots to do, he shut himself in his flat, took the phone off the hook and spent the next couple of days suffering the tortures of the damned all over again. Waking on Saturday red eyed and haggard with grief, he took himself off in the Jag. He spent a long time sitting watching the sea and the gulls wheeling above. He strolled along bridle paths wishing that he had a dog for company. When he felt like eating he found quiet inns and slept in quieter ones wondering if he would ever see these places again. For three days the sea and the country rolled before him until gradually he felt comforted and rested.

He finally returned to Ray's house and he after one look at Greg's gaunt face and tired eyes, phoned Dave and took his friend out on the boat for the next couple of days. Greg felt too unwell to talk much and Ray left him to himself concentrating on fishing and cooking them to tempt Greg's appetite.

Ray felt there was more to his illness than he had told him but he waited until Greg was ready to talk but it didn't look like soon, the best he could do was to be a true friend, help where he could and be there for him when he did. Ray was seriously worried about the farm bit and couldn't wait to see for himself what had caused his friend to change his life style. He had a bad feeling about all of this but wouldn't push; he would wait until the right time. They spent the following weekend on the boat as well but Greg now felt well enough to enjoy the company of a couple of girls and the time passed in sailing, picnics and pleasant evenings

The next couple of weeks saw all the loose ends tied and Greg signed the contract. "Longest two weeks of my life." He told Ray still not able to tell him why he found each day precious for its own sake and why he revelled in everything; sun, wind and rain. A new set of values had become Greg's, each day was like a lit candle and he watched it burn away sometimes with content, sometimes with fear always with a prayer.

It was now the end of May. Ray was taking his holidays when Greg moved, arranging with a cousin to hire his van and give them a hand; he looked at his friend strangely from time to time as he saw him flagging at what used to be simple tasks but he could see a decline in Greg's stamina and found it hard to accept. Tod looked a lot like Ray except he was darker but the same blue eyes and ready grin, unlike Ray he was shy although he had managed to get himself a fiancée and planned an autumn wedding. He was looking forward to staying for a few days and getting his first glimpse of the Welsh hills.

Chapter 9

It was a perfect spring day as Olwen left for Worcester, a cold clear day not a cloud in the sky, flowers beginning to bloom in the hedges and birds giving full voice to their plans. Usually Olwen enjoyed her early morning trip back from her grandmothers but today she had very mixed feelings. She was looking forward to her classes and eager to show them the new ideas that were flooding her mind but it was overshadowed by the fact that Aiden may not have left as she asked him to but was waiting for her to come back to continue the argument that he should stay and it was her that was being unreasonable. She was not afraid of him although he had shown a nasty temper at times; she was more afraid of him wearing her down until she was committed to something that she didn't want at all. she was not in love with him and she just wanted him to leave, however he was not the kind of person that you told to do anything, he pleased himself; he would try to charm her or dominate her into submission and although Olwen could stand up for herself she hated the conflict and pressure. She was determined this time it would not happen.

Parking her car she was relieved to see Aiden's space empty. With a sigh of relief she unloaded her bag, briefcase and Grannie's box of goodies she always brought back. The flat was quiet and very tidy she almost dared to hope when she saw the note on the table.

'I've gone to stay with Marcus until you come to your senses. You need space I'm giving you space, make good use of it. I'll see you next week. Don't be too long about it. Have fun. X'

"Shit" Olwen slung the note in the waste basket in disgust then kicking it across the floor. She slammed her fist on the table.

"How high handed, patronising and bloody minded is that" She was consumed with rage. How dare he make out she was going to be a pushover anymore? Enough was enough and she had taken all that she was going to take. She picked up the phone and rang the flats caretaker Dave stressing that it was urgent that her locks were changed right away. Dave had heard it all before there was always someone breaking up or breaking in; he promised to call around that evening. With a sigh of relief she unpacked showered and changed before heading off to her workshop firmly putting it all out of her mind as she greeted her students keen to see how they had individually handled their projects. Several asked if she had enjoyed her weekend and she could honestly reply that she had. Olwen settled into her day with a lighter heart now she had taken her first steps to independence.

Dave true to his word fitted her new locks early evening, teasing her about who she wanted to keep out. Later she sat with a glass of her favourite wine and allowed herself to dream about the little farm under the rock. How she would love to live there where the garden was full of flowers and the stream wandered through the yard. She could see herself wading in to clear it out having great fun. Of course she would have money to do the roof and who knows what state the inside would be in. She sighed there was no way that was going to happen, the little savings she had was not going to let her even think of buying it let alone what it would cost to do up. She only hoped the man that was buying it had good taste or at least a girlfriend who did. She wouldn't want to walk up there and find they had pulled it down to build another house or pulled it about until it didn't look anything like it was now. Well a girl could dream couldn't she? It was never going to happen that was for sure. She sighed longingly then smiled. She had better keep doing the lottery.

The next morning she filled black bags with Aiden's clothes, CDs and books, piling them in the boot of her car driving slowly around to Marcus's flat. She prayed she wouldn't meet either of them on the way. Luck was with her and with a sigh of relief she dumped it all in Marcus's bike shed pinning a note to the door. With a light heart she returned to her workshop. She didn't think for a moment he would let that stop him and waited with some trepidation for an angry phone call which to her surprise didn't come. She phoned Bronwyn telling her what she had done. "Good girl" was the reply but with a gentle warning to be careful in case of repercussions.

Chapter 10

The weather was fine and the journey uneventful. Once they were through Abergavenny the twisting lanes slowed the van, Greg wondered what Ray was thinking as he led them into the hills. When they at last pulled onto the cobbled yard, he grinned to see Ray's face as he jumped from the van and looked around.

"Bloody Hell! Greg we've done some things in our misspent youth but I reckon this beats the lot. Where are we for God's sake, surely you aren't going to live in that shed?'

"It's not a shed" Greg unlocked the door. "Come on in. Welcome to Graig-y-Dorth."

Ray stood very still, hands on hips surveying the mountain green now with a carpet of fern. Tod stood silent looking around with wide eyes.

"What in God's name are you going to do here? It's not big enough to farm. It's miles from anywhere and it's got a tin roof if you haven't noticed.'

Tod laughed. "I thought you liked mountains, Ray?'

"I do but not to squat under one doing sod all with my life. You gave up all that you had for this? Gone bonkers or what?" Ray lit a cigarette drawing heavily on it as if it might lead him to some understanding of the situation. Tod leaned on the van as if to get back in. Ray looked around.

"Beautiful site if you are going to pull it down and start again but what are you going to live on?'

"If I have been led here for some purpose, that question will take care of itself. You believe in fate and destiny and all that stuff more than I do. You should know. If all that stuff is true what choice do I have? Something will show up. Now get your butt in here, we have to sweep the chimney so that we can light a fire."

Ray said no more and Tod set to with the brushes they had brought. Later with a good fire going and some pies and coffee consumed, they swung into action. When the electric and water turned on, beds put up and essentials brought in, Ray began to show a bit more enthusiasm but before he would do any more he had to see the shed. When he saw the old Land Rover half buried under the tree he was sold, Greg almost had to remove him by force.

"Come on let's get some of the stuff in the house. It might rain."

Ray threw him a quick look and opened the van doors. They worked for the next three hours only stopping for more coffee. Although Greg could feel the ache building in his chest and his strength going he struggled to keep it from Tod and Ray. Finally he called a halt.

"Let's leave the rest until morning. I'm for bed it's been a long day.'

Ray gave him a searching glance usually Greg had the strength of ten men and certainly wouldn't have stopped until everything was in place; still he was ill and Ray didn't know much about lung shadows and things so he agreed to pack up for the night. He said nothing to Tod but he was worried, everything Greg was doing was completely out of character. He was certain this move was not a good idea. It just didn't make sense. He hoped in the next few days to be able to find some reason for the change in his friend. He felt certain it was not just this illness, there was something more and Ray was determined to find out.

The next few days kept them busy. Greg tried to pull his weight but it was beyond him and he found himself picking the easier jobs and leaving the lifting and tugging to Ray and Tod. He was fortunate here as Tod was a great one for pitching in without being asked. He was a strong lad and often took jobs off Greg without thinking. He knew Greg wasn't well and that was enough for Tod, he would have done it all by himself without thought, Ray worked hard but Tod worked harder so Greg slid under the net without much notice taken. He took it on himself to provide meals and keep the fires going. He also took on sorting out the kitchen so they had a sterile clean place to store food and eat.

Ray was beginning to enjoy himself. A couple of days and the place was coming to some sort of order, entering into the spirit of things he began to make a list of the sort of things that Greg could do to make a living, he and Tod were full of suggestions from market gardening, sheep farming and breeding dogs. Greg laughed with them and promised to think about it. Talk then led to Greg's finances. He had paid outright for the farm and was left with a couple of thousand to see him through until the flat sold.

'If and when the flat sells." Ray reminded him. The agent had not been too hopeful of a quick sale, too big and expensive for the average man, not large enough for a family.

"Surely it's a business man's flat?" Greg had argued with him.

"Yes. As long as he has enough income or two could share but don't hold your breaths for a quick sale will you? It will go eventually it's a nice flat."

Ray was bothered; he came back to the subject the next morning as they were painting the kitchen.

"If that flat doesn't sell for a year, what then?" If it doesn't sell for six months your money isn't going to last that long,"

"I'll think of something." Greg replied trying not to look worried. "The only pity is that I can't put this place to rights until it does sell. I do need a new roof and a decent bathroom and shower and I'd like to finish the extension."

"I'll give you a hand when you do need it." Tod wiped his paint brush and his hands. "Thanks! It'll give you a few more days holiday but what will your new bride think of it? You will be married by then and under the thumb"

"Nah, I'll still come" They laughed. Ray wiped his hands and opened a can of lager throwing a one to Tod. "I still don't understand why you couldn't have taken out a small mortgage. You could still do it at least it would give you a bit of leeway. I think you were mad to part with all that money when you knew the place was in this state. I didn't realise how bad it was I thought you were just painting a wilderness picture. Talking of wilderness where does the witch live?"

"Back down the hill I think. There are several cottages down there." Greg was relieved to get of the subject of mortgages. "There are a few neighbours around, haven't met any others yet."

"Witch where?" Tod looked around fearfully. Ray laughed. "Tod don't like things like that you'll scare him he'll jump in the van and be off. You will have to get a phone line in soon, the mobile's not enough very poor signal, I have to go up to the gate to get a good one." Ray stretched flinging down his brush. "Hell! This place is filthy, it's going to take gallons of this magnolia, good job we bought a good dose of it."

They had made a trip the day before and stocked up on rollers, brushes, nails, hooks and gallons of white and magnolia paint as well as a stack of freezer food and a larder of tins. Greg had sold his cooker with the flat so microwave and the range had to do for a while. The next item on the agenda was ordering or buying coal and cutting a supply of wood. He had to go out and buy a chainsaw tomorrow (more expense) but he couldn't chop wood. Money could be a problem sooner than he thought. He went to put the kettle on thinking very negative thoughts. Later however as he walked in the yard and saw smoke arising from the cleaned chimney in a soft grey plume and the lights shining through clean windows, Greg felt the magic return. Whatever happened in the future, however rough it would become, he was here for a new beginning. A Morgan had come home.

Chapter 11

After five days of scrubbing, repairing, burning and painting the old house took on a new life. Coming from town the following Saturday Tod remarked how homely and welcoming it looked. Ray's mother had sent a load of curtains and cushions with him which would have to do temporarily. Greg knew that his mother was dying to get her hands on the place only prevented by a bout of flu which she was certainly not bringing to him. Frequent phone calls warned him that a car full of goodies would be arriving as soon as she had the all clear. The answer to curtain hanging at the moment was for one of them to hold up the curtains while the other chopped them off at whatever level was required. The kitchen was now complete; only awaiting a cooker as Greg had brought freezer and washing machine with him. It was clean and fresh with a smell of pine from the new woodwork that Ray had spent a fair time on. Both Greg and Ray had always carried good tool kits; these now proving invaluable. Ray had hired a sander and as the upstairs floorboards were in good condition he had repaired and sanded them back to the original state. They looked good.

A days before he and Tod were due to leave, Ray came down one morning in a state of rebellion. "Greg have you seen my blisters? There is no way I am doing anymore chopping. We have to hire a chain saw. I haven't seen you chopping lately either and more important there is no way I am going to let another day go by without a look at that Land Rover. Let's go today and hire a saw for God's sake, I'll hire it if we can get it for a week then we can move the tree and see what treasures we have in the woodshed."

"We'll go halves on the hire" Greg filled the kettle, guilty about the way he had avoided any chopping because there was no way he could bring himself to tell Ray the truth when he was so happily settling him in. These were good times he knew Ray would always remember these weeks with pleasure.

"You are right about the Land Rover. I have been steeling myself to keep away from the shed with so much else to do. Let's call it a holiday and get at it. Having the tree cut will be a welcome bonus. We'll hire a saw for now but I am going to have to buy one soon"

Ray was frowning as he opened the gate, things were niggling at him; something felt wrong about the whole set up. He had never known Greg to lie to him but his whole being told him that the truth was being badly bent. If this farm was bigger and in good repair not so useless for anything, he might be able to understand that Greg wanted to move here. It had been in his family for many years after all but there was the fact that Greg didn't really want to work at anything making excuses to go and do something else when they were on a job as if he couldn't finish one damn job before starting another it just wasn't like him. He appeared nervy and preoccupied and Ray didn't like the way he turned an awful colour after any exertion making silly excuses about being out of training. Greg was a perfect specimen for Christ's sake fitter than himself surely a spot on a lung wouldn't do this. He knew they had done some daft and dangerous things in the past; he had seen Greg lift the front or backend of a car by himself before now, in fact it was Ray who had shouted at him about straining himself perhaps that is what he had done so why didn't he say so?' Deep in thought he came to as Greg slammed on the brakes.

"Damn the woman." He yelled. As they rounded the sharp bend by the church, Ray saw a tall gaunt woman jump into the hedge dragging a funny coloured dog with her.

"Why can't you look where you are going?" Greg wound the window down as he spoke. The woman straightened and as Ray met her strange light eyes, he realised that this was Greg's witch.

"Why don't you stop using these roads as a race track? Don't you realise there are animals about in these country lanes? You might put me in the ditch and think it funny but what about Samuel Peeps here? Do you get pleasure in running over dumb animals?"

"Just a moment---"Greg interrupted her flow. "Let's get a few facts straight here. First I was not speeding, secondly the dog should be on a lead and no I don't make a habit of killing animals nor find it funny to see people jump. Why do you see the worst in people? Look to yourself, you know the bends are there and cars are on the road. Why don't you take more care?"

Bronwyn Rhys released the dog which bounded over the road and into the gateway of a whitewashed cottage which stood end on to the road.

"Young man" she looked them both up and down, her light eyes sharp and steely. "I see who you are, we have met before. I am glad to see you have had the sense to get a more practical vehicle but it does not give you the right to drive around carelessly." She held her hand up as Greg moved to speak.

"Alright I admit I may be somewhat to blame in this instance." Greg's mouth dropped open. "I assume this thing has a horn of some kind; I suggest that you find where it is and use it." She crossed in front of the pick-up disappearing into the house after the dog. Ray was in stitches, Greg speechless. He put the truck in gear and moved slowly on. When Ray finally speak "So that's your witch, you didn't introduce me. You realise she will put a spell on you now don't you?"

Greg turned a scowling face on him. Ray spluttered. "You should have seen your face."

"How the bloody hell did I get put in the wrong? The silly woman was in the middle of the road, the dog off the lead and I get put in the wrong."

Ray shook with laughter. "Who the hell is Samuel Peeps?" he asked when he could speak.

"The dog." Greg snapped.

"For Pete's sake why a name like that?"

"Because he has wall eyes and peeps at you from the brown one."

This was too much for Ray and Greg could get no sense out of him until they reached Abergavenny. As they walked through the town looking for the hire shop, they noticed crowds gathering in the old market place.

"There's a sale." Greg stopped to look. "They have these in Swansea sometimes, wonder if there's anything good, let's have a look." The old green domed market was a hive of activity, pictures, tools, furniture and fittings of all kinds from baths to bedsteads filling the huge hall. People jammed the aisles all talking at once, pulling things about rummaging in boxes full of china, knick- knacks and rubbish. Tables full of books of all kinds while pictures of pastoral scenes leaned precariously against table legs along with portraits of gentlemen with moustaches in stiff collars and ladies held upright with pearl chockers and layers of lace. Someone was trying out a piano, kids banging the keys of another. The smell of dust and must mingled with the smell of humanity, sweat, perfume and tobacco. The enticing smell of frying bacon wafted from a cave like café at the side of the hall. Brown coated assistants hurried about. Women turned over curtains and bedding, inspected baby cots and prams. The overall noise was deafening.

Neither Greg nor Ray had experienced a sale of this magnitude before and they were fascinated. They enjoyed an hour of picking up and putting down as much as anyone there. Ray was amused to see a couple of boats in the main aisle, one hooked to a Cortina car both for sale. Presently a bell rang and the auctioneers began calling for attention. They watched proceedings for a while until Ray noticed that Greg was missing. He found him in the lower part of the market examining an apparently new three seater settee and two deep recliners in red leather.

"I fancy these, wonder how much they will fetch? We can't keep sitting on those old chairs."

"Go for it. Here he comes now."

Before they forced themselves away, Greg was the owner of the settee and recliners, a scrubbed pine table and four chairs. Half an hour later to his delight outside among the machinery was a chainsaw, in working condition and started up by an assistant to prove it. It ran to more than Greg wanted to give for a second hand one but it would do for the present. Ray had also become carried away in the heat of the moment buying himself a huge toolbox filled with all sorts of treasures. They rang Tod to bring the van and while they were waiting they enjoyed watching two dealers having a full scale row about who had purchased what. After a verbal row which looked to the delighted onlookers as if it might come to blows, one walked off leaving the other the victor; by the time Tod arrived with the van, they were sat with a mug of tea each, people watching with great amusement.

As they drove back through Graigwen following Tod with the van, Ray realised he had left his cigarettes in the market. He pulled up at the village shop. "Should give it up" Greg remarked who had never started the habit and was almost asleep. "Will one day" was the reply as Ray climbed back in the driving seat. "There's a notice in the window here a dance on Saturday at the village hall. Want to go?"

"I don't think so." Greg was feeling decidedly ill after the day's activities.

"Oh! Come on, we've earned a break, let's go if only for a laugh, haven't been to a village hop for years. Tod will go anyway."

"Okay." Greg realised that both the lads had given up their holidays to work like ten men into the bargain and there was no way he could find an excuse not to go with them. "Your right it could be fun."

The best of the day was gone by the time they had eaten but Ray was determined to get to grips with the tree. Greg felt more like going to bed but couldn't say anything. The lads were going home in a couple of days and he didn't want to spoil their fun. Unfortunately the saw which had fired up in the saleroom fired once then stopped. Taking it to pieces they found the petrol filter hanging loose and gummed up with sawdust. Ray washed the filter with petrol cleaning every part carefully then put back together it started first time. He started on the ash tree with Tod loading a wheelbarrow and making a log pile in the stable. To their disappointment they would have to wait for morning to get near the Land Rover. The problem was getting the logs and branches out of the way and the light was going. Ray took one look at Greg's colourless face and hearing him panting as he walked about, called a halt and sent him in to make tea.

Next day they were once again frustrated by the junk in the way. Ray could saw the branches and block them but there was nowhere to put them once he had. Tod had battles getting the wheelbarrow through and couldn't work quick enough to catch up with Ray who was sitting up in the tree waiting for him to come back. Tod had the sense as soon as he saw a break to pick up the chain harrows which were taking up most of the doorway and pull them out into the yard. Once this was done he had a clear run with his wheelbarrow and things moved on a pace. Greg found a set of garden tools with several scythes, bill hooks and other useful gadgets.

"Be careful up there." he called to Ray who was now astride the ladder as near to the main trunk of the tree as he could get. "It doesn't look rotten but you can't see what is holding it up"

"It's fine, it's caught on the two walls it's not going anywhere." Greg took himself off to start a fire the far side of the yard. When he came back the tree was gone but a huge pile of logs were still keeping Tod busy. The urge to see the Land Rover was too much for all of them. Ray jumped down to join them, his face red, his fair curly hair standing on end full of sawdust and twigs. They all approached the vehicle together.

"She looks bad outwardly, doesn't she?" The canvas roof hung in shreds one support rail badly twisted, the driver's door dented in. "I can't open that." Ray tugged. Windscreen was cracked and the tyres perished. "All repairable." muttered Greg walking around. "Ray if this is what I think it is we may have a nineteen forty-eight original here."

"Didn't they have a petrol cap under the seat?"

"Right on they did." Ray beat Greg to the passenger door which opened easily enough disturbing some mice which had nested in the leather seat. "Ugh I'm tied up in spider's webs."

"Serve you right for being first." Greg pushed his head in beside Ray who lay flat, feeling under the driver's seat. "Yes, it's here Greg."

"Great all we need now is an engine. Pray to God no one has taken it out. He tugged at the bonnet's rusty catch. Pain shot across his chest, he stepped back leaning against the wing. The engine was there alright, a twelve horse power cylinder rover. They stood gazing in awe. Mice had eaten all the rubber off the wires and hoses, made nests in the air filter. Tod rushed forward then jumped back. "Distributer cap cracked but the plugs are still in. Maybe the engine is okay. If there's a starter handle we could be alright if there isn't we are knackered, should be under the seat,"

Greg recovering reached under the seat. "Good Grief! We're in luck it's still here." Ray fitting it turning slowly, to their surprise the engine turned over.

"It's turning, I don't believe it, it's not seized. God Almighty all this time and it's not seized." Greg took a deep breath. "What now Ray? It won't actually start will it?"

"No battery, I'll get the one off the truck." Ray leapt the rubbish returning with the battery. It took moments to fix although he had to substitute a wire." I'll put a wire through the ignition switch and see what we've got. Jump in Greg, see what happens." Greg climbed over the passenger seat. "I can't find a starter button."

"Try the floor- button there somewhere." It was immediately beneath his leg, he pressed and the engine turned over. Greg held his breath pressed again nothing happened and again, nothing.

"Hang on Greg let me have a look again at the plugs. I've taken one out now try again. It's sparking, must be petrol." Ray took a sample from the carburettor. "Flat I'll have to drain the system."

"There's a spare can we bought for the pick-up in the shed." Tod came around to look. "I'll fetch it." When he returned he emptied it in the tank and Ray pumped it through putting the plug back. "Hope there's no dirt in it now. Pull the choke Greg and try again" Nothing. "Blast it, give it another go" The Land Rover juddered and fired. "Once more" The engine leaped into life.

Tod and Ray leaped around like children, slapping each other on the back and whooping their voices echoing back from the hill. Greg sat in the Land Rover on the mouse's nest grinning happily. "Well done Ray, great job. I knew your hot rodding days weren't wasted. What a find." Ray's oily face beamed back at him. "Get your pen out and your cheque book. You'll need. New distributer cap set of tyres, plugs, new lights, windscreen. I think I can hammer the door out, not a problem, need a new loom, I've only done a temporary job on the wiring. We'll get it priced up; might cost a bit but oh! What a find. We'll scout around see what we can pick up. I can get bits back at the garage know a few old contacts and more than a few scrap yards. I'll come back in a few weeks and give you a hand. That is if you want Greg? I'm taking over a bit, aren't I? Or do you want to do it yourself?"

"Ray." Greg put his hand on his friend's shoulder. "It's our project not just mine. I couldn't have done this without you. You and Tod have been a godsend these couple of weeks. Don't think that you are going off to Spain on your next holiday. You have got more time to come haven't you?"

"Yeah, Dave owes me. I've been months now without a break and it's always me that stays home and does the rush jobs. Dave gave himself six weeks in the Algarve last year so it's my turn. I'm taking a month now and some more in September but I'll come for a few long weekends now and then if you'll have me. Tod can't for a while as he's starting a new job when he gets back."

"You bet I will. I need the company and there's plenty more work to be done" a sly grin. "You'll earn your keep" Ray threw the oily rags at him.

"And there's the tractor!"

"We'll leave that for a while. Somehow I think we have enough on our plates and a lot of fun to be had on this. Don't let's push our luck but it could be an asset to this place if it can be got to go. Plenty of rainy day work here. Come on Tod, your turn to make the tea."

Chapter 12

It was a week later that Olwen returned from her classes to find Aiden at her door with a bottle of wine and a large bouquet of flowers. Her heart sank as she came up the steps. He smiled mocking and confident. He came forward and kissed her cheek. She drew back "What are you doing here?"

"I think we should be having a talk about things.'

"I don't want to talk to you." She turned away. He caught her arm. "Please, let's just sit down have a glass of wine and talk." She sighed 'Maybe it would be fair to him; reluctantly she opened the door and he followed her in. He tried to take her in his arms but she stepped sideways, switching on the light and dropping her bag on the table.

"You're being very unfriendly." He put the flowers in the sink, standing the bottle on the draining board he moved to fetch glasses from the cupboard.

"Olwen put up a hand. "Don't start; I don't want to know. I asked you to move out. I don't want to drink wine with you. I have had enough. Please leave, I am sorry it hasn't worked out. You are a lovely, talented man but we are not compatible and never will be, so please go now and maybe we can still be friends."

"I don't want to be friends. I want you to be marrying me. You know that."

"That's never going to happen, Aiden, so accept it and go."

"You are not getting rid of me that easily my girl." His voice changed, he came to her holding both her arms. "Don't play with me. You are playing games and I will not be doing with it. You listen to me; we are back together and it's going to stay that way. If you don't want to get married, fair enough. I can take that as long as we stay together.'

"No Aiden. I told you in my note and I'm telling you now. It's over. Now will you please leave me alone?"

"Don't be stupid Olwen. You know we go well together. You are just having a childish tantrum. I won't let you ruin my life or yours either for that matter and that's what you will be doing.'

She stepped back as far as the kitchen units allowed, he was beginning to worry her now. She prayed someone would come to the door or ring her phone but there was no one. She wasn't one for crying; tears were very close but they would show weakness and he would take full advantage of that. She slid sideways to reach the door but he grabbed her arms trying to kiss her. As she fought him, he picked her up carrying her into the bedroom. Panicking she screamed clawing at his face and pulling his hair. Kicking the door shut he threw her onto the bed. She screamed again, pleading with him as she tried to roll off the bed but he was on top of her pinning her down his hand sliding up her leg while his other hand caught and held both her wrists, she cursed herself for wearing a skirt that morning. There was no stopping him holding both hands above her head he raped her stopping her cries with his mouth. She thought it would never end when it was finally over she was sobbing bitterly her head turned into the pillow while he stood rearranging his clothing looking down at her.

"Now you be calming yourself, no harm done. Tidy yourself, I am going to my office and I expect you to be here for dinner. By the way I didn't use any protection so if you're pregnant it will be a bonus. Let's not have any more of your nonsense. You're mine so don't you be forgetting it." He left slamming the door behind him.

Olwen lay sobbing, consumed with guilt, fear and disgust. She raged at herself for allowing this situation to happen. The disgust she felt was mixed with fury. Did he honestly think he was going to get away with this? Did he really think that she was going to allow him anywhere near her ever again? Shaking with shock and rage she was off the bed and locking the door stayed in the shower sobbing for a long time, rubbing at her skin until she was raw, she finally staggered out wrapping herself in a thick blanket while she tried to think what to do. After a strong coffee (which she wished was whisky) she realised she had no time to lose. Aiden was going to be back. She quickly dressed in warm slacks and jumper; even after the hot shower she was so cold she didn't think she would ever be warm again; she quickly packed all she would need for a few days and standing where she could watch the car park; she rang Dave Tanner caretaker of the flats asking ask him to change the locks as soon as possible. Dave was used to this kind of request; relationships ended or someone tried to break in. He promised to do it this evening if she would leave her keys at his office and collect hers afterwards. Olwen rang her friend Alicia bursting into tears again as she heard her voice.

"Don't you stay there another minuet, come on over and bring your things with you. If you aren't here in half an hour I'll come and fetch you."

Olwen smiled through her tears. Alicia had been her friend since they had attended their first interviews together, she had never been too fond of Aiden; said he was domineering and full of himself and she only put up with him for Olwen's sake. She herself was married to a science teacher who was away on a course at the moment. Harry was a kind gentle man who would be horrified when he heard. Alicia wrapped Olwen in her arms when she arrived and they both cried together. On learning that Olwen hadn't eaten that day she immediately sent out for a Chinese meal pouring them a brandy each as they waited for it to arrive. Alicia insisted that they tell the police.

"If I do he'll lose his job and he is the best musician the college has ever had." Olwen picked at her sweet and sour chicken. She felt she might never eat again.

"Listen to me. He will be going out with other girls; you can't let it happen again. I'm pretty sure the college will side with you not him. They have a duty to protect their students. Talk to Professor Colby, see what he says but you must report it Olwen."

Olwen lay in bed unable to sleep tossing and turning, her mind going over and over the experience, sometimes crying sometimes so angry she just wanted to get up, find him and hurt him as he had hurt her. Had she encouraged him, led him on? Was he right, had she been playing games without realising it? She had only asked him to leave that wasn't playing games, was it? She knew it wasn't and she hadn't been unreasonable in telling him to go. What if she had married him? How would he have treated her then? "Like a doormat." Alicia had said. "Slapping you around when he felt like it. "You aren't that sort of girl; you are fiery, feisty and deserve so much better. You don't love him anyway so ditch him. let the law deal with him. If he loses his job so much better, we don't want the likes of him around here thank you."

Alicia made Olwen smile despite herself. She was right she must go to the authorities in the morning, she should have done so last night but she was in no state. Thinking this through it was dawn before she finally fell asleep.

Professor Colby was deeply distressed at her interview with him next day. He repeated what Alicia had said about protecting other students and was so understanding Olwen cried all over again. The white haired twinkly eyed Professor patted her shoulder awkwardly then without consulting her further rang a friend of his in the police force who came around almost immediately with a female colleague. They too were easy with her the policewoman leading Olwen to one side to discuss the incident. Olwen found it so hard to talk about such intimate things but Constable Wendy Wright was gentle but thorough, so Olwen was able to go with them for an examination by a police doctor. Unfortunately as they told her, she had showered and changed her clothes which they then asked her to collect and to bring in to them.

Collecting her keys from Dave she let herself into the flat. She really didn't want to be there and collected her things as quickly as possible. She was unable to ring her grandmother either it would have to wait until she see her which was going to be as soon as she could get away. Professor Colby had suggested that she take time off and go. He had gently questioned her about where and she talked to him for a while about her grandmother. He admitted that the Black Mountains were the ideal place to recover recalling he used to walk there every summer in his youth.

It was several days later that Olwen learned that Aiden had been relieved of his post. His case came up but was dismissed for lack of evidence. The fact that Olwen had bathed, dressed and left the flat, not reporting it until the next day went against her. It was with relief she heard that he had gone back to Ireland a few days later. Thankfully she decided to head for the mountains. She knew she would recover by talking to Bronwyn her astringent views would heal her more than anyone. She went back to tidy her flat, spoke a while to the girl who was taking her classes then with a sigh of thankfulness headed for the hills.

Chapter 13

The tree was gone from the shed, blocked and stacked. Ray had gone mad with the chainsaw clearing the trees from the brook so it could fall back into its proper course. He then went into the orchard cutting up the fallen trees there. Greg tried to help Tod but became so unwell that they told him to go in out of the smoke and dust. Greg consoled himself by sorting the tools in the shed. It was so much lighter now with the tree gone. Tod found some galvanised sheets left over from the house and did a temporary repair on the shed roof. He also made a quick journey into town bringing back a strip light and cable so the shed was well lit. The time was running out but Ray and Tod were happy that they had made things more comfortable for Greg. They were so tired at night they did very little talking for which Greg was grateful. He still couldn't bring himself to ruin Ray's holiday, in any case he didn't want to go into emotional issues while Tod was there. Ray fell asleep most nights in front of the television overcome with hard work, mountain air and several cans of lager failing to notice the means by which Greg avoided many jobs.

So busy were they it was a shock to find it was Saturday and the night of the dance. Although reluctant Greg was unable to tell the others so he set to stocking the range for hot water. It actually felt good after a hot bath to dress in a crisp white shirt and clean jeans, although feeling weary he looked incredible, his rich dark hair curling damply over his collar, his long lashes hiding the shadows in his green eyes, the beautiful mouth a little more stern than before was smiling now as Ray came downstairs. Another transformation had taken place; the dirty, oily Ray who had gone up bore little resemblance to the very attractive Ray that came down dressed in tight denims and a dark blue shirt that matched his sparkling eyes, his mop of curly fair hair falling over his brow and a cheeky grin on his face. He wouldn't be alone for long tonight. Tod was going western style, cowboy boots, check shirt and leather fringed denims. His straight red hair firmly plastered down, his lopsided grin more than made up for his dress sense.

The hall was already crowded when they arrived, the music loud. The Dancing Fireflies were a popular local group. Their rhythm already had the floor crowded and the bar deep in customers. Paying at the door Greg noticed the proceeds were going to disabled children. He was glad they had come. The lights were dim but it was obvious that this part of the evening was a family affair. A fair number of old folk were seated around the room seeming not to mind the noise, very young children raced back and fore until finally grabbed by parents and taken home to bed their time over. The dances in Hull had never been like this, Ray remarked, they were discos or clubs mostly for teenagers. This was a new concept of life in a rural community with a different kind of atmosphere. It might get a bit rough later on once the old ones had left but everyone knew everyone else and troublemakers would get short shrift. A couple of fathers and the local policeman stayed at the door as bouncers. As there were quite a lot of over thirties Greg didn't feel out of place as he had at some of the dances that he and Stephanie had been to.

Ray was already in a dilemma. He was just getting interested in the brown-eyed blond behind the bar when looking up he met the blue eyes of the blond from the post office with whom he exchanged banter when he bought his cigarettes. They were both attracted to him and showed it but as the brown eyed girl was stuck behind the bar until midnight; blue eyes won and Ray was soon lost in the dancers.

Greg watched the dancing, his athletic figure showing to advantage as he unconsciously leant one shoulder against the wall, his casual, sensual pose and striking good looks attracting as many female stares as the fact that he was also a newcomer to the scene. He knew he shouldn't dance unless it was a smooch so rested in sublime oblivion to the inquisitive probing stares and whispers of the local girls. He felt a pang as he remembered the dances that he and Steph had gone to when he could dance most of the night although thinking back he had ignored the breathlessness and the occasional dizzy spell blaming it at the time on tiredness or drink; he also remembered having some pain and Stephanie giving him indigestion tablets telling him he ate too quickly. Someone touched his arm turning he saw a brown imp dressed in a scarlet trouser suit, diminutively beautiful with many gold chains hung about her person, tossing back her long black hair she smiled "Would you care to dance?" The band was playing a very slow number and she asked so prettily, Greg was pleased to dance although she was so tiny he was half afraid of stepping on her. They managed another waltz after which she left to powder her nose and Greg was suddenly grabbed by a tall dark girl who seemed to have danced with everyone in the room. She did some strange steps of her own which left Greg to do his own quiet moves until she reappeared in his arms. He later learned that she was the local butcher's wife and more than a little eccentric; he wasn't sorry to lose her to a large red faced man who clutched her with glee He was immediately reclaimed by his tiny lady who told him her name was Tracy and she lived in Hay on Wye, she was here with her sister and their boyfriends. As he was trying to disentangle her arms from around his neck, he stepped back feeling some ones foot under his own, hearing a sharp exclamation he turned to apologise and found himself looking into a pair of wide angry eyes set in a heart-shaped face on a level with his own.

"Can't you be more careful? That really hurt."

"I am so sorry." The music drowned his words; as she turned away Greg caught his breath as her hair flowed around her like a cloak it was the most glorious red-gold reaching to her waist in a mass of living flame. Never had he seen hair of such colour and quantity. He wondered who she was and why he hadn't noticed her before.

"Who is that?" he asked his partner, she snuggled closer.

"Don't know don't think she's local. Get me another drink, Greg please"

Pushing his way to the bar he saw the red-haired girl sitting among a group around a side table. 'My God! What hair' It fell around her like a living shawl. He watched her as he waited for the drinks. He could buy her one to make up for hurting her, people kept passing between them and he wished she would look up. He barely listened to Tracy's chatter and was glad to find a red faced sweating Ray behind him.

"All right Mate?" he asked

"Fine. They're a great band. See you've clicked then?"

"You can shout." Ray had the blue eyed blond in tow to the chagrin of brown eyes on the bar who had one eye on Ray and one on the clock behind her, blue eyes wasn't going to reign much longer if she had anything to do with it.

"Hey!, Ray, see if you can find out who the redhead is" he turned to point her out but she was gone, a large hot looking woman fanning herself was in her place. "Damn!" Ray raised his eyebrows, disappearing into the crowd. As a group of youngsters gathered around them, Tracy stopped to talk so Greg escaped to the gents. On his return he saw with relief a tall dark haired boy grab Tracy's arm and drag her into the dance. Greg thankfully returned to the bar to get a fruit juice wishing that he could go home when he found himself once more gazing into wide grey eyes which had a strange compelling look that he found oddly familiar; although he knew he had never seen her before in his life. Her fabulous hair again took his attention he had to stop himself commenting on it

"Hello" he put out his hand. "I'm sorry if I hurt you earlier. Are you alright now?"

"I'm okay It's a bit overcrowded in here tonight but as it's for the disabled children then I am glad." Her voice was low and he had difficulty hearing.

"Would you like a drink?"

I am thinking that I've had enough for one night. Thank you all the same."

The band swung into a slow number. Greg took his chance. "Would you care to dance? I promise not to tread on you again" She smiled and nodded, they moved onto the floor. Soon he began to wish that he hadn't asked her he would rather have sat and talked to her, he wanted to know more about her. She moved lightly, intricately dancing well. As the music ended she smiled and began to move away but the band started playing 'Moon River' Greg held out his arms and to his delight she moved into them, She was almost as tall as himself, he was very aware of soft, creamy skin her perfume was hauntingly sweet, her hair swung around them like a curtain as she moved; there was enough light to see the red gold of it and feel the warm clinging curls falling over his bare arms as he held her, he longed to bury his hands in it. Tiny ripples of electricity prickled his skin. She wore no jewellery but her dress flowed around her with glints of violet and silver as she moved. Her eyes were almost level with his, he wished there was more light so he could see their depths. Her head fell to his shoulder as they moved slowly around the floor, he could have danced for ever just holding her but the music stopped to announce last orders. She smiled her thanks moving away to join her friends at the door before Greg could regain his voice. He swore softly to himself. People rushing to the bar or to leave pushed past him, moving out of their way he looked again but she was gone. Frantically his eyes searched the room but there was no sign of her. The girls who had sat with her at the table earlier were back, he made his way forward but lacked the courage to speak although he was desperate to know her name or where she was from but felt foolish to ask. He turned to see Ray now with the brown eyed barmaid doing the Lombardo to a storm of cheers and clapping. Of the red haired beauty there was no sign.

Chapter 14

'Vote we find a pub lunch somewhere.' Greg flung his paint brush down in frustration. He had opened his eyes that morning to a dismal depressing day. Mist hung in the trees and was rapidly turning into rain, the mountain was shrouded in cloud, visibility nil in all directions. The air was chilly and the bleating of sheep calling off the hill was lonely. He had stumbled down to light the fire feeling the cold, decidedly the worse for wear, not because of drink in fact he had drunk little but the smoky atmosphere of the dance hall, the lack of rest the day before had guaranteed him a bad night. Bodily discomfort kept him awake most of it and when he finally slept it was fitful with red haired people wandering in and out of half dreams. He was also feeling depressed that his helpers were leaving him that evening and he still hadn't been able to talk to Ray. Several cups of coffee later he had started to paint a wall but after a few brush strokes the impetus was gone. He wandered into the living room where Ray was sipping coffee and Rod, barely awake was struggling to watch television. Between their hangovers and the bad television picture, they were in no state to notice Greg. Tod flicked the remote uselessly before flinging it aside.

"You'll have to get a booster for this thing, in weather like this there's no picture at all."

'Vote we go for a pub lunch if you can face it' Greg repeated his invitation. "I don't feel like cooking, you don't feel like eating perhaps the hair of the dog might put us right. It's a stinking day anyway, can't do much else.'

Ray was so hungover that Greg's words took a while to penetrate. 'What? Oh right!, might as well'

The rain eased a little as they crept passed the Witches cottage. There was no one about although a red jeep stood in the yard. Greg smiled to himself.

"Hey! Tod, Do you suppose it's hers or do people actually visit her?" Ray yawned. "Wonder what colour her broomstick is.'

"Don't laugh it hurts" sighed Tod.

"Hair of the dog you need my boy. By the way where did you get to? I didn't see much of you all evening. Didn't forget you have a fiancée, did you?"

"Course not. I was there but you two were too busy to notice." Greg laughed. "What about you Ray? Who had the score of the evening then? Blue eyed girl or brown?"

"Brown" Ray answered when he had given it as much thought as his aching head would allow. "Seeing her again Thursday at some concert down the village, not really my scene but she's keen to go. Thought we might stay 'till then if it's alright with you. We're not in any fit state to drive today anyway.'

'It's fine by me. Damn and blast, look what you made me do. I meant to go to the village. I've turned wrong and now don't know where we are.'

Greg had come down a steep hill to a crossroads with no signpost. There was a house nearby but as it was now raining hard no one wanted to get out.

'Just keep going'. Ray leant his head against the window. 'It's bound to come out somewhere.'

After twisting and turning for what seemed like miles with no sign of habitation it was a shock to come out right in front of a pub; at least the sign swinging in the rain read. THE COPPER BEECH. B/ B. It stood with its back to the road with no immediate sign of entry, stone built, overhung with large trees dripping above it. A depressed looking horse stood tied in a lean -to, one leg resting, head drooping. A smart Land Rover Discovery and an old estate car were parked nearby so Greg pulled off the road and woke Ray who opened first one eye then the other in an effort to clear both. 'Where the devil are we? Copper Beech sounds more like a b/b in Surry. Come on Tod, wake up, get your butt out here, see what's on offer."

They found the path leading through bushes at the side of the building. It felt like some ones garden except for a load of tables and chairs standing on the sodden lawn. The sound of voices came from behind a studded door. Silence and the full battery of five pairs of eyes met them as they entered ducking under a beam that threatened to decapitate any one over five foot six. The room was dominated with a huge stone fireplace which was glowing with a welcoming log fire. The bar stretched the length of the room carrying an impressive amount of glasses and bottles; there didn't appear to be optics. Windows were set in walls at least eight foot thick not letting in a great deal of light through the heavy leaded panes. Chintz covered chairs stood around assorted tables. On a deep window seat slept the largest black cat they had ever seen. "A bit old fashioned" Tod remarked in an undertone. Almost sitting on top of the fire was a large fat man giving off a strong aroma of horses and wet straw. A couple of men perched on stools at the bar, one a surly looking lad with mucky straw on his boots the other a man with a long grey beard dressed in a navy blazer and slacks wearing a peaked cap looking very much like an admiral lost in the wilds without his ship. He eyed the new comers with sharp blue eyes over his pint glass.

Greg approached the bar while Tod and Ray slid behind a scrubbed deal table near the window.

"Good morning Sir. Both landlord and landlady leapt to attention at this intrusion into a Sunday morning routine. "Three halves of lager please."

"Certainly Sir, which would you prefer? I recommend the draught Pilsner."

"They might want bottled." His wife interrupted "Maybe the Heineken?"

"The draught will do." Greg was momentarily taken back over two fighting to serve him. "Thank you Sir" They chorused in unison. He could see no sign of a menu. As he took the drinks to the table "We may have to go farther afield for our dinner." he remarked looking about him, he saw the place was warm, clean and cosy. 'You could drive a horse and cart up the chimney' he remarked later on the phone to his father. There was a vast amount of horse brasses and old prints decorating the walls. The landlord however was completely out of character; a neat dapper man with a military moustache and brushed back silver hair; dressed in cream slacks, blue shirt and a spotted silk cravat. He would have looked more at home in the London West End. His wife was the opposite, round, plump and motherly, sandy coloured hair piled on her head in a bun, her pale blue eyes were heavily made up and she wore a flowery apron tied firmly around her middle. They formed an incongruous team.

As the kitchen door swung open a welcome smell of roast beef wafted out, a thin anaemic looking girl came through carrying a loaded tray which she deposited on the next table.

"Here you are Captain" she laid his cutlery and turned to leave.

"Thank you, Trudy. Looks good as always"

Even Ray in his delicate state couldn't resist the tempting sight. They found themselves studying a small hand written menu.

> Roast beef or roast chicken Sunday dinner.
> Homemade Shepherd's pie or Cottage
> Sausage and chips or Scampi and chips
> Followed by
> Apple pie or Raspberry
> Rhubarb and custard or ice cream
> Trifle or cheese and biscuits

Tod began to laugh. "Shh!" Greg grabbed the menu from him. "What are you two having? Roast beef or.......Stop laughing you two, she's coming back. Three roast beefs please.'

'Or---'began Ray.

'I see you're recovered.' "This is enough to make anyone recover.' as three huge dinners were placed in front of them.

"Hope it tastes as good as it looks.' It certainly did and although none of them did as well as usual, they had to admit they felt better afterwards.

When they came to know John and Patty better it was to realise the way the menu was written was simply a reflection of the type of conversation that passed between husband and wife most of the time; to the great amusement and delight of their regulars and the complete confusion of visitors. If John remarked how wet it was today, Patty said it would clear later. If Patty was cold, Len found it milder than yesterday. If someone asked the way to Hay-on-Wye a lively discussion would develop immediately between the couple as John directed them the hill road being the quickest way and Patty recommended them to keep to the valley road as better driving. The confused party left rather hurriedly. Trudy their daughter who did the waitressing ignored them going her own sweet way; it wasn't surprising to learn later that their son Jason left home at an early age to work abroad, returning only at Christmas or on a summer vacation.

The pub became busy as the Sunday lunch time progressed, attracted by traditional ales as well as the usual brands of cider and lager. The atmosphere became that of a country house as people gossiped over the Sunday papers as they waited for their lunch. They were surprised to learn the pub had a tremendous amount of summer trade; trekkers rode over the hill, hikers from the mountain roads while tourists travelled the lanes most of the year and campers used the adjoining fields during the summer. The locals made it their own on Saturday nights and long winter evenings. The pub boasted a games room at the back, cold and bare where children abandoned by parents having a drink could play Ludo, Snap and other games in various stages of imperfection, broken crayons and colouring books usually full unless renewed by Trudy when she went to town, magazines for cutting out (if one could find the scissors) and a huge box of toy and bricks with a large sign pinned to the side 'Not to be taken from this room'. Two small sized table games completed the entertainment for children who spent most of their time signalling parents for pop and crisps. In the summer a swing, slide and a small sandpit added to the fun outside, usually ending in tears as they fought over the swing pushed one another off the slide and flung sand in each other's faces. A pony of doubtful age lived in a nearby field where he was supposed to give rides, along with a cross donkey who wouldn't let any child near him except from the other side of the gate if they fed him carrots, apples or sweets, sometimes known to accept a chip or two if in the right mood.

After the best cooked meal the lads had eaten for some time, they were quite content to chat to the landlord and watch people coming and going. Presently the door opened and a group of youths entered. "A pint of cider and two lemonades, please.' called a fair –haired lad of about twenty who seemed to know everyone in the pub.

'Lemonade? Must have been a good night down the town?" enquired John

"Yes it was." The lad handed over a note. 'Has Sam been in yet?'

'About half an hour ago I think. Patty served him didn't you dear?'

'No, I don't remember but we have been very busy.'

'Slackening off.' nodded her husband. "He'll probably be in tonight.'

'No he won't' returned Patty. 'He's darts at the Green man.'

"It may be cancelled if they don't have enough turn up for a team.' The fair lad having spotted Sam near the fire drifted off. A tall dark man moved to the bar.

'Hey John, Has Olwen been in this weekend?'

"No, she hasn't and I couldn't miss that hair could I?" Greg's ears picked up 'Olwen?' was that the red-head he met last night? It wasn't likely that two girls with hair that noticeable would be in the neighbourhood.

"I thought she might have come up this morning." The man continued. I was surprised to see her at the dance. She doesn't come that often.'

'Oh! She does come to see her grandmother'

.I know." returned the man. "But it's not often she goes to a dance over here but there's been a split up and I thought she might have called in as she was here.'

"Bronwyn likes an occasional Sunday lunchtime drink I thought she may have come today.'

Here to Greg's frustration the conversation changed. Greg was so tired the connection between grandmother and Bronwyn eluded him and though he unashamedly listened to the conversation the names weren't mentioned again.

Chapter 15

The next few days passed quickly in last minute jobs of grass cutting, rubbish burning and Ray enjoying himself filling Greg's woodshed. Tod burned the old hay and straw, hosing out the stables with disinfectant and mending the doors. In between times they played with the Land rover, starting her up, ripping out the old seats and straightening out the roof struts. The boys were definite they must leave after the concert on Thursday having stayed longer than they should because of Ray wanting to meet the brown eyed girl from the pub again. He had already called in The Green Man twice since the weekend and the concert was the last time before he had to go. He was pleased he had got Greg off to a good start as he called it but was worried as he could see his friend far from well and couldn't fathom how he was going to manage after they had left. Greg was worried that he couldn't seem to find time to talk to Ray as Tod was constantly with them and Greg felt it was only fair to put Ray in the picture first before anyone one else but the days were flying by and Thursday morning was on them when Ray approached Greg.

"Are you coming to the concert tonight? Its local talent performing for the children's fund, tickets at the door."

"Right" Greg said with a grin. "Anything for a quiet life, we'll go but no setting up dates for me mind." Ray went to phone brown eyes.

"Count me out." Tod yawned. "I'm watching the match and there are a couple of beers with my name on them in the back. See you later." The concert had started when they arrived but they found they had seats saved for them by brown eyes now introduced as Megan Lewis a pretty girl in her twenties who apparently helped a lot with Save the Children events. There proved to be a lot of real talent here for a small mountain village, beautiful voices with harmony and rhythm. Small children kept forgetting words, the most unlikely farmers and their families doing almost professional comedy acts, duets, piano recitals and playing in small brass bands. Chapels and churches, Girl Guides, brownies, cubs and scouts, Women's Institute and The young Farmers all made worthwhile contributions many showing exceptional talent. While an attractive farmer's wife was singing a hauntingly beautiful song with a great deal of professionalism, Greg relaxed and looked around. A couple who were sitting in front of him, rose quietly collected coats and whispering apologies tiptoed out leaving a clear view through to the front row. He gave a start. Near to the aisle at the front was the red-haired girl, her beautiful hair now gathered in plats coiled around her head, next to her sat a white haired woman dressed in blue with which she exchanged an occasional remark. That it was the girl who had so intrigued him at the dance he was almost certain but as the

125

people who sat behind them kept leaning forward to whisper together he only had glimpses. The song ended in a storm of clapping, the lights came on and supper was announced.

Greg rose to his feet struggling past Ray who was deep in conversation with Megan and made his way resolutely to the side room where tea was being served. Pushing ruthlessly past a family who were trying to reach the buffet table, he came face to face with the same grey eyes he had met before. The green suit fitted a figure tall and slender. The mass of hair pulled back from a heart shaped face, creamy skin with a smattering of freckles, rather high cheek bones and a delightfully straight nose. Her full lips parted in a slight smile as she recognised him although slightly built she gave air of wiry fitness.

'Hello, we meet again.' Her voice was low and musical with a slight inflection. Greg felt his heart stop and his stomach lurch. He held out his hand.

'Hello, I'm Greg Morgan I've just bought Graig-y-dorth'

'We didn't get chance to introduce ourselves last week.'

'We did not.' The lilt in her voice didn't sound welsh. 'I'm Olwen Jameson.' They shook hands.

'And I'm thirsty, if you two want to stand there jabbering, let me through before the tea is all gone.'

"Oh! I'm sorry Granny. This is a young man I met the other night at the dance." She stood aside and to Greg's dismay behind her stood the witch, Bronwyn Rhys.

"I know him, we've met. He almost ran me and Samuel Peeps down the other day."

"Really I didn't." Greg managed to get out.

"Come on Granny. Let's get some tea while it's hot. I'm sure Mr Morgan wouldn't do any such thing on purpose. You're such a cross patch at times.'

126

"Please call me Greg. May I get you both some tea?"

"It's alright thanks, we can manage." In spite of her soft tones, Greg felt rather than heard the independence in her 'probably like her grandmother if crossed' he thought irritably. 'Why couldn't she have been on her own tonight? It must be her Jeep in the yard' he smiled to himself to think of the witch travelling in a Jeep.' Would Olwen have to drive very slowly and sound her horn on all the bends?'

Olwen turned and smiled at him "Maybe we'll meet again?" She murmured. Tucking her hand in her grandmother's arm they moved away. Later Greg saw them talking to the vicar at the door. At least he now knew her name. It suited her. 'Olwen 'he murmured over to himself as he finally turned to find Ray. As usual Ray was feeding his face and alternately Megan's, both fully occupied. Disconsolately Greg helped himself to coffee and a scone, later returning to his seat he was dragged into a long conversation about farming and the weather by a man in a brown suit and gaiters. It was only when the lights were lowered for the second half and everyone returned to their seats that he realised that Ray and Megan hadn't returned to theirs and he was free to watch the movements of the girl and her grandmother two rows in front and muse to himself. It was sod's law for her to be the grandchild of the one person that he always seemed to be out of favour with and Olwen herself to be slightly unapproachable. He thought of girls he had known, including Stephanie who had practically thrown themselves at him and now? 'I'm sure Mr Morgan didn't do it on purpose.' 'Who does she think she is?'. Then he remembered the feel of her hair under his hands and her head dropping to his shoulder. Whoever she was and whatever she is he knew he wanted to see her again. In spite of everything he had to see her again.

Chapter 16

It was a dull and cloudy day when Ray and Tod left. The house felt cold even with the fire lit and all the lights on. The mountain seemed to brood over the farm. Greg felt bereft and guilty. For the first time he wondered at his wisdom in coming here. At no time had he attempted to tell Ray the truth and had drifted along with them enjoying almost a holiday and a sense of adventure, except it wasn't a holiday for him and wasn't going to be an adventure. Ray's bright happy face and Tod's tireless energy had kept them all going. Greg hadn't experienced being here alone as yet and he was beginning to wonder what he was thinking of and what he had done. The sheds were stacked with wood and the garden cleaned off for Greg's father who had said he was coming up to plant it. Inside walls had been plastered and painted, windows cleaned and repaired, doors oiled, bedrooms cleaned and painted two of which were now serviceable and warm with a single bed and wardrobe in each; more furniture would have to wait until some money came in, the bathroom was clean and fully functional. Major repairs were still needed; ie new roof and the extension sorted out but at least the house was liveable for the present.

Greg had tried to work as best he could along with his friends, trying not to show when he was tired or in pain, now it was a relief to be on his own not having to hide how he felt, exhausted, with pain often not far away. He decided to do nothing but read and rest for a few days. An engineer had come to sort the television so although he couldn't get as many programs as he was used to, he could enjoy a good picture and some of his favourite shows, not that he was used to all this sitting around but he felt he had better discipline himself or he would be in real trouble. He hadn't heard about his driving but it was only a matter of time, the notification had probably gone to his old address and doctor; it would catch up any time now and he had no idea how he would manage then. He was such a fool to think everything was going to be alright here, he had visions of having to sell up again and go home.

He felt more than guilty about not talking to Ray when he had the chance. He knew Ray was not altogether taken in with his story about a lung spot. He'd caught him looking at him several times with real worry in his eyes but Greg had not been able to put it into words especially with Tod around and all the work they had done. Perhaps when Ray came back on his own it would be easier, he would be hurt and angry but at least they could talk it out. He would have to know sometime but Greg himself could push the shadows back in Ray's sunny presence and selfishly hang on to summer because once Ray knew; things would never be the same again. They had eaten their last meal together at The Copper Beech and been greeted as if they were old customers. Ray had kept them laughing with merry quips about different people and talking almost nonstop about Megan the brown eyed barmaid with whom he was obviously smitten. Now he was gone and Greg had to face his demons again. He reached for his mobile to ring his parents just as British Telecom drove in the yard to install his land line After they had finished it was a pleasure not to have to fight with the signal on his mobile. He usually had to go up to the road to get a good signal now he could ring from his armchair.

"Mum when you come bring your sewing kit there are several curtains needing your attention and a couple of your pies wouldn't go amiss and I miss you."

His mother thankful to hear he was alright and that he had a landline at last promised that her and his father would be there in a couple of days.

Greg decided he must explore Hay on Wye rather than mope here on his own so taking the chance of not getting lost he took the road past The Copper Beech and kept going. Hay was a delight, quaint old town full of bookshops and antiques; the small winding streets and old fashioned shops fascinated him. Parking in the huge open carpark that seemed as large as the town itself, he browsed happily around the town following wandering streets that always seemed to bring him back to where he started. He visited the arcade of antique shops, enjoying the lovely china, furnishings and products of a bygone age for an hour or two before lunching in the old Granary which sold homemade soups and much more. Afterwards he looked at the remains of the castle which had been badly burned a long time ago but was now partially restored. It was too steep for him to actually walk up to the castle itself today so he headed for the old cinema which was known to be one of the largest second hand book store in the country. Books were in every shop and one could spend hours in a shop that sold clothes, fishing tackle or greengrocery just browsing their book store. He chose the Cinema which even had books outside in what used to be the carpark where you paid in a honesty box if you chose something from under the many shed like shelves which saved the books from the rain. As he wandered along the outside racks of books in their display cases, he looked up to see Olwen walking into the bookstore itself. Hurrying inside he found her talking to a man behind the counter discussing a box of books she had brought in. He stood to one side until her business was completed. While she talked he was able to observe her more closely, realising this was the first time he had chance to see her in daylight. Dressed in jeans and a tan jacket almost the colour of her hair, he noticed now she was tall and slender, her movements quick and graceful, when talking she made full use of her hands and body almost physically expressing what she was saying. She concluded her business an was handed an envelope, she thanked him and was turning away when she saw Greg standing near a window, her face lit with a smile as if pleased to see him there.

"Hi" We meet again." Her large grey eyes gave him the same jolt as they met his as they had before. In daylight they were as clear and soft as rain clouds fringed with long thick lashes darker than her hair which was pulled back hanging in a huge plait down her back. Her face was strong with a determined jaw, the skin creamy with tiny laugh lines around her eyes and wide generous mouth. In the full light of day he could see she appeared older than he first thought when he had met her. He hazarded a guess she could be in her early thirties whereas at the concert he had thought her to be in her twenties. She held out her hand. "Have you come to drink at our enormous house of knowledge?" she asked. He laughed "I heard of this place and wondered if they had anything in these millions of books on Land Rover restoration."

As they released hands she turned with him to enter the main doors. Greg found himself telling her about the treasure they had found in the shed at Graig-y-dorth and she, to his delight showed great interest.

"Come on let's have a look." The place was huge but every section in every isle had signs and lists of what could be found At to Z in each subject. Greg had never seen so many books in his life. This is where he could come to browse on a winter's day he decided. There were books on every subject under the sun, the temptation to stop at each interesting subject overwhelming.

"Come on." Olwen laughed. "You'll get used to it if you come often enough and learn to head with your eyes down for what you want and ignore the rest."

Greg was delighted when they came to a section on mechanical restorations and could see more books on various subjects than he could ever hope to have. His interest in books however was secondary to his interest in his companion who was hunting the shelves as eagerly as himself.

"This is exciting." She exclaimed. "I love the old types of Land Rovers much better than the newer ones. You are lucky. I love jeeps too, most four wheel drives actually. I have a little red jeep. I adore it, it goes everywhere and anywhere; great for visiting granny and to fetch her shopping when it snows. Maybe you haven't seen a winter in the Black mountains though you come from the north don't you? They get some bad ones up there but of course you have a Subaru that will get you through. What will you be doing with the Land Rover? Will you be selling."

"Not if I can help it." Greg protested. "I would like to use it if I can do it up; it needs a lot of work though."

"I would love to see it sometime. Look! Here is a book on Land rovers. Does it cover yours?"

"Yes it does. Here's a picture of it."

"Which one is yours, is it this or this?" She moved close holding the book for Greg to lean over her shoulder to see. The same perfume she had worn on the night of the dance wafted as she moved, woodsy and sensual. He felt the same jolt he had felt before.

"Yes that's it I'll get this one and those other two. I had better stop or I shall be taking them all." Moving reluctantly away from her he picked up the books going out to the front desk to pay.

"Have you time for a coffee, Olwen?" He took pleasure in saying her name out loud at last. To his disappointment she shook her head.

"It's sorry I am but I don't have the time now." The inflection in her voice he still couldn't place, the accent or the twist of some of her words.

"But might I be coming to see your Land rover one day when I next come to Granny's or perhaps you wish to be keeping it to yourself until it's finished?"

"Of course not, I mean yes. I would like to show it to you if you are really keen to see it. It's in a bit of a mess at the moment---"Greg found himself stuttering and mentally cursed himself.

"Right, I must be getting back to work tomorrow. I have had a few days off but I must get to it again but I will call next time I'm down."

"What do you do?" He was loath to let her go.

"I teach Art and design at Worcester College. I have a flat there during term time but I like to come down to Granny's in the holidays or as often as I can. My mother can't make it often as she lives and works in London with a full social life. If I didn't have to be working at all, I would stay with Granny. It's wonderful there and I adore her." Greg tried hard not to show amusement as he hadn't found anything even remotely adorable about Bronwyn Rhys.

"Anyway Greg I must go, nice to see you again. I will call one day. See you."

She swung off down the street with a long striding walk, not waiting for a reply. Greg felt as if the sun had gone in, yet he was exultant, he had met her again and she wanted to see him again. He was well pleased by his visit to Hay on Wye, collecting his purchases and fish and chips which he ate as he drove he took the road to home almost happy, passing the Witch's cottage he grinned to himself 'Adorable indeed.' He couldn't help wondering as he put his shopping away and made up the fire, remembering the conversation at The Copper Beech he wished that he had paid more attention to it. How had it gone? 'surprised to see her at the dance hadn't seen her much since the split up' surely in heaven's name she wasn't married but then she was old enough to have been married and have a couple of kids as well. He was surprised to be dismayed at the thought. He mentally shook himself. What business of his was it anyway? He had only met her three times in all. She was just a very beautiful, unusual woman who intrigued him. What man wouldn't be? That combination of red hair, grey eyes and soft lilting voice; she was dynamite and he was vulnerable and stupid, a cold voice spoke in his head. What have you to offer any girl let alone one as special as this one appeared to be? You have no money, no job, no life, you dare not get involved with anyone ever unless you get a transplant and quickly, you don't even have time. Depression hit him with a force that he thought he'd conquered and he laid his head on his arms and wept with despair, self-pity and frustration. It was dark when he woke. He had managed with a terrible effort of will power to stop himself once more lashing out and had merely cried himself to sleep like a child once again longing for his mother- It had been a huge mistake to come here. He should pack up and go home. It had been great when Ray was here and he had been kept from thinking. He despised himself for not telling Ray the truth. He was weak minded, he should put the farm on the market and let his mother spoil him, he should spend his last months with his parents, God knows they would suffer enough when he went. The least he could do was to give them some time before it happened. He'd ring them first thing in the morning; at this point he must have fallen asleep, he wasn't sure what woke him. He was cold and saw the fire had burnt almost away he knelt to make it up with more logs. He'd take his medication and go to bed, sort it all out in the morning. Pain gripped his back and chest and he cursed as he took his drugs.

Suddenly he heard it again, the sound that had woken him, a whining noise and a faint scuffling, not rats surely as he and Ray had put down enough poison to kill an army and they hadn't seen one since. There it was again, a whine that was coming from the backdoor of the house. This had been overgrown and impossible to open but thanks to Tod, it was now clear and opened easily. Greg picked up his keys and a torch flicking on the house lights as he went. Opening the door he shone the torch down the garden. The wind was rising and rain spotted his face as he peered out. He stepped outside, the weather was deteriorating and a storm brewing, setting the trees creaking in a rush of wind. He flashed the torch over the garden and on to his watch; it was turned midnight and he couldn't see anything, it must have been the wind he decided turning back to the house. He heard a whine clearly this time nearer the door, flashing the torch he caught the gleam of animal eyes. He stepped forward warily as the animal whined again piteously, carefully Greg moved forward instinctively uttering soothing sounds, cursing when the wind caught the door slamming it shut. The animal never moved just gave another moan. Greg crouched down shining the torch on a black and brown head with a white blaze. "Hello boy who are you? Where are you hurt? Are you going to let me take a look?"

He extended a hand gingerly towards the dog but it appeared too distressed to be aggressive. He touched the head slowly, talking while creeping his fingers around its ears; the light showing a sticky mass of blood and mud around the animal's neck, gently he let his hand drop around----'God almighty! Who the hell has done this? I'll kill them. It's alright boy good dog. His creeping fingers had found a wire or string so deep around the animal's throat it felt embedded in the flesh itself. The poor creature was very weak but had somehow crawled from somewhere to his door. Greg dashed back into the house and grabbing a rug off the settee wrapped the dog as gently as possible carrying it back into the kitchen. It was a terrible sight, he could see the wire now but it had cut too deep into the dog's neck for him to remove it. He grabbed the phone book quickly finding the number for an emergency vet in Hay who arranged to meet him at the surgery in half an hour. He gave Greg directions, warning him not to give the dog food or water. Getting the dog into the pick-up was easy, although not small it was very light, probably half-starved thought Greg flying down the hill. The roads were empty and the vet waiting, after examining the animal he sedated him and started cutting away the fur showing clearly the wire which was as Greg feared embedded in the flesh. "Rabbit wire" muttered the vet as he removed it. An hour passed before the wound was cleansed, stitched and injections given.

"There you are fella.' The vet ripped off his gloves flinging them in the bin. "I think you will feel more comfortable tomorrow although I shall keep him tonight in case there is any trouble in the throat. I want to see him drink and eat some soft stuff before I let him go. He put his head in the wire intended for some poor fox or rabbit, dammed bloody practice, animal can't get free and either gets it's throat cut or suffocates. The amount of cats brought in is ridicules. This chap was lucky, he obviously was able to pull the stake out of the ground or break it at the spike. Whoever sets these things needs one around his balls in my opinion?"

"I quite agree" said Greg. "I'll take a look around tomorrow and see if I can find where he crawled from, might give us a clue if we know whose land it was on"

"Give me a call in the morning." Simon Hill placed the dog in a padded cage at the back of the surgery. "I'll look in on him later I'm off duty at six so you might get my colleague Sam when you phone. As I said provided he can breathe properly, eat and drink he can go. He's starved and his coat is rough as if he has been outside for some time. Maybe he's been abandoned. He's too dirty to see what he really looks like but he is a collie and someone could have lost their working dog. He's not very old either about two I would say there may be a reward out for him. Your locals may know, they usually know one others dogs. I'll put the word out.'

"I'll make enquiries too. Greg replied taking care of the bill. Thanks for all you've done.' The vet smiled and locked the door behind him.

The next morning Greg tried to follow a line in the direction that the dog may have come. It was difficult as rain in the night had obliterated any blood or paw marks although he found a gap in the garden hedge where there were traces of fur. Greg had to assume that he had come through the orchard so he followed coming out on the hill where the fern being young and tender showed where the dog had rolled in his agony. Going very slowly because his breath was going and the familiar pain starting, he realised that he shouldn't be doing this. He sat for a long while until he felt comfortable again. Continuing a while later he found himself in a short space of time under the great rock. Out of breath again he sat on a stone and looked at the great mass ahead of him. Here his grandfather had sheltered from storms and sent Rocky out across the hill to bring the sheep down for shearing or lambing. His granny had based all her stories on this place. Here his father had played as a child with neighbouring children having been warned to watch for adders, that deadly little snake that sunned itself on the rocks on hot days. Rocky had once been bitten on the face when he jumped on a rock where the snake was sleeping. Grandfather carried him over his shoulder to the farm and sent word to the local vet who travelled around on horseback. Rocky was given an antidote but had a swollen face for a couple of days, they thought they had lost Rocky then. Greg smiled to himself; it was here his father had brought his mother one summer day when they were courting and proposed on one knee in the fern; what was it the local lads called it when you went courting on the hill? Fern tickets that was it when you took a girl into the fern; bet father got a few. Greg grinned to himself. After a while he struggled to the foot of the rock itself it towered above him, how he would have loved to climb to the top. Grandad had told him that on a clear day you could see all the way to Hereford, Hay and beyond with the whole of the Golden Valley stretching out beneath you like a kingdom. What a sight it must have been when the valley was golden with corn and tiny cattle motionless like toys on a model farm. He sighed and looked about him at first he could only see broken fern but on moving around the base of the rock a little he found a cleft large enough to take a fox or a dog and his point was proved, something had been going in and out recently, hunting in wider circle he came to a space where something had threshed about violently bearing evidence of the agony the poor animal had suffered as it frantically tried to lose the noose about its throat. He noticed a stick lying in the fern picking it up he held the evidence; the pronged hook from the end of a rabbit wire snapped off at the base. 'Why was he hiding up here anyway?' There were no more answers here on the hill so Greg made his way very slowly down to phone the vet.

"Yes you can pick him up, he's on his feet. He's had some soft food and a drink of milk and although it's sore for him that will wear off in about a week. If you get any problems bring him back but he should be fine." Greg told him what he had found. The vet thought that had been the cause. 'He's been living rough and got unlucky. See you in about an hour then If you want to take him otherwise I'll ring the RSPCA'.

"Thanks." Greg replied. "I'll ring the local police to see if anybody's reported him missing and be with you as soon as I can.'

Police Constable Jeff Arnott had lived in the village for ten years and knew everyone around. "I've had no reports of a dog missing." He said when Greg rang him. "I'll have good look at him when you bring him back and put it about. No one's reported any sheep worrying either since last year but I would like to find the wire setter as well. Alright sir, let me know how the dog goes on and I will do my best to find his owner."

Greg collected the dog that afternoon. He was surprised to be greeted with a tail wag and allowed himself to be lifted into the truck.

"You are friendly aren't you for a wild dog? Let's get you home and feed you up a bit. Phew! You stink a warm

bath wouldn't go amiss and probably a flea treatment too."
Stopping only to pick up a selection of dog food mostly
tinned because of the soft content, a bottle of shampoo and
various other powders. Greg took him home, after a good
bath which he didn't enjoy, Greg wrapped him in a big towel
to dry him off, he emerged a very attractive black and white
collie with a brown and white face and white socks.

"I expect someone is looking for you but in the meantime
I shall call you Rocky like Granddad's dog. I would love to
keep you but someone must already own you." He took him
down stairs where he made a good meal of soft meat and
warm milk after which he curled up in the box that Greg
found for him and went to sleep.

Chapter 17

Olwen drove back to Worcester with some trepidation. She was looking forward to going back to her classes but with a reluctance to face her flat. She still had a lurking fear that somehow Aiden would still be around. She knew she was being irrational as he had left for Ireland, the college had written to her and Alicia had phoned her, other friends had texted her but still the feeling persisted. She knew she would get over it in time but the first thing she had to do was change her accommodation; she was sure the college would find her somewhere else in the circumstances but even the thought of the next week in the flat and the packing everything up worried her. Bronwyn had told her not to be so silly and to believe what she was told otherwise she was going to remain paranoid about the whole thing. Driving into the car park she found herself looking around for Aiden's car; telling herself not to be so stupid, she carried her packages to the front door hesitating before she put the key in the lock. The flat looked dusty but as she had left it except a red light was flashing on her answer machine. She felt sick dreading to pick it up. Determinedly she put the kettle on and made a cup of tea staring out of the window while she waited for it to boil only when she had drunk half of it did she gently press play. Her worst fears realised Aiden's voice.

"I'm glad it is you answering this. I hope you are pleased with yourself"- she backed away until she felt the table behind her; every instinct was telling her to turn it off and delete but she was frozen unable to move almost forced to listen.

"You didn't wait for me to apologise for startling you as I did but you above all people should have realised that I never meant to hurt you but you couldn't wait could you? You went running to people who don't have your best interests at heart. As a result you have lost everything we had together. You have cost me my job and my friends. I'm sorry but we can't be together anymore. I can't trust you not to shout every time we make love because that's all it was silly girl. Anyway this is goodbye. I am going back to Ireland. I have a job at a university in Belfast. They aren't so snobbish there. I did love you; knew that though didn't you? Bye! Be happy if you can. You may have to change a little though."

She stood still a long time until the feeling came back to her legs and she was able to move. She managed to get to the machine delete the message and switching it off. She was shaking, wanted to tell someone but didn't know who to call. She wasn't going to worry Bronwyn and Alicia was away. She had other friends but didn't think they would be very interested. Suddenly Greg Morgan came to mind, why she had no idea but she suddenly felt he would have understood. She gave herself a mental shake, she didn't know the man, she must be going daft, better to get on, have something to eat and plan her next move. First see about getting another flat and another phone she wouldn't put it past Aiden to try to reach her again when he felt like it.

Uneasy as she was she finally fell asleep but her sleep was muddled and full of dreams none of which she could remember with clarity when she woke. She couldn't wait for breakfast so keen she was to speak to the director and get back to her classes. It appeared that it might be several weeks until the college could accommodate her with housing as understanding as they were, her name was placed forward on the accommodation list but that was the best they could do. They advised her to try for an exchange among her friends and colleagues but after another restless night she made up her mind to rent privately in the town itself. After her classes she visited several estate agents coming away with a list of properties, she had no idea what time she would have to visit them all. Eight o'clock that evening after visiting several, she was tired out, hadn't liked any of them and dreaded going to bed; the phone rang, with her heart in her mouth hoping it was Bronwyn she slowly picked up the receiver, to her surprise it was her mother Alwen ringing from France. She had heard from Bronwyn and was worried about her daughter. 'First time for everything.' thought Olwen ungraciously but really thrilled and relieved to hear from her. They had never been really close but maybe now would be a good time to talk. The conversation took some time as Olwen relived the events for her mother filling in the gaps she had been embarrassed to tell her grandmother. Alwen listened in silence but her only advice was exactly what Olwen had decided for herself. She was unable to come over at the moment to be with her daughter as she had as she said 'commitments' without explaining what they were. She would be over later in the summer and advised Olwen not to get involved with anyone else until she was certain they were as she put it 'reliable'. After telling her to keep in touch and repeating how much she loved her and how shocked she had been to hear of Olwen's problems and how worried and upset she had been. 'I haven't slept for nights Darling, please be careful and let me know where you are. Bye Sweetheart. Keep in touch, Bye"

Olwen collapsed on a chair exhausted as she always felt after dealing with her mother, just then the phone rang again, she jumped to answer it thinking her mother had forgotten to tell her something. There was no response but whoever had rung hadn't rung off and was still holding the phone, "Hello, hello. Who's there please answer" There was no reply except the phone being quietly replaced. Olwen began to shake, she couldn't cope with this, she switched the phone off at the wall and went to bed but spent the night alternately dozing and listening. She drifted into a deep sleep somewhere around dawn, awaking to a realisation that she had been dreaming of a tall man with sparking green eyes who wanted her to go somewhere with him she didn't know where but she recognised him as the man she had met in Hay, Greg Morgan. Why she should dream about him she had no idea.

Later that morning she had just finished a project with her class and decided she would spend the afternoon working on one of her entries for the exhibition which was shortly coming up when her mobile rang; it was Aiden, she quickly deleted it but he rang again that afternoon. Furious that he could still upset her she quickly finished up and headed into town where she purchased a new phone, transferred her details and flicked her old sim card in a nearby skip. She couldn't have borne to go around unable to leave her phone switched on. Her luck must have changed with the new phone because as she left the shop she passed a newsagent. She stopped to glance at the adverts in the window.

A small flat to let in Market Street, usual offices, clean and very comfortable would suit professional lady with references. Olwen read it over again. The rent was more than she wanted to pay but it was in an ideal location. She hurriedly pulled out the new phone and set it to work. The lady who answered sounded surprised. "That was quick. I only put the advert in this morning. Please come around and have a look."

Olwen was delighted with the flat; pretty and spacious worth the extra cost. Two large rooms with a queen sized bed in one and a tiny kitchen off the other nicely fitted out, a shared bathroom but as there was only one other flat occupied by an elderly lady that too was fine. Her landlady was Italian aged about fifty with lovely dark eyes and a sweet smile. She told Olwen she had two daughters one married living in the city, the other a lawyer living in Bath engaged to be married to an Italian Barrister. Her husband was a fireman as well as owning a small café nearby. Olwen was delighted, giving the college director and her friend Alicia as references arranged to move in on the following weekend and treated herself to dinner at a local restaurant with a bottle of wine to take home. For the first time for weeks she felt safe. That night she slept well but dreamed of a green eyed man who held her hand and told her funny stories.

Chapter 18

Sally Morgan was so glad to be with her son. She had cried for days then she had been ill with a bout of flu that had lingered, she still hadn't fully recovered. She wouldn't come to Greg until she was no longer infectious but now could wait no longer. John's faith and support had pulled her through the worst of her shock and grief although she still suffered bitterly she firmly believed that a donor would be found in time. Now they both needed to be with Greg for a while. Sally was horrified at the state of the house but relieved to find Greg coping with himself. The weather was warm and the blossom out and it reminded her of the times she was here with John. It had once been such a pretty farmhouse she remembered, they had married at the little church down the road living for a while afterwards with John's parents. How she would have loved to have Greg do the same and Stephanie would have been so right for him. She sighed deeply as she felt the tears ready to flow again but she mustn't upset Greg so she wiped her eyes and went to admire the wild garden again where John was already at work making a vegetable patch. She had knitted Greg a sweater in deep green and brought several cakes and pies for the freezer, now she started on the house with vim and vigour. Greg looked so much better she thought and seeing him with Rocky in his own home reassured her. She set her mind to polishing, cleaning and rearranging, cooked tempting meals, sewing and rehanging the chopped off curtains while washing everything in sight. From Swansea she had brought a car full of lamps cushions and rugs; Greg laughing protested but didn't attempt to stop her having fun.

As Sally coped with the house so John tackled the garden fighting with years of brambles and overgrown shrubs until he had cleared a space for vegetables and planted the seeds he had brought with him. Tod had already cut back the rose bushes which had covered the back door, John now set about training the shoots over the porch. He took a trip into Abergavenny returning with a car full of shrubs and fir trees which he planted on the eastern side of the garden where the wind blew of the hill. The flowering shrubs he planted in four corners of the small plot he'd laid down for a lawn. Greg wanted to keep the beautiful wild garden as he had first seen it so except for some necessary pruning his father left it alone; in any case the birds that sang there had nests everywhere. The bulbs too were left to come again. John confined his main work to the vegetables and the lawn where Greg admitted it would be nice to eat out in the sun.

Greg turned down their offer of replacing the roof to Sally's distress; she pictured him lying ill under a leaking roof with the rain drumming in his ears. After a heated argument his parents had to give way as Greg assured them when his flat sold the roof was his first priority, only when he promised that if it was not sold by winter he would borrow the money from them, did they give in and took their frustrations out on the house and garden. Grey was looking better, the country was obviously doing him good and they blessed Ray who had done so much for him. Greg did not tell his parents that Ray did not yet know the whole truth, as they seldom saw him he felt safe that he would be able to tell him before they did.

"By the way, Greg, I rang Stephanie and told her about you." Sally told him firmly one night at dinner.

"What on earth for?" exclaimed Greg. "It's got nothing to do with her."

"Of course it is." She replied. "You lived together as far as we're concerned as man and wife. She had a right to know"

This was an old bone of contention. His parents had found it hard to accept that Greg and Stephanie had not married.

"She is so upset she will most likely contact you one day. She has to go to New York again but she was so distressed she almost didn't go. I am quite surprised that you haven't heard already."

Greg groaned. "I will no doubt. What am I supposed to say to her? I don't want to see her Mother. It's no good her contacting me."

"She has a right. At least you can talk to her. She is such a kind hearted girl I'm sure she could help."

'Yes.' Greg thought savagely 'I spent six months trying to get her from around my neck and Mother promptly puts her back. Thanks but no thanks.'

Aloud he said" I wouldn't bank on it. She's too selfish, too busy and always has friends and acquaintances more important to her."

His father said nothing. He knew Greg's feelings and was inclined to agree with him, he had a soft spot for Steph and had thought her a good choice for Greg but it was no use if there was no love between them anymore and he didn't want to see them both hurt all over again. He was cross with Sally for interfering. He had told his wife that Greg wouldn't want to be involved again but Sally was adamant that she was told and had invited Steph over one evening, both had been very upset. He believed she would be in touch when she returned from New York then everyone would be upset all over again.

"We'll see." Sally unfolded the ironing board. "I told her we would be here for a couple of weeks so maybe she will come after we have gone"

Stephanie arrived at Graig-y-dorth the following Sunday morning as his parents were packing ready to leave after lunch. Rocky barked and Greg looked up from his job of tying back some bushes to see Stephanie opening the road gate, his heart sank; why did his mother have to call her? He put down his tools and went to meet her cursing under his breath. On seeing him she ran down the path arms outstretched dramatically, before he could stop her she was in his arms shaking and sobbing.

"Greg! My Darling, why didn't you tell me? I am so sorry. You could have come to me. I can't bear it. Hold me close." As she was clinging around his neck like a limpet there was little else he could do at this point except cheerfully strangle his mother. Detaching Stephanie arms, he drew back to notice with a start that she was not alone. The car had followed her down the yard and a very tall, dark, good looking man got out carefully picking his way through the mud with an expression of distaste though he smiled as he came towards them.

"Good morning." Greg holding Stephanie at arm's length with one hand held out the other in greeting. The man shook hands with a firm grip. "Yes, it is a good morning. I am pleased to meet you." Stephanie pulled herself together

"Darling, I am so sorry but I am too upset to mind my manners. This is Joseph. He handles my designs but when he heard that I had to come here he insisted on bringing me. Joseph, this is poor Gregory Morgan and these are his parents John and Sally Morgan." They shook hands somewhat embarrassed.

"Shall we all have some coffee?" Sally after embracing Steph led the way inside leaving the men to follow. Greg was angry but there was no way he could show it either to his guests or his parents. His father understanding squeezed his shoulder. "Joseph. How kind of you to escort Stephanie on such short notice. Have you been to Wales before?"

"No I never have." His accent was strong maybe Norwegian or Swedish. "It is very beautiful but how do you cope with the silence and the mud."

"You get used to it. "Greg retorted. Would you join us for a coffee?"

"What a good idea." His father led the way into the house. As Greg followed Joseph he looked him over with interest. He obviously hadn't dressed for the country. Cream slacks, pale lilac shirt, cream shoes, he looked as uncomfortable as Greg felt but he must think a lot of Steph to drive into the hills with her. They found the women in the kitchen. Stephanie had recovered enough to place biscuits on a plate and load a tray as Sally made the coffee. Greg carefully kept the table between them he didn't want a repeat performance of the scene on the yard, knowing Steph that would happen if he so much as caught her eye. John set himself to making Joseph at ease and soon had him talking about stamp collecting which was John's lifetime hobby. A chance remark about the postal service and cost of postage led to the discovery that Joseph also had an impressive collection so they were soon deep in the delights of philately. Greg breathed a sigh of relief, with the best will in the world he didn't think he and Joseph would have much in common. Sally was asking Steph about her trip to New York and what she thought of the city. Greg took his coffee and with Rocky slid out of the front door and sat on the garden wall. Not only was he unable to find anything to talk to Joseph about but he didn't want to talk to Stephanie. He failed to see any purpose to them coming, a note or a phone call would have sufficed. He only hoped that she and her fancy sponsor would take themselves off after their coffee but knowing Steph so well, he knew that she never did anything without a motive and although they had parted last year, there was some reason for her presence here now. He was filled with foreboding.

"Where are you Greg?" Stephanie came through the back door towards him. "Oh! Darling there you are! I know you must be feeling wretched but don't go away from us all and brood by yourself." Greg set his teeth and stretched his lips into a smile. It was hard to remember that so long ago he had adored this woman and her way of life had been his.

Had she always been so gushing? He knew basically she was soft and kind and had been genuinely devastated when she had heard about him. She had always loved him and he had hurt her badly but for the life of him her couldn't remember her being so cloying, her baby blue eyes gazing into his as she laid her head on his shoulder, almost at once a vision of cool grey eyes and blazing hair slid into his mind, he recalled a low calm voice with a lilting accent. Suddenly it came into his mind what it was, that accent was Irish not Welsh as he had first thought. How come her grandmother didn't have it? She didn't sound Welsh or Irish. He mused for a moment but was roused by Stephanie tugging on his arm.

"Aren't you glad Darling? Doesn't it work out perfectly?"

"Sorry Steph, I didn't hear what you said."

You really need me, don't you? I was saying that when I heard how ill you were I just died inside and I had to talk to someone. I couldn't find the number and your mother gave me the wrong one so I went and cried all over Joseph. He has been wonderful I couldn't have coped without him"

"Come off it Steph. You could always cope with anything. If there is one thing I missed about you it was your efficiency"

"You are a Sweetie. Well that's what I am saying you don't need to any more. I am here now"

"What do you mean?" Greg was puzzled.

"Come inside, Joseph will explain."

"You explain."

"Well you see my New York collection was a huge success so they asked me to set up another next season. This year's theme was English Rose and I want to give them something different next time. When Joseph knew I needed to get to you quickly he suggested that I should look for colours and fabrics here. We have decided to go Welsh – base it all on daffodils, the heathers and the colours of the mountains. New Yorkers will go crazy for them. I can stay here take care of you while working on my new collection. Get you all sorted, see you keep your appointments and things, right sort of food; I'll work out a diet sheet, see you get plenty of rest no worries. I can collect all I need from local towns with a few trips to North Wales (it's so different from South Wales). Isn't it just perfect how things have worked out? Now your mum and I are going to prepare lunch and you can come and talk to Joseph. He'll tell you all about it."

"You brought her here Mother you will get rid of her." Greg was furious he'd marched into the house grinning at everyone with set teeth. "Just a word Mother dear" He marched her outside down to the orchard. He had seldom ever raised his voice to her and when he called her mother in that tone she knew he was very angry "I do not need her or want her, our relationship was over months ago but neither you or she will accept it will you? I do not love her, she must leave and that is final. I am not an invalid and quite capable of looking after myself and am still able to make my own decisions as to who I see or who I live with. Understood?" His mother was nearly in tears.

"Oh! Greg I am so sorry, I didn't know that she would come here with that in mind."

"You must have had an idea. You know Stephanie she never gives up and you are as bad. She will just not take no for an answer. Now get her out of here or I will go in there and tell her in front of her friend that I don't want her here. I will have to humiliate her and cause a scene. I was weeks convincing her before but I will do it again in one fell swoop and it won't be pleasant. Now you will back me up."

Oh Greg, I thought----

"I know what you thought and it won't work. I loved her once but it died a natural death and now I want peace to die mine."

She burst into tears. Greg groaned.

'I'm sorry Mother, I love you and I know I'm hurting you but if I don't have my way now when can I?" He put his arms around her. "I didn't mean to shout at you but you must admit that you are as bad as her and you just don't listen. Listen to me now please. When I go back in there and explain she must leave, you will back me up won't you? I know Dad will but it's you she talks to, you have some influence on her."

Sally wiped her eyes. "Alright but what are you going to say to her?"

Before Greg could answer a small red jeep shot into the driveway pulling up behind Josephs car.

"Hi" called Olwen from the open window as they walked towards her.

"I just thought I would be dropping in to look at the Land Rover " She saw Sally behind Greg wiping her eyes. "Oh I am sorry. You have visitors. I didn't mean to intrude."

Greg's heart missed a beat, what a time for her to come and how much he had hoped that she would sometime but now,

"Hello there." He raised his hand. "Come and meet my mother."

Olwen stepped from the jeep. She wore old cords none too clean and a faded sweatshirt. Her hair hung plaited to her waist, a green headband allowing wisps to curl around her face however she looked amazing and very attractive.

"Mother this is Olwen, her granny is my neighbour. Olwen I'd like you to meet my mother."

"Pleased I am to meet you, Mrs Morgan." They shook hands, Sally somewhat embarrassed, her eyes still weepy and conscious she was wearing her apron.

"I just came out for a quick drive and decided to call on Greg and see this Land Rover he is so keen on. It's such a lovely day."

Sally agreed smiling taking off the apron and turning to Greg. "You take Olwen to see the Land Rover. I will have a word with your father. I think Steph and Joseph will be leaving soon." She squeezed his arm meaningfully.

"Oh! Please don't let me interfere." Olwen begged. "Another time will do."

"No it's fine. Come on in." Greg opened the garden gate. He didn't know what his mother was up to but he would have to trust her. "My parents have been staying with me and some friends turned up out of the blue. You know how it is, not sure if they are staying for a meal or for the day."

"If you are sure that I am not interrupting." Olwen looked about her with interest.

"Isn't this something else? I'm just loving it but wouldn't it be a shame about the roof and isn't it noisy when it rains?"

"Isn't it just?" He smiled steering her away from the house and around to the shed. "I hope to get it done soon, must get a quote. Do you know anyone?"

"Dean and Len Graham in the village are qualified builders, excellent lads. Granny won't use anyone else and they are reasonable. I'll get you their number."

"Thanks, I could give them a ring,"

"They are busy I know because we have just had a quote off them for a chimney to be repointed and we have to wait two weeks but if they can fit you in they will. Now where is your pride and joy?"

"Here, take a look at this." He helped her over the boxes and tools that still littered the way in.

"Hey! What a find. When are you going to get it started?"

Greg showed her how much had been done and what the next steps would be. He was thrilled at her interest and they were soon deep in discussion, Olwen showing a considerable knowledge of mechanics to Greg's surprise, when his father came into the garage.

"Please excuse me Greg but we have decided to leave earlier than planned as we are taking Stephanie and Joseph for a meal on the way home. We have persuaded Steph to come and stay with us for a few days"

Oh! Thanks Dad." Greg turned. "Olwen this is my father John Morgan."

"I'm pleased to meet you and are you not alike so." Definitely Irish Greg decided hearing the lovely lilt in the soft low voice.

"Yes I believe we are only he is the one with the best looks." John laughed taking her hand. "I can see why Greg likes the hills so much now." A deep pink flushed the creamy skin.

"And you are the one with the charm." Olwen dimpled back.

John turned to his son. "Give us ten minutes and we will be ready with the goodbyes." He smiled at Olwen and left.

"I'm sorry." She said. "I'm afraid I have spoilt your afternoon when you should have been with your guests."

"On the contrary, Mum and Dad were leaving this afternoon anyway and I'm glad you were able to meet them. Listen I have an idea, are you busy later tonight?"

"I have to go back tonight, I have work tomorrow." Greg felt a pang of disappointment.

"Why? What did you have in mind?" She was certainly her grandmother's equal in directness. Greg decided to take the plunge.

"As everyone is deserting me I wondered if you might like a meal or a drink at the Copper Beech." A small frown creased her dark brows. After a moment's thought "I could be meeting you there about seven thirty or so although I can't drink I will have a juice with you. I love it there they are all such characters; the gang of us from Graigwen get there some Saturday nights taking it in turns to drive, there are usually about six of us that means you can get drunk five times before it's your turn again."

Greg laughed. "I like your logic. Will you think I'm rude if I ask if that's a touch of Irish in your accent?"

"Sure it is." She smiled. There are three reasons. One my father was Irish with an accent you could barely understand and we lived in Southern Ireland for ten years also my ex-boyfriend was Irish so it's no wonder is it?"

"It's very attractive, so keep talking.' The lovely pink crept over her cheeks again

"Now it's you and your father that have been kissing the Blarney Stone. You have more charm between you than the little folk."

"Do you believe in them as well?" Greg was watching her as he leant on the gate, his green eyes narrowed and smiling.

"Of course I do and what self-respecting Irish girl would take the risk not to? Now I must not keep you longer from your guests." As she spoke Stephanie and Joseph came out of the cottage door. Steph's eyes were hard as she looked Olwen up and down. Greg introduced them. Steph barely met Olwen's hand with a murmured greeting but Joseph put Olwen's hand to his lips in a continental gesture.

"To find such beauty in this wild place. When you get tired of the hills, my dear, I can always make room for a model of your colouring."

"Not for such a brownie as I am." Olwen laughed withdrawing her hand. "I'll move my jeep out of your way. It was so nice to have met you all. I'll see you later Greg, Goodbye everyone." Reversing down the drive she was gone.

"Oh! That's the way of it is it?" snapped Stephanie. "I might have known and have you bothered to tell her we were engaged? Now I know why you gave me the cool reception." Her eyes filled with tears. "It's not that way at all." John took her arm leading her to the car." You and Joseph follow us or we will be too late for lunch."

"Please Darling, can't we stay friends? Can I come and see you sometimes? What if I never see you again?"

"Look Stephanie, we said our goodbyes more than a year ago and if mother hadn't phoned, you wouldn't have known any different so please don't upset yourself all over again. We are friends but nothing more. Have a good life and remember the good things that we shared. Someday you will find someone else to enjoy life with and to love as you deserve to be loved. You probably would have lost me in a year or two it seems that way. Let's part while we are both alive and well. Remember me like that Steph please." She drew back and looked at him then with a sob threw herself into his arms. The others had walked to the cars and for a moment his arms tightened around her and he kissed her lips comforting her. He released her and she stepped back.

"Okay Greg, if that's how you want it. I appreciate what you are saying but I thought you may have needed me now. I'm sorry I made a mess of this. Her lips trembled tears lay on the long lashes, she raised her eyes to Greg's his dark with sympathy. He kissed her again gently. "Go Stephanie. Live your life. You are a lovely woman and one day someone will be so proud to have you at their side." Keeping his arm about her he led her to the car and handed her inside. He shook Joseph's hand.

"Thanks for bringing her Joseph. Goodbye, I am sorry that your visit was not more enjoyable."

"That is alright." Joseph pumped his hand. I am sorry for your trouble and wish you all the best. I hope they put you right. Don't worry about Stephanie I will take care of her. She is a beautiful talented lady and will go a long way. I am pleased to have met you. Good bye." He drove through the gate with a wave of his hand and a toot on the horn.

Greg took a deep breath going to his mother he folded her tightly in his arms.

"I'm sorry that I shouted at you but you do love a bit of matchmaking, don't you? Sorry I let you down."

"Don't be silly dear, my fault entirely. I never listen so your father keeps telling me. Don't worry we will give them a good time next week. They shall get their Welsh atmosphere and don't worry I won't let her come again but tell me about that lovely red-head. Where did you say she was from?"

Greg threw back his head laughing "Get in the car Mother, don't start." He kissed her tenderly and hugged his father. "Thank you for all the comforts. See you very soon."

"We need as much time with you as we can get."

"I know I'll be down in a week or two." John started the car. "We'll be back with you. That garden needs doing. Take care of Rocky hope you get to keep him. Your mother says your dinner is in the oven." Greg waved and closed the gate drawing a deep sigh of relief. "They have all gone, Rocky where are you?" he called. The dog came bounding out of the shed where he hidden when the house became too full of people. Not a social dog he approved of Greg's parents but drew the line at Joseph and Stephanie, after a lot of barking he had disappeared, now he was full of beans and shared Greg's lunch with enthusiasm.

Greg was exhausted and his chest ached. He lay on the settee with Rocky keeping guard and fell into a deep sleep.

Chapter 19

He awoke with a start wondering where he was, looking at his watch he saw that he had been asleep for several hours, it was seven o'clock.

"Damn it Rocky, why didn't you wake me? I'm going to be late and she will have gone, just my luck." Cursing there was no shower and no time to bath, he ran the sink full of hot water and did the best he could. Shirt after shirt was discarded until he settled on a soft green sweatshirt and green slacks, running a comb through his hair he groaned aloud as he noted the time. Shutting Rocky in with a couple of biscuits, racing the pickup down the mountain road he thanked God his heart had settled down. "I hope the witch isn't about tonight because I can't stop now" He kept his hand on the horn as he flew past her gate. The red jeep had gone and he pressed his foot down harder. It was well after eight when he reached the pub and pulled up with in a cloud of dust. There was no sign of the jeep and his heart sank. Why couldn't she have waited until at least eight thirty? He had no idea how far Worcester was but why didn't she say if it was too late for her? Better go in for a few moments he thought, then he saw the jeep coming down the lane from the opposite direction. She pulled up long side him and wound the window down.

"Not going are you?"

"No." said Greg. "I thought you had."

"I had to deliver some chickens to a couple at Old House Farm. Granny took advantage of me coming this way. Well I was late anyway, let's go in. It doesn't look as if there are many here tonight."

The bar was empty except for a couple sat in the window engrossed with each other.

"Evening both." called John who was filling a shelf behind the bar. "Be with you in a jiffy. Hello Olwen, nice to see you again."

"Hello John, all on your own? What have you done with Betty and Trudy?"

"Betty will be down directly and Trudy is with her young man, gone to the pictures in Brecon I believe."

"Good grief! People travel a long way for an hour's entertainment." remarked Greg.

"Well we are all used to it. Sometimes we have to go to Hereford or Hay twice in one day if we get busy and have a run on food especially in the summer."

Greg bought a lager and a pineapple juice, he and Olwen sitting near the bar. He would have liked to be a bit more private in a corner somewhere but she chose the place and he didn't like to insist they sat somewhere else. Olwen like himself was dressed in green, flowing skirt and soft floral top. She wore her hair in a coil on her neck but tendrils escaped clinging to her ears and cheeks. The light threw shadows under cheek bones, her eyes enormous in the soft light. They had no sooner sat down when the man they called the Captain came in.

"Hello John, beautiful night. Drop of the usual if you please, Sir and one for yourself."

"Thank you very much." John pushed a glass under the optic. "How is the leg?"

"Better today, thanks John. Good weather." He looked around as sipped his drink and to Greg's annoyance spotted them and came over.

"Hello Olwen, my dear. Nice to see you and this is a young man who was in here a week back, I believe." Olwen introduced him.

"Greg, meet Captain Grant Andrews. He lives at the top of the village in a lovely old farmhouse right under the hill. This is Greg Morgan he has bought Graig-y-dorth and tidied it up already."

"Is that so? Glad to hear it, it needs a lot doing. How are you getting on? Were those friends I saw you with? Come to give you a hand I suppose? Getting it all shipshape? Greg while replying civilly could feel his frustration mounting. The Captain was the sort of man who could talk for hours without listening to the replies. Here was a golden opportunity to talk to Olwen maybe get to know her a little better and here they were talking to this nosy fake Captain. (he was sure he wasn't a real one)and time was slipping away. He replied to as many questions as pleasantly as he could.

"Well done my boy. Another rum and whatever our two young friends are having" He wiped his thick moustache with a snowy white handkerchief. He was immaculately dressed in navy slacks and jumper his peaked cap set at a jaunty angle, a good looking man with a weather beaten face and bright blue eyes he certainly looked the part. His smile was jovial but Greg sensed he could be a tough man to cross. However to Greg he looked like someone who had wandered out of the script of some navel play. Olwen hung on to her glass.

"No thanks Captain, I mustn't stay long. I am on my way back to Worcester."

Greg's heart sank, a few moments and she would be gone.

"Still teaching with the college then my dear?"

"Yes I am worse luck. I would much rather be here."

"Of course you would. Granny alright? I haven't had a chance to call this week, must pop over to see her soon. Come on have another juice and you sir, a lager?"

"I'm alright thanks." Greg was beginning to feel desperate.

"Nonsense, fill them up John."

"Evening Captain." The Landlady was standing at the bar dressed for the evening in a flowered dress, hair piled high fixed with diamante combs, matching lipstick and nail varnish, not an apron in sight. She brought their drinks with a smile. "It's lovely to see you Olwen. Not going back tonight are you?"

"Yes." replied Olwen. "I'm still there."

"Sorry to hear of your problems. Bit embarrassing isn't it love? You know what I mean." Olwen flushed angrily Greg thought and wondered.

"Not at all, we're civilised over there." John came to the rescue. "Now dear, let the people enjoy their drinks." Betty returned disgruntled to the bar.

Meanwhile the Captain had been pressed into playing cards with two elderly men who had just come in. Greg breathed a sigh of relief as they moved to the far end of the room. Olwen hearing his sigh laughed. "Don't you be minding, he lives on his own and he gets lonely, only granny and those two old boys go to see him. Granny and he are old friends, go back a long way.'

'Why do they call him Captain?'

"Well he was apparently, many years ago and something happened and he lost his ship and was thrown out of the Navy but he never admits anything and never talks about it. He has convinced himself that he left with honours and we all humour him. It does no harm and he is a nice old boy."

"Am I speaking out of turn or was Betty getting a bit personal just then? You seemed angry."

Olwen was so silent, Greg thought he had gone too far finally she spoke slowly.

"I will tell you although I don't usually talk about myself but I wouldn't want you to be hearing things from others and Trudy from here is at college not in my class but would have known all about it, thus Betty's remarks." She paused again as if reluctant to speak further.

"Please don't if it bothers you." He wished he hadn't mentioned it. She took a sip of her drink.

"The man involved was a professor of music and taught at the college. He was brilliant and the Irish ex I mentioned earlier. We were together a long time but never got any further with a future together. He was charming, talented and extremely good looking and all the girls were stupid about him but they didn't know how domineering and bossy he was behind closed doors. Everything was about him and how it affected him. Most of our rows were because I am my own person and couldn't take the smothering. He especially hated me to come here to grannie's and would think of any means to stop me, a dinner or a film pre booked of course or meeting friends who were expecting us. He wanted us to get married but I had doubts. In the beginning, the first year I would have but he wasn't so keen then. These last six months he has been bossy trying to control me who I saw and where I went I couldn't cope. This last row was awful, I defied him about coming to Granny's then it got worse so I told him that I wanted him out by the time I came back. He stayed with a friend for a few days (for me to come to my senses as he put it) then he came back"——- She paused for so long Greg thought she wasn't going to continue. Anger was already in him that this moron could have upset her so much. She lowered her voice until he had difficulty in hearing her words. "He wouldn't take no as an answer so I had to report him, he lost his job over it and thankfully has gone back to Ireland."

"Are you over it all now?" Greg asked gently though he was raging inside. He only wished he could have been around then.

"I think so I had a bad time but it is over and life goes on. It's sorry I am to have told you all this. You didn't need to know but you are great at letting people talk and I wanted you to know the truth. It is surprising how things get known about even when they occur miles apart." Greg flinched thinking of his own problems that he had yet to share with anyone.

"Had you nobody to talk to? Where are your parents?"

"My father died four years ago and I miss him. He was a wonderful, wonderful man. "My mother is in France. She is a fashion writer for a French newspaper. She is with her currant boyfriend who is a journalist. I haven't met him yet but she is coming over soon. He has a flat in London and a business in France. They lead a great social life. I haven't told her or Granny the whole truth of the matter only my best friend Alicia, I went to stay with her afterwards for a while. She was wonderful and her husband Harry is a darling man, they were so good to me I don't know what I would have done without them."

"Thank you for telling me. I didn't mean to push you about your private life."

She smiled and rose to her feet. "I haven't started on you yet but I really must go or I shall never be up in the morning."

They left to a chorus of goodnights from the bar. As they walked to the jeep, Greg cursed the fact that it was Sunday not Saturday. A thought struck him.

"Surely there is no college at the moment?"

"No there is not but I have to prepare next terms work so I spend some of the holiday time on it. I have been lazy with all that has happened and had to lose some time last term so it is easier to pretend it is a normal college day, get up and work as usual. I don't do it every day but I also have a holiday job temping for a firm of solicitors so I keep busy."

"When will you be coming down again?"

I hope to get away Friday for a week. Why?"

"I was wondering; do you like picnics?"

Olwen laughed. "When the weather is good I do."

"What would you say to a picnic next weekend with luck the weather will be fine." He held his breath. Olwen thought for a moment.

"I don't see why not. Where are you planning to go?"

"I don't know the area, you tell me."

"Tell you what you arrange the picnic and I will take you to a good whinberry patch. Accept the challenge?"

"I would if I knew what a whinberry patch was." Greg laughed.

"I will show you and the loser buys the beers when we get back." She climbed in the jeep winding down the window. "Thank you for the drink and for listening. Next time we talk about you instead."

Greg leant on the door; the urge to kiss her inviting mouth inches from his own was almost too much. She started the engine and with a little wave she was gone. As he watched the lights disappear around a bend, he was filled with elation. She had accepted his invitation and told him confidential things about herself. How he wished he could get his hands on that Irish bloke. He only hoped it hadn't put her off being alone with a man. She seemed alright about it so now all he had to do was pray for fine weather and prepare a picnic she would remember. He was very tired as he drove home but slept a deep refreshing sleep until towards dawn he dreamt that he asked Olwen out but the Captain turned up instead.

Chapter 20

The next day Greg felt he was a prize idiot. Not only was he becoming involved when he shouldn't but he was not even thinking straight, so woolly headed he hadn't fixed a day for this picnic neither had he got Olwen's phone number or her address, he hadn't asked what she liked or disliked to eat and hadn't taken into account he most probably not be able to walk anywhere she suggested neither had he asked for the phone number of the builders. He found the builders by enquiring in the village shop and was directed to a house with a JCB in the back garden. There was no one at home except a ginger and white cat in the garden who loudly enquired his business but couldn't supply answers. Greg scribbled a note and dropping it through the letterbox. He was rewarded the following evening by a cheerful voice on the phone.

"Good evening, Mr Morgan. Len Graham here I found your note and see you're in need of a builder. How can we help?'

"Hi yes thanks for calling. You may have heard that I bought Graig- y-Dorth and you probably know about the roof."

"Everyone has heard about the roof, it caused quite a laugh down the pub a few years back. How do you sleep when it rains?'

'Actually, part of the roof is felted and there is an attic over the main cottage. It's not too bad now but winter isn't here yet.'

"No, Len laughed "Obviously the sooner it's done the better. Do you want us to take a look? We are up to our eyes at the moment; can't do anything for at least two months.'

"That's fine, I can't either. I have a flat in Hull that is on the market but I would like an estimate and your views on an extension.'

"Okay, Sunday at ten if that suits?'

"Fine, see you then.' Greg felt better things felt more progressive. Then a thought struck him, suppose Sunday was the only day that Olwen could come and another thought suppose this weekend was a bad time for him what if he had pain and couldn't walk. He felt a right idiot, it wasn't something you could blurt out to a girl you had just met 'sorry about this but I will have to sit down every few yards and I can only walk zig-zag up a slope or I might drop dead'. He wished he had never asked her or started anything in the first place. He could feel the now familiar depression coming on.

Pulling himself together Rocky following closely he spent an hour on the Land rover carefully taking out the broken windscreen ready for the day when he could afford a new one. The money situation was beginning to bug him he had noticed from his bank statements he didn't have a lot left. Where did it all go? Admittedly he had have to have the phone put in, he couldn't rely on his mobile the signal here was not good, then there had been the vet's bill, paint for the house and the bits and pieces to make it liveable, petrol, food it all adding to a frightening figure. Greg realised that he had never actually been short of money and the sudden cutting back on his lifestyle was going to be hard. Soon the phone bill would be in and the council tax, supposing next winter was a bad one, he had to get in stores for himself and Rocky (if he still had him no one had come forward as yet) Greg paused in his work. He knew his parents would want to help but they couldn't afford to subsidise him even for a short time. He had to prove his independence and find some sort of income because once it came to asking for help it would be time to sell up and go home; at least the farm wouldn't then be a drain on his parents. He couldn't bear his thoughts; Grai-y-dorth was home. He should be looking for some kind of job. He would go to the job centre tomorrow. He could surely get a desk job of some kind but then how would he get to any kind of job; he was supposed to stop driving he couldn't keep pretending it wasn't a reality, supposing he collapsed and killed someone else as well as himself. He had been ignoring the situation but it couldn't be ignored any longer. As if in response a dull ache spread heavily over his chest crept to his shoulders and down his arms, quickly slipping one of the capsules he carried into his mouth he lay back in the seat until it passed. That he thought savagely answered that question. If there was only something he could do from home.

The pain eventually subsiding he sat a long time thinking. It was a big mistake to come here, he should have stayed in his flat and kept his money, it would have kept him, and there were people there to help. It was mistake to be going out with Olwen, he could already feel a powerful attraction; he had to be careful, he dare not become involved. It would hurt too much to break another relationship, supposing she felt the same, she would be facing heartache of the worst kind especially after what she had already been through. He must tell her the truth and never see her again.

He was interrupted in his thoughts by Rocky's angry barking. He struggled to his feet still feeling groggy but managed to walk to the gate where an agitated Rocky was keeping a man outside it. Usually a friendly dog, every time the man put his hand on the latch, Rocky threw himself against the gate snarling and snapping his teeth. Greg called him off.

"Good afternoon. Can I help you?'

The man opened the gate and came through. Greg grabbed Rocky's collar as the dog leapt forward. He was a short man of about fifty years of age wearing a ragged raincoat tied around his waist with string and wellington boots thick with ripe smelling dung. His dirty cap was pulled well down only allowing a few strands of greasy black hair to escape on to his collar. He was unshaven, a week's growth of stubble crept like grey fungi over his cheeks and chin. His eyes were of indeterminate colour, shifty, never still with an unwholesome flickering movement. His voice when he spoke was harsh when Rocky heard it he snarled.

'Nice day.' His eyes slid on to Greg and away around the yard.

"Not bad. How can I help you?' Greg kept a firm hold on the quivering growling dog. The eyes flickered onto the dog and away over the mountain; Greg felt his skin crawl.

"I believe you've got my dog there." He went missing a couple of months back." Greg swallowed and his grip on Rocky tightened.

"How come if he's yours why didn't he come back?'

"Well!" The drawing voice hesitated. "He's a bit queer like, a stone fell on him off the wall back last winter and it's as if he's lost his memory goes off for weeks, can't seem to find his way back but this is the longest yet but then you've been feeding him ain't yer?'

"Can you prove that he is yours?' Greg was shaking with anger. There was no way Rocky was going with this shifty eyed tramp. "Where do you live?" he asked."

The man waved his stick, pointing over the fields. "Penry Farm. It's down the mountain road about two miles from the village.'

"How are you going to prove it?" Greg asked again.

"I don't ave to, e's mine right enough, ent yer Mick? I bought more sheep at market Tuesday and I need two dogs. I only got Jack at 'ome now and e's getting past it so I need Mick back." Greg didn't believe a word of it but without prove there was no way he could stop him taking the dog except one- he released Rocky. 'Call him' He commanded.

"Come on Mick, remember me?" Greg felt sick but Rocky taking matters into his own paws leapt forward. As the man turned to open the gate the dog sank his teeth into his leg. Greg rushed to grab Rocky's collar hauling him gobbling and choking off his victim who with a stream of curses sank to the ground in pain.

"Bloody dog, I'll get 'im for this and yer, yer bloody interfering townie, taking our farms and animals. Why don't yer get from yer? The dog's mad, needs to be put down. Next time I seed 'im I'll shoot the bloody swine."

"No you won't." Greg's eyes were steel flints. "This is not your dog and never has been. You saw him on the mountain and wanted him, you tried to trap him. If I could prove it was you setting those traps I'd hang you with them. Get off my property and don't ever come back. I'll mention your visit to Jeff Arnott. He will be very interested. Funny how he had never seen the dog before, if he belonged to you. Why hadn't you reported him missing? You just thought you would get yourself a working dog to save buying one. When the plan didn't work you came lying your way in here. You didn't bargain on the dog not liking or trusting you. He would have never worked for you. Of course if you are badly injured—(the man was hobbling away to a battered Land rover at the end of the drive)--- I'll run you to the vet that sewed up the dog's neck. He would enjoy treating you, soon make you better, Bastard.'

The man climbed with great difficulty into his vehicle, after two attempts to start it he drove off.

"Well Rocky old son?" Greg bent down to caress the quivering dog. "That got rid of him whoever he was. "Don't look so sheepish I wouldn't scold you for biting him; teach him a lesson. Let's go and give Jeff a ring.'

Jeff was brief and to the point. "That old scoundrel never owned that dog. He has been barred from keeping dogs for five years. Cruel as hell, name of Luke Jeffries. Nasty cruel and small minded; watch yourself he could be dangerous given half a chance. Was on an assault charge;

he attacked the RSPCA man. He may be a bit wary as you are a stranger around here but watch your back and watch your dog. He would shoot him if he sees him about alone. I'll call by and have a word but we can't prove anything so be careful what you say to neighbours. I'll put the frighteners on him take a look around his sheds and stock. There's sure to be something I can have him for. Just keep an eye for a while. Thanks for telling me."

"Enemy no one' thought Greg putting down the phone. 'Bound to get one I suppose but I wish that Rocky wasn't involved'.

Olwen rang the following Thusday. "Would the picnic still be on?" she enquired.

"Oh! Yes." Said Greg, all his good intentions vanished like smoke.

"Saturday would be a good day for me." She said, "Could you pick me up about eleven?'

"Yes Ma'm." He grinned down the phone.

"That's if it's convenient. Sir" she picked up the ball.

"Fine." said Greg. "See you then and pray for fine weather."

"Here we go boy." He shouted to Rocky. "Now we have to put together the perfect picnic and we have to face the witch again." He was to face the witch before that. She was at his gate the following morning.

Chapter 21

Rocky barked and Greg came out to see the dog on his hind legs being petted while Samuel Peeps nosed at him. "Hello" Greg was mindful of their last encounter. "Are you coming to see me?"

"Wouldn't be here if I wasn't." She let herself in through the gate. For a wild moment Greg thought she had come because he was taking Olwen out but her next words took him by surprise. "I hear you have gained a dog and made an enemy."

"It seems I have. He's a nasty piece of work that man."

"He is and worse, he's dangerous; he does silly tricks to amuse himself, they do a lot of harm. He carries a gun too, have often met him with one. He does have a licence unfortunately he hasn't done anything yet to get himself banned from holding one. Samuel Peeps doesn't like him, keeps away growling hackles up. I know your dog bit him yesterday." "How did you hear about that?" Greg interrupted.

"Well if you must know he came to me for some herbs to heal his leg. I expect you have heard I'm the local witch or White witch as they used to call any one dabbling in medicines" Was there the ghost of a smile in those strange light eyes? "I refused to treat him, not because I couldn't or wouldn't because every living thing has a right to be treated or cured at some time but he needed a tetanus injection and stitches, if I did it and something went wrong he would be spiteful enough to make me or mine pay for it. Also he told me how he came by it and I knew you must have had a good reason not to have driven him to casualty yourself. I really don't like handling a man as evil as him so I rang young Glen from the farm to take him to the hospital and kept my conscience clear. I thought I should warn you if he can pay you out he will. Don't let your dog anywhere he can get at him. He really will kill him and say he was sheep worrying or some such tale.'

'Thanks for the tip. I really do appreciate it.'

'Just remember it.' Bronwyn turned to leave. 'By the way, in passing I've six hens and a cockerel would do you just fine, you should be eating free range eggs not ones you don't know where they're from. I'll send them up with Olwen. I have a crate for them.'

"Really it's very kind of you but no thank you. I don't think I need chickens--- Greg began.

"Nonsense there's plenty of room for them. I'll not charge you seeing you are a newcomer. Call it a welcome gift. Need a bit of netting on the garden wall or you'll have no cabbage come autumn.' She was through the gate before he could reply, where she was joined by Samuel Peeps who sat waiting for her rather than trespass on Rocky's territory. As she started down the road she suddenly turned around.

'By the way, next time you pass, keep your hand off that horn. Don't you know that it's not allowed after seven o'clock?' She was gone before Greg could think of a reply.

Greg stood in the yard almost incapable of speech. He looked at Rocky whose tail was beating the ground as he waited for him to say something.

'Well I'll be damned.' Greg finally spoke. 'Did you ever see the like, Rocky?' The tail beat a steady tattoo. 'First she very kindly warns me about old Luke, then she forces me to have chickens that I don't want, then I get a telling off for using the horn that I had a telling off for not using before. A self-confessed witch too. Remember that, Rocky. Yes, she had you fawning too, don't deny it while her own dog sat and waited for her. I think we are being manipulated whether we like it or not.'

That evening Greg drove around the mountain road to see if he could spot where Luke Jeffries lived. He drove slowly following the road which ran along the foot of the mountain. He passed two derelict cottages set back in the woodland also a deserted chapel. The first farm that he passed belonged according to Jeff Arnott to Cliff Edwards known to be a good neighbour always willing to lend a hand. Some of his hedges formed the boundary to Graig-y-dorth and were in excellent condition. Greg noticed that his cattle looked well and Jeff had told him that Cliff's sheep ran the hill. Greg meant to call one day and introduce himself; he had seen the man in the distance and had learned from Bronwyn that the Glen she talked about was one of his sons. The next house belonged to an artist who lived in London where he exhibited his paintings. He was usually; when on vacation at the cottage to be found in The Copper

Beech where Greg later met him. He spotted a farm down in the fields where Jeff had told him a family lived with four children; Greg had not seen anything of them.

A mile or so farther he came to a drive leading across a field where a tumble down farm house sat in a circle of tall pine trees which added to its air of dilapidation and depression. It looked so rundown it appeared empty but for torn curtains at the window and a towel and a pair of trousers hanging on a line slung between two trees. The battered Land Rover standing on the yard Greg recognised immediately as Luke's. A cattle grid led across a field in which several steers stood in mud up to their hocks, sheep wandered at random over several fields in which large areas of docks and ferns were left untreated. In another field a tractor stood where someone had started to cut grass but left it. Greg slowed down as much as he dared without attracting attention. Taking in the whole sorry state, his lip curled seeing as he drove fields with stones fallen from walls and several barns standing empty and dilapidated. This then was the home of an idle man always ripe for mischief, never minding his own business, trying to get something for nothing not caring how he got it. Greg put his foot down and drove on he must keep Rocky with him never leaving him home on his own. He was half inclined to return now to collect him but time was getting on so he would hurry to get his shopping first. Uneasy all the time he was in town he was relieved to see the dog safe on his return.

'I won't risk it again Boy. You come to town with me because I would rather he broke into the house than he injured you.' Rocky barked an agreement and ate his supper with gusto.

Saturday dawned sunny, a typical July day. There was no wind and it was hot from early morning until by eleven almost too hot. Greg put the cool box and Rocky in the pickup. Olwen was going to have to share her seat with the dog as there was no way Greg was going to leave him and he didn't trust Rocky to ride in the back. He picked up his lead in case they were going near sheep. He was still worried about himself; he only hoped she wasn't taking them up a mountain. When he arrived at the cottage there was no sign of anyone although her jeep stood on the yard. Greg was just deciding whether he had enough courage to knock on the door when it opened and Olwen came out carrying a basket. She wore jeans and a blue open necked shirt. Greg opened the truck door for her.

'I hope you don't mind sharing with Rocky'

'Of course not, Gran told me. It's wise to bring him with you. Luke is such a dreadful man.'

'I went past his place yesterday. You certainly wouldn't call it home would you?'

'No indeed not.' agreed Olwen. 'Granny and I walk past there sometimes and she told him off about the state of his cattle once a couple of years back. I was nervous for her after that and dreading she might upset him one day but I think he is more scared of her and her reputation than she is of him. She can be very formidable sometimes; that she can.'

'I know.' Greg replied. 'What's with the chickens?'

'The what?' she looked puzzled. He told her of Bronwyn's visit.

She laughed. "Gran rears them under the hen and when they are grown she sells the cockerels at market and gives little sets of hens to anyone she thinks needs eggs. Actually you are the honoured one. She never gives to newcomers and only to deserving cases.'

'Great. I don't know that I want them.'

'Oh you will' It could have been her grandmother speaking. 'Think of the food value, they don't cost much to keep. You can always sell the eggs that you don't use.'

'Hey! Where are we going?' He suddenly realised that they were approaching the main road.

'Abergavenny; drive right through the town. We are going Whinberry picking.'

'Is that what the basket is for? Are we going to find that many?'

'Wait and see.' Greg smiled at her, his strong hands steady on the wheel. She sat with an arm around Rocky, completely at ease. Her ponytail cascading red-gold down her back, her eyes smoky grey, alight with fun, he noticed tiny gold lights glowing in their depths as her eyes met Greg's; his heart jolted (this wasn't good for him but it was nice.) Rocky looked ahead giving each of his subjects a licked ear now and then.

As they approached the Sugarloaf Mountain, Greg put his worries out of his mind giving himself up to the pleasures of the day. The mountain did indeed resemble a loaf of bread or sugar. It swept majestically and smoothly into a hazy blue sky as they drove onto its lower slopes. They parked and with Rocky jumping around them began a gentle walk in which the gradient increased so slowly that it required little effort. Much of the lower slopes were flat with acres of wild thyme filling the air with perfume. Heather spread for miles and would be a wonderful sight come autumn. Larks sent droplets of song while giant bumble bees hummed busily in tiny white flowers. The day was still hot and clear although the surrounding hills were a haze of blue.

'This is beautiful." Greg took deep breathes of perfumed air while giving silent thanks that he was not called upon to show weakness. The actual summit was a good way off and he fervently prayed that Olwen had no intention of going that far. She suddenly began racing Rocky across wide sheep tracks, startling rabbits sending the dog wild with excitement. At all times an obedient dog he was nevertheless sorely tempted not to come back when called. The grass flowed soft and green in a natural lawn beneath their feet. Sheep and rabbit droppings showed what a busy thoroughfare this was when no humans were around. There were no sheep to be seen at present and only a couple of people in the distance so Rocky could run to his heart's content but he didn't go far too excited by the many rabbit holes he tried to get down. They chattered about non consequential things as they strolled. After a while Olwen turned across a track looking carefully each side of the path. Suddenly she stopped and showed Greg the small black berries hidden on the stems of a tough little shrub which grew in profusion through the heather and wild thyme.

'This will do nicely.' Olwen spread the rug while Greg reached in the cool box for cold drinks and a bottle of water for Rocky. They sat a moment enjoying the shade of a small rowan tree. 'Don't you be getting too comfortable.' laughed Olwen. "Start picking." She knelt putting the basket between them. For a moment Greg couldn't see any berries then his eyes began to find them amongst their grey-green leaves, then he could see there was a good harvest but so difficult to pick he didn't think he would make much impression on the crop. Olwen already had both hands deep in the bushes and his eyes preferred to linger on the lovely picture she made. The ponytail had already loosened, tendrils escaping about her face and neck. She looked up and catching his eyes upon her, blushed deepening the sun kissed rose of her cheeks.

"Pick" she ordered. "Yes Mam" They picked in silence for a while. Rocky dashing backwards and forwards between two rabbit holes bouncing back every now and then to lick faces, stamp all over the berries and do his best to upset the basket. After being shouted at a few times he flung himself on the rug and went to sleep. The basket didn't seem very full when Greg looked at his watch. It was one- thirty. He looked around for Olwen she had taken a plastic bag and worked her way off a little, picking busily.

'Hey! Busy Bee, Lunchtime.' he called. She rose at once, coming back to empty her bag in the basket. 'It's too warm and I'm thirsty.'

'I've just the thing for you then.' He opened the cool box producing two paper cups and two cartons of apple juice sharp and cold.

"Lovely, Do we have one each?"

"We sure do." He brought out paper plates, napkins then boxes of sliced chicken, soft white buttered rolls, small garlic cheeses, a pot of prawn salad, crisps and two slices of watermelon.

"Heavenly; I give you full marks for the picnic." She grabbed a roll and a cheese. "This is sheer heaven."

They sat under the little rowan tree which dappled patterns over them while a slight breeze blew from the mountain. It was so hot Greg took his shirt off. His hard muscular body tanned tapering to a slim waist.

"Two can play at that game." Olwen promptly removed hers to Greg's delight. She wore a white bikini top her creamy skin lightly freckled. He swallowed; she was deliciously tempting and appeared completely oblivious to the effect she had on him They ate hungrily, Rocky demanding bits until Greg poured him a dish of water unwrapped a meaty bone then led him off a little way to gnaw in peace.

"You thought of everything didn't you?" What's in the bag?"

"Desert" He pulled out peaches. a bunch of huge black grapes then an ice cold bottle of wine from the cool box.

"I can't bear it." Olwen hid her face in her hands. "I shall be asleep."

"It's very low alcohol." Greg poured it into the paper cups. The sun filtered through the leaves making pattern play on their bodies. Greg rolled onto his back and within minutes was fast asleep. Olwen propped herself on her elbow watching him, noticing the fine dark hairs on his arms, his strong chest muscles moving with each breath beneath his bronzed skin. Her eyes slowly travelled upwards. He was beautiful, his mouth relaxed like a young boys. She found herself wondering what it would be like to kiss those firm lips now slightly apart his breathing even and steady. She liked the straight nose and wide set eyes closed now with long fringed lashes that any girl would envy. The eyes she knew were an unusual green. She had an irresistible urge ro sweep back the tangle of dark curls from around his ears while he slept. He attracted her strongly attracted her she had been thinking about him all week, she was finding the long lines of his body sensual, his green eyes held a mystery that she was longing to solve. She sensed there was more to this man that she wanted to know about, the tiny lines around his eyes and about the cleft in his chin. This man was mature and held secrets in his heart and she found she quite badly wanted to share them. Above all she felt completely safe in his company. She rested her head on her arms watching him until her eyes closed and she too slept.

Something tickling her nose woke her. She opened her eyes to see a pair of laughing green ones inches from her own. A fine strand of heather was lightly brushing her cheeks. She did not move. His eyes locked into hers. He leant over her. She slightly lifted her head; his lips met hers. Fire flicked through them both. The kiss was long and deep yet gentle with first kiss sweetness. Lightning flickered through nerves.

A cold wet nose was thrust rudely between them followed by a rough hairy head. They moved apart. Greg rose pulling her up with him. He kissed her again, leaning her back against the little tree. The second kiss was deeper searching, asking- answering, responding. They both felt passion flair between them his hands following the curve of her body then losing themselves in the wildness of her hair. She locked hands behind his head, drowning, giving. Rocky barking and the sound of voices brought them apart. Greg's eyes dark with desire, Olwen's huge pleading-

A man was moving across the berry patch followed by two women and a child running. Greg grabbed Rocky and slipped on his lead, picking up his shirt and Olwen's silently handing it to her. The magic broken he turned to pack up the picnic replacing everything in the cool box while Olwen grabbed the basket and was once again picking. The family moved towards them calling a greeting. Rocky growled but with a wagging tail. Olwen straightened up waved to the group and came back to Greg.

"Shall we call it a day then? The basket is half full and that's very good for a first pick" her smile was strained. Greg mentally shook himself, forcing a smile.

"Great! Yes let's get back now." Relenting he caught her berry stained hand and kissed the palm. "Come on Sweetheart, you win the challenge, it's a beautiful berry patch." She laughed and relaxed.

'That was a gorgeous picnic, the best I ever had. Let's call it a draw.'

"Okay." Greg slung the rug over his shoulder picking up the cool box. ''Can you manage the basket?'

'I can.'

He would have liked to put an arm around her but with Rocky in one hand and the box in the other it was impossible; he had hoped to release the dog again but there were suddenly more people on the path now with children and dogs. They found themselves at the pickup with little said except the undesirability of bringing dogs on picnics and the hope to have another later in the summer. As they drove back with Rocky again between them, the strain was almost unbearable. So much needed to be said but neither could say the words which would release the tension.

Greg stopped at the witch's gate. "Are you coming in?" Olwen asked.

"No I had better get back. I have several things to do." He came around the vehicle to take her basket. Concealed from the house as she slid out, he trapped her against the pickup.

"I'm sorry, Olwen."

"Don't." She laid a finger against his lips, in an instant she was in his arms, his mouth on hers. "Oh! Greg" he stopped her with another kiss.

'Come back to the farm with me, I want you to.'

"I can't now, Granny will have heard the pickup and wonder what's wrong. I have promised to take her to her friends tonight but I will come before I go back to Worcester.'

"When Olwen? When do you go?"

"Tomorrow night. I will come tomorrow afternoon. I'll be making you a pie and I have to bring the chickens." She slipped from his arms. "Thank you for a lovely day." She turned to the house, waving from the door.

Greg barely remembered driving home the truck was on the yard Rocky out and running around before he came to his senses.

'I am in love, really in love and God help me for now I am in real trouble because I can't have her. She will have to told and quick.' But the exultation wouldn't leave him. Depression would not return oh but it would but not now. Love was here. Magic was here. He was much too high to come down. It was enough to be in love and to believe that most probably she was too.

Chapter 22

It was late the following morning when Greg awoke. After tossing and turning most of the night reliving each kiss and each word, cursing himself over and over for being such a fool as to allow it to happen, then hugging himself for the very joy that it had. He had fallen into a troubled sleep at dawn, realisation hitting him again as he woke. He was wondering if she was thinking about him in the same way when his watch alarm warned him it was ten o'clock and the builders were due any minute. He dressed rushing down to put the kettle on and let Rocky out. Sudden dizziness warned him against rushing. It was well after ten before Rocky's bark announced the arrival of a pickup. As Greg opened the door two lads unmistakably brothers, smiled a greeting.

"Hi" Greg welcomed them in. "You just smelt the tea brewing."

"Builders always do." The taller of the two held out a hand. "I'm Len Bateman, this is my brother Dean." They shook hands.

"Let's take a look around then we can have that tea and a chat."

"Greg showed them inside. It amused the lads immensely that anyone would put a tin roof on a dwelling house. They speculated as to what had happened to the original stone tiles. They could throw no light on the subject but had heard talk at the pub when it happened, but apparently no one in the village had noticed the stone going or galvanise going on until it was an accomplished fact.

As they sat down to their tea, Greg knew he was going to get on with them. Len was tall with bright hazel eyes and a ready smile, broad muscular arms and chest. Greg wasn't surprised to learn he spent his spare time in the gym. Dean, a few inches shorter with fair curly hair and large blue-grey eyes wore a moustache, a more slender build than his brother although he too had the muscular arms and hands of a stone mason which Greg learned was his speciality. He was also married with two young children. Both their attitudes were friendly and helpful, Greg felt at ease. He could see that they knew their job and if their prices were right once he sold his flat he knew he would like these men to handle his home. He explained his position.

"That's fine." said Dean. "No problem. We are pretty busy at the moment. We'll try to get some of it done so by the time you are ready we should be as well. We should be able to get the roof done before the autumn anyway. Any offers on your flat? A big flat in that location shouldn't take too long to sell."

"I haven't heard a word but two agents have it. I'll give them a ring in the morning." They all agreed that the roof was top priority. Len was of the opinion that grants were available owing to the age of the property and the unsuitability of the galvanised as a roof on a house. He offered to look into it for Greg as he knew some people who would know.

"I'm grateful to you and I like the way you are talking. Seriously we will go ahead as soon as I can but it may take a little time I'm afraid." He sighed, he would have liked for them to start straight away. He felt that time was running away from him. Dean had wandered off and was looking at the old range.

"I like these." he said. "But they are dirty and hard work. How would you like a Rayburn in the kitchen for the hot water, to run upstairs radiators then we could convert this into an original stone fireplace with basket and dogs, lovely for a log fire in the winter evenings?"

"I never gave it a thought." Greg admitted. "Could you do that?"

"Of course, no problem is our motto. Chimney may give a bit of a problem though depends where it runs and what condition it's in." He disappeared upstairs.

"He's into fireplaces at the moment." laughed Len. "He is right though make a lot of difference to this room. The winters up here are something else. A Rayburn and a log fire are a must. We haven't had a bad one for a year or two and we are about due." They walked outside.

"These Subaru's are just the job around here aren't they?" Greg remarked.

"We couldn't be without this one." Len was just about to climb in when Dean came out wiping a sooty hand.

"Not much that we can't fix." He looked up at the chimney.

"Before you go come and see what I found." Greg led the way to the shed." Take a look at that.'

"My God it's a 1948 model." The lads spoke almost in unison. "Wow! That's the job for here." Dean walked carefully around the Land Rover. "It needs a lot doing though. Does it go?"

"We can turn it over." Greg told them how he and Ray had been working on it.

"Great! We'll keep an eye down the village for you when you get it going. It's worth a bit."

"The mice knew a good thing when they saw it, pity."

"More damage from them than years of disuse." Greg agreed.

"Of course you'll keep it won't you?" Dean asked. "I know they are worth a lot but think of actually using one again especially up here."

"I am, I am." laughed Greg. "Hang on I hear the phone." He tried not to run thinking it might be Olwen. He tried to steady his heart rate. To his surprise it was Dave, Ray's partner.

"Hello Greg. Ray's just asked me to phone you, he's on his way down for a couple of days." Dave sounded terse as if he couldn't spare the time to speak. Greg wondered what was wrong. "He should be with you about five. He's got a loom for the land Rover. Hope things go well. Bye."

'What's the matter with him?' Greg wondered. 'Hope Ray isn't taking too much time off.' Len put his head around the door. "We are off now. Will let you have an estimate for the roof and a rough plan of the other work that you can mull over at your leisure. We do an estimate for that when you are ready and know what you want.'

"Fine thanks a lot. As I said I will let you know when the finances are right and maybe we'll have some luck with the grants as you suggested. You never know. See you now.' They waved and were gone.

Greg wearily made himself something to eat then found that he couldn't eat it. Twice he picked up his mobile and put it down again. 'She said she would come' Oh! God how he wanted to see her but he had let the unthinkable happen. What should he say or do? He shrank from telling her the truth. Now he had the problem of Ray as well, not that he wouldn't be delighted to see him but he couldn't talk about important issues with them both here and his feelings for Olwen getting in the way. It was two o'clock before he heard the jeep turn in the gate. He had been on hooks all day.

"I always fancied this place whenever Gran and I walked by. It looked as if it were waiting for someone to love it. It looked so sad and neglected. I would be loving to come to help when you are doing it up. You will need someone to advise you on curtains and carpets won't you?"

"I certainly will and I'll hold you to that." Greg put his arms around her. She turned and was in his arms. He was kissing her, running his fingers through her hair which today was only held back with a ribbon. She was returning his kisses with passion.

"How beautiful you are." He whispered hoarsely. She ran her fingers lightly up and down his spine. He loosened the ribbon from her hair.

"I know it's too soon but I believe I am falling in love with you.'

"It's sure I am that I might be falling myself.' She pulled back her head. Grey eyes locked into green ones dark with

193

passion. "You're very handsome yourself and who's to say it's too soon. Aren't you after believing in love at first sight?'

"I do now.' He gathered her close, her breath soft on his neck, his lips kissing her eyes, ears, lips again and again, exploring with hands that trembled. Opening the tiny buttons of her silk shirt, his fingers slid into the lacy bra finding flesh soft and warm. She moaned as he gently rubbed his thumb over her hardening nipple. She felt him harden as he moved against her. He lowered his head taking her nipples gently between his teeth. She gasped clutching his thick curling hair. He straightened to find her lips again then with a groan lowered her to the rug. There was nothing now but their mounting passion, clothing discarded as flesh demanded flesh and exploring fingers. She gasped as he entered her. Greg was normally a gentle lover but his need for this girl drove him to demand and take with a deeper power that he had ever felt before. She rose to him, thrust for thrust until with a wild cry she came and he claimed her with shuddering gasps; sated they lay in each other's arms time forgotten; the magic complete.

Greg came to with a jolt of pain. He gasped, caught by its severity. Olwen lay half asleep wrapped in her shawl of hair. She smiled at him not understanding. He kissed her running his hand over her thigh and hips. He moved very slowly, pain thudding through his chest and arms. He reached for his jeans and the capsule that would bring relief.

"What are you doing?" Olwen yawned and sat up winding her arms around his chest.

"'Just a touch of cramp.' He lay back the pain ebbing away into a dull ache leaving him tired and drained. He drew her close pulling their clothes around them waiting for the pain to subside. Olwen laid her head on his chest, curled up in her hair like a cat; it flowed over them both a warm living cloak. Greg tried to keep perfectly still, cursing himself for several kinds of fool even though he was filled with love, tenderness and a deep sense of peace. They both woke an hour later feeling chilly. Holding each other tenderly they twined fingers, traced eyebrows and lips as lovers do.

"The only thing keeping us warm is your hair, Rapunzel.' Greg spread it over them loving the riot of red and gold waves. "Don't ever have it cut will you?"

"Well! I have not for the last twenty year or so. I don't suppose I shall now." She replied.

"You don't look old enough to have been growing it for twenty years." Greg had recovered now thanking his lucky stars that Olwen suspected nothing.

'Rubbish; I'm thirty two if you must know.' She laughed.

'Honestly? I would have said about twenty five.'

'Flatterer; now tell me how old you are or have I got a toy boy?'

'As old as my tongue and a bit older than my teeth.' Greg quipped reaching for his clothes. "Come on love, it's getting cold.'

'Let me be warming you up then.' She reached for him caressing his hair and back. Greg worried about making love again with such passion so he teased, kissed and tickled her instead until she begged for mercy.

'Right; kettle on woman, your job, mine fire.'

Olwen looked at him puzzled, for a young man so early in love to turn down a chance to make love again seemed unusual especially as she was almost sure that he hadn't had a relationship in a while but she dressed swiftly and went to put the kettle on as requested. They ate tea as children might, cutting bits of bread and cake, feeding each other with much laughter and little kisses. She was a born mimic, by exaggerating her accent, she enacted little stories so between kisses, tea and laughter they spent precious time getting to know one another. Tea would have turned into supper, they enjoyed each other so much but a car turning in the gate brought them swiftly back to earth.

"My God it's Ray. I clean forgot he was coming." Greg leapt to his feet.

"Your friend I saw at the dance hall?" Olwen smiled. "He looked a good fun person."

"He's the greatest friend one could have. We have been mates for years." Greg pulled on his shoes. Rocky was barking a welcome as Greg opened the door. Ray was slowly climbing out of the Jaguar. It gave Greg a strange feeling to see his car again. He was surprised at Ray bringing it onto the yard except the yard was very dry. Ray parked neatly by the jeep.

"Hi" called Greg. "Good to see you. Kettle's on the boil or a beer if you prefer. There is someone I want you to meet." Ray lifted his bag out of the car making no answer except to lift a hand in greeting. Olwen still barefoot came to the door and leant on Greg's shoulder. Ray straightened his shoulders as if a mighty weight sat upon them.

"Hello both." His smile was strained. Greg was shocked at his appearance as he came forward. Gone was the happy go lucky lad with the sparkling eyes and merry smile, an older man stepped forward a man with a deep sorrow. In the glance Ray gave Greg before putting down his bag and greeting Olwen, Greg saw that Ray knew the truth.

Chapter 23

"Why? Greg, why in God's name didn't you tell me? Am I your best mate or what?" Did you think that I wouldn't find out until they carted you off to hospital or out in a wooden box? Did you expect me to wait until the worst happened and you wouldn't be able to see me running around like a chicken with its head cut off?" Ray stood head on arm against the wall.

"Ray, I--- Greg tried to stop the savage flow of words pouring from his friend. Ray shrugged off the hand he'd placed on his shoulder and straightened up.

"Oh! I can guess what you were thinking. Good old Ray, alright to fool about with the girls or some bloody old car but of course he wouldn't be expected to handle the fact that his best friend has a terminal illness."

"I was going to tell you as soon as I could find the right time.'

"Were you? By God, how good of you. Christ! Greg you are a bastard. Can't you begin to see how I feel? I was here with you all those weeks. I don't bloody believe it. There was I whistling away, going back to Dave's after work to pick up that effing loom for you and I walk straight into Tom Gregson and what does he say? Ray I am so sorry about Greg and it must be hard on you being such great mates. How are you coping Ray? How is he Ray? Me? I'm stood there like an imbecile. Christ Almighty! Fuck you Greg.'

"I am sorry Ray. I just couldn't tell you. I knew it would hurt you and it would have made it more real. You were always so full of fun-------"

"Fun be damned." Ray spun around his blue eyes blazing. "You bloody idiot. Is that what it is? You don't deserve sympathy. "I know you but hell and damnation to be with you half the summer and not to know, wondering why you let me do most of the graft and looked such a damned awful colour half of the time. How do you think that makes me feel? I'll tell you. Great, fucking great, that's what." He swung back staring out of the darkening window. "You just can't be sorry enough Greg. Your parents and that poor girl I feel sorry for. Poor cow, screw her first tell her after, that's about right.'

Greg half rose, fists clenched though he was aware that Ray's justifiable anger masked a terrible grief. He spoke quietly.

"My parents have known since Spring and it almost killed them and me. No, Olwen doesn't know yet.'

"Doesn't she, by God?" Ray swung round and leant across the table. "When are you going to tell her then. I can see what's between you two without counting the time you spent at the jeep saying goodnight. If I hadn't come she would have stayed the night. Well that's fine, that's your business good luck to you. I would be the first to say good luck to you both but she doesn't know Greg; She doesn't bloody know and she is going to get hurt one way or another if you don't snuff it one night on top of her."

He crashed his fist down on the table smashing dishes and overturning the milk.

"Don't you damn well care at all about anyone." His shoulders shook and tears splashed on to the table and his clenched fists.

"Greg jumped to his feet. "Of course I care. It's because I care I haven't told you, idiot. Can't you see the only ray of sunshine in my life since I was told has been you; your wit, your escapades, your fun loving personality; Thoughts of you have brought a smile, kept me sane. You weren't there when I smashed up my flat and thought about suicide rather than a slower death. I have suffered and learned to cope by myself. I spend a lot of time alone. I couldn't put that burden on you, not yet. I knew that once you knew, the light would go out for both of us and selfishly I didn't want that to happen. I looked to you for normality. I kept thinking I will tell him tomorrow, the next day or next week and you were enjoying your time here so much and I was too. You made me forget most of the time you know what your friendship means to me. It was very hard, Ray.' He stretched out a hand to his friend.

"I know." Ray slowly took his outstretched hand and gripped it tightly before pulling him into a bear hug. After a while moving apart he wiped his eyes.

"It was hard admitting to Tom that I didn't know. It shook him a bit too.'

"I never gave him a thought. He seldom goes over to your neck of the woods I didn't think he knew you anyway.'

Ray wiped his face in the tea towel. "He does come very occasionally. Dave knows him and would have told him we were friends. Don't forget he would have heard you speak of me anyway. Dave is pretty cut up about it too; says if there is anything he can do for you just let him know.'

"I thought he was a bit abrupt on the phone earlier.' Greg frowned. 'I seem to be upsetting everyone. I can only say I'm sorry mate. I just haven't been able to think straight.'

'I'll say.' Ray had calmed now and flung himself into a chair near the fire. "Come on Greg; I want to know what's going on. Why isn't there a cure and when are they going to find a donor? What are you doing living out here when you should be resting? What gives with Olwen and when are you going to tell her? You'll have to tell her fast or she might fall in love with you.'

"I'm afraid it's too late for that.' Greg murmured dropping his head in his hands. "I know that I love her. It's happened so fast. "I told myself not to but when I am with her everything flies out of my head except how much I need her, until something awful recalls it, like making love to her and almost having an attack bad enough to finish me and managing to keep it from her. Oh God! Ray. What am I going to do? I can't bear it and I have to. I have to tell her, see pity in her eyes then send her away. Suppose she won't go, wants to stay and nurse me." He told him about Stephanie's visit. "Right mess I've made of everything already instead of putting my affairs in order, I bloody louse them up leaving heartbreak for everyone else. Why has it all happened Ray? Why?'

"I can't answer that. There must be something positive. Most likely you are going to get well and this is only an interlude to teach us some lessons.'

Greg stood up shakily putting a hand on Ray's shoulder. "Make us some tea while I feed Rocky and the chickens then I will tell you all. How do you like my dog then?'

"When you told me how you found him I wanted to kill the bastard that done it. You haven't found out yet? What did you say about chickens?" Ray stopped half way to the kitchen.

"Olwen's grandmother sent them more or less insisted I had them"

"You'll make a farmer yet but tell me do you feel comfortable making it with a witch's granddaughter." Ray grinned then turned abruptly away.

They sat until the early hours in spite of the long day Greg had spent on the Sugarloaf. He felt such relief that Ray was here and knew the score that time slipped away with a few beers and the chance to really talk. He explained his illness, able to talk at last about his thoughts and fears. How he felt about the operation, about dying. Ray listened looking into the fire. Greg had never before felt the strength Ray concealed beneath his fun loving nature. He proved a quiet listener but quickly grasped all that Greg was telling him and Greg felt his heart lifting. Ray could share and understand feelings that Greg's parents hadn't been able to for the emotions they could not control. After a long silence Ray spoke.

"Sorry I shot my mouth of earlier."

"I would have done the same, it was stupidity on my part to try and hide things, you always get found out. I must talk to Olwen. You are right I can't let it get any deeper with her. God knows its deep enough with me already. All those years with Steph, now I find a girl I can love with all my heart and its barren no future at all. If only I had a few more years to make something of my life.'

"How long is the best Greg? Honestly.'

"They don't really know but not more than two McLoughlin thought but he also said that you can never tell, maybe more maybe less. The medication helps; I go days without pain and feel very normal. Other days I just can't do anything much, the pain just grabs me. Since I have been here on the whole I feel much better, haven't had time to think about things too much.'

"Shouldn't you be home Greg, not on your own? Your mum would love to look after you.'

"I know but I don't want that. I want to feel that I am doing something on my own before I die. I don't want to be nursed, treated like an invalid before I need to be. At least here I can pretend to be well although I don't know what to do with the place or how to make a living."

"I could stay with you." Ray spoke quietly. "I've fallen for this place. If it was a proper farm and could support us I'd pack in the garage.'

"I think you have been phoning Megan in Graigwen. How is it going?'

Ray was slow in answering. After a long pause he said. "You knew she came up to Hull after I left here didn't you? Well she came again last week and here's something that you never thought you'd hear. Megan is different to all the others. She is sweet and clean in a way I can't explain, no side, no sophistication but so pretty and handles herself well even in the posh nightclubs and restaurants that I took her to. Says what she thinks rather like your Olwen; perhaps mountain girls are different. She is such a worker too. She came out on the boat last weekend, she didn't know anything about it but somehow made herself useful and was picking it all up like mad. Things got done without asking or telling. All the others would be cooking and cleaning or not as the case maybe bu always with one eye on me' look what I can do' sort of thing. Megan just got on with whatever had to be done as if it didn't enter her head that I might be noticing or not simply it was there to do and it was done. I just can't explain.'

"I know what you mean, it just feels right.'

"That's right it does. I want to see her for herself not because she is good in bed or fun to be with(she is both as it happens) but I respect her too. It's becoming important how she feels, how she is and I know without a doubt that she loves me already. I never felt that anyone really wanted me for myself before and my parents loved her on sight. That's another reason that I want you to tell Olwen, if she feels about you half of what I'm feeling for Megan, she is going to be just about killed.'

"I know, I know.' Greg stood up. 'Come on, let's get some sleep. Thanks Ray for making me face a few facts. You are a good mate to me in more ways than one. Wish you were living here, it gets lonely sometimes and now you know everything it's a relief to have someone to talk to."

"Find me a job and I'll come. Don't worry about the money side of it, as long as it feeds me and runs the car.'

"Come off it, Megan lives down the village.' Greg laughed. "I'm no fool; someone will be looking for a house here soon.'

"Well! She has talked about coming to work in Hull. We'll see but remember Greg, if you need me I'll come straight away."

Greg lost for words clapped him on his shoulder.

Chapter 24

Fitting the new loom in the Land Rover was a day of pleasure for them both. They were in their element, troubles set aside, and they almost forgot to eat. Ray was staying until Wednesday but was spending Tuesday with Megan. They spent all of Monday fitting the loom and sorting out the electrics. Ray had found a set of original headlamps at a scrap yard in Hull, fitted them and had them working. Olwen phoned to say she would be down the following weekend. Greg promised to ring later in the week but there was no way he was going to say anything over the phone although after his talk with Ray; he was determined it must end. The sick feeling of desolation at the very thought of it he firmly conquered and gave a loving message over the phone. One more week he thought.

"You know I'm right." Ray saw his face as he came back to the table where they were having a late dinner. Greg pushed his plate away.

"I just don't want to face it. Let's get on." They went back to the shed where they worked until late.

The post came unusually early on Wednesday. They were having breakfast as Ray had to be away early. Greg threw a wad of letters on to the table. "Two circulars" he muttered aloud. "An invitation to join a book club, how do they find you when you have only just moved?" A sudden loud whoop from Greg, made Ray, who never good in the mornings, drop his toast, marmalade side down on the floor. "For God's sakes Greg" he muttered.

"I've sold the flat," whooped Greg again. "Just in bloody time, I've sold the flat. Bloke's very keen and in a hurry, he's paid the full asking price. I'll ring as soon as the office is open."

"Great stuff" Ray busy scraping marmalade off the carpet. "What are you going to do with this sudden wealth?"

"Put this place right for the winter. Get the builders in, roof done, shower in, Rayburn, the works. Ray my old son, you've brought me luck. I said you were a little ray of sunshine."

"Oh! Shut up, it's too early for your larking about. Don't forget to keep some back to live on, will you? I have to go or Megan will never forgive me if I don't see her before she goes to work. She hasn't forgiven me yet for working all day on the Land Rover." Greg knew it was not that. Ray had come with a purpose on Sunday. Megan would not have been allowed to come near at that time.

"Now I can order those parts for the Land Rover then she will be on the road. By the way I haven't paid you for the loom and those lamps. How much do I owe you?"

"No you don't, the loom is a present from me and the lamps were cheap from the scrap. I intend to see what else they have lurking about there. So don't go ordering until I give you a ring. I think they have stuff out of the ark and I don't think they even know what's there. So see you in a month, old son." He slapped Greg on the back. "Watch yourself and don't forget if you need me I'm only at the end of the phone."

"Sure thing and Ray, I really am sorry for what I put you through and thanks for being there."

"I know and me for blowing my top but that's what friends are for. What say you, Rocky?" he bent down to caress the dog. "Look out for that old Luke what is name, don't you let him get to you or I'll come down with a gun myself. See you." Ray turned the car and was gone.

Chapter 25

As the days passed Greg's depression grew. He missed Ray and their discussions played on his mind. He knew that Ray was right in all he had said he must let Olwen go, there was no future in it. He felt lonely and far from well. He phoned Olwen forcing himself to laugh and talk about Ray and his budding romance with Megan but not a word about the row they had. Told of the fun they had putting the loom in, talked about Rocky and the chickens. He told her that he loved her and would see her the weekend but not a word about himself.

Next day he spoke to his parents and feeling better went to Hay to order tyres then to Hereford to the market, still the weekend would not come, his body would not rest or his mind settle. He alternately wished it all over but dreaded it happening. He managed to put some wire on the garden wall to stop the chickens, tried to weed a bit of the garden but failed the work bringing on pain and breathlessness. Too much thinking drove his brain crazy. It was a bad week ending in Friday when he went to the local surgery appointment for check -ups, blood tests and medication. Nothing changed, keep in touch take things easy.

As he was driving back through the village, Bronwyn Rhys was walking towards him, he stopped to thank her for the hens.

"How are they doing?" she asked, her light piercing eyes almost too much for him this morning with his thoughts on Olwen.

"Fine thanks, except for the cockerel' She threw back her head and laughed, Olwen's ringing laugh, he thought her snowy hair had probably once been red.

"Good. Gets a body going in the morning young man like you shouldn't lie a bed. Not sick are you?"

"Here was golden opportunity, tell Bronwyn, she can tell Olwen and you never need see her again. Make it easy on yourself. What came out of his mouth was entirely different. "Not really, bit of strain in the chest muscles."

She spoke her voice harsh. "Knowing Dr Vane, he's given you pain killers or some such rubbish. Call by the cottage I have some liniment you can rub in. do you more good and I have a herb tea that will ease the pain more softly and less harmful than tablets. Drugs should be kept for serious illness not little things like strain. Call by later and don't do any lifting for a while." She marched off head high reminding him again of her granddaughter's queenly bearing. They both walked tall.

"Oh! Shit!" Greg slammed the truck door. Rocky looked at him in alarm.

"Shit! Shit! Shit! Why do I do it? I just can't talk to that woman, when I do I get into trouble of some sort and she gets me in deeper; now she will tell Olwen and she will rush up all sympathy and tender loving care. Then I will have to admit that I lied and instead tell her things to tear her heart out. Hell! I wish I had never started this. Wish I had never come here." He slammed the truck into reverse, spun around and took to the hill road.

Luke Jeffries was on his way down as Greg raced up. Greasy cap pulled well down, huddled into an old army greatcoat in spite of the sun, he looked up as Greg passed. Sullen faced there was no flicker of recognition yet Greg knew he spotted Rocky on the seat beside him. 'If he touches you Boy, I'll nail him heart or no heart' he muttered.

His bad temper lasted all day and the heavy rain that beat on the windows in the late afternoon did nothing to help. It broke the new shrubs from their supports, lashed the flowers to the ground and beat a loud tattoo on the galvanised roof. The room grew dark as he paced the floor. The television jumped and flickered when he turned it on, after trying to watch for a while he swore and turned it off. 'I don't want to go out in this. I don't want to go to the witch's house. I don't need her medication and least of all do I want to tell Olwen anything tonight but if I don't go and fetch the blasted stuff she will sense that I'm lying and if I don't tell Olwen tonight…..'. he groaned flinging himself in a chair turning the television on again to drown his thoughts. An hour of sport partly took his attention when he turned it off the rain had stopped but with every intention of starting again.

"Better go and get it over with Rocky. I shall be glad when this day is over." The dog leapt up, he didn't mind another trip.

Greg left Rocky in the truck with a swift glance up and down the road he locked it. Samuel Peeps wouldn't want Rocky invading his territory anyway. The wet bushes slapped against his jeans as he walked up the path, before he could knock the door opened. Bronwyn stood with Samuel Peepes beside her in the porch with his tail wagging.

"Come in lad. Glad to see you waited until the storm passed, mighty heavy at one time." Greg entered not sure what to expect, wiping his feet carefully on the mat he looked around. The heavy porch door led directly into a large lounge. It took Greg by surprise. Whether he had been subconsciously expecting something akin to Wokey Hole, filled with herbs, toads and black cats, the reality was very different. Deep chintz covered chairs were comfortably placed near amber reading lamps. The soft tonnes of the tan and cream carpet were inhanced that lit a warm welcome in the lovely Adam fireplace. A rosewood piano stood open invitingly and dainty china adorned an Elizabethan sideboard which occupied the wholw of one wall. Bowls of leaves and flowers stood around with several silver-framed photgraphs. A big desk was positioned near the window with a computer and piles of paper giving evidence of her recent occupation. The whole room spoke of comfort, charm and taste.

"Don't stand there staring, come in, take your wet jacket off and sit down. Not there –you will sit on Marmalade Macaverty, it's his favourite chair. Eliza Doolittle is hiding underneath. She will come out presently to see you."

Greg turned to see if she was laughing at him but she had gone into the kitchen and he could hear her rattling cups. From under the fringes of the chair emerged very slowly a huge white Persian cat with vivid blue eyes fixing him with a steady stare so like her owner's he felt slightly unnerved. Holding him with her eyes for several minutes until she had inspected him thoroughly she then jumped into another chair disturbing another cat Greg hadn't noticed, Ginger and white he was the exact shade of the cushions on which he slept; Greg realised he could have easily sat on him without realising he was there. As Eliza jumped on him marmalade rose and stretched, he was the biggest cat Greg had ever seen, he yawned showing sharp pointed teeth as his mouth snapped shut, his eyes opened large and green, they blazed an instant before they closed again and he disappeared into the cushions and his own fur.

"Don't tell me, Macavity ignored you while Liza inspected you while acting every inch a lady." Bronwyn entered carrying a tray. "But then you expected black ones didn't you?" This was so near the truth that Greg rising to take the tray found himself flushing. She laughed although her speaking voice was harsh her laugh had a ringing quality very like Olwen's.

"I know what people think of me. I have been about too many years and have too many eccentricities for this neighbourhood not to gossip. I don't encourage visitors and curiosity breeds rumours. You'll take tea? Most men like cake.'

Greg recovered his composure and his good manners at the same time.

"I'm sorry, I am rather rude,… I like your cats."

"They are characters. Eliza is very curious and has to be told and shown everything while Macaverty is exactly like the one in the musical Cats; whatever happens he is never there."

Greg tried to balance cup, saucer and plate. Bronwyn lifted books off a small table and carried it to him.

"Eliza Dolittle was a favourite character of mine and a female Persian is such a lady yet her curiosity is straight out of the gutter, she will kill anything that moves, explore anywhere, try anything but comes in perfectly clean and snowy white, extremely choosy over her food, only the best or she would rather starve to death, very small portions at a time as a lady should. She never eats what she kills and never breaks anything when she climbs around. Nothing at all is what she does best for days at a time. When I was given Macavity he was neutered, thin and lanky and I named him Marmalade for his colour, Then I saw the musical and named him Macavity because it fits him to a tee. If anything gets broken he is never in the room. He eats anything and everything, if no one is around he steals, frays cushions, scratches furniture, knocks over plants but you'll never see him do it, as far as he's concerned either he's out or asleep on the chair. Never catches anything but is loyal and affectionate.

Greg laughed. Great, they are two beautiful creatures.'

"They keep me company along with Samuel Peeps here.' The blue sheepdog had crept behind her chair and was pretending to be asleep.

Greg stole a look at Bronwyn as she bent to caress the dog. The term witch didn't suit her in this room dressed in a soft blue suit, her white hair piled on her head, on her wrist a silver watch. Several large emerald rings gave her hands the appearance of delicacy, the fingers long and slender, not the hands of the average country woman. The air of elegance became her and Greg felt himself in the presence of a lady.

"Now, young man.' Greg brought himself from his musings. "What are we going to treat you with? Can't have you delicate when Olwen comes home, can we?" Greg found himself flushing like a girl again. 'Damn the woman, she always has this effect on me.' The light eyes were steady now fixed on his.

"I know that you and Olwen are already lovers.'

Greg started up. "Good God! How.?'

"Don't blaspheme, young man. Olwen tells me most things but she didn't tell me that; neither would I expect her too. It's your own business after all but I can read faces and body language. She is a Gemini and although they are several people in one astronomically they are also extremely easy to read. You are Aquarius so you should get on well, depending of course on your ascendant and emotional signs. I will read them one day for you if you're so inclined. Olwen's main problem is having a nasty temper, being a red-head and a good bit Irish it often gets her into trouble. You have a short sharp temper and although short lived sparks will fly."

"How do you know I'm Aquarius?' Greg was deeply perturbed.

"Your face, your hands and your sunny disposition when you are not fretting over some inner worry as you are now.' Oh God! Greg's plea to the Almighty was a silent one this time.

"Now I think you have some explaining to do. What is worrying you so much and how does it affect my girl?' Greg's first reaction to this barrage was to tell Bronwyn to go to hell, mind her own business and to get out fast. Then came a feeling of relief; stop fighting, tell her everything. The coward's way out Great!

"I am single, thirty-five and in love with Olwen but I have a terminal heart condition called Myocarditis and I can't tell her.' He listened to the words in amazement as if someone else had spoken them. The silence was broken only by the crackling of the fire, Samuel Peeps snoring and the rain beating on the window. If he had planned to blurt it out that way he could never have done it. The silence deepened as the dog stopped snoring and Greg became aware of the grandfather clock ticking behind him. He watched Eliza Dolittle delicately wash a paw. The silence seemed to last forever but it could have only been minutes.

"When are you going to tell her?" the usually harsh voice was very gentle.

"I don't know. I just can't. I told my parents, that was hell for all of us. My friend Ray who is like a brother to me found out from my ex- boss. I hurt him badly by not telling him myself. Damn it I'm afraid to tell her." His words came out disjointed and full of pain. He looked up. "Not because I want to keep it a secret but I don't know what effect it will have on her. Will it be revulsion or pity? Will she want to smother me to death as my mother does? I don't know her well enough to even guess her reaction.'

His green eyes were dark now, hard as flint but unflinching as they met Bronwyn's. She saw beyond to the anguish inside the man. Again silence Greg waited for her to speak nails biting into his palms.

"Tell me the medical facts as you know them." came a surprising reply. Greg told her his case history and Mr McLoughlin's final words. She answered slowly. A donor probably be found, it's always a matter of how much time you have. What medication are you on?' Greg told her surprised at her clinical interest.

"It's the best. The chance of a donor in your circumstances is a lot more difficult of course. You've already accepted that.

The medication you are on does its job or you would be in hospital by now. I can see you're a fighter Greg the positive attitude can actually slow the process for some people. Do you eat carefully and not over exert yourself?'

"Yes, I do most of the time.'

"All of the time young man, all of the time. I shall be keeping an eye on you. You interest me. If I had met you some years ago I would have tried alternative medicine on you. I am a great believer in it. Do you believe in faith healers?"

Greg with a thousand questions on his mind found himself deep in a discussion on fith healing and herbs. They talked for an hour without mentioning Olwen once. Was she going to tell her? He felt bitterness rising at the blows that life was dealing him. Bronwyn stood up as did Samuel Peeps padding to her side.

"Well interview over. I must get ready for the girl. I presume that you aren't taking her for a meal tonight?" Greg at a loss for words could only shake his head.

"We hadn't planned" he stammered. Then angrily his head came up. "No we hadn't planned because tonight I was going to finish with her, tell her how sick I am and tell her to find someone else." He was almost shouting now in his agitation. "Then she could spend the rest of the weekend feeling hurt for herself and sorry for me and herself.'

"You think I am going to tell her don't you? Let you off the hook. Well I'm not. Olwen wouldn't thank me for and would resent you and me. I don't think you are usually dull but it stands to reason that you aren't thinking straight at the moment. It's a miracle that you can think at all it's a lot to bear for a youngster. if you were my age you might not be so bothered perhaps. So you pick your time and place, say your piece and Olwen will speak for herself of that you can be sure." She led the way to the door pausing, her hand on the knob… "I like you. You are a good lad, a good looking one too. I know Olwen better than her own mother does. Whatever she says or does one thing I know for sure, she will not stay with you out of pity. If you are ever in trouble up there give me a ring"… Good night." She closed the door firmly behind him.

Chapter 26

The night was chilly the rain was bringing in thoughts of autumn. The daylight had slid into an early twilight and the wind had risen, first leaves swirling reluctantly from the trees. The brook was loud as it carried water from the hill. Rocky lay by the hearth breaking his summer habit of lying in the porch. Greg made up the fire until the old range glowed. He was a credible cook but not hungry himself knowing Bronwyn had prepared a meal for Olwen, he put a bottle of wine in the fridge. Washed, carefully shaved he changed into grey slacks and green sweatshirt, putting a Debussy CD on the music centre turning it low then sitting in the flickering firelight to wait, his heart sick. Remembering the growing darkness, he rose again to put on the outside light and open the road gate. He stood a moment in the rising wind, listening to the brook. It had stopped raining and the air was fresh, dampness seeping through his clothes. His thoughts jumbled and unsettled, he wanted to wait out in the dark as if by not seeing he would not feel, then shivering with nerves and cold he returned to the house. Rocky had deserted him and stayed by the fire. He sat again staring into the flames trying to keep his thoughts away from what he intended to say, thinking again about Bronwyn and the cats smiling a little at their names and characters desperately remembering the lovely quiet room still unable to relate the charming, educated woman of today with the witch in her old clothes tramping the hills with Samuel Peeps. As his thoughts roamed he remembered the photographs on her piano. The large one of Olwen a studio portrait that captured her wide grey eyes, cascade of red hair and her half smile he would love a photo of her like that. He switched the thoughts away, think about something else. What was he to do with this place when the builders had finished? He speculated again with some of the ideas that he and Ray had tossed around. Was that the Jeep? He started to his feet but it was only a Land Rover on the mountain road. He sat down again. He felt he would like animals of some kind. Rocky and the chickens were good but the fields needed to be used or they would become wilder than they already were unless he ploughed them for a market garden. No too high for that, should have gone further south; in any case there was one field that could not be ploughed, rare flowers and plants grew there, one of them Autumn crocus. He must go and look find out more, it must be nearly time for them to flower now. Why didn't she come? Was Bronwyn deliberately keeping her? What did they talk about? Would she give a hint about his illness? He knew she wouldn't, it wasn't her way, He now realised that for all her brusque speech she was a very private person and would grant to others the same privilege. What would Olwen do? Where would she go afterwards? That she might stay with him never entered his head. He could only see her face twisted in pity or hidden from him in pain. He wished she would come, at the same time he was glad of the delay. Thoughts tossed to and fro until he was exhausted and suddenly fell asleep, the flickering firelight moving across his face.

Greg awoke to Rocky barking and the slam of the jeep door. Oh God! She was here, he no more wanted to face her than fly yet his heart leapt he and Rocky made it to the door together. The rain drove across the yard and Olwen entered with a swirl of leaves and raindrops, black shiny mac and tangled hair. The room became alive with colour and movement as if it had been waiting for this moment. Greg found his arms full, hair on his lips, rain on his face, clinging as the room swung in a bubble of delight. All thoughts suspended, this moment was theirs alone, lips on lips, hands tangled in hair, ice cold cheek against warm, storm and stillness, passion and peace, one perfect whole. Nothing else existed; all was here in a kind of magic. Along while later they moved apart, she sliding out of her mac and boots, he taking them from her in silence; no need for speech. He poured her a glass of wine. She glowed up at him dressed in a bright yellow ski suit, curled on the hearth rug she was summer come again. Greg poured his own wine and sat on the arm of a chair where he could enjoy the picture she made. Everything fled from his mind in the joy of having her here with him.

"Oh! I have had such a week. I wanted to come home yesterday but I couldn't cut anything at all. Every lecture went on and on and I was given extra classes. I thought it would be never ending. What have you been doing with yourself?" He told her the bits and bobs of his week, not very exciting he admitted then fell silent. Olwen chattered on. The choir was starting up again and she had two solo parts. "You haven't heard me sing yet, have you? Poor you the pleasure is to come."

Drama classes were difficult because they couldn't decide on a production. Her mother was coming to stay with Gran for a week but they wouldn't get on for long but Greg would be able to meet her. He listened in silence filling his senses. The movements of her exquisite mouth, the picture she made as her red-gold hair swung over her yellow suit, sparkles deep in her eyes, her perfume and lilting tones as she enacted her stories. How he longed once more to possess this beauty who so invited him, from the soft hollow where her throat swept into the deep swell of her breasts to her long flexing feet now held to the fire. His heart thumped painfully as he remembered what he must say and what he must not do. The moments of madness when she first arrived must not be repeated or he would be lost forever. She fell silent at last staring into the fire then holding out her hand she caught his trying to pull him down to her. Gently he took her hand in both his. "Olwen…" he began. She knelt up in one fluid movement and laid her arm across his knee.

"You know what happened the last time I was here don't you?" She asked almost anxiously

"Of course, how could I forget?" he whispered hoarsely.

"Well you are going to think it's the brazen hussy that I am but never have I felt about anyone like this in my whole life. Hush now." As Greg tried to speak…

"Listen and let me finish then you can tell me what you think and I will listen but if you feel the way I am feeling you will be knowing the answer. We are both in our thirties and we have both been in long relationships that went nowhere at all. We are running out of time Greg and I am thinking that I know what we both want. I want to pack up Worcester after next term. I have enjoyed it but I think it is time I tried something different. You need help here and something to work for. The fun we could be having. It would be a good life Greg, we could be doing something with this place but…" again as he went to speak she held up her hand.

"Don't you feel that we need some form of commitment? Oh" I can't be waiting for you to ask me. I'm asking you. Will you marry me Greg? Now soon so we can get on with our lives together?"

The silence was deathly. Greg tried desperately to speak. Mist came before his eyes, his heart hammering. How he longed to say yes and take her in his arms. He swallowed, rose staggering and turned away. Olwen sat back on her heels the colour draining from her face.

"Greg, what is it? What's the matter?"

He moved away shaking to the far side of the room facing the wall. To save his life he couldn't speak at all. As he fought for control a log fell in the grate in a shower of sparks. Olwen rose slowly to her feet.

"Greg, answer me." She shouted. "What the hell is the matter? Did you hear what I said?" Anger and fear were in her voice now. Greg turned very slowly, rigid with shock, his face haggard, eyes stony. The music had long stopped it was as if the room was waiting. Olwen stood on the hearth, a flame of red and gold, head held high, eyes blazing face white as death itself, hands clenched into fists at her side. His eyes took in the scene even as his brain made his lips form the words.

"I can't.'

"You what?' her tone was incredulous. "What did you say? I thought you cared. Did I get it wrong?" Her lips suddenly trembled. "Don't you care for me that way?" In two strides he was across the room but kept from touching her with an iron will.

"Of course I did and I do." Go on finish it now his head prompted while his heart bled. "It's been lovely sweetheart, but I can't marry you I must make you see that" his tongue was running away with him now. The words were coming out wrong, all wrong, too fast and wrong. "We had a great time, it was fun getting to know you and making friends but you will soon see it was just a beautiful interlude that has no future for you. It was wonderful of you to ask me and I only wish that I could say yes but it is impossible. If you will sit down and let me explain you will see."

Olwen choked back tears, her eyes blazing fury.

'Friends, fun, interlude?' How dare you? What kind of man are you? Making love the way we did after only a few weeks, the magic the fitness of it all and you can stand there like an idiot, hear me make a complete fool of myself like the brazen hussy I feel and call this an interlude. What kind of bastard are you?"

Greg tried in vain to stop the angry flow of words.

"Please listen, Olwen. I didn't mean it like that. All the wrong things are coming out. Please sit down and listen I will try to explain."

"Explain will you? That's what you think. I'll not be needing explanations. You could have explained before that you were not really interested in commitment. You used me but I don't need you. I don't want to see you ever again and that will be too soon so." As she spoke she was pulling on her boots, grabbing her mac the tears pouring down her ashen face. Greg grabbed her arm.

"Please Darling don't do this. I can't let you go like this. There is a reason. Please listen." He heard the slap before he felt the pain.

"Let me go, don't be coming near me. How could I be such a fool? As if you'd want to be marrying me. You who have the fine looks, little farm and the money to do as you like with your bachelor friends, girls too most like. Stephanie wanted you back she can have you and most welcome." The door slammed so hard it shook the house. He ran, determined to stop her but she was gone into the jeep reversing in such a hurry she hit the stone wall of the garden. Straightening up and reversing down the lane, she hit the mountain road at such a speed Greg raced for the phone for Jeff Arnold to stop her. He changed his mind spotting his keys on the table, he ran for the pick-up instead. Slow to start Greg was cursing the truck furiously as he took to the hill after her.

At every bend he expected to see her piled in a ditch or over the hedge. He felt sick when he thought about the bad bends at the bottom of the hill road. She had a good start. He followed the hill road around and back to Bronwyn's cottage the jeep was not there. There were no lights except a glow in an upper window. He rang her mobile again and again but it was switched off; now he didn't know which way to go or what to do.

It was raining again but he drove around like a maniac for over an hour. It was hopeless, too many lanes and she knew them well and he didn't. Several times he wasted precious time killing the engine to listen for sounds on the other roads, wasted more time following lights up the mountain road, only to find his neighbour going home the other way, raced to The Copper Beech although crowded there was no sign of the jeep. He tried The Green man, again drew a blank. Two hours later, almost out of fuel he was forced to give up and go home. He had left the door wide open and all the lights on, he realised with fear he had left Rocky alone but the dog was waiting for him on the yard barking as he drove wearily in. He shut the gate and stood shivering and heart-sick for a long while, straining ears and eyes for a sign of the jeep returning. At last a set of lights were coming slowly down the hill above him. He ran back down the drive and stood in the road willing it to be her. As it drew near he saw it was just another car, probably a couple who had been courting on the hill road. Sick at heart, soaked through, he finally went in and closed the door. There was simply nothing he could do. She may have driven straight back to Worcester also she had many friends she could go to. There was no one he knew of to ring. He would talk to Bronwyn in the morning. He glanced at his watch, gone midnight, no good now he would only worry her. He spent the night on the settee with a blanket waiting for what; he didn't know. she was badly hurt and had a nasty temper but surely she would calm down and come back to talk it through.

He had tried to tell her, it was her fault for flying off like that. 'No it was your fault.' His conscience told him. 'You should have told her when you made love to her, should have told her as soon as she came last night. Anytime you could have told her, Phoned, written. It's your fault.' He beat his fist on the arm of the settee 'Last night you should have been gentle, not stood the other side of the room like a mute. She took me by surprise, I couldn't handle it, should have held her, kissed her, told her why. A fat lot of good that would have done. Really this is better, now she doesn't have to know at all. You have achieved what you wanted. Olwen's gone you never need see her again.' The pain grew as he tossed and turned. When Rocky heard the hard sobs, he put his furry head against the dark one on the cushion until a hand came down and caressed him. Finally they both slept.

The cockerel woke before real light. Rocky hearing him rose and shook himself, he hated the cockerel and stalked him whenever he could. Greg showed no signs of waking but his bare feet hung over the arm of the settee, his head deep in cushions. Rocky set to with a thorough washing of them the only bits he could find. With a groan Greg woke. "Leave off Rocky, it's too early. All right you can go out and torment the cockerel but you'll find he's not out yet."

He staggered to the door as soon as it opened Rocky shot off barking at the pigeons that were feeding off the new lawn. The early light sprinkled diamonds everywhere but the rain had gone and a clear sky promised a fair day. Greg remembered with sudden clarity and a deep sick sensation the events of the night before. He sat back on the settee his head in his hands. He seemed to be lurching from one crisis to another. He wasn't worried now about money although he would have to find an income soon. God knows what his health was like after all the stress. He had a hospital appointment Friday. He dare not think about Olwen except he must ring Bronwyn tell her what happened she could find out if she was safe. She must have gone back to Worcester;

eventually she might have calmed down and would listen if he could speak to her this morning. Surely she would listen, he had a right damn it. At nine o'clock he rang Bronwyn.

"I'm sorry she has gone.' Came the answer to his questions. 'She came in during the early hours and left me a note to say she had gone straight back to Worcester about four o'clock this morning. Fine goings on, I take it you told her. What happened?" There came a sharp intake of breath as Greg found himself telling her of Olwen's proposal. There was a silence before she spoke.

"I see." A pause, "Let her get over it, lot of pride that girl, too much for her own good. She will come back when she is good and ready. You were too slow, should have beaten her to the door and made her listen. Still what will be will be. I have chickens to feed. Thanks for checking on her, good lad." The phone went dead.

Greg stared at it for a while then slowly replaced the receiver. He tried Olwen's mobile with his own again, no reply. He spent the morning finishing small jobs on the Land Rover put in some petrol and started her up. She fired almost at once and Greg moved her back and fore in the small space but it was clear it was impossible to get her out until the tractor was moved. He then tried to move some more junk from the front of the shed but tired, ill and dispirited he found himself listening unreasonably for the jeep to return. Later he tried to eat, failed then went to bed for a couple of hours. He felt better at teatime and decided to go to the pub to see if the food there would tempt him. He almost phoned Ray or his parents to say what happened but Ray would only say 'I told you so' and his parents would want to rush up and he knew his mother wasn't well anyway he decided that he couldn't talk it all over again. He put Rocky in the truck while he locked the house but as he went to open the gate a quick movement caught his eye as Luke Jeffries scuttled down the drive and a few seconds later his Land Rover was going up the hill road. Greg worried as he drove to the pub as to why he would be in his drive, another attempt on Rocky perhaps? What was the matter with the man? Was the dog that valuable? It was certain that he had never owned him or was he just unbalanced? He sighed. 'More problems for us, dog. You have to come in with me tonight. Not leaving you anywhere.' He parked up and not at all in the mood entered the pub

Chapter 27

The captain was sat at the bar talking to John. The fat farmer who had come as usual on horseback was talking to a white-haired old man Greg had not seen before. Several lads he had seen at the dance were playing cards in the corner. Trudy came out of the kitchen and smiled at Greg.

"Hello there. Are you having a meal or a drink tonight?'

"Both. What do you recommend?"

"It's all good depends how hungry you are," Trudy dimpled, pleased to have his full attention.

"Not very but I could manage egg, chips and a half of cider"

"Good. I won't keep you long." She laid his place and brought his cider before disappearing into the kitchen.

"Good evening everyone." Betty made her entrance and the Captain rose to his feet. "You are a vision of loveliness, my dear." He raised her hand to his lips in a theatrical gesture. "How are you? Is everything ship-shape and Bristol fashion?"

"You are an old flatterer, Captain. I bet you had a girl in every port didn't he John?"

"All ships have to come to dry dock sometime and it's a dry one tonight. I'll have another small glass of rum if you don't mind."

"Okay Captain." The talk irritated Greg tonight he found no amusement in what sounded like an overdone script rehearsal. He took his drink and sat in the far window seat wishing that Ray was here or that Olwen would walk in. He felt very alone. Two lads came in who Greg recognised as his neighbour's sons. They nodded to Greg and joined the Captain at the bar. His meal finished Greg sat with Rocky on his feet feeling less and less like returning home. His thoughts were too depressing, the warmth and light making him sleepy. He was feeling the effects of the previous night. Half asleep in his window seat he was startled awake by the white-haired man who had been talking with the Captain. His drink in his hand he pulled up a chair. "Can I join you for a moment? You look as if you could do with a little company."

"Yes of course." Greg forced himself awake. "Please do" The man appeared to be in his seventies or thereabouts, fresh faced, clean shaven with a pair of twinkling blue eyes. His thick white hair gave him a grandfatherly appearance.

"Let me introduce myself. My name is Fred Barnes from Tynewedd, the farm you can just see in the valley when yer stand on the road above yer gate. You see I already know who you are. Your name is Greg Morgan, you come from Hull, bought Greg-y-Dorth. There is not a body about here who knows what yer came here to do and they're all guessing. A young single man from away taking a old mountain place like that and not going to farm?" He sat back eyeing Greg with delight as if he had just solved the whole puzzle himself. Greg laughed. "You've got it in one but the truth is I don't know what to do with it myself. It's not big enough to farm properly and I am limited as to what I can do. I have a health problem. Too much hard work is out of the question."

"A strong handsome fellow like you? You do surprise me. Do you mind?" he pulled a pipe out of his pocket.

"Not at all" Greg replied.

'Not lungs is it?' The old man was lighting up with much puffing. 'Smoke won't affect you?"

"No it's fine. What do you do?" Greg changed the subject.

"Oh! I'm retired now; used to have the trekking around here until ten years ago. My son does it now over the other valley but I takes an interest and often have a couple of ponies here for the grazing over the winter. I help out where I can. The missus likes to put up a few people for bed and breakfast, keeps her young she sez." He laughed a wheezy laugh. Greg smiled. "Now yer be wondering what I be chattering on to yer for, ain't yer?. Well I thought you might be putting a few sheep on the mountain seeing you've got a dog." He sat back puffing. 'but if you're not fit to go rounding sheep, we 'as to look at it another way.' Greg was puzzled, what was the old boy getting at?

"Now I've got yer flummoxed, ain't I. My old girl always says I go's by way of Hay to get to Aber." He leaned forward taking his pipe from his mouth and waving it at Greg. "If yer was going fer sheep on the hill, yer'd need a pony to look around and I have the very thing."

"I don't think that I need one but thanks all the same."

"Ha! But yer ain't thought about it. What's better than a cob to ride on a frosty morning up on the hill, take all the stress out of yer."

"It's very kind of you. I can't see me needing one."

"Well, young Sir. Are you using the fields at the moment?"

"No" Greg said thoughtfully.

"Tell yer what"—the pipe was going well now. "If I rent's a bit of grazing off yer for two nice cobs (only fer a couple of weeks mind as the grass is goin' over now I'd ave to bring a bit of hay over for 'em,) yer might fancy a ride. I'll bring a saddle, yer can try one out and I'll bet in a week yer'll want one and I'd do yer a good deal. Watcher say?" Greg thought for a moment, he'd liked the old boy on sight and the fields were lying idle. The rent would come in useful too.

"Okay, as long as I'm not responsible for them. I'll make sure the fences and hedges are good but it's up to you to feed and water and I can't promise that I will take you up on your offer." Fred's hand shot out. "Bet yer bottom dollar, in a couple of weeks one will be staying. I'll come up and have a look tomorrer."

It was with a lighter heart Greg drove home. It would be good to see some life in the fields and amuse Ray when he came. He and Greg had trekked in the summer holidays when they were younger and enjoyed it. He hadn't thought about a horse, it might be fun. At least Fred had taken his mind off his troubles for an hour or so.

The phone was ringing as he entered the house, rushing to pick it up he tripped over Rocky. It stopped as he picked it up, he re-dialled, it could have been Olwen but it rang a long time until a woman answered. She was sorry but there was no answer when she knocked on Olwen's door, she hadn't seen her all day and didn't know who might have rung him. 'Was there a message?' "No thanks" Greg replied. "I'll try again." He put the phone down slowly then after a few minutes rang her mobile, no answer. Depression washed over him. She wasn't there and hadn't rung he wouldn't either, not again. This time next year he might not be here. Let it go. It was over. Frustration and anguish welled inside him. The brief summer love affair was over like a butterfly's life, short lived, beautiful only to die days after being born. So would he, young life cut short all its promises unfulfilled. Someone else would live in his house, someone else have his girl. There would be nothing to show that that he had ever lived. Instead of violence flaring in him this time, cold despair froze him to numbness. Lying on the settee by the dying fire he let his life's memories pour through him. Nothing moved him. Thoughts of his childhood passed, his mother's love, his father's pride, the mates he had left on the rig, Steph his life with her, he viewed it all like photographs. Ray; for a moment his thoughts hurt. Ray would live, grieve for his friend then one day laugh again, marry Megan, raise a family his life running its normal course. Olwen would cry when she heard, later love again and in future years in the middle of her full life something would occasionally remind her, for a brief moment touch her. The scent of heather, the sight of whinberries on a mountain walk, someone would see a tear in her eye then it would all be gone again for ever.

Suddenly he couldn't bear any more, crying aloud like a lost child he raced from the house, Rocky hard on his heels. He fled through the gate not knowing or caring where he went blundering like someone drunk he fled upwards towards the hill. He ran until tears choked him and pain seized him, unable to go on he fell down in the wet grass and knew no more.

He was a long time floating, first wet then cold he shivered then burned with heat. Lights came and went for periods of time; pain slamming into blackness deep as night. The darkness lifted, voices ebbed and flowed, a clear sentence came through 'Hold that dog'. He heard a bark then heard no more.

A long, long time later he came to as one returning from a journey unsure of his welcome. A lighted lamp was near him and he could feel blankets rough and warm. He had no pain, now so relaxed his limbs seemed not to belong to him. He could se the lamp and a glass beside it; near it stood some sort of cylinder with pipes. He felt good, safe, warm but so very tired. He closed his eyes and slept.

"How is he today, Mrs Rhys? Just thought I'd call and see."

"He'll do. Good job you were about last night Glen, you and Martin. He probably wouldn't have been found until this morning and that would have been too late." Greg heard voices through the open window as he awoke.

"We had a drop on and thought someone had been murdered, feet sticking out of a ditch and a dog howling his head off. We were sure he was dead."

"Well you did the right thing that's for sure. Call by later he will be awake by then and I know he will want to thank you."

"Oh! That's alright. He'll be fine with you. I'll see to the chickens for him and everything's locked up. Here are his keys."

"You're a good lad, thanks a lot Glen I will tell him."
A door closed and a vehicle moved off. Greg sat up but his
head swam alarmingly, so he thought better of it and lay
back down. The voice belonged to Bronwyn Rhys but the
room was certainly not his. He wasn't at Graig-y-Dorth
either. Where the devil was he? He stared around, it was
certainly a woman's room, a deep green dressing gown
hung behind the door, pot's and jars on the dressing table,
duvet covers and curtains peach and green, all frilled and
matching; definitely a woman's room. An Oxygen cylinder
stood beside the bed. He heard the door open again and
Bronwyn's voice calling. "Here Mac, Puss, Puss, Come on
Liza, hurry up or he will eat it all including yours.' He gave
a gasp. He now knew where he was. he was at the witch's
cottage. She was downstairs calling the cat's. This must be
Olwen's room. He doubted it would be Bronwyn's, too girlie
and all that makeup. What the devil was he doing here, his
head ached with the effort of trying to remember. The last
thing he could recall was coming from the pub, the rest was
a nightmare of shadows and sensations. He remembered
Rocky barking and someone saying. 'Hold that dog....
Rocky and where was Rocky and the chickens should be
fed and shut in? What time was it? He made it onto his feet
by hanging on to the bedside cabinet while he swung his legs
over the side of the bed. This was difficult as he seemed to be
wrapped in a cocoon of blankets. He realised he was mother
naked. He flushed, had Bronwyn got him in here? How?
why? He wished he could think straight and remember. His
chest ached but he pulled himself to his feet. He heard dogs
bark recognising Rocky he gave a sigh of relief. Thank God
the dog was here too but where on earth were his clothes, he

couldn't see them anywhere? He managed to reach the door and pulled on the thick fluffy dressing gown. It was huge more than enough to go around him but as he recognised Olwen's perfume painful memories began to stir. He tried to shut them out. A bathroom door stood open opposite as he left the room so he quickly used the facilities avoiding the mirror, cold water on his face helped clear his head which spun on sudden movement, his chest ached with a dull heavy sensation and several bruises were beginning to appear on various parts of his body. As he reached the top of the stairs he met Bronwyn coming up with a tray.

"Who told you to get up? Back you go this instant."

"What happened? Where are my clothes? I must get home; why am I here?"

"Alright you can come down for a few minutes, no longer. Now sit in that chair and don't move until you have eaten this. While you are eating I will tell you all I know. you alone know what happened before." She gave him a sharp glance as she settled the tray on his knees. The room seemed more of a haven than ever. Firelight flickered on the polished wood and china. An air of tranquillity even at this time of day pervaded it like incense. He felt himself relax a little. He looked at the tray on his lap.

"I can't, I'm sorry. I really can't.—he began.

"You can and you will or back to bed you go now. You gave us all enough trouble last night and the best way you can repay is to do as you're told. Doctor will be back in a while to have a look at you. You are very lucky that you aren't in hospital this morning.'

"I don't need him. I go to the hospital Friday anyway. What day is it now?'

"Stop your rattle or your soup will spoil, eat and I will tell you.' Greg resigned himself to obey in any case he was too tired to argue. He was glad he did, the soup was hot and delicious, the bread homemade and he managed a decent slice of it before putting the tray aside. After Bronwyn made a pot of tea, she sat down opposite in the rocking chair. There were no sign of cats or dogs. She saw him looking around.

"The cats are eating. Your Rocky is fed, safe and sound in the porch. Samuel Peeps has been banished to the shed. Rocky was agitated over you. The boys had terrible trouble getting anywhere near you and when they brought him here he and Samuel had a fight so I let Rocky stay on guard and banished Samuel for a while. They will be alright." Seeing Greg's impatience she continued. "I don't know how you got there but you were in a ditch on the hill road with Rocky standing guard. Glen and Martin Edwards were coming home from The Green Man, for sheer devilment they drove past their own house and up the hill road, why heaven knows probably spotted Jeff Arnott's car somewhere and thought they'd get out of the way for a bit. Anyway they saw two feet sticking out of the ditch and a howling dog, otherwise you would have still been there. They would have taken you to Roberts house and phoned an ambulance from there(neither of them had phones on them, would you believe?) but the Roberts are away this weekend and it was quicker to come down here, I sent for the doctor. You had an attack brought on by over exertion and stress, much more of that and your time is up. What you have been up to I don't know, only the end result. Something to do with the girl I imagine.'

Greg felt annoyed. Who did she think she was? Why hadn't she or the doctor sent for an ambulance if he was that bad? What medicines had he been given? He was uncertain how to voice this without giving offence after all they had probably saved his life between them. Bronwyn's strange penetrating eyes read his face.

"I know what you are thinking. Why no ambulance and flashing lights? Is it because you are a lost cause? I can assure you that's not so." Greg stirred uneasily before he could speak she went on.

"Let me put you right on a few things while you are at my mercy. The boys brought you here at one o'clock in the morning, they had been drinking after hours, although hey were going to do their best for you, they were also thinking about their own skins. There was no way they were going to take you into town. I sent for the doctor because you were coming round and you were not going to need urgent medical attention. The doctor had your case notes and it would be up to him to send you in if he thought necessary. The hospital could do no more for you than I could once the doctor had confirmed my own thoughts. The oxygen beside your bed is there because you were breathing badly and to stop your heart labouring unnecessary. The doctor agreed with me that the oxygen, warmth and a couple of injections were all that was required and I would most certainly have sent for an ambulance if there was any sign of further problems. The doctor is coming to see you anytime now, in fact I hear his car. If he feels you should be in hospital that is where you will go."

There was a knock on the door and Rocky had to be forcibly removed from the porch. Doctor Davies was a quiet little man who always seemed to be talking to himself. His wife Nicole was the district nurse. They had four children the oldest of which was away at university also studying to be a doctor. Dr Davies was very much on Greg's case and had exchanged letters and phone calls with Mr McLoughlin. He now examined Greg from top to toe muttering to himself all the while. Presently he closed his case and sat down.

"I have been in touch with Mr McLouglin and his team this morning. No news yet I'm afraid but don't give up hope, it's early days yet, lots of time. You are in fine shape considering. A fit man, shame about the heart; never mind it will come. You must not run around mountains in the middle of the night or the day for that matter. What happened?" Greg stumbled over his explanation that he had been out for a walk and suddenly been taken ill. The doctor gave him a keen glance from under his ginger eyebrows. Greg was in no state to remember that the doctor already knew that he had been running at an unlikely hour of the morning. He wrote vigorously in his notebook.

"There you are then. Come and see me sometime next week. You have a hospital check-up on Friday, see what they say, you may need to go in for a rest. In the meantime take it easy. You should have someone with you up there on the farm, not good to be there on your own in your condition. Think about it there must be someone, bit lonely for you especially at night." Doctor Davies gave him a searching look. "I'm going to give you another injection now so back into bed with you. Mrs Rhys will look after you for a few days, she will give you another injection tomorrow."

"Hey! Doctor how come she is able to give injections and what is it with this medical knowledge she seems to have?'

Doctor Davies laughed. "Oh! You are alright with her, she is more qualified to treat you than I am. Ask her about it sometime. Don't know if she will tell you all but believe me you couldn't be in better hands." He left leaving Greg more puzzled than ever. Bronwyn came in bringing the cats with her. "Sorry I can't let Rocky in because of these two but he's alright and has been fed. By the way don't worry about the farm or the chickens. Glen locked up for you last night, made sure everything was alright, he will see to the fowls until you get back. He's a good lad. You may not remember leaving the doors open and the lights burning." She gave Greg the same look as had the doctor but asked no questions.

"I'm sorry to have caused so much trouble. I feel much better now. Thank you for everything but I think I can manage if I get home. My parents will come as soon as my mother is better.'

"Rubbish. You are staying put for a few days. You are still very tired and haven't eaten yet and you must have a couple more injections to calm everything down. You wouldn't make it to the gate, so into bed with you. In any case your clothes are in the washing machine, they were wet and muddy.' She indicated a small table. 'There are your wallet, car and house keys. Glen saw them on your table when he checked the fire, lights and locked up. Your watch you are wearing, so no worries, bed and relax.'

"Doctor Davies told me about your ability to give injections." Greg began hesitatingly. Bronwyn frowned. "What else did he say?'

"He said you probably wouldn't tell me why and that you were more qualified than him.'

239

"Humph. Don't know about that, it's been a long time but once you are trained you never forget. There was silence as Bronwyn weighed something in her mind. She studied Greg intently. He managed to hold her gaze without shrinking from her all seeing eyes. After a moment she went to her desk, opening a draw she took out a folder and a small card.

"Because I like you and Olwen cares enough about you to want to marry you and I know you can keep secrets even when it's not in your interests to do so, I am entrusting you with knowledge that's not known around here. I don't want it known about here. Doctor Davies and two others at the hospital know and the Captain; yes you may look surprised but he and I are old friends, we have known each other for many years. I expect some of those around here think he's a fake. He is most certainly no fake. His wife left him running off with another man leaving him to bring up his daughter even though he was at sea most of the time.'

"He is a real Captain?" Greg was astonished.

"Yes in his younger days. Unfortunately after his wife left he took to drink and eventually lost everything, his ship, his reputation along with his so called friends. He had to sell his big house, lost a lot of his money in drink and unwise investments. He moved here bringing his sixteen year old daughter with him. She was very delicate and became extremely ill a few years later, I was able to help him with her but she died with complications of her condition. It was so sad. Strangely enough although the Captain was heartbroken, it seemed to be the incentive he needed. All the time Elizabeth was ill I never saw a drop pass his lips. He enjoys a drink now but it's always rum and never more than two tots. I was worried that the old habits would return but he went away for a time, when he came back he was as you see him now. He has a small private pension and his cottage at the top of the village. People that don't know his history make fun of him and his ways, I wouldn't like you or your friends to make that mistake because under that jovial exterior is a lonely old man. he comes here some evenings I cook him a meal and let him talk. I am the only one he can talk to about Elizabeth we listen to music and play cards. That is when you see the real man.'

There was a long pause. Greg hesitated to break it although he wondered how this tied in with Bronwyn's own story. Liza Dolittle suddenly came out to sit on Greg's feet searching his face with intent eyes after a while she slipped away to her own secret hideaway. Macaverty had made himself comfortable on his cushion and faded away into the tawny background. Bronwyn leant forward putting a card on Greg's knee.

"This is who I was and will never be again. I have taken that name out of my life. I became Bronwyn Rhys which was my mother's name.'

Greg picked up the card and gasped. The name on the card was that of a famous heart surgeon at an address in Harley Street. When he was in his early twenties he recalled the name in the newspapers but couldn't remember why. She handed him a newspaper cutting. The headlines read- Top Harley Street consultant acquitted. Harley Street consultant Barbara DeLeon was today acquitted at the Crown Court of charges relating to the death of Architect Michael Sean Jamieson of Clear Water, Kilkenny Ridge, Southern Ireland who died of a heart condition last May. Mrs DeLeon had been arrested following complaints by Mrs Anwen Jamieson wife of the deceased that her husband had left off taking vital drugs for his condition after a consultation with Mrs DeLeon at her rooms in Harley Street on January the twenty sixth nineteen eighty one. Mr Jamieson died in the May of that same year. Mr Jamieson who was being treated for a serious heart condition by Mr Daniel Hathaway a London consultant had stopped his medication following a discussion with his mother- in-law at her consulting rooms, alleged his wife. He had later died at his home. Today the judge, Sir John Barclay, acquitted Barbara DeLion of all charges. He ruled out the charge of interference with the patient's treatment. The discussion had not been a medical discussion and had only briefly mentioned his condition after a general inquiry as to how he was feeling. Mr Jamieson was fully aware of his condition and knew what the result would be if he failed to take his medication. The judge could find nothing in the evidence shown to suggest that any such recommendation had been made to Mr Jamieson and that he was under no delusions whatsoever that by ceasing his medication he would die. The fact that he chose to do so could not be laid at Barbara DeLion's door and he therefore acquitted her of all blame in the matter.

Greg looked up horrified. Bronwyn was sat quietly looking into the fire. After a while she spoke. "The judge acquitted me, my daughter Anwen didn't; she pretends to believe the evidence but things will never be right between us. She pays a short visit occasionally maybe once or twice in two or three years more for Olwen's sake than anything else. Of course Olwen being the girl she is fished the whole story out in her teens. She has always been hot in my defence, has had many a row with her mother. I tell her to let it be. I was rather thankful that my husband was dead before it all happened. He was a surgeon too and it would have affected his good name as well as mine; not that he would have worried about that, he would have fully supported me but it would have hurt him to believe for one minute that Anwen could have done such a thing.'

"But you were acquitted." Greg protested. "Why couldn't she accept that? After all you were her mother and proven innocent.'

"Perhaps I was and perhaps I wasn't entirely. You see Michael had only called in to discuss some family matters while he was in London seeing Mr Hathaway. It was unfortunate that he came to my actual consulting rooms but he was anxious to get to another meeting before returning to Ireland. We discussed family business for a while then he talked about his health saying that he wasn't entirely satisfied with Mr Hathaway's treatment. I told him that I couldn't interfere or discuss, it would not ethical also I knew Dan Hathaway to be the best there was. I did not know that Michael had gone home and thrown all his tablets into the fire and I still don't know why. Their housekeeper saw him do it but as he didn't speak to her, she assumed his doctor advised him so she said nothing. All was well for a time then in the beginning of May Anwen and Olwen went on holiday for three weeks with friends, soon after their return Michael suffered a massive heart attack in the night. Afterwards Anwen remembered he had been to see me, she also remembered my opinion of those particular drugs but never in a million years would have I told him or anyone else to come off them unless there was an appropriate substitute and much consultation on it. The worst of all Anwen remembered me saying to Michael at their house a couple of years previously that if he had come to me five years earlier before he became so ill he would not have had to take those things at all. Idle words like that may have made him think but I still don't understand, he knew he had to take those tablets and I had not mentioned them or given him any advice or instructions to the contrary. As I said I'd refused to discuss it with him; that saved the day for me but I could not practise after that. I knew it was time to leave it all behind me. I could hear my William speaking as clearly as if he stood beside me 'Get out of it girl. You are one of the best and you have done your best. There are other ways of healing the world.' So I retired here, I write articles, a thesis, two books to date on alternative medicine and similar topics. They have been well received so I know I'm on the right track. I am on my third book. I love country ways, I have my dog and the cats, friends around me as I said no one knows but the Captain, he knows it all and will never say a word. He was there at the time of Elizabeth and stood by me all the way through." Greg handed back the folder. She took it with a sigh.

"All I have left are the memories of a lifetime of curing and easing the suffering of a few.'

He looked at her as she sat gently rocking staring into the fire. How could he have thought of her as witch like? With sympathy and a deeper understanding, he saw a woman of great intellect and courage who although innocent of the accusations hurled against her chose to take another path to heal the people she loved. Behind the harsh and abrupt manner dwelt a woman of integrity and pride. With new eyes he saw some of the characteristics which had helped to form Olwen. The pride, the beauty, the refusal to be silenced, maybe she would have stayed with him out of love not pity. It had been him that was afraid. Greg leant forward laying his hand over her folded ones.

Thank you for telling me, I appreciate it and will respect your confidence with my life.'

"Thank you Greg. You have a face to trust and I felt it was only fair that you should know a little of Olwen's background. You were honest with me about her. Do you want to tell me what happened the other night?' Greg told her all.

The following morning Greg felt much better. It had been a great relief to pour out his feelings and to know Bronwyn understood. There was no one but her that could appreciate what he was going through. Afterwards she had sent him to bed and he had slept deeply and more restfully than for a long time. She had woken him about six with a light meal exquisitely cooked and served, tempted he had cleared his plate. He had gone back downstairs for an hour listening to music while Bronwyn worked at her desk, her presence restful. When she settled him for the night it was with efficiency yet as tenderly as one of her own. He had slept until morning.

Chapter 28

The next few days were one of those exquisite Autumn ones of mist, sun and falling leaves. The air was crisp and tangy with the scent of chrysanthemums in the garden beds, beech leaves giving off smoke which drifted up the valley from some ones bonfire. Greg and Bronwyn slowly walked the dogs along a grassy lane where the leaves were alight with fire leaves from the maple trees and a faint rustling in the hedge of falling nuts. The sun was warm bringing swarms of bluebottles and wasps onto the decaying blackberries. A Squirrel dared the dogs, racing down the lane then taking a flying leap into the safety of a tree to the great disgust of the dogs who still only barely tolerated each other. Bronwyn now talked to Greg freely and he enjoyed her caustic wit realising that her apparent rudeness was a crabby sense of humour. She positively enjoyed peoples shocked or angry faces. Her knowledge and love of wildlife and country lore amazed him and he found himself thoroughly enjoying her company. She would not allow him to walk far and they soon returned to the comfort of the fire. That evening they enjoyed a film on television which proved so amusing that Bronwyn feared for Greg's health although as she said later 'Laughter is the best medicine of all'.

Greg was to return home the following day but as he sat considering all he had to do, he sat up suddenly horrified.

"Oh Lord! The parents will be going scatty, they phone usually every couple of days and my phone has been switched off. I never gave it a thought.'

"Ring them now." He reached for his phone. As he suspected his mother was frantic, they were leaving almost at once to come up. He more or less had to tell them what had happened without worrying them too much but despite his protestations that he was alright, his mother insisted they would come for a few days to see for themselves.

"I'm afraid you will have to put up with being cosseted." Bronwyn remarked when he told her. "You can see their point of view although it makes you feel like a child, it's not easy for them you know; in fact it is very hard for those who have to wait in the wings.'

"I know, I am a bit short in understanding. What am I going to do about Olwen? I love her, Bronwyn tough I know I mustn't.'

"Who says?" the piercing eyes met his unhappy ones. "Loving is very good for you. Sometimes it's all we have. Olwen's pride is her downfall and her lack of patience, if she had waited to listen to you it could have been talked through and a decision made between you. It's the one sided ones that hurt. I can't interfere, it would only send her rushing back with some notion or other. Leave her be, she is staying away from here at the moment because she knows I will get after her for dashing off in a temper but until she comes to me I can do nothing, I'll not phone. See what happens when she calms down. I know you feel it's some sort of a way out for you but sometimes fate takes a hand then there is nothing one can do but go along. Now then I've had an idea. Something to fill your head and your time.'

"Fire away." Greg picked up Macavity who yawned and relaxed hanging like a limp bag over his arm.

'How do you fancy running a model farm for handicapped children to visit?'

Greg stared at her in amazement. "How on earth could I do that?' he asked returning Macavity to his cushion.

"I take it that money isn't an immediate problem?'

"No but I am using it to get the place done up, the boys are starting next week.'

"Yes, you'll have to get that done first of course. I'm not sure what grants and things are available also the place would have to be in good condition before you could get anywhere. I don't know whether you would need or could get planning permission either; as you are having the house done up anyway I had this idea. Listen while I talk, ask questions afterwards. A big farmhouse kitchen where meals could be eaten as they were in the old days; an extension to take a couple more bedrooms big enough to take a couple of bunk beds in each, couple of bathrooms, downstairs showers and toilets. You may have other ideas perhaps another building in the grounds. Think about it carefully. Outside some Jacob sheep about a dozen, pig pen in the orchard with a couple of pot- bellied pigs that children love, goats, small cow Jersey or Dexter, hens, those I gave you are unusual; those are Silver Lace, what about small Orpingtons, make lovely pets very tame, some Rabbits, Guinea pigs ducks and geese. Find an old tractor, paint it in bright colours, make it safe, swings and things. You have the hill behind you for those fit enough to climb it.'

"Hey! Stop! I've just remembered Fred Barnes was coming with two cobs today he wants me to try one.'

"Excellent idea, Fred is a good man and fit as a fiddle although he has turned seventy. He'll give you a hand and enjoy doing it.'

"It sounds a wonderful idea but aren't you forgetting that I can't work, don't have that much money and not much time left either? How could disabled children cope on a mountain farm, how would I cope with them?'

"Didn't you tell me yesterday that your friend Ray wanted to live here if you could find him a job? Well here's one tailor made; he's a happy go lucky chap and hard working so I hear, just what you need. You would need a woman or two in the house though but I'm sure there is someone who would love to come and help with a project like that.'

"Ray has a girl- friend here who he is serious about. Megan Lewis; perhaps you know her?'

'Megan Lewis she works at The Green Man; a nice little girl although her skirts are too short. I always think after twenty they should get longer not shorter. Well! it's a thought, sleep on it and turn it over in your mind. Thinking about it that big shed with the rubbish in it would make a good extension to the house. It all depends what you can afford and what help is available. Sponsorships are the thing.'

"Aren't you forgetting something?'

"What?' Bronwyn rose to stir the fire.

"My health.'

"No I am not. You don't need me to remind you not to do anything yourself, get people in, delegate, take an administrative role. You see the children I am thinking of aren't incapacitated, they will have some form of disability, maybe deaf, partial sighted, lost a limb or there are other forms of disability, problems after operations, broken homes, disturbed for various reasons. You know Greg we all have disabilities, you know yours, others are not always easy to see. Some carry guilt or bitterness, resentment or anger to dangerous levels, so much so that it affects their lives and the lives of those around them then families suffer too. Some it is easy to help, others you mey not see the problem or understand it but these too need help where and how we can. It can be a hard task and we may only be able to do little but even someone to talk to as we have these two days to each other can start a healing process. Wouldn't it be wonderful to feel that your suffering has not been in vain and some little child would remember the times on your farm where he learned about animals and someone there hed time to learn about him as well.'

"how would it be funded?" Greg asked, now very interested.

"Sponsors. I'm sure you would not have any trouble getting those. I would put in a few thousand; if you are interested and I have friends who are very keen on worthwhile cases. I'm sure you too have friends, business acquaintances and contacts. It is surprising who you can come up with if you try.'

"I can't believe it." Greg's eyes sparkled. It would give me something to do; a focal point. Then if the worst happens for me at least I would leave something to show for my life, an achievement.'

Bronwyn watched him, the sudden animation in his face, his green eyes sparkling and saw what a handsome happy man he was without the tired pallor and worry which was usually on his face.

"Right, you think it over, discuss it with your friend, see what you both come up with, there are all sorts of possibilities. I am here I will help where ever I can as I told you.' To her great surprise and his own, Greg put his arms around her and kissed her gently on the cheek.

"Thank you.' He said. 'Thank you for everything.'

"Get on with you." She was smiling even though a tear stood in her light eyes. "That's enough of that. I'm making you a hot drink then it's bed for you. I know that once you are home and your friend gets here there will be enough late nights." Long after he was asleep, she sat staring into the fire. 'Poor lad. I hope something good happens for him before long. I hope McLoughlin knows the value of him. Wish I had a son like him. Olwen's no fool once she comes to her senses but she should have given him half a chance by stopping to listen to him. It won't be easy whichever way it goes but maybe I have given him something else to think about for a while.'

Chapter 29

Graig –y-Dorth in the Autumn was beautiful. The trees threw their leaves in golden bands through the green, the big Sycamore burned red and in the garden neglected clumps of Golden Rod and Michaelmas daisies bloomed in profusion. Spindle and Rowan trees glowed like minute fires in the dusk that each evening came a little earlier. Soft mist gathered in the mornings and mushrooms appeared in the fields. Hot sunshine at midday drew the smell of bracken and fresh earth as John turned over the garden for winter. When it rained heavy clouds wrapped around the mountains and the brook roared all night.

John and Sally had arrived almost as soon as Greg was home, to their relief he appeared to have recovered but then came the worry that he was living here on his own and winter was approaching. They said nothing to him but secretly decided to call on Bronwyn to thank her for her care of him. Greg could say nothing of about her except for her nursing and how good she had been. They said nothing to him of their worries but concentrated on the gathering of the damsons, apples and plums of which there was an abundance this year while John worked on the garden, Sally made jams, pickles and filled the freezer with fruit, pies, cakes and scones. Greg decided against telling them of Bronwyn's ideas about the farm and spent a restful few days enjoying their company. He finally protested though when he found his mother scrubbing out the porch and restacking the logs on the stone seat. His father took him to one side.

"Leave her be. It's the only way she can cope, if she can put you right it acts as therapy for her. I expect like me you let things slip a bit when you are on your own." Greg didn't argue about the apple pies and lasagne filling his freezer in fact it gave him food for thought as well but he would wait until he talked to Ray because if he couldn't help there might be a problem. Monday saw the arrival of Dean Bateman and a lorry load of felt batons and tiles. The weather was cold but clear, the forecast good. It was time to make a start on the roof. Dean and his labourer Colin had made good time stripping the galvanised before Greg approached the matter of lunch. Afterwards when his parents had gone back out to the orchard he and Dean had a chat about some of the new ideas that Greg had floating about in his mind.

"I'm not sure how far to go with the extension and the new roof. I don't want you to have to undo the good work for some future project."

Dean downed his third cup of tea. "Let's get the roof on the house that you are actually living in and we'll sort the extension when you have settled your mind."

"I won't keep you too long." Greg replied. "I just have to get some answers to some questions first and find out a bit more about grants."

"As I said we'll go as far as we can, then wait for your go ahead. Len will be along tomorrow, we can have another chat then. In the meantime if you need this galvanised for something we can stack it in the orchard or take it away if you prefer."

Greg liked Dean, they talked more that afternoon and Dean filled Greg in on some of the villagers including Luke Jeffries. He was horrified to hear about Rocky.

"I know that he is a nasty piece of work, a lot of the villagers don't like him, some even seem afraid of him. he has caused some nasty incidents over the years. If someone complains about him they always get some kind of trouble either their gates are left open or something is pinched. He threatened one woman who reported him about the state of the roads around his farm saying he would lie in wait for her husband one dark night. Didn't tackle the man mind, just frightened his wife. He emptied a trailer load of swedes outside his neighbour's gate blocking the road, over some cattle deal that went wrong. No proof mind but everybody knew it was him. If he gives you any trouble let us know and a few of us will sort him out."

"Thanks." Greg laughed. Dean was very interested in Greg's proposal about converting the farm to a model farm for disabled children. A bit dubious at first but as they talked the idea caught hold, he suggested Greg should talk to the doctor's wife as she had done marvels for local kids projects and for charities. "She might have some helpful ideas." As Dean passed the open window on his way back to work, he stuck his head in. "Think it's a great idea, more work for us." Greg threw an apple at him and he disappeared laughing.

The roof seemed to go on at a great pace until it reached the extension site now they had to wait for Greg's decisions. They sealed the roof at this point and Greg invited them back one evening and cooked them a dinner. Afterwards they discussed his ideas.

"If I should go ahead—if" Greg poured them fresh drinks. "I think I would need three more bedrooms at least, two more bathrooms upstairs and toilets and showers down stairs"

"Wait a minute." Len pulled out a notepad. "If we were to extend the present kitchen towards the edge of the yard and the width of the house, It would give you a hell of a kitchen; quite adequate for your requirements. This sitting room would surely be your own private lounge though you would still need rooms for your visitors as well as yourself. You may marry and have a family one day so you will have to enough to start with, it's too late after anyway you wouldn't want the whole house overrun with children and the people that come with them would you? You'd have no peace at all. I don't know how you are fixed financially or if you can get the sponsors you need or how we come off with the planning authorities but how about that shed you showed us? It's part brick, build on a proper site so no planning needed for that except maybe change of use and other official problems which always seem to crop up as soon as you start to do anything but if we could convert that into dormitories, toilet and shower facilities study and rest room, it would mean the house could cope with the catering, an extra bathroom couple of extra bedrooms en suite for the family then turn the rest into a small flat for whoever's going to help you. You would still have three private bedrooms as well." he paused for breath. Meanwhile Dean had been quietly sketching.'

"Look! You would want single rooms as well as doubles for tutors, parents or whoever, a boiler room for the central heating, more showers, utility room and really large games and television rooms. If we use that site you would have room for all those.'

"Good grief.'Greg was incredulous. "You have both got it all sewn up haven't you? Have you been talking to Bronwyn by any chance?" they laughed. Len put down his knife and waved his fork about. "It makes sense Greg. If you are going to do it, use all the space you have to get the best right off, no need going over old ground or grtting things done then regretting you didn't go bigger."

"Right draw up the plans for me to take to the authorities and I'll see if I can raise some help and money. I've got to try I really want to do this. Do you know where I can get some pot- bellied pigs?" The meal ended in laughter and lewd jokes.

The new roof made the house much warmer and quieter. Greg had tried to phone Ray but Dave informed him that he was off on a fishing trip with an old friend. Megan hadn't been seen about the village so maybe she had gone too.

It was almost a week later that Ray phoned, sounding like his old self as if his trip had done him good.

"Hi Greg I'm sorry to have been out of reach. I have been thinking about you but Jim came over unexpectedly and I grabbed the chance to get some good fish. Have you been alright and have you seen Megan?"

"No thought she may have been with you. Do you know when you're coming down? Several things are going on and I have ideas I want to mull over with you before I throw it to the parents. Mother is going to flip and say it's all too much for me or something.'

"What have you been up to now? For an invalid you lead a pretty hectic life. Yes I can make it Saturday until Tuesday; Dave will cuss but what the hell? Make that Friday and I'll see yer.'

Ray arrived late with an air of supressed excitement. It was a more serious Ray than before but some of the old sparkle was definitely back.

"You look as if you've lost sixpence and found a pound." Greg eyed him with amusement.

"Hell! Do I? Better tell you then before I burst. Megan and I are getting married next Feb and I want you for best man.' Greg slapped him on the back then hugged him.

"Good man. Congratulations, of course I will, if I survive the winter."

"You'd better had. Don't even joke about it Greg.'

"Sorry but I am pleased. You were the king of love 'em and leave 'em, caught at last, never thought I'd see the day. When did you ask her if you've been away?"

"Last night on the phone, I asked if you had seen her. Well I'd rung several times and got no reply Then I reached her mother who told me she was away staying with a friend coming back late. God alive was I ever jealous? I couldn't remember her telling me about any friend called Nancy. I just didn't believe it, anyway I waited until midnight and rang again, she had just come in, then we had a row on the phone but before she could slam it down I asked her to marry me. She was so surprised she couldn't speak for a moment then she said yes. I still can't believe it, I didn't tell her I was coming here tonight she expects me tomorrow afternoon so we can have our talk tonight. I'll ring her later. Tomorrow I'll take her to town to buy a ring.'

"Great. Where will the wedding be, here or in Hull?'

"Here I should think, in Graigwen, it's the Brides choice of course." Greg felt a stab of envy, a fleeting thought that had he accepted Olwen's proposal they might have had a double wedding. He pushed the thought aside. For a while they talked of Megan, then Ray's fishing trip. After a while Ray looked closely at his friend, noticing that he looked tired and sad.

"Where's Olwen, Greg?" He told him what had happened.

"God you are dumb, why didn't you get out before it got that far? Now what are you going to do?'

"I'm just leaving it. She rushed out, didn't give me time to explain so if that's the way she wants it so be it; makes it easier this way." Ray gave him a searching look.

"You still love her don't you? I'm damned sure she loves you or she wouldn't have gone that far. Why didn't you accept then tell her later?'

"Could you have done that?'

"I guess not.' He answered slowly. "But then I'm not such a high moral flier as you. I would have been tempted.'

"Not if it was Megan's whole future at stake you wouldn't. You might have wanted to but you wouldn't in the end. No, it's done so leave well alone. Anyway listen to this. Bronwyn had to look after me the other day. She was really great." He went on to telling what happened and the outcome. Ray was astounded.

"Then" Greg continued. "She had this brilliant idea about something I could do with this farm in the time I have left, a contribution to someone's future that I could set up which could continue after I am gone. I would like you in on it Ray. Do you still want to move here?'

"You know I would like to but I have shares in Dave's business and I would need to find somewhere to live. Whatever I do I must have the secure income which I now have. Megan and I will want a family someday." Greg was finding it hard to believe this was light hearted Ray he was having this conversation with but one look at his serious face convinced him.

"Well listen, don't say a word." He told of the ideas and plans that he, Bronwyn and the builders had talked about. Before he had finished Ray's eyes were shining. With his old impulsiveness he leapt to his feet.

"That's brilliant man, brilliant. Of course I would have to talk to Megan but I know she would like to stay near her family rather than move to Hull. If I could get a guaranteed regular wage and somewhere decent to live then I'm your man. I think it's a fantastic idea. What do the parents think?'

"I haven't dared to tell them yet, you know my mother will worry herself to death that I am taking on too much. No, I wanted to see what you thought and if it could be done first. What if I said that you and Megan could live here at Graig-y-dorth? The builders seemed to think there is room for a decent flat over the extension, it would be a bit small but would it do until you are ready to start a family, maybe then you could buy a house somewhere in the valley?'

"This gets better. It would be brilliant." Ray was almost leaping about the room in his excitement. He finally flung himself back in his chair. "How would it be funded?'

"Sponsors mainly, perhaps ministry or grants anything we can pull in and we would have to make it fairly self-sufficient food wise; I have yet to research all that. Bronwyn is into sponsorships, she has offered to handle that side of it. She has offered to invest herself.'

"Where would she get that sort of money?' Ray looked puzzled.

"Oh! She used to have a business when she was younger." Greg evaded the question by putting the kettle on. Ray was sat slowly thinking things through.

"I could sell my share of the garage, the house and boat. I could sell the Jaguar too if you didn't mind. It would certainly be of no use here. I could invest some savings into this. It's got to come off it's such a brilliant idea. What about Tom and your mates on the rig? Wouldn't they cough up for a good cause?'

"Some of them might. Tom is worth a bit and I know for a fact that he knows some seriously wealthy people who might sponsor us. I know of a few connected with off shore business." He reached for a pen scrabbling about on the windowsill for paper. "It's amazing how many people with money I can recall dealing with over the years, if they are approached in the right way they surely would put up something." He started writing busily. "Lee and Patsy Ross are certainly worth asking then there are all the people at home, the clubs, good for fund raising maybe. It's as Bronwyn said when you start looking the list seems endless. We'll get the estimate off the boys then we'll have to set up a trust fund for the running of the place and for long term funding. Getting the place ready is the first thing red tape by the mile; fire regs, health and safety, water, sewerage, insurance—Greg was writing furiously while Ray did complicated sums of his own. "Then there will be the animals, health care, safety, I'll have a chat with the vet. Don't know if the environmental people come into this, we will have to see.'

They talked making plans and suggestions until the early hours. Greg realised that he had been afraid that when it came to the point Ray would not really want to come. People often long to do something until the opportunity actually arises then have a change of heart but Ray actually seemed keener than he was himself. Greg felt it only fair to give him time to think things through as well as discussing it all with Megan. He had a lot more to lose than Greg financially, a good job, sound investments, house and this was one hell of a risk with no guarantees of any kind, Greg could die leaving everything in mid- air. They could draw up all the contracts and agreements but in the end it was a great risk for all concerned but especially Ray. Ray listened carefully as Greg pointed all this out the next day.

"I hear you Greg I understand all that you say and you are right but look what happened to you. You had security, good job, home and never expected to lose it. I have been pretty free and easy with my life putting it all about, enjoying myself with no thought to the future. Then what happened to you made me stop and think. It could happen to anyone, who's to say I may have a giant hiccup which would change my way of life. We all live on chance but this place is something else, it has a strange kind of magic and a pull once you have stayed here and worked for a while it's like home. It's rough and ready but there is some quality in the air or the mountains, I don't know what, I'm not good at explaining this sort of thing but there is a magical feel that makes you want to work and do something better with your time. Who knows how much time any of us has got? We all take it for granted, I know I have. This maybe rough but its magic that's the only way I can describe it. I want more than material possessions. I have Megan now and she means everything, I never thought that would happen to me. I may be taking this for granted answering for her but as much as she enjoyed visiting Hull and would live there if I asked her but this is her home where she would prefer to stay. I know perhaps we could find her a job as well?'

Greg stood up putting his hand on Ray's shoulder. "I know what you mean I felt it as soon as I came here. If I'm to survive, body and soul it will be from here.'

He forced away thoughts of Olwen.

Chapter 30

Snakes alive! Where did they come from? You never said anything last night.'Ray's voice floated in from the yard where he had gone to feed the fowls.

"What? Where? Greg came to the door ladle in hand. It was his job to cook breakfast and he had already burnt the toast.

"Don't tell me you didn't know there were two bloody great horses in your field?'

Greg could see two heads, one grey, one brown bobbing up and down over the gate. "Hell! I forgot old Fred was bringing them. They are for us to ride. Get your hunting gear on.'

"You've got to be joking. Are they really here for us?'

"Let's take a look in the stables.' The smell of burning bacon wafted out of the kitchen. "Damn.' Greg fled back inside.

There were two sets of harness in the stable with a short note. 'Bit of apple or carrot will catch either of them. The grey is Muffin the other Oxo, enjoy yourselves'. It was an exhilarating experience riding across the heather covered hill, much further than Greg could have walked. The fresh breeze, larks darting up into the hazy blue sky, the horses sure footed and steady. Once over the ridge there was a broad stretch of turf where they were able to give them their heads for a short stretch. When they returned home Greg found that he was only pleasantly tired, both agreed that Fred was right this was a must for Greg to get a little exercise without over exerting. Ray was thrilled as he hadn't ridden since a boy when they used to go trekking, thankfully he hadn't forgotten how. They met other trekkers on the hill and promised themselves a quiet ride one day to the old Abbey Inn where Greg had first stayed. After rubbing the horses down then turning them back in the field they heated one of Sally's casseroles and were sat talking when Megan arrived. She was soon hauled into deep discussions on the new project. Although Greg had only met her a couple of times he now looked at her with new respect. The change in Ray was mainly due to her so he wanted to get to know her properly. He hoped for Ray's sake she would agree to fit into the scheme of things and that he and Ray would keep their friendship which sometimes became lost when a partner came on the scene. He soon realised that he need have no such fears as he watched her with Ray writing notes with their heads close together, she looking up from time to time including him, asking his opinion on some point. Megan was very small, corn coloured hair rioting in a cap of curls over her head, big brown eyes alight with excitement and a touch of mischief. She soon proved to be as light –hearted as Ray but with a deeply sensitive yet practical nature which would bring out the best in him. Greg was to find when he knew her better that she was organised, possessed a wiry strength and determination; she adored Ray which she was inclined to hide unlike his previous girlfriends. Megan didn't wait on him with adoring eyes, she fended for herself and made him do the same, Ray found himself the submissive partner, thus becoming her slave. It amused Greg to see Ray, so used to bossing his girlfriends about now waiting on Megan with tender care. She took it as her right with a sweet dimpled smile and shy response. They were well matched. The evening passed quickly with plans, ideas and laughter.

Megan was delighted with it all and full of suggestions. As she was cook at The Green Man she was very interested in the idea that she might like to cook for the children and staff also the thought that her and Ray might share the flat that was to be built. Sunday found them out on the horses again while Megan cooked lunch. Afterwards when Greg rested, her and Ray sorted the stuff in the shed in preparation for getting the Land rover out. Ray filled his truck with scrap to dispose of next day. "Bit more money for the petty cash box." He laughed. Megan rescued the garden tools taking then aside for cleaning and sharpening. A set of chain harrows Ray set aside. "Ideal for the fields but we are going to have to get a small tractor, this one is useless except as scrap.'

"Why don't we strip it, paint it, making it safe for children to play on?" Megan brushed her hair from her eyes with an oily hand.

"Brilliant idea, you do the painting while I do the stripping." Ray gave a suggestive leer. Megan rubbed her oily hands over his face.

"Get on with your work, boy or you get no tea that Greg is making. I've done enough for today.'

"Thanks a bunch I know who my friends are." Greg came up behind her making her jump. "We'll need a tractor to pull all this heavy stuff. I'll give Glen a ring and see if he could perhaps come next weekend if you are coming down.'

"I hope to, I am going to talk to Dave when I get back but I can't give him warning until we know whether we can go ahead. I think there is an answer to that too but I want to be sure before I say anything.'

'Give me a ring when you're ready and I'll get hold of Glen' Greg threw the remains of his tea onto the ground.

There was no sight or sound of Olwen, even her grandmother had heard nothing when she phoned the answer phone cut in or it was engaged for ages. Bronwyn left her alone after the initial attempts, as she told Greg who had also been trying it was no good pushing her, she would emerge in her own time. Greg fought with his heartache much as he fought with the fact of his illness. It was a daily battle that he often felt that he was losing. He definitely found he could do less and was getting very tired more often.

Work on the house moved on a pace, the kitchen being of prime importance. Nothing else could really be tackle until such time as he had the go ahead from the powers that be also a main backing sponsor other than Bronwyn had promised a substantial amount which hadn't yet cleared. As finding and dealing with sponsors had been taken over by Bronwyn, Greg was left dealing with the authorities. He decided to talk to Mrs Davies the doctor's wife before he fell into a tangle of red tape. She was so excited by the project she arrived the same day he phoned, a bright green Mini pulling onto the yard a couple of hours later. Rocky's excited barking brought Greg to the door where a plump lady was giving him a fussing that sent the delighted dog crazy, obviously thinking her no threat to his master's wellbeing.

"Good day to you. Thank you for calling me. My name is Gwen and I am so pleased to meet you." Bright blue eyes surveyed him from beneath the brim of a man's waterproof hat although it wasn't raining. Greg later learned that she wore it rain or shine.

"Isn't this wonderful? I can see a lot needs doing but I think your plans are marvellous. My husband told me about you moving in. I am sorry you needed to see him professionally so soon. Now tell me about your plans and how I may help you.'

Greg found that she hopped from subject to subject with ease leaving him slightly bewildered and breathless but he soon learned that she was extremely efficient and knew a good many people in the right places. What she took on things got done. Greg made her coffee and within the hour felt he had known her all his life. She was delighted with his plans, added a few ideas of her own, gave him names of a few people she felt would be delighted to support such a cause. Gwen Davies had Greg writing at high speed in a very short space of time. Before she left he knew exactly who to contact and where. As he walked her to her car he felt he had gained a friend.

"Leave it to me Greg. I know just the man to get this through the parish council and he, if you believe it has very good ears in the district council. We have been grateful to him before for several things and this is the sort of project very dear to his heart for personal reasons that I won't go into. I am off to see him this very afternoon." They shook hands then as she turned to get in her car- "You are not overdoing things I hope?'

Greg assured her he was being very careful wondering how confidential the doctor's notes were if she knew so much. When he next saw Bronwyn he mentioned this and she laughed. "Doctor never discusses patients with her'.

It was more than two weeks before he heard from Ray and Greg was beginning to worry that perhaps things weren't working out for him. Megan didn't seem to be about the village either. He rang a couple of times but there was no reply, he was determined not to bother him too much until Ray had fully considered all his options. In the meantime the builders made good progress. Len had given him an estimate of things that could be done before winter to make the house weather proof as first priority. Within this was the kitchen, installation of the Rayburn and wood burner. Also they could make a start on the extension and flat. This would make no difference to future plans, should they come about, as most of the work was necessary anyway. It was a case of going steady until Ray decided what he was doing as he had offered to contribute to the flat if he was going to be living there. It was the new building on the shed site which would cost the most and could not be started until plans were passed and the farmhouse alterations complete. Len and Dean were moving as quickly as possible now bringing in labourers. "You need to be prepared here in case snow comes early." Dean pointed out to him. 'It is quite possible to be marooned here and you may not see us for weeks. You should be able to get out with the truck but it can get bad here. You should get in some stores.'

This so bothered Greg that he bought another large deep chest freezer phoning his mother for another baking. He bought a large diesel tank for the central heating and a smaller one for the Land rover which was now almost ready for the road. Restored now to its former glory it stood beside the pickup where Greg couldn't keep his eyes off it, itching to get it on the road. It was only waiting on Ray for a few things he was bringing next time he came. The builders were taking Greg to task on the stocking of supplies, taking great delight in thinking of new items that he couldn't possibly survive the winter without, going into fits of laughter when without fail he took their advice and brought it back from town. As he drove off they called after him.

"Cooking oil Greg better get a drum. Don't forget a string of onions and candles; you will certainly get power cuts out here.'

He took it all in good part. One of the great finds in the shed as it was cleared was an old generator which later when he had time Ray managed to get going.

The awaited call from Ray came late one night. Greg was feeling very low. He was troubled by thoughts of Olwen and he didn't feel well, not hearing from Ray was getting him down and he was steeling himself to phone him again anyway when the house phone rang almost under his hand.

"It's all on." Came Ray's cheerful voice. "Dave was upset but he likes the sound of the venture and wished us luck. He's buying me out but I think he has an eye on his brother-in- law coming in. If things go well for him he'll consider making a contribution to our funds himself.'

"Great. When are you coming down?" Greg felt his spirits rise a little.

"This weekend hopefully for a couple of days but I have to be back then for a week or two as I have to sell the boat and put the house on the market. I think I have a buyer for the Jaguar but he can't take it until the end of the month.'

Greg was silent with a momentary pang at the thought of the Jag going to someone else pulling himself together he began to feel the rising excitement of having some of their plans coming to fruition.

"So see you Friday. Get the tractor, we'll clear the shed and get started. I've got the bits for the Land Rover so with a bit of luck she will be on the road; that should cheer you up. Megan is over the moon. Is there any news of Olwen?'

"Neither sight nor sound. Bronwyn hasn't seen or heard from her either."

"Best way perhaps if she is as touchy as all that.' Greg was silent. "See you Friday anyway.'

As the nights were drawing in the builders often worked late inside the house. The kitchen was taking shape which Greg liked very much. Dean spent several nights taking out the old range and building a wider space for the new one. Taking Bronwyn's advice he bought the biggest calor gas cooker in the show room with a mind for power cuts, it would also act as a booster for the Rayburn which stood waiting to be connected. The excitement this weekend would be getting the Land rover on the road. Ray had done a great job on the repairs and windscreen, new seats and canvas hood had been delivered from Hay-on-wye; Greg managing to fit them when he had felt well enough. Great care had been taken with anything purchased and she was as near the original as they could make her. The canvas hood had been the most difficult to find so although expensive Greg had one made.

Ray arrived early on Friday and within a couple of hours the jobs on the Land rover were finished. Greg had bought a bottle of champagne and invited Bronwyn to do the honours. She greatly amused agreed and arrived just as the builders returned from town with the pipes for the Rayburn.

'Come on, you two.' Ray was revving up. 'Just in time for a launching, call the other lads they have all been looking forward to this.'

Plasterers, plumbers and painters arrived from all directions and Ray who had never seen Bronwyn in a frivolous mood before stared in astonishment as she stepped forward and carefully cracking the bottle on the bonnet spoke in a loud clear voice.

"I name thee Patience. God bless all who ride in her." Everyone laughed as Greg produced another bottle and paper cups for a toast to Patience and the new centre. Laughing they all climbed in, Greg bowing to Bronwyn as he held the door for her, she entering into the spirit of the occasion to the amazement of all; bowed back before climbing in. Ray insisting that Greg drove, they set off for a lap of the mountain road. Heads turned as they drove through Graigwen the old Land Rover taking to the roads as they had dreamt.

"Why call her Patience?" Greg asked as they drove back on the yard. Her eyes twinkled. "Obvious isn't it? She waited many years to be discovered. You had the patience to restore her with the faith you could do it and she fulfilled the promise you saw in her. Faith and patience inherit the promise.'

"Well it's a great name. Thanks.'

"It works in other ways too lad. Faith and patience work side by side, no good one without the other. Don't forget that.'

"I'll remember. You know Bronwyn I wish Olwen had been here today. She loved the Land Rover." Greg's green eyes darkened at the memory of those wide grey eyes and tender smile.

"Ha! Remember faith and patience.'She wagged her finger at him.

"Not in this case I'm afraid." Greg turned to look at the lads around the Land rover, his face drawn.

"You don't know what is around the corner Greg. It's not for us to know and just as well. Have the faith if you don't have the patience. It's time I went home, jobs to do, no time to be idling around here watching a lot of strong young men make fools of themselves over a piece of machinery when they could be finding something better to do with their time." There was a twinkle in her sharp eyes even as she spoke and didn't take much persuading for Greg to show her around before she left.

"It's a good job coming along well. You think my idea may work then?'

"I hope so. I'm relying on it more than I can say.' He ran his fingers through his hair. "But how much further we get depends on many things.'

"I still think my last words still apply. Anyway I can't stand time wasting any longer. I'm off see you shortly." She turned at the gate and walked back.

"I would carry on if I were you. I have already had quite a few replies to my appeals. There should be a few cheques in the post soon and several people coming to see you shortly, they want to talk to you about some of your ideas but don't worry they will go along with you. They owe me." She strode out of the gate and down the road her old barber jacket flapping around her. Greg stood as he often stood when she left him, speechless. Dean came up to him.

"She's a funny old bird, isn't she? Always makes me feel as if she's caught me behind the bike shed. She'll praise your work then wipes your nose with some comment, pays you well for the job so you end up going back for more of the same.'

"She used to give me the shivers." Ray closed the bonnet on the Land rover 'But I'm getting used to her now.' Greg smiled.

Chapter 31

At the end of October the weather turned bitterly cold. All night the wind howled bringing down the leaves which lay in a thick carpet, then came rain when the pretty gold and red carpet became a slippery hazard for wheels and feet. Greg's parents came for a weekend and John cleared the mess from around the doors as best he could but the builder's vehicles made the job impossible. Icy rain blew in at the sides of untreated windows and under the doors. Clouds hid the mountain and hung in the trees all day. Everywhere was damp and depressing, an early winter was forecast on the news and everyone Greg met seemed to be saying the same. The temperature began to drop everyday seemed to grow steadily colder. The new fireplace in the lounge was lit every day Greg shivered and was glad when the Rayburn and wood burner were finally in place. The house with its unfinished rooms felt hollow and chill. His parents were glad to be going home begging him to come with them until the work was completed. He couldn't as he was waiting for the oil tanker to arrive so that the Rayburn could be lit. A load of dry logs arrived and the wood burner was lit which made such a difference, where the open fire had burnt sluggish giving out little heat the wood burner gave warmth through all the rooms even heating the bedrooms which meant the central heating boiler didn't have to work so hard, gradually the house warmed through. Sally sighed with thankfulness but still packed to go home. She had baked for the new freezer and shopped as if Greg didn't have enough stores already. "You never know." she said checking the kitchen cupboards. After they left Greg felt lonely as there were no builders at work this week. Len had been called to another urgent job in the village while Dean had gone to court over some unpaid bill. The painters hadn't turned up. Fred had repaired the stable doors then he and his grandson had hauled straw, hay and nuts for the horses in case it snowed. It was too cold and wet to turn them out.

Shots fired late one afternoon had Greg worried, they seemed too close to the house for comfort. He rang Jeff Arnott but there was nothing he could do. Local farmers were known to go shooting rabbits or foxes on the hill and there was no proof that shots had been aimed at Greg's yard but it made him more careful to keep Rocky by him at all times. He was certain that Luke nosed around when he was out and even more certain that he would help himself to anything lying about. It was a nuisance to have to keep locking everything up but after coming home one day when there were no builders around to find the stable doors open(luckily the horses were out that time) Greg wasn't prepared to take chances. He told Fred and the stables were locked when he knew he was going out, until Ray moved in there was nothing else to do.

Greg felt that Graig-y-dorth was becoming his home more each day. The extension was taking shape and the men could work in the dry so an air of camaraderie sprang up which he enjoyed missing it on days the lads didn't come. The new roof was his delight, he loved to stand at the gate looking at it firm and secure against the background of the mountain especially late afternoon when a fire was lit in the dining room and soft grey smoke drifted across the evening sky. The Rayburn stood now warm and welcoming saving a lot of work as a casserole or a pot of stew could simmer away until needed plus plenty of hot water. The kitchen was now enormous just waiting a final coat of paint. How he wished Olwen was here to share his delight, how his heart ached wondering where she was now. Bronwyn had received one very brief phone call, not revealing much and not giving time for much to be said. Greg kept telling himself it was for the best but his heart leapt every time the phone rang or his mobile trilled. When he was alone in the evenings his hand would move towards his phone to call her but his head told him to leave well alone. He grew thinner and his eyes were shadowed. His mother noticed each time she came and begged him to come home for winter. Ray noticed and redoubled his efforts to move more quickly to Graig-y-dorth. The builders were now working on the flat it promised to be a very attractive apartment in which to start married life. The lounge was bigger than anticipated with views over the trees to Graigwen. There was large bedroom en suite and small kitchen for when Ray and Megan wanted some privacy to cook a meal for friends. The whole heated by radiators run by the wood burner in Greg's lounge. Megan was delighted with the whole flat and enjoyed planning to furnish it out aided by her mother Sylvia who adored Ray and offered to support Greg when the centre opened.

Bronwyn was kept busy as the sponsorships began to come in. It was surprising what amounts were promised. A large mail order conglomerate had sent a staggering amount and no one seemed to know how or why they had done so. Bronwyn seemed to think it had probably been approached by another sponsor who had some influence she was delighted and redoubled her efforts. She had opened an account initially with her own contribution and Rays impute from the sale of his boat and shares from the garage so the huge check from this company swelled the coffers and allowed the building work to continue. Ray's house was on the market, the sale of the Jaguar confirmed; he stated this money was to go into sponsor ship but Bronwyn insisted he keep it in his own account as he might want to buy a house at some point. "There's plenty more to come in and a lot of fund raising going on so don't you be worrying at the moment." As other monies began to pour in Greg was hopeful for a go ahead to start the new building. The parish council had passed the plans as Gwen Davies had promised these were now in the hands of the district council's planning office with several recommending letters. Greg spent a lot of time contacting people in his own circle and was amazed at the encouragement and support. Although there wasn't an hour went by that something didn't remind him of Olwen he was beginning to believe that the dream for his farm might come true.

It was Halloween and Greg was alone. No one had been on site all day but Greg was getting used to builders habits of appearing and disappearing. He had spent the morning staining the kitchen doors with antique pine, enjoying the warmth and serenity of the house. He was not feeling well and a quiet job suited him. While waiting the doors to dry he was making lists of furniture needed for the new rooms. It had been a bleak enough morning but after lunch the day deteriorated with a cold wind and icy rain. Fred called in to say he had seen to the horses. He stayed for a coffee and to admire the new kitchen. Greg showed him over the house telling him about the plans for the new building. Fred was very interested.

"I've never seen the like but good on yer. Anything I can do fer yer lad, yer've only ter ask. There'll be a few animals about soon no doubt. I won't charge yer, I'll enjoy it. Keep me out of mischief." His eyes twinkled behind the cloud of pipe smoke that Greg hadn't the heart to ask him to put out. "Young Joe'll help me, he enjoys it too as yer may 'ave noticed, mind ee looks for a bit o cash come Saturdays so yer'd better keep 'im sweet but not me mind, this u'll be my contribution fer the poor things that'll come ere." Greg hid his smile. "Thank you Fred I do appreciate it and you were right about the horses. Ray and I have enjoyed them quite a bit and others will too later on.'

"Didn't I tell ee? I knows yer can get about better on a horse. How yer feeling, young chap, yer don't look so clever of late?'

"Oh! I guess I've been doing too much lately. It'll pass." Fred peered at him as he tapped his pipe out laying it on the table.

"Look 'ere, I've been about a bit an' I knows yer ain't tellin the truth, I knows, I can tell it in the grandchildren and yer ain't no different don't worry fer now as yer as yer reasons but when yer want ter talk old Fred don't tell a soul and I'll be waitin. Yer might need some 'elp before long. Yer need lass to come and work with yer. I know yer friend is coming. Good job too. Anyway I'll be off. I'll do the chickens on my way out its goin ter get dark early ter night.'

Greg shook his hand as Fred levered himself out of his chair. "Thanks Fred I'll remember what you've said. I need all the friends I can get. Don't forget your pipe.'

I doubt I'll be smoking in front of yer agin, don't care what yer say. I can see it's no good ter yer. No don't come out, get on with the job yer doin. Remember the phone is there if yer needs anything.'

"Thanks again Fred. Good night.'

Greg felt very comforted when he thought of the good friends he had made since he came to the mountains. Noticing how dark it was getting although only early afternoon, he brought in a pile of logs for the wood burner. When he finished the varnishing a film on the television seemed a good idea. Rocky had gone with Fred to see to the chickens then headed for his blanket. After tea Greg was deciding between a video or a new book he was itching to read when the sound of a vehicle sent Rocky barking to the door. "All right Rocky, it's only one of the boys. Come on in its open." He called at the tap on the door. Rocky was barking but his tail wagged furiously. As Greg carried on putting his video into the machine the door opened and an icy blast whirled inside.

"Come on in and get that blasted door shut its cold enough to freeze a brass monkey" A low voice behind him. "Is it too late to say that I'm sorry? Can I come in?"

279

"You are in."

She closed the door behind her bending to fuss Rocky who was beside himself with delight. Greg remained motionless, so totally unexpected the scene he had so longed for but dreaded so much. Rocky temporarily satisfied retreated to his bed as Greg very carefully put down his video and rose to his feet. He turned his eyes meeting hers. She stood just inside the closed door, not moving. Her eyes appeared huge with dark violet shadows beneath them. The blue tracksuit she wore drained the colour from her face leaving her freckles standing livid across her cheekbones. She looked ill and tired. Greg ached to take her in his arms and kiss away the strain in her eyes, the droop from her mouth.

"Why have you come?" he asked at last.

"I had too. I know I was wrong not to hear what you had to say to me." Her voice was weary, trembling.

"Oh! You have spoken to your grandmother?" his heart was hammering, his throat dry.

"Yes I've been there since this morning.'

"So!" thought Greg "She knows now; that's why she looks so ill and I thought I could trust Bronwyn with my life.'

"I wanted to come a long time ago but I was hurt and embarrassed and you never phoned or came to look for me. It was all so bad I thought it best I didn't come so.

I thought it best to leave well alone.' Greg's tones were wary. He wished she would hurry and say her piece then he could send her on her way. He had dreaded this; now it would start again all the pain and hunger but this time it would be worse because knowing the truth she would want to stay with him. He couldn't bear that; all her bright flame fading out as they waited for the end. He turned away fiddling with the videos pushing them in and out of the cases; anything rather than look at that haunted beloved face. Damn Bronwyn.

"How have you been?" he asked when she didn't speak.

"Fine, just fine." she answered brightly, too brightly.

"You don't look well." he retorted. "You've been working too hard.'

"No not recently. Look Greg. I've said I'm sorry. I was too hasty, my filthy temper just took me out of the door and I just couldn't come back." She sat down suddenly on a chair, slouched hands deep in her pockets. Her tracksuit hood covered her hair but in the heat of the room she shook it off. Her hair was tied back tightly with a shoelace, red-gold wisps clinging to her face and neck. He glanced at her quickly then away, his face as white as her own his jaw set.

"Well maybe I was a bit stupid but you took me by surprise and I'm not good at surprises as you found out.'

"I realised that later and didn't know what to do, then I phoned Gran but she never mentioned you until I came back today then she had a right go at me.'

Greg felt betrayed. "Well it doesn't matter now, does it?" he said coldly. "I accept your apology in the spirit you give it. I was wrong too. We'll call it quits shall we?" He realised as he spoke how pompous he sounded and could have bitten his tongue out. She stared at him stunned.

"You are a cold bastard aren't you? Well let me be telling you this----rising to her feet. "If it wasn't for Granny, I wouldn.t be here now. I let her talk me round. I was for managing nicely thank you very much. I think she was wrong going on and on about temper and pride. Sometimes it's all one has left." She turned to the door. "I won't be bothering you any more, I've said my piece and you've said yours as you are saying we're quits. You are after getting the place nice now as I can see. I hope you meet someone one day that you can really love or maybe this has put you off women for good. Anyway I wish you good luck for the future." She turned back now and smiled eyes full of tears, her smile tremulous. "I won't be coming this way for a long time. I am going to my mother in London. I'll probably go back to France with her. Please Greg, marry someone nice and have a lovely life, I do sincerely wish it for you. I only wish it could have been me. May God and all the fairies bless you and keep you safe." She fumbled with the door. "Bye Rocky, look after him." Her voice broke as she flung open the door, fumbling for the outer one.

"Olwen!" before she could find the latch Greg had caught her arm and whirled her to face him. "Come back in here quickly, there is something I must know." she was sobbing helplessly now trying to pull away. He pushed her back into the warm room and into a chair where he knelt keeping his arms around her.

"Olwen, I must know word for word what your Granny has been saying to you. Please Olwen it's very important to me." She stared at him her grey eyes drowned dark as a lake in rain.

"Only that I should have been slapped more for losing my temper as a child and if I carried on the way I do I would never have a relationship at all, other people had rights to their opinions and points of view as well as me and it was about time that I grew up, stopped running away when things got tough, that I acted more like a teenager than a thirty year old. She said it wasn't clever to hit out and stamp out that it took courage to calm down and wait your turn. Oh! She was for saying more, much more all in the same vein, she hardly drew breath; most of which I realised before I reached Worcester and knew what I had done.'

"She said nothing about me?" Greg was insistent.

"No." Olwen withdrew her hands to wipe her eyes. "Only that you were the finest man she had met for a long time and I was the biggest fool going. Why, what else would she be saying?'

"A great deal more that should have been said earlier. That was my fault, I am far guiltier than you realise, Sweetheart." At the endearment Olwen's eyes filled again, tears spilling over down her cheeks. Greg mopped them away tenderly with the tea towel.

"Come and sit with me on the settee. We must talk as we should have done in the beginning. Can I get you a drink first?'

"In a minute, only I must take this jacket off it's so hot in here, I see you have a wood burner now what a great idea." He helped her off with her jacket then sitting beside her caught her hand in his. "It was darling of you to want to marry me.'

"It doesn't matter—she began.

"Hush now, it's my turn. I need you to listen to me. This is something I hoped never to have to tell you but I was wrong there too. It's your right to know. As I said it was a wonderful idea of yours to get married in any other circumstances I would have beaten you to it but there is a very good reason why I have to say no." His hands tightened on hers. "It's not because I am already married with six kids or anything like that. It's because it wouldn't be fair to you. In another year I may not be here. I have an illness called Obstructive Cardiomyopathy or another name is Myocarditis which means that the heart the heart muscle becomes inflamed and degenerates into fibrous tissue. There is no cure." Her gasp made him reach for her other hand and hold both tightly. She was deathly pale.

"The only hope is a transplant." As her face brightened he squeezed her hands hard "But for me that is not simple either. I have a rare blood group O Rhesus Positive with rare antibodies. The chances of finding a donor in time are slim to non- existent I do carry a---- He caught her as she slid forward in a dead faint, laying her back on the couch, he rushed for water sprinkling her face and neck, slapping her hands. Frantic he pushed the couch back from the fire and opened the windows. She came to slowly.

"Greg, Greg.'

"I'm here darling it's alright, I shouldn't have put it so bluntly and it is hot in here. But you had to know and I should have told you when we first met.'

"Just hold me Greg, just hold me" Her voice was so low he could barely hear the words. He cradled her to him, his eyes full of tears. Presently she murmured.

"Go on, tell me everything." He brought her a drink and watched her slip slowly after a few sips he took the cup from her shaking hands. "Are you alright Sweetheart?'

"Yes please go on.'

"Well! I found this place which was my grandfathers. I haven't done much in my life that was worthwhile and it was your grandmother that sowed the seed that I could do something with the time I have left to prove my life hasn't been a waste. With help I could make this place into something I could leave for others. If things don't go well with me, I may have existed a while to help others." He helped Olwen to sit up and keeping his arms around her pulling her into his shoulder. She resisted, her eyes never leaving his face, her hands twisting restlessly in her lap.

"I want this place to be a model farm, a happy visiting place for small groups of children who are disabled mentally or physically deprived in some way. I have come to realise that we all suffer from some sort of disablement if it is only bad temper." He smiled at her. "Some suffer more than others and many never realise the burden they are carrying, they may be someone else's worries, just as I am putting mine on you now. If I can help children with problems enjoy a holiday or some time away from whatever they are trying to cope with and they can have good memories to take home with them, then I know that I have not lived in vain, someone will benefit from my dreams. There is so much to do and so little time to do it. When you asked me to marry you I wanted to say yes because I fell in love with you although I knew that I shouldn't. It was a wonderful idea but I didn't dare. At that time I didn't know what I was going to do with the place or even if I would survive the winter without collapsing or going mad with depression. I was taken ill after you left." Olwen caught his arm. "No it wasn't your fault I get turns like that and they are frightening. Bronwyn took me in and nursed me we became very good friends after I told her everything that I couldn't tell you.'

"She didn't tell me." Olwen was distraught. "Why didn't she tell me? I had a right, I would have come straight back to you.'

"That's where I was wrong. I didn't want your pity. I don't want your pity and I don't want you to see me die either, so I can't keep you my lovely Darling. I love you but you must go now.' Greg was crying hard sobs that stopped him continuing. Her arms came around him, they held each other as they mouthed incoherent words of love and comfort, rocking each other they wept with abandonment, caressing and kissing, stopping with mouths, half spoken words.

Rocky suddenly woke realising that his two favourite people were in some kind of trouble came whining and trying to climb in their laps, his rough tongue washing their faces, finding they were holding more Rocky than each other they were forced apart still trembling from the storm, half smiling tremulously at the dog's persistence. Greg rose to let him out. Olwen sitting up straight blew her nose on her already sodden handkerchief a determined look on her face. She took control of her voice.

"Come and sit down. Darling, it's my turn. I know that you still have things you want to say but it's my turn. Let me tell you this. I know that you love me and was not intending to humiliate me as I thought when I ran away. I should have recognised the type of man you were.'

"I'm sorry you thought that but you never gave me a chance.'

I know that now also I know I love you more than I dreamt I would love anyone which is amazing as we have only known each other for a short time. I don't pity you Greg. You break my heart but I can't pity a man with courage like yours and I can't change the way things are, we are both adult enough to know that, whether we can cope with it we must just wait and see. I am not leaving you Greg, not ever.

Your life is mine and mine yours, we can't be changing that either---don't interrupt yet. Please don't let's be wasting a precious moment, let's spend every one together building a future however long or short it may be. I have faith. I believe if it's God's will a donor will be found and I want to be there Greg; please don't shut me out of your dreams. You will be killing me if you send me away. I want to share everything with you for as long as we have. Will you marry me Greg? Not from pity but as a partner and a lover.'

"Oh! My Darling it's not fair on you." Greg's head went down.

"Yes it is because we have a fight on our hands, to get you well and this place running as a real home where we share everything for better for worse, in sickness and in health; remember how it does?'

"Yes, my brave girl. I know now. If you really want me in this state I will marry you but I wish I could promise you happiness and a future.'

"You, Sweetheart have given me great happiness and more to come. You have to fight to get well and stay positive. We will pray every day for a donor to be found because you have everything to live for because I'm pregnant. You must live for your son.

Chapter 32

As the wedding approached Olwen spent more time with her grandmother and her mother Anwen who had arrived from London to help with the arrangements. Although it was to be a quiet affair there was no way Anwen was allowing her daughter to get out of some of the traditions she considered essential, although Bronwyn and Olwen were insistent on low key due to the circumstances. Anwen had her way when she dragged them off to Gloucester to shop for outfits and hats so there was no one at the farm when Greg had his next collapse. He'd fed the chickens and seen to the horses for Fred who had business elsewhere and wouldn't be back until dark. Rocky was enjoying a bone on the porch. Greg started back to the house with logs for the wood burner when pain slammed into his chest driving him into swirling blackness. It seemed a long time until he came to in a puddle of rainwater feeling bruised all over, his chest hurting like hell, limbs useless. He tried to roll over preparatory to getting up but nausea, dizziness and loss of movement in his legs frightened him. He lay very quiet trying to steady his erratic breathing, trying to remember if his pills were in his pocket, adding to his discomfort it began to rain. His breathing slowed and the pain subsiding he decided that he had no intention of dying outside in a cold puddle so began a slow crawl towards the house. His progress was hampered by Rocky who decided this was a new sort of game barked incessantly while licking Greg's face at intervals. Greg hadn't managed more than a few feet when a car turned into the drive, lifting his head as the driver opened the gate, Greg realised it was his father. He gave a sigh of thankfulness and rested his head on the ground. John looking across the yard at Rocky's agitated barking saw Greg's huddled form and raced forward praying as he ran. Sally looking to see what the commotion was about screamed, flung herself out of the car and ran too.

"It's alright dad." Greg gasped as his father reached him. "I'm over the worst. Don't let mother panic." Too late Sally had reached them, flinging herself on the ground lifting his head into her lap crying-----

"John! Ring an ambulance or the doctor. Do something."

Greg was recovering now but very breathless. His father got him to his feet and supporting him they moved slowly towards the house. Greg put a hand out to his mother. "Mam, be a dear and fetch my pills off the kitchen table once I have had them I shall be okay." He panted for breath, mentally crossing his fingers, the sweat of his fear still damp on his brow. "I probably won't have another for months." His father lowered him onto the couch.

"I never realised you had turns like this. Dear Lord, can nothing be done?"

"They are trying Dad. I had a check- up a week ago and they are still looking for a donor as well as keeping an eye on me. Don't let mother get the doctor out, he will only put me in hospital for rest and I can do that here. It's my fault for doing too much. The pain is going now.' Still shaking he was glad of his father's help to sponge him down and get him into his dressing gown. After his mother had given him a hot drink, he was almost recovered. Badly frightened, Sally was almost in tears so took herself into the kitchen to prepare a meal for John who hadn't eaten and Greg who insisted that he wasn't hungry but nibbled at some toast to please her most of which he surreptitiously fed to Rocky. Into this scene walked Ray and Megan.

"What's going on?" Ray dropped his overnight bag and took the tea tray from Sally.

"Greg had one of his turns but he is getting better now." John pulled out a chair for Megan who was looking at Greg worriedly.

"Shouldn't you have the doctor or go to the hospital for a check-up." She asked. Greg had to reassure everyone again that there was no need. An hour later Olwen drove onto the yard. Sally ran outside to meet her before anyone else knew that she was back, as Olwen went to kiss her Sally burst into tears.

"What's wrong?" Olwen was suddenly frightened.

"It's Greg he's had one of his attacks and I'm so frightened. He shouldn't be left here on his own. I didn't know they were so severe, I don't know how he survived. He had this one outside he was down in the yard when we came. He could have died from the cold alone. We don't know how long he was there. I know how ill he is but I've never seen him like this.'

"How is he now? Where is he?" before Sally could answer Olwen was running for the house she slammed open the door as Greg looked up.

"Darling, don't get upset. I'm fine now only tired. It was just one of my warnings that I've done too much." He drew her down beside him.

"I didn't realise, I'm not leaving you again." Olwen held him tightly.

"Well either that or we come and live here until the wedding or Ray can move in. I'm not having this happen again." Sally slammed the dishes down on the table her mind made up.

"I'll not be leaving him again." Olwen trembling as she tried to pull off her gloves.

"I'm sorry, it's just that we don't know each other properly or your family yet. I shouldn't have sounded off like that." Sally hugged her. "I know you love Greg and I can tell that you are a beautiful caring girl. We are pleased about the baby though we have never approved of marriage coming second to the child but these are special circumstances it will help Greg to stay positive; anyway he's so good looking I don't suppose you could help yourself "Olwen laughed.

"I see a woman after my own heart. Please don't worry as I won't leave him alone here again and Ray moves in very soon don't you Ray?" Ray and Megan who had been inspecting the flat came back into the room bringing their cups for a refill.

"Yes and the sooner the better as far as I can see. Greg won't be messing with even the smallest jobs when I get here.

Sally, trust us he won't be doing a thing." Sally managed a smile. "I'll believe that when I see it knowing my son. Megan, I'm sure someone can finish up that pie." She turned in the doorway. "As a matter of interest, Olwen, am I hearing a good Irish accent there?'

"To be sure you are." Olwen laughed. "I did kiss the Blarney Stone once when I was a girl." She bent and kissed Greg whispering in his ear. He smiled at her. She pulled a funny face at him then turned to greet John who embraced her warmly.

"Hello Lass, good to see you again. I am pleased for you both, you are good for him I can see that.'

It's sorry I am if we have upset you about the baby, John but you know it's going to be loved and welcome when it arrives."

"These things are sometimes sent for strange or special reasons and the wrong actions sometimes have the right reasons. We must not judge." He replied gently.

"I'll have that kiss now, Olwen." Ray swung her around and planted a kiss full on her lips. "I've promised myself this. Greg can't do anything and Megan isn't looking.'

"Megan is looking." a voice spoke from the doorway. "Much more of that and there will be no February wedding." She winked at Olwen. "Put him down you don't know where he's been." At her warning delivered in her soft Welsh accent they all laughed. As they went about their jobs of making up beds and settling things for the night, Olwen knelt by Greg's chair.

"Sweetheart I can't bear to see you suffering so, I'll not leave you again for anything. Mother and Gran must get on with their shopping themselves.'

"No Olwen, they want the best for you. You must go with them, I'll be alright.'

John and Ray helped Greg to bed where he fell into a deep sleep while downstairs they gathered to discuss the situation. Sally burst into tears.

"What can we do? We can't stay until the wedding although we will be back up that week. Can you stay now Ray?"

"I would gladly but I have to get back to settle things up as I shall be moving everything up very shortly for good." Ray frowned worriedly.

"There is really no need I only have a very small amount of shopping left which I can do when Fred is here."

Megan broke in. "I am coming up with my mother to sort out the flat and we can do that when Olwen goes with her mother, so I will be here anyway."

"Thanks Megan." everyone breathed a sigh of relief and Olwen hugged her. It was with a better frame of mind they all went to bed.

The following afternoon brought Bronwyn up to meet the family and to see how Greg was faring. He was better after a restful night and greeted her warmly introducing her to his parents. While they thanked her for her care of Greg, his mother confessed to him later that she didn't know if she cared for Olwen's grandmother.

"She is very strange. There is something uncanny about her eyes, they are so light and they look right through you." She shivered; John frowned at her.

"She seemed very honest and straight, one cannot take her to task for the colour of her eyes." Sally gave herself a little shake. Ray admitted that he still felt a little nervous in her company. It was little Megan although she only knew Bronwyn from events in the village, greeted her as an old friend proudly leading her off to see the new flat and inviting her to her own wedding in February.

"I love seeing them all but it's glad I am to have you to myself." Olwen stretched out on her favourite position on the rug. Greg from his chair reached out a hand to play with her hair. Megan and Ray were down the village at her parents.

"I know it has felt more like a week than a weekend but just think what Christmas will be like. It won't be too much for you and our baby will it?" he asked tenderly.

"Of course not, I'm as strong as an ox. I just like having you to myself."

"Be honest with me Olwen. Do you think this plan will work and children will come here to enjoy the farm? Sometimes I get scared that I have taken on so much when I have so little to give." Olwen put her head on her knees so her hair swung forward hiding her sudden tears. After a moment she raised her head looking Greg full in the eyes. Grey clouds meeting troubled green water.

"Listen, me darlin. You are the bravest most splendid man I know. You have a dream and you have made us see your dream. You have already brought life to a child and a derelict farm plus you have given work to local people. You set this up and will see it working providing a future for our child and the welfare of other people's children that we haven't yet met. Do you think Ray and Megan would have given up their jobs on a whim? They believe in your dream, they see a future. It will happen and Greg…" her voice faltered as Greg put his arm around her shoulders, she caught his wrist.* "We must face it just in case, if you should leave us. If God in his knowledge of things doesn't want you to live, your dream will come true anyway. I pledge myself to you. I will see this little farm be the happy place you want it to be for the children that you intend to share it with, your child will grow up here strong remembering through my memories the wonderful man who gave him life and a future and he will learn the same values as his father. It's sure I am that Ray and Megan will pledge you the same. It will happen. Graig-y –dorth will mean the world to our child and many, many other children too, whatever happens."

The silence was long, a log fell in a shower of sparks, the clock ticked loudly Rocky sighed in his sleep. Greg finally spoke his voice husky with emotion.

"What if our little one is a girl, she may not want our dreams?"

"She will still be a Morgan of Graig-y-dorth until she marries then it is up to her to do what is best for her but be sure the farm will go on as a refuge for disabled children whatever happens." Greg buried his face in her hair.

"I want to live Olwen, be a part of it all for many years and watch our child grow."

"You will darlin, just faith that's all." He smiled putting both arms around her. "I am so glad Ray is coming here and isn't Megan a dear? They do suit each other."

"I'll bet he's been a bit of a lad, hasn't he?"

"Just a bit but I think he's a reformed character. Megan seems to have him on a collar and lead. I never thought that I would see the day." They laughed.

"Tell me---Greg said after a while. "How did you feel in Worcester when you found out about the baby, were you frightened?"

"Yes I used to walk the nearby common with my friend's dog trying to sort my heal out. All over the common were patches of thick green grass with circles of toadstools in them; my father called them fairy rings and he told me that if you turned three times in the centre of one and wished hard enough your wish would come true." "And did they?" Greg laughed twisting one of her long ringlets around his fingers.

"Sure I did it night and morning. Anyone who saw me would think it was mad I was for sure but it worked. I soon knew that I must come back and sort it all out." She rested her arms on his knees. Now I must find some more and wish you well again, It'll work you'll see

"I'm beginning to believe in your sort of magic. Ray once said that this place had a rough kind of magic and I believe him but you bring faith and fairyland right into our home."

"And aren't they one and the same thing?" Her face was serious.

"I love you my darling and that's the best magic of all"

"Faith and patience inherit the promises" Olwen murmured softly.

"I believe you're right." Greg hugged her tightly.

Chapter 33

Christmas and the wedding drew nearer. The wet and windy weather turned bitterly cold and frosty. There was talk of snow before Christmas. Olwen had been frantically shopping for kitchen utensils, curtains, bedding and food. The things from her flat at Worcester had arrived to be placed and sorted. There was a regular coming of people, builders, electricians, painters and decorators. Ray's flat was almost finished and shutters for the house had to be put up. There always seemed to be some little job to be finished or a delivery was on the yard. Megan and her mother Gina were working on the flat's essentials. Greg kept himself quiet much as he longed to be in the thick of things as he knew That the wedding and Christmas would be hectic so he paced himself with small jobs and rested as much as possible.

It was only a week to the wedding on Christmas Eve and for once Greg was alone this was rare as since his last attack there had always been someone in the house. Olwen was having a final dress fitting at Bronwyn's, Megan had just left and Ray was due to arrive at any moment. Rocky was let for a few moments for his last run but dashed barking and growling across the yard and for the first time ever refused to come to Greg's call or whistle. Greg hurried to find his wellingtons. There was no sign of the dog but frenzied barking down the road sent Greg hurrying as fast as he dared calling as he went. It was with a sigh of relief the dog came through the gate just as he reached it. Rocky was still disturbed although Greg could see no one about or hear any vehicle. Once in the house he kept growling at the door and pacing the downstairs rooms. Greg did a tour of the house but could find nothing amiss. He ended in the kitchen making his tea when a bang at the door heralded the arrival of Ray who entered with his arms full of parcels and bags. He stood at the doorway full of admiration.

"Wow! When did you get all this done? Haven't been overdoing it again have you?'

"No, this is Olwen's doing. She has been at it all week. Like it?'

'I'll say.' Ray dropped his bags gazing around with pleasure.

The long wide room glowed with the warmth of the Rayburn, its rich red colour echoed in the quarry tiled floor, a large earth coloured rug lay before it. The deep window seats filled with autumn coloured cushions matched the curtains and two deep armchairs which stood each side of the Rayburn where Rocky had taken advantage of no one noticing him and gone to sleep. Greg's first kitchen cupboards were still in place blending well with newer wall units, while the old dresser which had been in the house when Greg bought it; now stood cleaned and polished between the two windows filled with leaf patterned china. The far side of the room hosted a large American fridge, an even larger deep freezer and an enormous electric cooker with a copper hood were built with a commercial dishwasher were built into the pine units and central stood a farmhouse table with matching chairs. At the far end of the room an arch led into a utility room containing wsing machine, dryer and another big chest freezer. The whole made up a beautiful practical home where one could work and relax afterwards. Olwen had done her job well. Ray was speechless. "I could never have imagined it would be like this when all those workmen were here. It's come together very quickly in the end." Greg agreed.

"The children will be coming from all sorts of backgrounds and we want them to find a warm, welcoming, efficient but homely place where they feel they belong even for a short time and everyone here cares about their needs."

Ray had seen all this in preparation but in the last two weeks all these goodies had been delivered so only now could he see the full effect. "Where did all these things come from? You win the lottery or something.'

"Or something--" Greg grinned "Bronwyn's wedding present to us was the larder fridge and deep freeze for this room then Olwen's mother wasn't going to be beaten so she bought a new washing machine and dryer and my parents brought the big chest freezer(our old stuff is all out in the shed might go in the new build somewhere) Their excuses were that they had to buy wedding presents anyway, we are out in the sticks when the snow comes and thirdly we don't know what children we may get that have special needs or diets so what else could they give us?"

"That's brill, Greg and you haven't had mine yet.'

"Not another deep freeze?'

"You wait and see.'

The bright modern kitchen made the old living room look dull and shabby but at the weekend Olwen pressed Ray and Megan into service. Dean came up and whitened the ceiling doing a few minor repairs as he did so, then papering the walls with a soft old- rose patterned wallpaper which everyone told her would drown the room in roses, her only reply being 'you ain't seen nothing yet.' She was right, the room was transformed appearing much larger and warmer. The furniture that had come from the sale room was cleaned and polished to be put in place.

"No point in buying more. The kitchen cost the earth so we have to manage but I'm sorry boys, the curtain and carpet will have to go, they are odd and I hate the thought of blue with rose paper. I'll buy them as a wedding present to myself that's reminded me Greg, I hope you are well enough for town tomorrow, there is something very important to buy." Greg groaned but there was a smile on his face when they returned. Olwen wearing a diamond flower engagement ring in white gold with a matching wedding ring in a little blue box which he handed to Ray for safe keeping. Ray took one look clapping his hand to his mouth. "Oh! My God" and fled from the room. Greg and Olwen stared at each other wide eyed as they heard the motor racing down the lane, Greg began to laugh.

"What? What?" shrieked Olwen; Greg creased up and fell into the armchair.

"Ray hasn't bought Megan a ring yet; bet you a pound.'

"Oh! No. Wouldn't she have said something to him?'

"Not Megan, she would think that he would want them to use the money to buy things for the flat.'

Later that evening a sheepish Ray brought Megan in to show off her hoop of sapphires. Both girls exclaimed in delight over each other's rings then went off to discuss weddings. "What happened to you then?" Greg tried to look stern.

"I clean forgot about rings. Megan mentioned it once and I promised we would look that weekend you were ill. Then I went back to Hull and forgot all about it. I've had to pretend I hadn't of course but that was a narrow squeak, if she had come here tonight and seen Olwen's and hadn't got hers I would have been dead meat. Thanks man, you saved my life." They both exploded into laughter. Greg didn't tell him that Olwen had bought his ring at the same time and it bore an inscription. 'Gregory—Olwen December 24th always Christmas' with a set of gold cuff links for his wedding shirt. He would leave all that to Megan. While they were in town they had purchased a soft green carpet and curtains with brass rods to hang them on. Olwen was happy.

"When we get rich we will have a new three - piece suite until then these will do fine. Thank goodness the bedrooms are painted. I have a weakness for pretty duvets and matching curtains, they are all down at Granny's with the rest of the stuff from my flat, I'll fetch them up tomorrow, hopefully the curtains will fit but they are long so they should.'

The days moved towards Christmas and the wedding with indecent haste. Olwen worked like a slave but refused to let Greg do more than supervise. If Greg could be happy it was now, getting ready for his wedding and the baby making its presence felt the second week in December. Their home building around them, surrounded by family and friends, for the first time he felt the faint stirrings of hope.

The house was almost finished when Greg's parents returned for the wedding. Thrilled, they wandered from room to room, congratulating Olwen on her taste. Sally was in raptures over the kitchen and settled happily to a couple of days baking, willingly helped by Megan in the evenings leaving Olwen to get her rooms ready and wait for her mother to return from London where she had gone a week earlier to meet her husband David who had been in France on business.

John went to help Fred to prepare for guests parking and do what he could to tidy up outside although the weather was against them, it rained or snowed incessantly, never enough to stick but often froze making Greg worry over Olwen driving up and down although the jeep was four-wheel drive; she used to mountain roads and bad winters on the Welsh borders merely laughed and settled him down to write wedding invitations, Christmas cards and thank you letters for the presents that were beginning to arrive. There was so much coming and going that Greg felt very tired and made a habit of going to bed for an hour or so every afternoon. The first time he did this he frightened everyone to death until he explained how much better he felt by doing it. He would have preferred a wedding with only his parent's, Ray, Megan and Bronwyn but wouldn't say so for worlds.

Then it was Christmas Eve and the morning of the wedding. The sun rose glittering on a fairy world. After a hard frost every tree was made of spun glass, every leaf etched in silver with tiny droplets gleaming like jewels in the air. If ever there was a perfect day for a winter wedding this was it. Greg had risen early to exercise and feed Rocky before he was shut in for the day. He was very out of breath although he had only taken the dog around the smallest field. On his return he stopped to lean on the gate and look at the farm in its fairy tale setting. No winter in Hull had prepared him for a sight such as this where everything was so clean, bright and new. Last night had been the hardest frost of the winter so far but how appropriate for a wedding day. There were signs of stirring in the house as lights came on. There was still a great deal to do before twelve o'clock when the wedding was to take place. He hadn't seen Olwen she had been banished to Bronwyn's the afternoon before. Yesterday everyone had been cooking cleaning and decorating the house, Greg had been glad to escape for a time with Ray, Fred, John and David to the Green man for a quiet meal and a drink. He had met David and Anwen for the first time yesterday. He had liked David, a good looking man in his fifties. They had spent some time chatting, he showed great interest in Greg's project. He didn't think that he would get on so well with Anwen, a pretty dark haired woman not resembling Olwen at all except for her big grey eyes. She didn't seem a lot like Bronwyn either she had a sulky mouth and slightly demanding way of speaking. Greg could see why they might not get on too well. After his talk with Bronwyn he could see how things had turned out between them. However she was charming to Greg but he was secretly rather glad she lived in France and wouldn't be inclined to visit too often.

The men had been told not to come back until Olwen had left with her mother in the afternoon. Greg was glad when his mobile rang, he had been feeling tired and weak for the past hour but not for the world would he admit it and spoil the others enjoyment. They had been joined in the pub with the builders Dean and Len, Martin Chimes and Glen Roberts who had refused to let Greg buy any drinks and kept everyone laughing.

This morning Greg could only pray that his heart behaved and allowed him to enjoy this day. He watched Rocky rolling in the frosty grass making soft ecstatic snorts of delight. He would soon be shut in so that he didn't jump over the guests wedding finery. He would be safe here today as two women from the village and their teenage daughters who were going to wait on tables would be arriving any time soon. Although nothing had been seen of Luke Jeffries lately due to the hive of activity, He still had that funny feeling that the man was biding his time to do something unpleasant.

Greg sent up a fervent prayer that he might be spared to see his little one born and safe and the farm ready to provide an income for his family also the others who would be dependent upon it. He had talked with Olwen long and deeply on this subject and he knew beyond doubt that although heart –broken, if something should happen to Greg she was adamant that the project would go on not only for his sake but because she believed in it too. He was amazed at the response already to Bronwyn's appeals. The bank account opened was growing at a good rate while the money that she herself had put forward was enough for the builders to start on the new building, already the shed was down and the site cleared, it only waited on the frost to let up before the foundations would go in.

It had been a surprise to find that David had been so interested in the project. He was a business man, involved in tourism, he had questioned everything deeply and then to Greg's surprise offered to help in any way he could."

"If you wouldn't be offended Greg, I have a brilliant accountant who has a feel for charity work. He practices in London but I could bring him down for a break after Christmas. He is a friend of mine and we play golf together here and in France. Are you a golfer?" Greg had to admit he wasn't but said he would like to meet his friend.

"Good, I'll get in touch with him when you are settled after the wedding. I will have a word with my colleagues too. I should think we could find a few more sponsors there. Bye the way, don't think of buying frozen foods for the farm when you start up. I will take care of that as my contribution, just send me an order when you need it and I will set it up so that you can just order and it will be delivered to your door. Just another tax dodge you know." he was laughing.

"David, what can I say except thank you very much, I do appreciate it." He shook his hand. "All this and you haven't seen the farm yet.'

"I am looking forward to doing so tomorrow but later on I would like you to talk over your plans if you would?'

John who had been listening to this exchange with interest, moved closer.

"My wife and I are looking forward to meeting Olwen's mother tomorrow and getting to know you better, Sally especially is dying to meet her.'

Greg smiled to himself. Anyone less similar to his mother than Anwen would be hard to find... Still it would be interesting to see them all interacting tomorrowSomeone calling from the house startled him out of his reverie. He whistled Rocky shutting him in the stables with food and water until they returned from church. Entering the warm kitchen shivering he realised how cold he had become.

"Where have you been? Your breakfast has been ready this last half hour." Sally still in her dressing gown was bustling about the kitchen. "I have to get on. There are still things to do and Joan and the others won't be here for another hour. Megan is making beds and tidying upstairs. I can't think where your father and Ray have gone.'

"I've just had a bath and Ray is seeing to the fires. Calm down woman or you'll be worn out before the day is over else.'

Greg made himself tea and toast, he couldn't face anything else. Sounds of the hoover came from upstairs. Ray came in for his lighter, gave him a wink and disappeared again. Greg looked around the room, everything was transformed. He hadn't realised until now how much had been achieved. The long pine table had been extended to form a horseshoe, draped with white lace and sprinkled with confetti. Ivy trailed along the centre with tiny golden chrysanthemums set at intervals along it. Gold table mats waited for the hot dishes which were set near the Rayburn to be warmed at the last minute. He had already seen great dishes of salads, cold meats and vol-au-vents which stood in the pantry along with fruit flans and jellies. There was enough food to feed an army without a sign of the roast turkey dinner scheduled for tomorrow, Christmas Day. He peeked in the lounge, while they had been at the pub last night, someone had brought in a Christmas tree and it stood glowing with tiny coloured lights in a corner of the room while holly, ivy and mistletoe were woven into a canopy in the beams above. Rooms had been raided for side lamps to shed a golden glow over two side tables set one each side of the tree filled to overflowing with gifts one side marked wedding the other Christmas, more piled beneath the tree. Large bowls that Greg had never seen before stood on a rosewood bookcase and were filled with holly and Christmas roses. Every easy chair that could be fitted in had been brought in and arranged. Christmas and wedding cards ran in strips along the beams, pinned into place with red ribbon amid green boughs. The wood burner was beginning to give warmth bringing out the scents of the fir tree and the oranges, nuts and rosy apples which stood in baskets on the hearth. Ray could be seen running coloured lights through the trees outside the door through the porch and back inside around a small bar that he had set up in the deep window recess. Although Greg had bought quite lavishly himself, he had no idea where the more exotic bottles he could see had come from. He was suddenly childishly weepy. The house was under some magic spell, transformed from the tumbledown ruin with a tin roof to a glowing country farmhouse filled with celebrations. He turned brushing his hand over his eyes almost bumping into Megan who was pulling on her anorak.

"Greg! Will you please make your mother sit down for five minutes and eat something or she is going to collapse?"

"Where are you going?"

"To get your bride dressed. I am her bridesmaid so I had better be off. See you in Church." Pausing only to kiss Ray under the mistletoe, she drove away.

For the next two hours the house was a beehive with everyone getting ready at once.Fred arrived to see to the horses and chickens. He and Mrs Fred would see them all in church he was followed by the postman with armfuls of parcels, letters and cards. John hauled him in for a coffee and a hot sausage sandwich for which he was grateful as the frost had not given in the slightest. When the women arrived from the village Sally was sent upstairs with a cup of tea and a biscuit, they assuring her they could manage and she had better get her bath before the men took all the hot water. It was almost time to go.

Chapter 34

In the old church at Graigwen, the organ played softly piece after piece which seemed to Greg to go on for ever. His heart raced he surreptitiously slid a capsule out of his pocket praying he wouldn't have a turn now.

"Are you alright?" Ray leaned forward.

"Sure." But his hands were shaking. He took a quick look around at his mother, pretty in a soft brown coat and pink feathered hat. She smiled at him. Bronwyn regal in royal blue sat behind with the Captain. Anwen beside them wearing lime green with a silver fox fur over her shoulders complimenting her dark hair, next to her his Aunt Eddie in grey tweeds, Uncle Walter beside her. He noticed a plain woman wearing heavy glasses who he believed to be Olwen's great Aunt Glenys. Tom Gregson entered, Betty in furs. There seemed to be a lot of people arriving that he couldn't see properly and he wondered who they were. The vicar's wife continued to play softly, a blond woman was sitting near her at the organ; he wondered who she was. A rustle of expectancy, a change of tone from the organ, Olwen had arrived. To the wedding march she entered the church on David's arm. Greg turned to look and was stunned, always lovely, on this her wedding day Olwen was beautiful. Her medieval style dress, cream velvet, its soft folds gathered at the front swooping into a train which swept the floor behind her. Long sleeves hung in points below her waist. In the folds of her dress and in her hair which she wore in a coronet of braids tiny stars gleamed as she moved. She wore no veil and carried a sheaf of dark red roses and green ferns which trailed to the hem of her gown. Head high she swept glorious to where Greg stood his eyes misty at the sight of her. Following her walked Megan breath taking in ink-blue velvet, her curls caught in a hoop of Christmas roses, carrying cream carnations she was a perfect foil for Olwen. There were murmurs and gasps of admiration from the congregation as they rose to their feet several women sobbed audibly.

Olwen came to Greg, her great grey eyes smiling into his as they turned to take their vows the vicar meeting them at the steps as he nodded to his wife at the organ. The woman in blue rose stepping to the altar rail she sang' I know that My Redeemer liveth' in a clear haunting soprano. This was a surprise to Greg who had left all arrangements to Olwen after he had seen the vicar and helped pick the music. Olwen whispered "This is a wedding present to you, Darling," He squeezed her hand, tears in his eyes. The wedding continued traditionally but very moving.

They left the church to the sound of the bells in the frosty air. Another surprise waited at the gate. Ray had driven Greg down in his car but someone had brought the

Land Rover covered in fake snow, ribbons and flowers, the inside fitted with a red carpet with white material laid across the seats. 'Patience waited to take them home.' Too cold to stand long for photos, these were kept to the minimum then in a shower of confetti they climbed in the Land rover, Olwen first throwing her bouquet which was caught with much laughter by Glen Robert's girlfriend, Jenifer to Glen's embarrassment as he had only been going out with her a few months. Greg drove them slowly home to wait for their guests.

Bronwyn lent them her cottage for their wedding night while she stayed with a friend. It was bitter-sweet longing to consummate their marriage, they made love gently, undemanding aware that it could trigger severe pain for Greg. They held each other, holding back the passion with kisses, caresses and tender words. The fact she carried his baby was almost enough for Greg who prayed he would live to see the day of its birth.

At the end of December they went to Swansea to stay with Greg's parents for the new year, Olwen met more of Greg's relatives and renewed her acquaintance with those she had met at the wedding, they took in a few shows and walked a little on the beach with Rocky who thought it a wonderful idea but only went once in the sea preferring to catch sticks. Greg kept fairly well with Olwen and his mother watching him he did little more than rest; of which he was secretly glad. They returned home on the third of January to find a furious Fred. He had caught Luke poking around the house and buildings. As Ray had returned home to prepare for his move and Fred had only been coming morning and evening Luke obviously thought he was safe to visit after Fred had left at lunchtime but that morning Fred had worried that a hinge had come loose on the stable door so had come back early to see to it, catching sight of Luke slipping around the corner of the house. He had run off down the lane when Fred spotted him. "If I had been a few moments earlier or a few years younger he wouldn't have got away" Fred fumed "Especially when I saw him trying the back door. I rang Jeff Arnott I did as soon as I got home. Told the missus I wouldn't be back fer a day or two and camped in yer kitchen fer two nights. Good job yer gave the key ter see ter the stove. Op yer didn't mind? I went 'ome fer me dinner and fetched a bit of bread and cheese fer me supper but I don't trust that varmint. Jeff said as e couldn't do much about it as nothing 'ad 'happened but I seed 'im drive up and down more than a couple of times.'

"thank you Fred but you could have slept in a proper bed rather than the sofa and you should have helped yourself to food, there's any amount here since the wedding and you are always welcome; we are more than grateful.'

"That's not my way. Missus said mind yer come 'om fer yer dinner Fred, when they're away, I shouldn't like someone poking in my pantry when I was away.'

Olwen hugged him. "You are always welcome Fred. What on earth can the man be wanting here all the time.'

"I don't know but I'm glad the dog was along o you. I wouldn't leave 'im here with that one about fer a thousand pound.'

"No it will be a relief when Ray moves in, then there will always be someone about. Thanks again Fred.'

"No need, now I must get on. Glad yer back safe 'om'

Rocky was racing up and down glad to be back. It was good to be home. They spent the next couple of hours enjoying the opening of wedding presents that were oiled on the table with letters and more cards and two large parcels that had arrived while they were away. The first was marked fragile, Greg took his time getting through the straw and packing. Inside was the most exquisite tea service bone china, tiny pink rosebuds on a cream background with a matching tea-pot.

"This must have cost the earth." gasped Olwen. "There's no card.'

"It must be from Ray.'

"No, Ray and his parents and sister gave us that beautiful dinner service. They wouldn't have done this as well.'

"Perhaps it's from one of the aunts?'

"No. They were towels and sheets. Your parent gave us this coffee table and coffee set. Mother was duvets and towels. Oh! I don't know. How can we thank anyone? They are so beautiful. I never could afford to buy them. Let's clear the rubbish and see if there are any clues.' On clearing away the straw Greg found an envelope attached to an inner wrapping, tearing it open Greg drew a sharp breath. "I don't believe this.'

"Who is it?" Olwen looked up from the card she was reading.

"Listen to this Dear Greg and Olwen, you might want to send this back or put it in the Charity shop. Congratulations to you both, I really mean it. We are so pleased for you and hope all goes well. I know tea sets are out of date now but a girl must always have a nice one to show off in a cabinet. Joseph and I are getting married in March. I loved you Greg but you deserved an Olwen. Joseph is a lovely man and now I'm glad I didn't marry you. We both pray all goes well with the operation. Get well, be happy, Good Luck. Stephanie and Joseph.

"How lovely is that? I like that, she's put the record straight. I felt guilty that I've got you and she hasn't. I hope they are happy.'

so do I." Greg replied firmly. You shouldn't feel guilty. It was over a long time ago for me. I only hope she is marrying for all the right reasons. Funny fellow Joseph bit of a poser I thought.'

"Well I hope they will be half as happy s we are." Olwen pulled him down beside her. Who are all these letters from and what is in the other parcel?'

The second parcel was well wrapped and took some getting into. "Darn the knots I'm going to use my knife." A small packet was fastened to a larger one, as Greg opened it he gave an exclamation of pleasure.

"How fantastic! Look Olwen a packet of cards and messages from the lads on the rig.'

"Wonderful, read them to me slowly.'

Greg was very touched. Some of the men had just sent a line of congratulations, others pages of gossip about the men Greg had known and worked with. Cards of every sort from sentimental to gross indecency, he loved them all sitting on the floor reading them aloud to Olwen with little descriptions of the men who had written them.

"This one with a huge leg of pork cooking is from Fatty Jessop, the cook who is not fat but very skinny in fact he doesn't look like a cook at all. He has written- I am coming over in summer for Welsh cakes and Herefordshire steak. Tell Olwen she will be cooking for me for a change. Best of luck to both of you. This one is from my Jamaican mate who told me to go to Jamaica for a holiday. He's a great lad to work with. He writes 'Won't ask about the honeymoon but hope baby's fine. When Greg is fit again come and cook in the Jamaican sunshine with my family. Don't forget now and don't forget your old buddy Jo-jo'." When the messages were all read they opened the parcel. It contained a huge conch shell made into a delightful lamp with a message tied to it. 'To light your way through a happy future from your mates on Varda'

"How lovely aren't they dears? Please say we can visit sometime. I would love to meet them all" "I'll fix something with Tom when the weather is better. They are kind of special. Oh! What is this?" A large envelope was taped to the base of the lamp and addressed to Mr and Mrs Morgan from Tom and Betty Gregson and all the crew on Varda.

"We had a lovely pair of vases and a basket of silk flowers from them. What else would they be sending?" Olwen sat with finger on lip as Greg opened the envelope.

"Glory be listen to this. We are so excited to see that you are making your mark in the world in spite of everything. You are the sort of chap that never gives up so we know that you are going to get well. Congratulations on your venture. Betty and I so enjoyed your beautiful wedding and the chaps enjoyed the masses of photos we sent out to the rig with photos of the farm as well. Please send more as the work develops. The boys are delighted. You can see the result. They all to a man wish you well both in your own future and that of the farm for disabled children. The men are planning a big concert in April to raise some more dosh. Good luck. Tom. The envelope contained three cheques, fifteen hundred pounds from the crew, two thousand from Tom and family and five thousand from the company.

Greg put his head in Olwen's lap and cried. Too choked to speak, she rocked him her tears dripping into his hair. Much later they opened the rest of the mail. It contained Cards, circulars, bills and cheques from five thousand to the promise of eight thousand from an old friend of Bronwyn's late husband. Others promised food, games, beds and household appliances. One firm offered a combined washer-drier. A garden firm were holding trees and shrubs until requested. A branded clothing firm offered to supply anoraks, trainers, waterproof clothing and wellington boots as soon as required. The lists and offers seemed endless. Bronwyn had done her work well. It seemed impossible that there should be generosity on such a large scale when there had been no media publicity.

"Granny knows her stuff she said she would get them. Oh! Greg I think your dream is going to come true quickly.'

"I feel such a fool." he said blowing his nose hard. "I never guessed I can't handle this. I was so worried that we had started something we couldn't afford to finish and would look fools.'

Olwen began to laugh. "Do we want two goats in kid for the children to enjoy, a Trogenberg and an Alpine two years old also some rabbits suitable for children to handle, a tortoiseshell (I thought that was a cat) rabbit. Pair of Dutch Dwarfs an Andulaisian something or other—I can't make it out and two guinea pigs. They also say they can offer some rare breeds of chickens and geese and best of all a pair of Pot-bellied pigs. Oh! Greg!'

"I just don't know where to start." Greg looked bewildered. "We have nothing prepared for this." He picked up another letter. "Oh! Heavens above; this is from a lady in Berkshire. Lady Saunders-Smiles- Medlington- where do they get their names from? She heard via her doctor- (that's Bronwyn's hand again) she is sending two peacocks. I don't believe this- they are arriving by train on January twentieth, she thinks they will amuse the children. That's this month Olwen. Don't laugh help me.'

"Olwen rolled on the rug helpless with laughter. She sat up wiping her eyes. "When is Ray coming?'

"Not until the twentieth and his wedding is on the sixth. He won't have time.'

"We'll manage I'll talk to Fred in the morning." Olwen sat up a smile still tugging at the corners of her mouth. "It's not as bad as it looks. We can ring the goat woman she will have to keep them until after Ray's wedding, we don't have time for them anyway; same for the rabbits. I'll ring the pet shop and tell them we have to get pens; they can go in the stables anyway out of the cold. We'll buy a couple of hutches." Her mouth twitched again and catching Greg's anxious green eyes, she exploded while he watched helplessly as she laughed until she cried. His lips twisted involuntarily as her laughter infected him. In future times the word peacocks brought instant laughter to them both.

The peacocks duly arrived at Abergavenny station with a bag of food and elaborate instructions as to their care and diet, which Fred promptly lost and shut them in with the chickens to the cockerel's disgust' letting them out a few days later to shout their melancholy call over the mountains,

317

Olwen thought them beautiful but extremely noisy and feared they would be frightening to city bred children. Bronwyn when she heard came striding up the road to urge Olwento get rid of them as they were known to be extremely unlucky.

"Do you know that a Gypsy will not visit a house where there are peacocks? They bring bad luck and so do their tail feathers.' This started Greg off.

"Sure it's good luck to keep the Gypsies off and what did the feathers have to do with anything." He laughed. Olwen gave him a level look and said that if Granny thought they were unlucky so did she so she sold them and bought some Chinese Geese and fluffy Dorking chickens instead.

Chapter 35

At the end of January it snowed heavily and they woke one morning to a winter wonderland. Light and crisp it coated the trees like blossom. They enjoyed a snowball fight until Greg complained that his chest hurt whereupon Olwen pushed him into a chair and forbade him to move a finger.

"It's always when I try to forget and enjoy myself a little" he moaned.

"It's my fault." Olwen insisted. "I should watch more carefully."

Ray arrived that evening, the Pick-up piled high with boxes, trunks and bags. A furniture van was to arrive in the morning. After supper and a catch-up on the news (he was disappointed to miss the Peacocks) he went off to see Megan who was working. Olwen was clearing the meal while Greg dozed beside a roaring fire in the lounge Rocky went to the front door growling softly in his throat. Olwen went to let him out but Greg suddenly motioned her back. Taking her hand he led her softly up the stairs to the landing window.

Rocky was now barking and growling at the garden door. Creeping from window to window in the dark rooms they peered out. Nothing stirred the snow which had started to melt clung in corners and crevices leaving the areas between black and mysterious. They could see nothing on the yard but a slight movement in the garden caught Greg's eye. He opened the window yelling which made a figure which had been in the garden and was now climbing over the wall leap down, run down the yard through the gate and disappear through the orchard.

"Two guesses as to who that was." Greg muttered shutting the window.

"Surely it can't be Luke" Olwen breathed in his ear. "What can he want after all this time and in this weather an all? He must be crazy."

"He's queer. Ask your Granny. It just comes into his head to see if he can catch Rocky or just to upset him because we stopped him. Who knows?"

"What can we do to stop him?"

"Don't let Rocky out on his own for any reason we must always take him with us. At night Ray or I will take him out. The moon must affect him or something."

"Are you sure it's Rocky he's after?"

"There is nothing else of interest to him is there? He's banned from keeping dogs but if he could get Rocky, he is a damn good sheepdog, he could keep him hidden, just using him when he wanted but he is cruel enough to destroy him out of spite if he can't have him."

"Greg, what are we going to do?'

"What we have always done. Everyone knows the situation. Bronwyn, Fred, Jeff, the builders and the local farmers; they all keep an eye. Ray is here now and Megan.' Olwen wasn't convinced and decided to have a chat with Jeff in the morning.

The next few days were hectic for everyone except Greg who was supervisory only except for a little paperwork. Megan came every day but wouldn't move in until she was married.

"I'm an old fashioned girl and I have to go home overnight to get married anyway." Ray moaned and complained but she was adamant. "It's not long now calm yourself.'

Carpets arrived and were laid. Curtains hung, Ray's boxes unpacked and furniture sorted then it was Megan's turn to bring all her belongings and the contents of her bottom drawer to every ones amusement and curiosity. "I told you I'm an old fashioned girl and that is what they did.'

"I'll bet Ray got her into bed already though.' Greg whispered in Olwen's ear. "Fact I know because he told me.'

"You can talk, can't you?" Olwen whisked out of the door before he could say any more.

Megan was thrilled to have Ray's grandmother's things. "They are beautiful and I am one lucky girl to have them." She told Olwen who when she saw them had to agree.The flat was spacious and comfortable. The sitting room where the plaster was still drying was to be decorated later. The two bedrooms were painted in pretty sweet-pea colours with matching covers, curtains and shades. The bathroom was an exciting combination of royal blue, pale green and white while the kitchen washed in cream with gingham curtains was just big enough for them to cook a meal in private or if they had guests. The garden door which Greg and Olwen seldom used made a private entrance to the back stairs (once the only stairs) where from the landing a small flight of steps led up to the flat. Greg was amazed every time he came to it that so much had happened in so short a time. Graig-y-dorth was now an impressive house with a flat, two staircases, five bedrooms, two bathrooms, an enormous kitchen and utility and a large lounge, a far cry from the dilapidated cottage with a tin roof. There was still a lot to be done but the worst was over now as soon as the weather improved it would be all systems go to build the new unit for the children. Ray and Megan were delighted with their first home if they needed more room later they would buy house as near as possible but for the moment everyone was pleased with the way things had worked out, if there were shadows in Greg's eyes, a haunted look in Olwen's when alone and worry dimming the joy of the coming wedding, it was because of the ominous silence of Greg's bleeper.

The sky was heavy threatening more snow. A cold wind blew over the mountain and the chickens returned to their hutch after feeding. It was two days to the wedding at Graigwen church and afterwards at 'The Green Man' where Megan worked. Greg went to the doctor's and to collect a few bits of shopping from the village. He drove very little now and only enjoyed a short trip to the village in 'Patience' if he was feeling well. Olwen told him to make the most of this outing as Doctor Davies had already warned him not to drive so his notification from D.V.L.S would shortly arrive. It was only luck for him it hadn't already. Megan was at work, Ray had gone into town on wedding errands and Olwen had much to do. Several guests would be staying with them Greg's parents and Dave, Liz and their two boys. Ray's parents sister jenny and husband Ken would arrive tomorrow and although staying with Megan's parents would be coming with them to dinner in the evening. Olwen was glad that Sally and John would be here to help her.

After a light lunch the urge to leave her chores and take Rocky for a good walk was overwhelming. Giving herself several reasons why she shouldn't, thoughts of a walk before everyone including the forecast snow arrived was enticing. Wrapping up warmly she set off Rocky at her heels although stopping every now and then for exciting smells he still stayed close to her. Although Greg's dog he regarded Olwen as his sacred charge and spent much time with her. It felt good to have some time to herself in the cold fresh air, she enjoyed being alone. It was the first time for a while she had time to herself to think. The baby was very much a presence now although fit and carrying easily she did get very tired and uncomfortable at times. Today was a good day as she strode onwards and upwards. The hill road curved as it climbed so one never realised how high one had gone until they reached the top where there was a car park and picnic area where tourists could sit admiring the Black Mountains which lay ahead and the view which covered three counties. Here in summer crowds ate their packed lunches before changing their shoes ready for the climb ahead. This time of year there was not a soul in sight. The air was clear and cold in spite of heavy cloud and Olwen breathed deeply as she walked convinced it was good for the baby. Through matted grass at the roadside tiny shoots were emerging, a reminder that Spring could not be far away. In a sheltered spot she noticed a gleam of yellow, delighted she spotted a lone primrose in bud.

"Good grief." With a struggle she bent down to stroke it with one finger, loathe picking it out of its nest in last year's

grass "You are too early, don't you let the frost get you."
She straightened and walked on noticing there were tiny
catkins on the hazel bushes and a green sheen on the pussy
willows. In the car park she sat on a large stone gazing at
the hills and the village of Graigwen below her. The cloud
was beginning to come down now and within minutes the
village was hidden from view. Olwen suddenly felt very
lonely and slightly melancholy thinking about Greg, sitting
here she allowed thoughts that she usually kept at bay to
come in. She looked hard at the situation. He was definitely
worse and in more pain than he showed her. She tried to
make him rest taking on more jobs each day to spare him
but it was hard and she longed desperately for the time when
Ray and Megan would be back from their honeymoon and
settled in. They had suggested putting the honeymoon off
until later in the year but as she pointed out he could get
worse and she would need them then more than ever. 'Why
wouldn't that blasted bleeper go off?' Surely there must be
a heart somewhere for Greg before it was too late. Heart
transplants were common these days. Why did his have to
be so difficult to find? How did his father and mother stand
it? She knew Sally had a bad time of it and wondered how
she coped. She realised with dreadful feelings of guilt that
she had never told Greg about the rape. How could she when
he had so much to bear already? That dreadful time had
never left her mind but why should she put that on his mind
when he already had so much to bear? No she would keep it
to herself where it couldn't hurt anyone else. Tears slid down
her cheeks as fear stalked closer mostly she could keep it at
bay as they both kept eyes firmly on the future and their
dreams, now alone, tired and snow pressure building she sat

and cried. Her eyes blurred with tears, the first inkling of anyone about came from Rocky who suddenly left her side and went barking through the woods below. Brushing away her tears she stood up calling, only the sound of barking came back to her.

'Damn the dog I should have brought a lead but he never leaves me like that. I bet he saw a rabbit but he always comes when he's called. That's not an excited bark anyway it's a threatening one. Please God, don't let it be Luke.' She started after the dog hurrying the best she could over the uneven ground calling and shouting as she went. The sound of his barking faded into silence. She tried to run but dead bracken and roots caught her feet, the baby weighing heavy and cumbersome. Several times she almost lost her footing or a branch whipped across her face bringing teas to her eyes. She began to weep openly now with fear and frustration. She had to stop for breath with a stitch in her side trying to listen. There was no sound save for a dog barking a long way away across the valley. She rushed on again; a pheasant fled from under her feet, her side hurting she sobbed aloud. Suddenly far away to her right a shot rang out, a dog's sharp cry of pain then silence. She screamed. "Rocky, Rocky." There was total silence. Flakes of snow hissed through the leaves and drifted into her mouth as she called again and again in desperation. The faster she moved the faster the flakes seemed to fall settling quickly on the fallen leaves, the rustle of snow the only sound on the darkening hillside.

She stumbled onto a bridle path, it was easier going now. Stopping to get her bearings she recognised where she was, she had walked this path before with her grandmother all she had to do was to keep going. It was no use to go looking for Rocky herself, better to try to reach the farm for help. As she reached the road her feet caught in briars, she stumbled and fell into the ditch which ran along side the road. Luckily it was full of leaves which softened her fall but she could feel mud on her hands and her feet were wet in her boots. Hurrying as best she was able, she could see a car on the yard where Ray was talking to Greg's parents. She screamed something she didn't know what as she reached the gate then bent to get her breath. The words came in a jumble as she tripped again measuring her length on the yard. Pain jolted through her then she knew no more.

She surfaced slowly almost reluctantly, to find herself in bed. It was warm and secure but she couldn't think why she was here or why it was dark. She could hear a mummer of voices but couldn't make out what they were saying. She tried to sit up but failing finding she ached from head to toe. Her knee and wrist were bandaged and her face felt sore and stung, putting up a hand she discovered a long sore scratch running the length of her face. Her movements brought Greg and Bronwyn to her side.

"Oh! Greg what's happened? Oh! I remember now I got Rocky killed." She began to cry the tears burning her scratched face. "The baby? Greg, have I hurt the baby?'

"No Olwen sweetheart. It's alright. It's you we are worried about. Granny thinks the baby is alright but Dr Davies will be here any moment to check you over. He will send you to the hospital if he's at all worried. Rocky is fine.'

Bronwyn handed her a cup of tea propping her up to drink it.

"Who's a naughty girl then, racing about the countryside at seven months pregnant? How do you feel now girl?'

"Terrible. Did you say Rocky is alright? How come? I heard a shot and he cried out.'

"Yes." Greg squeezed her good hand. "Someone winged him, Ray and Dad went looking but didn't find him then he came back about an hour ago with a grazed shoulder and a pellet in his leg. Dad took him to the vet but he's fine, it's you that sent us off our heads with worry when you fell on the yard and wouldn't come round. Mother panicked as usual. Ray carried you up to bed, I sent for the doctor, he was out as usual but we tracked him down and he'll be here soon. I rang Bronwyn, Ray went to fetch her. We were going to send for an ambulance.'

"I felt you were better kept quiet until the doctor got here. I examined you and baby is alright at the moment.' Bronwyn took her cup.

Greg was trembling and Olwen realised how afraid he had been for her.

"I'm alright Darling." She tried to sit up but pain and dizziness sent her back to her pillows.

"No you don't, you don't move a muscle until doctor has seen you. You are thoroughly shocked and tired out. At the moment all is well but we are not taking anything for granted." Bronwyn tucked her in and felt her brow. "Get some sleep if you can.'

"How can I we have houseful of guests arriving? What are we to do?'

"They are all capable of looking after themselves. Sally is here and coping well at the moment." At this point Sally hurried in. "Is she alright Greg?" She crossed to the bed and bent to kiss Olwen, visibly shaken herself, her eyes searching Olwen's face.

"She has to take care, Mum. We are hoping that a few days in bed will do the trick'

"I can't be doing that. The wedding is on Saturday and I'm Megan's dresser.'

"They will understand Darling." Greg soothed her. "Let's just see how you are.'

Later that evening Olwen started to contract. Distraught she clung to Greg sobbing.

"If I have hurt our baby you will never forgive me, I will never forgive me. I can't lose him now. I must not. Granny, can't you do something?'

"The doctor has just phoned he is on his way," Bronwyn was stripping away the pillows as she spoke and placing them under her hips. "You must relax.'

"I can't" sobbed the frightened girl. To every ones relief Doctor Davies arrived. He examined her gently then turned to Bronwyn and Greg.

"It's mostly shock. I'm sure the baby is safe. It's not time to send her to hospital it will only cause her more distress. I am going to give her an injection and leave one with you to give her if the contractions continue. If she starts to bleed that that is a different story, send for the ambulance at once. The contractions are very slight baby is moving about a lot and there is bruising" He turned to Olwen. Now young lady I am going to put you out until morning, the contractions should stop and you will go into a deep sleep. Will you stay with her Mrs Rhys?'

"Of course I will and this young man won't move far, I'll be bound.'

"Good call me if you need anything. I hope you all have a good night's sleep.' After he had gone Olwen sank into a deep sleep only waking once in the night to find Greg sleeping in the deep armchair beside her bed. She slept again until a cold wet nose on her face woke her to daylight and Greg trying to coax Rocky back downstairs.

"Sorry Darling, bad leg or not he had to come up to see you.'

"Is he alright?" Olwen spoke groggily licking her dry lips.

"He's fine. How are you? How do you feel?'

"As if I've been run over by a truck but no pain thanks be to God.'

"I'll second that." He kissed her tenderly. "Now you keep quiet. Here's Granny with your breakfast. I must go down I hear people arriving already. See you in a little while and tell you all about it." Another kiss and he was gone.

"I must be getting up." Wincing she flung back the bed clothes.

"No you don't, young lady. You stay there, you are not getting up. You will wat this egg and toast then you may have a shower and back into bed.'

"But Granny I am fine now except for being very stiff and my knee hurts. If I have a hot bath most of it would be gone.'

"Certainly not." The light eyes locked firmly with the grey. "A shower only then back to bed doctor's orders." Olwen began to colour up. "If I don't get on my feet to even see how I feel, how will I be getting to Megan's wedding and I will be going.'

"We'll see eat your breakfast then get under that shower." Bronwyn took her temperature and left the room. Ray stood at the foot of the stairs.

"What's up? Is Olwen alright?'

Bronwyn sniffed. "She's getting a mood on her. She will be downstairs two minutes after that shower and there's no reasoning with her. I can only say so much. She is not a child I can't smack her and keep her in bed. Now the contractions have stopped we can't sedate her either.'

"Ok then. Greg. With your permission Sir, can Uncle Ray have a go?'

"Sure." Greg replied worriedly. "My kingdom is yours but she has a hell of a temper if you make her mad.'

'Leave her to me.' He tapped at Olwen's door and went in. the door closed behind him. Bronwyn and Greg looked at each other, Greg shivered. Bronwyn could see he was overtired, worried and far from well. This last drama was proving too much, He would not be able to cope much longer. They both went slowly downstairs, she sent him to sit in the lounge with his parents and guests.

Ray crossed the room and pulled up a chair to where Olwen sat upright in her bed an angry frown on her face and a sulky pout to her lips.

'Hi. How's the invalid and junior coming along?'

Olwen answered moodily her grey eyes stormy. 'I feel fine, bit sore but I must get up and see everyone. My hair is a mess and it's your wedding tomorrow.'

'You look great to me except for a few bruises.' Ray pulled a chair up to the bed. Mind it's a good job that you turned Megan down when she wanted you to be matron of honour.'

'Matron is the word with my bump, I feel like a house.'

'You don't look like one. You look a very attractive woman to me. Mind you do have a bruise on your face that suggests Greg knocked you down the stairs and you would obviously walk with a limp. I watched Bronwyn dressing

330

that knee last night, not a pretty sight.' He shuddered watching her under his lids.'

'Have I really a bruise on my face that bad?' He nodded slowly bringing her the mirror from the chest.

'Oh! Glory, no wonder my face hurts. Why didn't Greg tell me?'

'Greg is too worried about other things. He loves you too much to risk you in any way.'

'I should be knowing that but I am strong.'

'You are. He's not.'

'What do you mean?' Olwen laid down the mirror and looked at him.

'Have you noticed his breathing lately, Olwen?'

'Yes I have, it's getting worse even though he is doing a lot less. He used to manage small jobs but now he has to use his inhaler most of the time. He is so tired a lot of the time and not hungry either. Oh! Ray, it's so frightened that I am. That wretched bleeper stays as silent as if it doesn't work at all. Do you think it's working?'

'Of course it is. The police would be out here and the phone ringing off its hook if it didn't anyway he checks it.'

'I don't wish anyone to die but surely, there is someone somewhere?'

'It has to be right Olwen. They can't just use any old heart. It must be perfect for him or his body will reject it. They will call when the time and the heart is right for him. You can help in fact you have a vital part to play.'

'What do you mean? How can I help?'

'You can keep him free from worry, you know this baby is very important to him as well as you but if anything should happen to him(God forbid) it would be all you'd have left of him but face it Olwen, you are young and strong you could have more children, Greg may never be able to have another. You are the most important person in his life before anyone including the baby. Can you see the tonic will be for him if he can see it born and know it will inherit this place one day? He is still young Olwen but he is never going to get the chance to set the world on fire even if he gets a donor. At the moment his time is running out fast and if that donor is not found.......' Olwen covered her face and wept.

'I know I am a selfish cow, always was.'

'No sweetheart never that.' Ray put his arms around her. 'Just give in to that good-looking hulk of a husband of yours for a couple more months. He's got it rough, don't make it worse.'

Olwen wiped her eyes and kissed his cheek. 'Thanks Uncle Ray I deserved that.' She managed a watery smile. 'Although I did want to be at your wedding.'

'You shall see it Cinderella. We are having it videoed so you will be able to see it all while we honeymoon in Egypt, loafing about in the sun, pyramids by moonlight eating Turkish Delight, drinking coffee. We'll bring you back some sand and sand-flies, Camel's ----'

'Oh! Do shut up; Torment.' Olwen hit him with a pillow. 'You had better bring Turkish Delight and Coffee. Now go and tell Granny that I am ready for my shower but please ask Greg to come to me first and tell Megan I need to see her if she has a spare moment.'

'She is coming this afternoon. Oh! Lady of the fairest night. Your slightest wish is my deepest command' he salaamed his way to the door.

'Fool.' Olwen called---- and Ray'-- he turned at the door his blond curls tousled, his blue eyes glinting wickedly. 'My Lady you called?'

'Thanks.'

He bowed 'My pleasure.' He left closing the door quietly.

When Greg came slowly into her room, Olwen held out her arms.

'It's so sorry I am, I just wasn't thinking straight.'

'What did he say?' asked Greg curious but relieved.

'Told me I was a selfish old cow.'

'He didn't?'

'No, silly, he didn't, he wouldn't but I was and I'm sorry. I will stay here and be good but tell everyone to come and see me, please don't leave me out.'

'Of course they will. Rest up then put on your prettiest nightie and hold court for everyone here this evening. Seven thirty, your room, everyone brings a bottle. Right?'

'Right.' Olwen's eyes were very bright as her grandmother called her to the shower. Although she was still bruised and sore after a shower Olwen felt much better. Her invitation was accepted, everyone coming to her room that evening to drink the health of the bride and groom except Megan who returned home after her chat with Olwen so she didn't run into Ray but her parents came tobe introduced along with his sister Jenny and husband Ken. Ray's father Ralph Bowers was a large florid friendly man much quieter than his son but with the same fair features and the merry twinkle in his eyes. Jenny featured their mother Lynda both being small and dark though it was soon clear where Ray's vivacious nature came from for Lynda was at home where ever she went and soon had every one under her spell. Jenny and Ken were very engrossed in their delightful daughter Emma who at ten months old held everyone's attention until her father took her off to bed. Ralph took Olwen's hand.

'My dear if we had known of your accident sooner we would not have come here to worry you. We should not be here it is too much. It was that husband and that boy of ours that insisted that we come to see you this evening. Are you sure you are up to all this?'

'Sure I am. I am fine. Please sit down and have a beer, tell me all about tomorrow. Is everything ready?'

'Yes and Sally has been showing us the flat.' Lynda sat on the end of the bed. 'It's gorgeous Pet. I wish we'd had one like that when we were first married.' She passed her glass to John who was acting barman. @We had to live with Ralph's mother until Jenny was born. We have a lovely house now. Greg must bring you down to see us later on. He is like a second son to us. We have been so upset that he is ill but I'm sure he will have a heart soon. Mind living with Granny was good she was a dear. I was rather sorry that Ray sold her house but the money is better invested here, she would have liked that. It's is a fantastic idea, Greg what made you think of it?' She chattered on and no one noticed that Ray was missing until Greg turning to thank him for talking with Olwen realised that he and Rocky were missing.

He slipped down to the kitchen where rocky was shut in whining at the door but no sign of Ray although all the outside security lights were on. As he opened the back door Rocky rushed out passed him barking running for the gate but was grabbed by Ray who was coming back through.

'Thanks, old boy but I don't need you now.' Ray was panting so hard he could scarcely hold the dog. Greg took Rocky by the collar and pushed him back into the house. He could see the state of Ray.

'Good God Ray! You are bleeding man. What's happened, have you been attacked?'

'No I was doing the attacking. Let's get in, it'll be alright now.' As they came into the kitchen Greg could see the state he was in. 'Hell! Ray. Are you hurt bad? Why didn't you shout? There are enough blokes here tonight. Who was it? I'll ring Jeff.'

'I'm not hurt as much as that fucking bastard Luke. I only busted my fist on him but he kicked me in the ribs when I slipped over then I grabbed his foot, that's when he kicked me in the face but I got him and I don't care whether he's got home or not.'

'We'd better make sure. We don't want him to go and die on us. What sort of shape is he in? It's bloody freezing out there.'

'Sod the bastard. He was out there with all these people in here creeping around the wall of the house with a shotgun. So you tell me what he's up too, he could have killed any of us not just Rocky. Some one needs to go and round up the chickens, he'd let them out first. Don't know why he hadn't killed them?'

'How did you hear him? I never heard a thing.' While he was talking Greg had poured warm water into a bowl, grabbing lint from the medicine cabinet above the sink and began bathing the cut on Ray's face and his swelling hand.

'God! My ribs hurt.'

'You've probably cracked one. Let's take a look, better still I'll call Bronwyn down.'

'It'll be a weight off if that lunatic never comes here again. Just give me a minute and I'll ring Jeff. He must go and look for him but I have to tell him what I've done and why. Bye the way, the gun is somewhere in the garden. I just threw it. The police had better have that.' Greg lifted Ray's shirt to inspect his ribs and the discolouration already forming.

'I came down because I thought I had left my keys in the truck, Rocky was growling in the porch so I brought him through and shut him in the kitchen, went out through the garden door and crept around the wall. As I came past the sitting room window there was a dark shape of someone crouching and waiting so I jumped him, then I realised that he had a gun so I got that off him and chucked it as far as I could while still holding on to Luke but he gave me the heave ho and legged it through the orchard. Well I can run a lot faster than him so I caught him and hammered him good but I slipped and that's when he got me.' Ray regarded his battered knuckles with relish. 'I thought if I didn't give him a hiding that he wouldn't forget, any time Megan or Olwen might be here alone for some reason, it may not be Rocky he'd go for. He is queer enough for anything.'

Greg's face was ashen as Ray spoke. He went to the phone and dialled the number handing it to Ray going to the stairs he called Bronwyn. Ray explained what had happened. Jeff promised to find Luke and call at the farm later.

Bronwyn examined Ray's side and hand. 'No bones broken but gosh boy, it's your wedding day tomorrow and you are going to look a pretty sight.'

'So it is and I can't stand make-up.' They laughed though Ray complained it hurt.

'I'll run you a hot bath.' Bronwyn not approving or disapproving left the room.

'Thanks Ray' Greg gripped his shoulder. 'You never know what might happen with someone as unbalanced as Luke'

It was almost an hour until the police arrived. Ray's parents had come down to hear the story again and of Luke's previous exploits. They were in full agreement that the man was unbalanced and needed a lesson. When the police arrived they only stayed a moment to confirm that they had heard nothing be for slipping away to bed.

Jeff Arnott had another constable with him whom he introduced as Steven Shaw who came from town but had been at Jeff's house when the call came through. They had found Luke on the road making for home. He told them he had been hit by a car which didn't stop. Greg and Ray exchanged surprised glances. Jeff looked from one to the other.

'Do either of you wish to add anything to what Mr Bower told me on the telephone? You will need to make a full statement. Luke could change his tale by morning. We will need all the details now.'

'Greg had nothing to do with it.' Ray put in quickly. He knew nothing about it until he came down to let the dog out and I came in.'

'You are sure about that?' Jeff looked hard at Greg. 'You didn't both wade in did you?' Before Greg could reply,

'No. He was upstairs with everyone else, anyway look at him then look at me.' Both policemen smiled wrote the details and Ray signed them.

'Well we can't do more tonight. If Luke persists in his story about a car, you are in the clear but if he's hurt and decides to sue you, it's a different story; regardless that he was trespassing with some motive in mind. We will let you know in the morning when we have spoken to him again.'

'Ray is getting married at twelve o'clock, Jeff and flying at midnight to Egypt for their honeymoon.'

'We'll early enough if there is any news. Let's hope there isn't and Luke has the sense to take his medicine without trouble or causing trouble. I can't say that I blame you under the circumstances but better you had dragged him in here and rang me, not taken the law into your own hands but I know how you must feel. Let's go and find this gun.' They all went into the garden with flashlights. Greg found the gun handing it to Jeff, a double barrel shot gun with the safety catch on.

'I wonder what Like was hunting with this; definitely a word in his ear in the morning. He must have a strange story to tell, lost his gun and got hit by a car late at night. With a bit of luck he hasn't got a licence. Good night to you both and good luck for tomorrow.'

'That's torn it. Megan will go spare instead of getting married I could be going to jail.'

'Come on you don't know that. Ring Megan put her in the picture.'

'I can't look at the time it's half past one. No wonder it's quiet upstairs. I'll have to wait 'till morning. Just keep praying.' He turned at the stairs.

'I'm not sorry. I'm glad I hit him.'

Greg laughed and turned out the light.

Chapter 36

At ten o'clock the phone rang. Everyone was rushing around getting ready and getting in everyone else's way except Olwen who slowed everybody down by demanding to see how they looked or give some vital instructions. John answered the phone shouting to Ray who was trying unsuccessfully to fix a sticking plaster to his face making more of a mess than if he left it alone.

'Mr Bower.' Jeff was brusque. 'Luke Jeffries is not a pretty sight this morning. He has two broken ribs, broken nose, two black eyes and other cuts and bruises. He is in so much pain that he called Doctor Davies this morning; in fact he was there when I arrived this morning. Luke is going to Casualty to be patched up. More to the point he still says a car hit him but he doesn't know who was driving and didn't see the make. That he made that statement in front of the doctor means he doesn't have a leg to stand on. I asked the doctor if the injuries were consistent with a car accident and he seemed to think they could be so you could be in the clear if he doesn't change his statement. The gun, unfortunately he does have a licence but he doesn't know how it got into your garden, he lost it one night when he fell down the other side of your hedge when he was shooting rabbits one night with a torch and he hasn't had time to look for it.' Jeff was laughing openly now. 'I read him the riot act about fire arms being left in the open unattended, warned him about the possible trespass when rabbiting and warned him there had been reports of a peeping tom in the neighbourhood and unless he wasn't more careful about roaming about at night he could be blamed. I think that's enough to be going on with. Congratulations on the day, enjoy your honeymoon but don't let the bride hug you too tight for a day or two.' He rang off before Ray could thank him.' I'm in the clear Greg, so far, so, good. Now let's get a move on. Hell! My side hurts.'

'What is Megan going to say about those hands?' John inspected them. 'You'll never get a ring over those knuckles.'

'Oh! Laws. I'd better ring and warn her.'

'No you don't.' Sally took the phone from him. 'I'll do that you don't see or speak to her before twelve o'clock. Go and get ready and take that ridiculous plaster off, it's curling at the edges.'

Bronwyn elected to stay with Olwen with apologies to Ray.

'I shall be alright Granny, please go.

'No indeed, I am not a relation, only know Megan really. They won't miss me. Ray understands so does Megan, I rung her.'

'So did I this morning.' Olwen said sorrowfully. 'I mean she knew about me yesterday but I rang this morning to wish her luck. Did you see the present we gave jointly with Greg's parents?'

'Yes I did. A reclining chair and a rocker, I bet they laughed over that.'

'Megan said it was just right. Ray will lounge about while she rocks and knits. They were both pleased anyway.' The morning passed slowly for Olwen she kept putting her book down and looking from the window. The afternoon wore slowly on. The promise of more snow hung over the mountains and it was bitterly cold. The thought of Megan in a wedding dress made her shiver. What the dress was like was a well kept secret still she would see the video later. She dozed but awoke suddenly to the sound of a car, voices on the stairs, quick light footsteps and the door flew open It was Megan in her bridal gown, her big brown eyes sparkling with excitement, dressed in white silk over covered in lace. Her veil was lace and hung to the hem of her gown her hair piled high and held in place with a glittering tiara. She wore a white fur cape against the cold and carried white Freesias and Carnations which trailed through maidenhair fern which clung to her gown. Spangled with confetti she glowed with happiness.

'You're beautiful' gasped Olwen. 'You're a lovely, lovely snow queen. Come and let me look at you. Really, really married?' Megan laughed and flashed her gold band.

'Really, really and I had to come straight away for you to see, better than waiting for the video, isn't?'

'Oh! it is. Thank you so much. I did so much want to be there.'

'I did too but you must take care, you all seem to have been in the wars. Have you seen the state of Ray's hands? I won't be able to hug him for a while either.'

'No but he'll be able to hug you. Have a splendid time Megan. Give our love to Egypt and send a postcard if you have time.'

'I'll do better than that I'll bring a bag of sand for the baby's sand pit.' They laughed and hugged. Just then Bronwyn brought Olwen's tea.

'My, My, You look good enough to eat.' Her eyes were misty. Megan laughed again and kissed her. 'I'll send cake and champagne up with Greg. 'You take care now. Bye.'

'She looks fantastic.' Olwen sighed.

'Nice girl Megan always was even as a youngster which seems like yesterday. Nicer than her sister Jean who's all right I suppose, very pretty but sharper nature. Bronwyn sank into a nearby chair while Olwen drank her tea.

'Gran, I am really worried about Greg. He is worse isn't he? He was in pain and breathless this morning. It was a real effort to be Ray's best man but he wouldn't hear of letting him down. Do you notice that he can do less and less; he doesn't look at all well either.' Olwen pushed her almost untouched plate away. 'It is so frightened I am.'

'I know girl but what can't be cured must be endured. You must stay strong for his sake and the little one.'

'I know that was what Ray was saying.'

'I thought that boy had some sense for all his flighty ways.'

'Have you noticed Ray has become quieter and more mature since Greg has become less well? I do wish a donor would be found soon,'

'So do I.' Bronwyn picked up the tray. 'Now you rest some more then maybe you could get up for an hour or two when your guests come back.'

'Thanks Gran. What would I do without you?'

Greg was thrilled to see Olwen in the big chair when he came back but seeing how exhausted and drawn he looked she packed him off to bed in her place while she chatted with his parents and Bronwyn. John and Sally were leaving the next day but Sally confessed she was very worried about Greg and they were only rushing back because they had urgent business to see to and some appointments, they would come back as soon as possible and would ring every day. The next morning saw them leave with tears from Sally as she hugged Greg who looked no better for his early night.

Ray's parents came to say goodbye and were glad to see Olwen about again. They weren't staying for the evening and left early for the long drive home while Jenny, Ken and Emma stayed at the Green Man after the evening do and left next morning.

'Thank goodness they have all gone.' Greg sighed as Olwen prepared for bed that evening. 'I have enjoyed them but can't stand too many people for long.'

'No more now until the honeymooners get back except the parents of course and by the christening you will have a new heart.'

'Will I? I often doubt it.' Greg's eyes were clouded. 'I am teaching myself to accept that it may never happen but I do want to see our project started but most of all I want to see our baby born and to be able to take you in my arms making love as we did the first time not gentle fumbling as we have managed about twice since.' His voice was bitter. 'I so much want to make passionate love to you so much Olwen so much but I dare not and it's not fair on you, my darling. Olwen took him in her arms. Greg was the first to recover. 'Don't cry sweetheart. Promise me that you won't cry over me. I am so happy with you and lucky enough to marry you and have our baby.'

'Stop it Greg.' She fought hard to control her tears. 'It hasn't happened yet. It won't be happening. Now keep your chin up. I love you and I'll wait to make love until your new heart comes. Listen I have some good news for you, did you know that the builders will be back on Monday? There is no frost forcast so they are going to take a chance on the weather and start on the foundations.'

'Are they?' Greg's face lit up. 'When did you hear?'

'Len rang while you were out with Rocky this evening. All systems go for Monday.' Having something else to think about might help Greg to sleep. He did and looked better for it the next day.

True to their word the builders arrived in the morning with three men and two diggers, they definitely intended to get a move on while the weather was right. Within the next week the foundations were in; thankfully the promised snow did not materialise but they were only just in time for at the end of February the frost returned and Ray and Megan arrived home shivering into minus three degrees. Everything ground to a halt. The foursome back together again didn't mind too much. It was quite pleasant to get the chores done and settle in the evenings to talk and T.V. They took turns to do exciting little suppers for each other in their kitchens while they discussed plans for the new build. Greg seemed a little better for the enforced rest and time passed quickly enough.

At the beginning of March the snow came back but not in any quantity but enough to give everyone "cabin fever" To everyone's surprise it was Greg who roused the demon of his old self by suggesting a visit to The Copper Beech. They looked up startled. Greg had not lately moved far from his chair.

'I am not mad. I know it's cold and dark outside and the roads aren't that special but Hell! I'm sick of being cooped up here and you lot must be. I feel good tonight so how about an adventure.'

They didn't need much persuasion but only Olwen's jeep had room for them all. She held her breath as they passed her grandmother's house.

'I always feel as if she can see what I'm doing and she would be shocked at me going out on a snowy night at eight months pregnant so she would, in fact I would never be hearing the last of it.'

Chapter 37

Inside the pub the welcome was warm as was the fire, with very few people in they managed to bag the seats near it.

'It's lovely to see you all. How are you Olwen? We heard that you had a fall way back.' Betty was hurrying to serve them. 'Are you alright now?'

'Of course she is, Betty.' John spoke before Olwen could answer. 'She wouldn't be here now otherwise. How are you dear? It's an awful night out there tonight surprised you could make it down here.'

'It's lovely out there tonight.' Betty brought their drinks on a tray. 'All sparkly like fairyland now the moon's come up.' The foursome exchanged amused glances.

'Are you all recovered from the weddings then.' John leant on the bar fingering his moustache.

'Of course they have.' Betty handed Greg his change. 'Have you heard about Luke Jeffries?' 'She went on 'Seeing he lives your way.'

'He doesn't, Betty. He lives the other side of the village.'

'Now John, he lives nearer them than us. A car hit him a while back he's out of hospital but keeps himself to himself lately. His daughter has been staying with him they say.'

'They say, they say. You listen to too much gossip, woman.' John wiped the bar with a towel. 'Have you seen his daughter? No one else has.'

'Oh! yes they have. She was on the market bus a week ago Mrs Lacey was talking to her. The Laceys knew Maddy when she was in school. They say she left here when her mother died or did she just leave him? I can't remember.'

'You remember too much Dear, that's the trouble.' He turned as the door opened to admit two local farmers who were often in here and the weather had been no deterrent. The girls were giggling now concealing it with great difficulty.

'It's always good.' Megan was struggling to keep a straight face.' They have always been like this especially when there are not too many customers then they have time to listen to each other. It's a real entertainment sometimes.'

'Why do they keep contradicting each other?' asked Ray who didn't get it.

'Don't know but they always have. It's awful trying not to laugh in their faces sometimes.'

"That's Albert Price at the bar.' Olwen interrupted. He and his wife live in the hills about three miles from here. When it snows someone usually Jeff Arnott or Doctor Davies go to see if they are okay for supplies They don't have any means of getting out except by tractor or a very old unreliable Morris Oxford. That's where I was taking the chickens when I met you.' She smiled at Greg.

'People are funny.' Ray remarked lighting a cigarette. 'If I lived up there I would make sure I had a four-wheel drive.'

'Like Patience.' Greg laughed. 'Like Patience. What a find that was. I enjoyed that project.'

'So did I.' Talk between the men became technical. Megan turned to Olwen.

'When do we start thinking positive? I was talking to Len the other day and he seemed to think we might be opening in June if things go alright, he is prepared to put more men on to get it finished in time.'

The unspoken thought passed between them, it needed to be soon if Greg was to see it finished if the heart didn't come in time.

'Shouldn't we be thinking about how we are going to decorate? We should start calling in some of the sponsors or they forget half of what they intended to give us.'

'To be sure' Olwen sipped her orange juice. 'There is so much stuff ordered and promised but nowhere to put it all at the moment. Most people are hanging on to the goods until we give them the go ahead but some parcels have arrived already; two very large ones this morning. I forgot to tell you. I think you and I should be opening them tomorrow and list who from and what they contain then find somewhere to store them depending what they contain of course.'

Megan thought for a moment. 'Mightn't Fred have a dry shed or something?'

'That's an idea. He doesn't come up so often in this weather now that Ray does the horses and chickens so I'll ring him in the morning. Now you mention it Mrs Fred said she had a spare room if we needed it, whether for people or goods I didn't ask.'

'It's great I am dying to get started.'

/Albert Price and the old man with him came and sat near them. He nodded at them'

'There's more snow to come for sure' Greg looked surprised. 'Do you really think so, it won't come to much though will it?'

"Don't you believe it.' laughed the other man who introduced himself as Dave Hughes. His laugh sounded like branches creaking in the wind and he himself sounded more than anything a small gnarled tree, brown of feature like a walnut and just as lined. He was bent at the shoulder like someone walking permanently in a strong wind, sparse grey hair and old grey overcoat completed the image of a wintry, hazel bush.

He went on 'I live towards Hay and I've seen it mild as milk, all the daffodils out, we thought spring had come, and then it turned quick as a flash to three feet or more and bitter cold. Remember eighty- three Albert?'

'Yes I do. We were here in the village but we never saw you for nigh on three weeks or more.'

'I know I got the tractor down to Hay for bread and stuff ten days atter the first fall. We was very near starved out, then a weak later the council came up with a snowplough and grit and some grub, seems some people in hay where we deal was worried about us but blow me next night we 'ad another blizzard and that as the end of that. Always keep a stock of supplies by us 'as yer knows Albert? But that lot nearly finished us.'

'Sure did.' Albert pushed back his greasy cap scratching his bald head; in contrast to Dave he was round and rosy with apple cheeks and dark snapping eyes but seemed to have no eyebrows which gave him a startled look, grey fuzz covered his chin.

'It must get lonely when you're cut off for so long.' Olwen remarked. 'Although Granny enjoys it (so she says) she can't go anywhere so she shuts the door, catches up on her reading and writing.'

'I wouldn't like to live where she does.' Albert rearranged his cap. 'Our place is over spooky but hers is haunted for sure.' They all sat forward in a piece. Ray laughed.

'What does he mean?' Greg turned to Olwen. 'Do you know about this?'

'Well- she began with a smile---

'I heard of this before but never taken notice.' Megan interrupted eagerly. 'Tell us Olwen.'

'You'll have heard of the white lady then, Megan?' Dave tapped his pipe into the hearth. At this point Fred Barnes came through and waved at them. 'Do ee all have a drink with me?' Glasses refilled, Fred pulled up a chair. Megan turned back to Olwen.

'Go on what were you going to tell us about the white lady.?

'Ah! That one.' Fred smacked his lips over his pint and took out his pipe.

'Is it true?' Ray asked nervously.

'Yes, it's true alright.' Dave leaned back in his chair. 'But only on Midsummer's Eve, Lady day and such like and only on a full moon,' Megan's eyes were wide. 'What does she do?'

'Stands on our landing and can be seen from the road outside the house.' Olwen put in.

'Not really?' Ray was leant forward his elbows on the table. 'Have you or your Gran seen her?'

'Well its funny but yes in a way.' Megan's eyes grew rounder.

'You see if you are coming up the road towards the house on a full moon, you can certainly see a white shape in the window but can't quite make it out but as soon as you come into the house, of course there is nothing there. Granny laughs and say's that whoever she is she must be friendly because the cats don't mind her and neither does Samuel Peeps, although to be sure…..she lowered her voice and looked thoughtful. ….Tis strange the cats never stay on the landing though there's a comfortable chair there, anywhere else in the house but never on the landing.' There was a silence.

'Have yer seen the black dog yet?' Fred took a pull at his pint.

'What black dog?' they all spoke in unison.

'The one that walks the lanes on a wild night, great black thing with red eyes, wild as the weather, slinks along the roadsides and through the hedges.'

'Come off it, I don't believe that.' Greg pulled himself together.

'Tis true.' Dave and Albert nodded agreement. 'We've all sin im over the years. Never knows when or why e appears, just does.' Megan moved closer to Ray, Greg smiled somewhat dubiously.

'Mind, that were a strange thing what happened when me and the missus was coming back from Hay rather late after dark a few years back.' Albert pulled off his cap stretching it over his knees. 'We'd been to see the daughter and left a bit later than usual, we'd come over the hill and round the double bends, missus saw it fust. 'What's that

351

Albert?' she says. 'I never see anything like that afore. Look.' So I slows up and there on the bank above us is a pair of devil's eyes if ever I saw 'em sort of greeny yellow like a cats slanted at the corners and big big as oranges glowing sort of almond shaped.'

'That u'll be a horse, Albert.' Fred struck a match. 'They as eyes like that at night.'

'No. It were too low down on the bank, horse could never stand that low. We went back next morning ter take a look and the ground were damp but no hoof marks or any other marks only broken fern. Mind we scuttled from there sharpish I can tell yer. Missus won't let me come that way after dark since. Gotta go all way around the main road if it's anyways near dusk, can't say I'm too keen myself.'

'Some say there is a big cat out on the hill escaped from somewhere.' Dave remarked. 'Never saw signs myself.' The old men puffed thoughtfully. Ray grabbed Megan's hand under the table. Olwen moved up to Greg and pulled his arm around her. Presently Dave spoke.

'Tell you a story about old Bill Shanklin a few years back, lives over Kington way now but then he lived the other end of Graigwen where the old church is now a house.' The others nodded. Olwen clutched Greg's arm tightly. 'Well Bill was coming down to the pub one windy night and always took the short cut past the churchyard. Yer knows it Albert?' Albert nodded agreement. 'We allus cut down by church if we was coming from Bill's or Stacy's farm.'

'Well! Bill comes flying into the pub this night, we was all there. Dashes up to the bar and demands a double brandy, now Bill was always a cider man, so we all looks up (playing cards we was)

Jeff Thomas as was landlord then looks at Bill.' Are you alright Bill? You look as if you've seen a ghost?'

'Ghost be damned.' Bill downed his brandy in one gulp and held out his glass fer another.' Then he said.' Yer won't believe what I just eard. God and the Devil are up in the churchyard sorting out the dead.' Well some laughed some jumped up and came over to 'im. 'How's this Bill?' What did yer see?'

'Didn't see nothing'. By now e was a shaking and a shiverin. 'But 'eard all right, where that old yew tree hangs over the wall I hear this voice very low and whispery. 'One fer you, and one fer me, two fer you and two fer me. 'I tell yer I ain't goin up that lane no more.' 'Course away went the youngsters to see fer themselves. Bill begged them not to go but off they went while Bill downed another brandy. Just now came a roar of laughter as they all come trooping back. One of 'em Jake Newton as I recall come followed by the others, slapped Bill on the back and told 'im to hold 'is hand out. Bill all of a tremble olds out 'is hand and Jake drops two apples in it. 'There you are Bill not God and the Devil but young Trevor and Li Thomas been scrumming apples and went in the churchyard to share them out.' Everyone burst out laughing but Bill drew himself up and turned to go, as 'e reached the door 'e turned back and said. 'I don't care what yer found, I know what I 'eard and away 'e went cause everyone laughed'. Dave paused and leant forward. 'But I'll tell yer this old Bill never came that way agin day or night and never touched a drop of cider or an apple until the day 'e died two year ago. So it was a fair fright 'e got and everyone else allus wondered what else 'e saw or 'eard'. Megan shuddered.

'Oh! Oh! I have often come down that lane. The yew tree is still there although the church is now a house and all the gravestones have gone into another field but I won't go that way again ever.'

'No you won't'. Ray drew her close. They all laughed.

'I mind my grandfather when I was a lad.' Fred tended his pipe carefully while Ray went to refill their glasses, when he was seated again Fred continued.

'There was eight of us at home and we lived near an old mansion at Cwm du. We lived in the gatehouse. There were a lot of old parklands witth a high wall all around. The only ones left of the family that owned it and lived in days of splender, was two old ladies, sisters, always went about together but not a lot, kept themselves to themselves. When they ad some little problem like a leak in the roof or windows wouldn't shut or a fuss with a tradesman, they would call by and ask grandfather's advice and 'e always got it sorted for them. Well both came by one morning, very agitated they was. Mr Barnes they called to 'im. I was in the garden with 'im at the time, this is 'ow I come to 'ear it. 'Mr Barnes, we have a worrying problem and we are very frightened.

'What is it Miss Hadley?' Grandfather touched 'is cap.

'We don't know what to do' They says. 'There's a ghost in our grounds. We have never believed 'til now but both my sister and I 'ave seen it three nights in a row. First we thought it was a white horse or such seen through the trees. Second night we weren't so sure just something white on the edge of the lawn white and swaying about. Last night it came right under our windows floating about the lawn and moaning that it 'ad lost its grave over and over. Mr Barnes, Can you please do something. We are very frightened and didn't sleep a wink.'

Well grandfather frowned, e didn't believe in ghosts and 'ated tricks of any kind so 'e agreed to go up the following night. A few neighbours 'ad got to 'ear about it and when grandfather went up the night a few bold ones went up as far as the shrubbery and all waited. Grandfather unlocks the gate and slips through. Sure enough about an hour later 'ere comes this white thing floating back and fore through the trees moaning to itself 'I lost my grave---------- I lost my grave'. Someone outside the gate called to Grandfather.

'Speak to it in the Lord's name, Will, speak to it in the Lords name.'

'I'll speak to it alright.' Was his response and being spry for his age 'e takes off after it. It ran from 'im still calling it 'ad lost its grave. Grandfather catches 'old of the end of the sheet; for that's all it were, gave the bloke under it a good kick up the arse and said 'You've no business out of it this time of night.' Some bloke it were wanting ter frighten old ladies into selling the place.' There were no troubles after that.'

By that time everyone was laughing. Ray so much that he choked on his drink and Megan had to bang him on the back.

'That's the sort of ghost story worth telling.' Greg tried to control his laughter as it made him wheeze. 'How come there are so many around here?'

Dave cleared his throat. 'Would you believe there are ninety stories of hauntings in this area between Graigwen and Hay –on-Wye. But why I don't know.'

'I do.' Fred put down his pipe. 'Yer see, we are on what they call Ley Lines, right across this valley, same ones run across the country from Stonehenge and links all the abbeys, castles and churches. All churches are built on 'em and it's a kind of build of power. Old folks never built an important building unless it were in a special place.' He turned to Olwen. 'You ask your granny about lay lines. She wrote an article once in our local paper about the effect of Lay lines on people's health and temper. I'm no reader but I read that one and it were good.'

'We'll do that.' Greg made a move for his coat. 'Now we had better make a move. Thank you all for the drinks and great company. It's throwing out time by the sound of that bell. We look forward to seeing you all again.'

'Just a minute' Ray leant across the table. 'Tell me why is this pub called The Copper Beech, seems a strange name for a Welsh border pub?'

The three old men looked at each other. Albert chuckled, his round red cheeks glowing in the firelight. 'Are yer sure yer want's ter know?'

'Of course.' Olwen and Greg spoke together while a muffled 'No' came from Megan. Albert glanced at Fred. 'Many years ago, about sixteen something or other, where Graig-y-dorth is now, there was only a little old cottage where lived a witch.' Here Ray spluttered into his beer and Olwen's hand stole to her mouth. Greg's eyes sparkled very green and a smile stole over his carefully held together lips. Albert went on. 'Her was very beautiful and her name was Bethany. She was a very good witch, cured animals and folk too when they were sick, made love potions too' Ray choked again and Megan removed his glass mopping up the table, her lips twitching.

'Down 'ere where this pub stands was an old 'ostelry fer travellers of the mountains. It was called then Dial Cerrig or in English' the Revenge Stone' No one knows why it was called that but in it lived an evil man called Harold Blackstone; of course 'e got called Black Harry and black hearted 'e was too. Many a traveller 'ad 'is beer watered and 'is food poisoned and 'is money pinched. 'Arry would fight with any who offended 'im and rumour is that some customers never left 'ere alive.' The girls shuddered, moved closer to the men, glancing at the dark shadows around the room.

'Well! It seems Black 'arry fell deep in love with Bethany who naturally enough would have nothing to do with 'im. Every day 'e would ride up on '(is big horse all shinny and black as coal) with a 'andsome face and a rotten heart. 'e kept proposing and she kept refusing, each time 'e became more and more evil. He stole farmers stock for the pubs kitchens and if they complained e would do something bad agin 'em. 'A bit like Luke. 'Megan whispered.

'Aye that 'e was, 'e seduced every woman 'e laid eyes on willing or not until the very name of Dial Cerrig made everyone cross themselves against the evil eye. It was said if a maid gave birth to a babe with black eyes it was 'is fer sure. Men 'ated 'im, wimmin feared 'im and they went to Bethany begging fer 'elp ter put a spell on 'im. She said she couldn't that she weren't that sort of witch only a 'herb woman. After a lot of persuasion she tried some spells but they didn't work. So she went up into the black mountains ter pray an ask fer guidance. When she came back she went ter bed and 'ad a dream, woke up knowing what ter do. Going inter the woods she dug up three little beech trees and in the dead of night come ter Dial Cerrig. All alone she planted them at the back of the building. She tried ter be quiet but 'e came out and caught 'er asking what she was at. She showed no fear but stood tall and looked 'im in the eye. 'Harold Blackstone' she said. If these three trees live fer three years and yer black 'eart becomes as gold as their leaves. I will wed yer but if they shrivels and dies in three years so will ye.' And back she went ter Graig-y-dorth. Well! Black 'Arry must 'ave loved ''er for e was a changed person after that. E cleaned up the inn, banned gaming and gambling, paid the farmers for the meat 'e wanted. The trees grew and flourished, 'e guarded them like gold. When the three years was up Bethany married 'im with great celebrations. She moved in, changes the name of the inn and Black 'Arry ter a changed man. They 'ad fifteen childer and all lived and it's said they earned a family crest with a beech tree on it and every one was teetotal.'

'That's a great story, I love that one.' Olwen smiled at Albert. 'I've never heard it before and always wondered.'

'Is it really true?' asked Ray who had now recovered. 'How do you know?'

'Well! Albert's eyes twinkled. 'ain't yer noticed the three great Copper Beeches at the back of this pub, very old they are and never shows it and isn't it a bit strange there are four families of Blackstone's living in the district?'

'Oh!' Megan clapped her hands together. 'Of course there are, I know some of them. I wonder if they know/'

'Come on you lot, Pub's shut.' Greg got stiffly to his feet. 'Thanks everyone for a smashing evening.' They all called goodnights as they moved out of the door.

'Hey! It's snowing hard out here'. came a shout from someone outside. 'Better get a move on, we're in for a heavy fall.'

True enough, outside all tracks had vanished and the air was thick with driving snow hissing gently as it filled the hedges. After many shouts of 'Take care, good night.' The company were all lost to sight in the swirling mists of white.

Chapter 38

The snow lasted two weeks and the wind blew chill over the hills, swirling it around in drifts, as fast as Ray and Megan dug it from the paths, clearing a way to the sheds and the chickens, so next day it had to be done all over again. Ray managed to get to town one day to step up supplies, taking Bronwyn with him, he also managed to get down to Fred Barnes' to make sure he and his wife was alright as the cold intensified. They were snug in their tiny farmhouse with only two horses and some poultry to take care of. Reassuring them about Greg and warning Fred not to come up until the snow cleared, Ray promised to look after everything and to let them know if there was any news. Fred prophesised that the weather would break in a week and he proved right, almost to the day the wind changed and it began to rain.

As it became warmer and wetter so the stream became swollen breaking its banks flooding the fields below the farm and bringing the ford over the road to the depth of two feet which still kept them home. The mountain road remained icy and treacherous. Olwen phoned her grandmother to be told she was fine, busy with her book and didn't need anything or anyone. At last the rain stopped, the water subsided, almost overnight the sun came out and a warm breeze blew down the hill bringing the whole valley suddenly into spring. Birds made a mad dash to continue nesting but not forgetting their dawn chorus which Greg made everyone get up one morning to hear. Daffodils and Narcissi made a great splash of colour almost running late into bluebells, between birds, flowers and sun it was like a new world emerging as everything fought to get born at once. Lambs called from the hill, great flocks of little birds squabbled in the trees over nesting rights and fat buds began to form in the orchard. Everyone felt a new surge of hope and renewal. Ray had been cleaning the chickens and horses as Fred's grandson hadn't been able to come but half term saw him back so Ray was able to work on opening clogged ditches in fields now bright with dandelions, cowslips and new grass. He also made pens for the rabbits which arrived safe and sound to the girls delight. His next job; with Fred giving a hand, was building shelters for the goats in the rough ground which ran along at the back of the farm. These were barely finished when the goats arrived one evening in a van. The Trogenberg was already in milk although also in kid and Megan had a new job night and morning, which she enjoyed, talking about the cheese and butter she would make when both goats had kidded down. A week after they arrived so did Bronwyn, eager to see the new arrivals. They walked over to the corner of the field where they were tethered. The goats stared back out of yellow devil's eyes.

'Aren't they great?' Olwen held out a cabbage leaf to each in turn. 'The alpine is very pretty, so well dressed in black and white.'

'Yes! well on in kid too' Bronwyn leant on the door of the shelter eyeing them both with consternation. 'You'll soon have your hands full or Megan will, she seems to be goat woman here.'

"Megan thought it would be soon. The person we had them from just said sometime in late spring. I wonder when, it will be lovely to have babies about the place when mine is born.'

'They won't stay babies long though, will they? Then what will you do with them?'

'If it's only one we will keep it.' Olwen replied with a fine disregard for the fact that there were two goats both in kid with a strong suspicion of twins on the Alpine's side. 'We have called them Heather and Magpie because of their colours.

'Oh well!' Bronwyn turned back to the house. 'How are the builders getting on'

'Come and have a look.' Olwen urged. 'We think its too small but the builders laughed and said it was huge'

The walls were up and roof rafters on. It appeared to be a warren of tiny rooms and passages but in reality it would be a building of some size. Len had brought in more men to get the roof on quickly so they could begin work inside. The days were filled with the sound of hammering, whistling and sounds of laughter from the big grey, structure with its many windows which looked so out of place at this stage in its construction. Everyone found it difficult to believe so much had been done in so short a time, yet it didn't seem possible it would be ready to open in July.

Ray to everyone's amusement was now working on a project of his own in the orchard, two pigsties ready for his own contribution to the menagerie. He and Greg had promised themselves a visit to a rare breed farm to purchase some pigs, he had in mind a pair of Gloucester Old Spot and a pair of pot- bellied pigs that children love so much, so was rushing to build really comfortable homes for them, easy to clean, for contrary to belief pigs like their bedding to be clean and dry. Ray had discovered he really liked pigs and had begun reading everything about them he could lay hands on. He was also hurrying because he felt Greg would be unable to make the short trip to the centre and he knew it would upset him if he couldn't go with him. Greg was far from well, the deep worry they all felt was fast becoming a nightmare as they watched him daily leaning on something to get his breath, his inhaler almost useless, attacks of pain were frequent although not severe, there was always the ever present fear of a really bad attack. Ray watched him like a hawk. Doctor Davies dropped in almost every other day begging him to go into hospital for a rest telling Olwen to call him any time of day or night if he worsened in the slightest. Greg refused to go anywhere until the baby was born. Greg's parents phoned daily and came up most weekends. The unspoken grew heavier on them all.

Olwen grew big and clumsy. Her worry over Greg sending her blood pressure up until the doctor threatened to send both of them into hospital unless she rested more, knowing it was not the lack of rest that was the problem. Bronwyn dropped in most days, watching both, her sharp eyes noting every change. She dosed Olwen with raspberry tea and set her diet. She organised anti natal classes of her own, devising and watching her carry them out properly. She also began helping Megan with the enormous task of writing thank you letters to sponsors, banking cheques, paying the bills and making lists of jobs which became urgent as the building progressed. They were all thankful for her help in this. It would have been mainly Olwen's job to book keep in the scheme of things but with the shadow that loomed she stayed close to Greg and watched for him and her baby. Greg's bleeper remained silent. Mr McLoughlin sent a letter which sent hopes soaring, but it was only to tell Greg that a bed was still available and the search was still on, also asking him to consider a bed rest on his doctor's recommendation and maybe some more tests to ascertain how his condition was at the moment. Greg flung it down in despair.

'I am not leaving here with the baby so near, my time is so precious, imagine being trapped in hospital, our baby comes and I die anyway. I would rather die in my own home thanks.' He turned to Olwen.

'I told you how it would be, you wouldn't listen. You will be left on your own to cope with all of this. I should never have started this farm thing. We should not have a baby coming. It's all far, far too much.' He hurled a cup across the room. It hit the wall but bounced onto the carpet unbroken. Ray, Megan and Olwen stood stunned at the sudden out-burst.

'Come on old chap. You know it's not like that.' Ray stepped forward.

'Don't patronise me Ray. It's exactly like that. We are all living in fantasy land dreaming it's all going to come right. Well! we are bloody well fooling ourselves and it's not bloody well going to come right. It might be for you lot but I won't be fucking here to see it, will I?' He slammed out of the room

'Greg' Olwen turned to run after him. Ray and Megan looked at each other helplessly. There was simply no answer. Olwen came back in slowly, tears pouring down her cheeks.

'He's gone, jumped in the Land rover and gone up the mountain road. Oh! Ray I am so frightened.

'Sit down, stay with her Megan I'll fetch him back.' Ray took off at a run for the Pick-up.

It was an hour before Ray came back alone, no sight of Greg.

'I'm sure he won't do anything silly.' He reassured a frantic Olwen. 'He has too much to fight for. He would have done it last year when he first knew and all those weeks here on his own.'

'That doesn't help, Ray, what if he has an attack now when he is all stressed out and driving. You know he has had his licence taken off him until he's had the op.'

.I knew he left it to us but I never gave it a thought, I am going back out, I won't come back until I find him or you give me a call if he's back.'

Before Ray could get in the truck, 'Patience came slowly back on the yard and a dejected Greg got out. Ray rushed forward.

'Are you alright? Where did you go? I drove all over the place.' Greg walked slowly with him back to the house where Olwen went into his arms the tears pouring down her face. 'Are you alright darling? You frightened me.'

'Sweetheart I'm a selfish sod. This thing is getting on top of me. I'm sorry folks for worrying you all to death. I just wanted to run away from myself. I'll get over it. Olwen you needed rest not worry. Come upstairs and talk to me about our baby. I need a lot of that right now.'

Ray caught his wife's hand and hurried her up to their flat where he closed the door and frightened her to death by bursting into tears and crying his heart out, tangling his fingers in her hair, hot tears running down her neck. His sobs finally subsiding she led him into their bedroom where she took him to bed.

The next day Ray finished the pig sties and Magpie produced triplets with ease tiny replicas of herself. The girls were ecstatic but the men exchanged glances of concern. Heather had yet to produce and the sudden increase of goats was alarming. Heather promptly adopted one of the triplets which ever after became hers which caused a major problem as a day later she had twins rejecting one in favour of her adopted daughter resisting Megan's efforts to right the situation. Finally she had to bottle feed the one. It became a daily battle until the kids were three months old when Megan phoned the goat woman who collected all the kids bar one which been bottle fed which Ray named Tubby because of the amount of food it ate.

The day after the kids were born, Ray decided to go for the pigs. Making sure Greg was up to it and had his bleeper and inhaler they set off early in Patience with a borrowed horsebox. Olwen and Megan were busy sorting a huge delivery of wellingtons and rain coats which arrived that morning half an hour after the men had left. Forbidding Olwen to do anything except check them off on the delivery sheet while she loaded them into the Pick-up and the jeep. After a call to Mrs Fred taking up her offer of a room where they could be stored for a time

As well as macs of every size and colour they found a box of mittens, thick woolly socks and several waterproof sheets. The list appeared endless and even when the vehicles were loaded there still seemed to be a lot over.

'I don't understand this list at all' Olwen held a hand to her aching back. 'There seems to be double to what the note says.'

'Oh Lord! Let's take a look.' Megan pondered the pages. 'I think I can see what's happened. There are two different firms here from the same industrial estate, see they are two different dispatch notes, it looks as if two firms got together with the transport. Seems odd but something like that has happened but what are we do do with all this stuff? We can't send it back.'

'Don't worry about it we'll just thank them both. We'll store it at least we won't have to ask for more when the things wear out. This will last us for years. We don't intend to have more than six children at one time and about three adults so it should last a long time.'

'Never mind.' Olwen struggled to her feet off the parcel she had been sitting on. 'I'm not going to worry about it and they will all be different sizes anyway but we can't send all this to Mrs Fred. We'll get Ray or Fred to put it in the attic until the store room here is ready. Mrs Fred has already taken in kitchen stuff and bedding, we can't just send all of this as well.'

'Fine' Megan sat firmly in the Pickup driving seat. 'I always wanted a job where you had to do the same thing over and over again. I've packed both vehicles so carefully, but don't mind me I'm just a robot' Olwen began to laugh.

'If only you could see your face. You look just like Ray when he's had enough'

'I know.' Megan murmured. 'It's catching.' She paused. 'Wait a moment Ray won't be able to lift this great box into the attic, it's too much for one and Greg can't. why don't we pack it into the garden shed? Take the tools into the stables and put it in the shed. It's dry.'

'I can't do much carrying.' Olwen protested.

'Not you silly, wait here.' With a wicked glint in her eye she walked over to where the builders were busy unloading cement. She soon returned with a satisfied grin on her pretty face. 'Done' she said. 'Off you go for a rest although you can make some bacon butties and a jug of tea before you lie down.'

'Charming. And what may I ask are you going to do?'

'Clear the shed and when the men break for lunch they will carry it in for us but it will cost tea and bacon butties this morning, tea and your fruit cake this afternoon. And a can of beer all round.' She called after Olwen who turned at the door with a thumb up sign.

By two all was clear and the parcels had disappeared into the garden shed which Megan then padlocked hanging the key in the kitchen. Looking for Olwen after giving the builders their tea and cake at four o'clock, she found her under the stairs. 'Whatever are you doing?'

'I'm cleaning.' Came the reply. 'It's filthy and room for a lot more stuff if it comes.'

'You be careful,' Megan pulled on her apron to start the evening meal. An hour later everything prepared she was horrified to find Olwen on a stepladder taking down the landing curtains.

'Now what are you doing? Come down off that ladder at once. Give them to me I'll put them in the machine but please go and sit down.' Presently the noise of the hoover drifted down the stairs. 'Oh God! I can't bear this.' Megan rushed up the stairs to find Olwen turning out the guest rooms. She looked up from the drawer she was lining 'Sorry Megan, I know you did all the bedrooms a couple of days ago, but I thought that the drawers needed some of that scented paper, I've made a bit of a mess so I had to clean it up.'

'That baby is coming, isn't it and you are making your nest.'

'I do feel all strung up and energetic. I must do something.'

'Save it you will need it soon enough.' Megan put the hoover away. 'Come on down, the men will be back anytime now then it's dinner then bed for you'Shoo.'

'Alright Mum' Olwen giggling headed off to the bathroom. Running her bath she sank into the scented water, the baby leaping as if it too felt the warm silken water. She lay her hand on the bump feeling the tiny limbs moving.

'Hi Babe, Can you feel me? She whispered. Love you so much. When are you coming out for a cuddle, please come in time for your Daddy to see and hold you. We may be on our own soon baby. I'll break my heart but you will never know what you have missed. I'll make sure of that and that you know every single thing about him. I have an album in my drawer with photos and little mementos

'We will keep him alive for you, Sweetheart but please God we won't need to. Please God, give him a new heart and let him stay with us until at least you are old yourself.' Her thoughts drifted as she dozed in the cooling water. The call of a cuckoo floated through the open window. She smiled; a spring baby coming with cherry blossom and floods of bluebells. How many more springs would Greg see? She closed her eyes forcing her thoughts into more pleasant channels, thinking of the pigs and how soon they would be here. She lay half asleep.

The sound of an engine roused her. Quickly drying herself and wrapping in a fluffy robe, she leant from the bedroom window, not able to see properly she hurried downstairs.

'Don't shout or you'll alarm her.' Ray was trying to keep a straight face. Olwen looked from one to the other. 'What have you done now?' She demanded. A shriek from Megan sent her outside.

'Come quick, it's a Llama.'

'A Llama?' echoed Olwen. 'What the hell are you doing with a Llama? You went for pigs.' There was an ominous silence as Olwen rushed out to the trailer. Greg was just leading the animal out. The Llama stepped daintily over to Megan and thoughtfully nibbled her blouse. Megan drew back too stunned to speak. Ray tugged the Llama away and tied her to the fence.'

'She is very quiet and friendly' he said in a subdued tone. Greg said nothing but watched Olwen's face with a grin on his own. Olwen began to laugh but Megan looked at her in dismay. The men both looked at Olwen hopefully.

'This reminds me of Saunders-Smiles and the peacocks' she choked. Greg gave a shout of laughter and Ray's face cleared in relief. Megan immediately pounced on him.

'This is your doing, isn't it? You put Greg up to it, I can tell. What on earth possessed you? Where did it come from and where are the pigs?'

'Hang on I'll put her in with the goats then tell you all about it. Give me a hand woman and don't stand there asking so many questions all at once.'

'It's not Ray's fault it's mine. Olwen love, we could murder a cup of tea.'

'Of course but you had better come clean.'

'I don't believe you Ray.' Megan followed Ray and the Llama up the meadow. 'You are unreal. How much did she cost? What are we going to do with it and where are the pigs? Didn't you get any?'

'Yes we did. They are coming on the weekend, a pair of Gloucester Old spot and two Tamworth year old both females. We couldn't get them in the trailer because of Natalie, so they are delivering them on Saturday'

'Right.' Olwen poured the tea and sat down. 'Now both of you come clean. Where does Natalie come into the picture?'

'Well! Greg leant back and started. 'We had reached Tenbury and found the road for the farm but although we had the flask we were hungry. Not fancying a main road pub we cut down a lane and found a real old English village, duck pond and all. We'll take you there one day. There was a huge oak tree in the middle of the green where three old men were sitting on a bench having a smoke. All around were little cottages with thatched roofs' He paused.

'Go on' the girls shouted in unison.

'Alright I am going on. Well! The pub was next to the church as it should be in all the best villages, so in we went, the food was excellent. We really must take you there sometime.'

'Greg?' warned Olwen picking up her folk.

'Okay, okay. We had a ploughman's each and half of cider, just about to leave when this Llama comes across the yard and into the bar. Everyone laughs (the pub was quite full) but the landlord comes rushing across cursing the animal. We follow him out and he leads it back to a small field. Ray shouts something about the joys of farming, when he turns around shouting 'Do you want her? She is a bloody nuisance, always getting out, going to cause an accident on the road one day.' Mind we weren't surprised that she had got out as the fence was useless, he obviously thought that a few sticks and a roll of wire would stop her, the idiot. So then Ray opens his mouth and say's 'How much?'

'Motor mouth' muttered Ray with a glance at Megan. Greg grinned 'This fellow then say's how much and how old is she?'

'She is two by the way.' Ray interrupted. 'Now the good bit, the man say's 'Give me twenty –five quid and you can have her, she is nothing but a nuisance here and I don't have time to see to her or mess about advertising. Apparently his wife had bought her from somewhere as an attraction but he had never liked her but she is so tame and friendly' Waving his arms around Ray knocked over his tea.

'Who the wife or the Llama?' Olwen remarked dryly. Greg glanced at her but Megan began to laugh. Ignoring the comment Ray rushed on while mopping his tea with his sleeve as well as his napkin. 'So we did all the asking and paying and here she is.' There was silence for a moment. Olwen passing around the apple pie remarked. 'She is here now. I suppose as we are having sheep and goats it's not a problem but we don't know a thing about Llamas. We must go to Hay and get a book. I want to go shopping tomorrow, it's our turn and I need things for the baby. Megan and I are going in early.'

'More baby things? Ray asked puzzled. 'How much does one little person need? You seem to have a shop full already?'

'You'd be surprised' Greg replied. Our bedroom is full, the nursery is full. I'd have never believed it.'

'Glad we are hanging fire until we get a house then'. Ray pushed back his chair carrying dishes to the sink. Megan and Olwen exchanged glances. 'Let's go and see how Natalie is getting on.'

'I'm going to bed if no one minds.' Greg very pale had a hand to his chest.

'Darling, are you alright?' Olwen looked up anxiously.

'Fine but I won't be unless I can lie down or something.'

'Go on up, I'll bring you another cuppa in a minuet'

'Thanks Sweetie.' He kissed the top of her head and wound one of her red ringlets around her throat. As he left the room they could hear his slow steps on the stairs. Ray turned to Olwen. 'We must put in a stair lift as soon as possible, he won't like it but we should have done it earlier. I'll ask about it tomorrow. He wasn't well this morning on the journey that's really why we stopped. I don't honestly thing he will travel around much more.'

'I know.' Olwen bit her lip, her grey eyes dark with anguish. 'I just have to watch him get worse. Why don't they do something? That wretched bleeper is silent while he…. She choked. Megan put her arms around her.

'Go and take him a cup of tea, see that he's okay then we'll go and look at Natalie. What a grand name for a Llama'

Chapter 39

Natalie was pacing up and down the goat field seeking a way out. Ray had however done a great job of fencing.

'She'll settle in a few days. We must think about a few sheep, the grass is getting too long in the meadows and we don't want goats and Llamas jumping all over them. I think we should keep two of the meadows for hay. We'll need it come winter, probably have to buy some as well as straw. I know Glen Edwards will cut it for us, I have already asked him.'

'You know more and more here will fall on you Ray, don't you'. Olwen put her arm through his. 'Can you manage when the centre opens as well? You weren't brought up a country boy were you?'

'Of course I can. I am in my element and I can learn. Fred is teaching me all the time and the Edward boys are okay too. I am enjoying it. Megan and I must earn our keep and Greg must rest before and after the op. You will have your hands full soon. If this farm were any bigger I wouldn't be able to cope but I know as it is I can give Dean and Len a hand now and then as well. Isn't it coming on well?'

They walked back down the field to the site of the old machinery shed where now stood a long brick and stone building, garish and new against the mountain which rose above it. When the builders were finished a firm of landscapers would be arriving to lay out a lawn near the orchard with flowerbeds all around and creeping plants, climbers and trees so that in years to come the brashness would disappear under their softening influence. Approaching from the gate where the old stone track was to have a coat of tarmac, the water had been piped to form a new stream that ran away from the yard. The building was almost finished, the entrance a strong oak door into a wide hallway where Olwen planned to have a reception desk like a hotel. To the left a huge lounge ran the length of the building with a wide view over the valley towards Hay –on-Wye. Here board games, books and various occupational therapies would be available while at the far end a huge television and video alcove would be surrounded by two settees and deep armchairs. Another large ground floor room was to be used for interviews, meetings or lectures and instructional studies while an annex at the rear of the building was to contain a pool table and dart board also a small soft drinks and crisp bar mocking the image of a real bar with stools and small tables. The rest of the ground floor housed showers, toilets and a big utility room where a large boiler would heat the whole building and provide drying space for wet weather. The connecting porch was large enough to take coats, macs and wellington boots. A lift for wheelchairs and luggage was tucked snugly into a convenient corner. On the next floor were five bedrooms of equal size, two would be dormitories, two for carers and a separate one away from the others where a sick child could be kept quiet and nursed if necessary The rest of the top floor contained two bathrooms, separate toilets. The corridors which ran through the building all contained huge sliding cupboards for storage. The bedrooms contained wardrobes and small chests of drawers with a mirror and bucket chair. Carers rooms televisions and a phone. The whole was designed for easy care and a pleasant comfortable atmosphere where children and accompanying adults could enjoy their holidays. Most activities would be outdoor based but the centre was designed so several indoor activities could go on at the same time should the weather be restrictive. Ray queried as to why the centre did not contain a dining room and cooking facilities but Greg explained they did not want the children to be cut off from what was basically their home for a few weeks. The big farm kitchen in Graig-y-dorth he believed would play a vital role in the establishing a family atmosphere. Everyone would gather around the big table for their meals with the family and carers they brought with them including any staff or visitors at the time. The plans for each day could be discussed, if there were problems all could share them and have lively discussions. Any celebrations such as birthdays etcetera would have a party atmosphere and each child would have a chance to join in and show something of their personalities. Olwen planned to have a kitchen morning each week where they could learn to make things and cook little simple dishes 'not only the girls either. 'She told Megan when they were planning. 'It would be fun to have a boys cook day too' Megan pointed out it would be good to have facilities over in the centre, snack meals or hot drinks in case someone wanted a night cap. After some thought and discussion, the snack bar was set up in a corner of the conference room with a small stove and fridge, and a big cupboard, so easy things like a pot noodle, cup-a-soup, tea coffee and other beverages, cake and biscuits could quickly be prepared.

'Gosh! It looks big now.' Olwen collapsed on a window seat. 'Im sure we have gone over the top.'

'We'll need it, even if there are only six children, don't forget there will be two carers, sometimes an extra child, sometimes they will stay two weeks sometimes a whole summer if there is a problem at home. We haven't worked out the costings yet, sometimes it worries me.' Megan rubbed her forehead as if she had a headache.

The accountant thought it was alright and so did the bank manager so it must be. Anyway my lovely you are a very good book keeper and so are you Olwen so between you all there is no need to worry.' Ray twined his arms around Megan's waist.

'Time will tell.' Olwen stood up a hand to her aching back. 'I'm glad it's happening so quickly. I just keep praying that Greg will see our first customers. I get so afraid sometimes.'

'So do I.' Ray reached an arm to her. 'I always used to be such a flippant sort of fellow, but since I knew about Greg I haven't forgotten even for a day what might happen.' He turned around placing his hands on her shoulders. 'You know we have to keep this place going, between us, for Greg's sake and have no fear but I will take care of you and the baby. Megan has agreed with me on that. We know how independent you are and it is you're and Greg's dream but we are both here for you. We won't leave you whatever happens. I love Greg as a brother and I will never let him down.' Olwen raised a hand to his cheek.

'I know you won't Ray and I know why Greg thinks so much of you. You are truly one of the best friends a man or girl could have. We do appreciate you. Thank you for being you.' She kissed him and turned to Megan. 'I haven't known you that long but I can see that you are made of the same stuff.' Megan hugged her.

'Now, right' said the deeply embarrassed Ray. 'I declare the mutual admiration society closed. I declare time for a bedtime drink and a toast. To Graig-y-dorth and junior, may they come together all right and keep Greg into old age.'

'I second that, let's go and find him and the sherry bottle.'

Chapter 40

As April came in with flowers and birdsong, April showers came as well. Tempers became fraught as time drew nearer to Olwen's birth date and the opening of the centre only months away. Greg's bleeper remained silent and he became worse. Every one begged him to go in to hospital for a short time to have a complete rest but he stubbornly refused.

'Maybe after the baby is born and Olwen is alright. I've told you before I'm not leaving. I shall be going in with her anyways so we'll all be in together if anything should go wrong with either of us we shall be in the right place, won't we?'

The weather became unseasonably hot for the time of the year, even thunder had been forecast, without much sun the air had become heavy and humid. Greg could only move slowly from room to room spending most of his time sitting in the window or outside when the sun came out with some paperwork but even that tired him and he was forced to give it up. Ray bought the stair-lift and had it installed within a couple of days and it proved a great help as Greg was able to sleep in his own bed instead of down stairs which had been first suggested. The deep unhappiness as his health failed crept like a blight in their midst. Sally near to tears for most of the time finally said to Olwen that she couldn't bear being away for days at a time.

'Why don't you and Dad come and stay for a while until we have the baby? Olwen rubbed her on her back. You are only going to make yourselves ill rushing back and fore worrying. Come and be with us instead at least you will be on hand when things happen.' The day they moved in John told his son that he needed to be in the garden every day this time of year. Greg was so weary he offered no comment merely squeezing his father's hand. Ray spent time he could ill afford to sit and chat, keeping him up to date with all that was going on outside.

Bronwyn called in some part of the day every day when she walked Samuel Peeps. Olwen seldom left his side. She read books and newspapers to him, talked about everything she could think of but felt his interest slipping away day by day, though her chatter enchanted him as she leapt from subject to subject. He watched her and listened, living for her bright laugh and expressive face, fretting because he could not hold her and kiss her with passion or make love to her and may never ever again. He dare not think beyond each day.

The weather grew warmer each day, everyone said it wouldn't last this early in the year but enjoyed the chance to see the flowers and trees put on their summer dress Birds were flew madly around the garden, singing everyone awake every morning, diving about every day excited about nests and nestlings. One of the hens went broody as if it were summer so Megan sat her on a clutch of eggs which gave her yet another job to do, her and Ray now had their hands full, taking over all the jobs that Greg and Olwen could no longer do. Sally filled Megan's place in the kitchen while John planted every vegetable he could think off and approached Olwen about getting a greenhouse if he could purchase it himself. She thanked him and told him to do whatever he saw fit. So he went ahead, when it arrived a few days later he soon had it up and filled with compost. In went cucumbers and tomatoes, early lettuce and boxes of seeds. It seemed to Sally as if he was trying to blot out what was happening by filling every minuet with growing things. She was doing similar therapy in the kitchen, filling the cake tins and the freezer with all she could manage. In the evenings they sat and talked to Greg about all they were doing. Later in bed they would hold each other either to cry or lay in the dark silent unable to speak.

Ray went to town with Fred one market day returning with a dozen Jacob sheep and a ram which was sold with them but Fred didn't consider him much good and offered to resell him at a later date and buy better. However the ewes were in lamb and the first day after they arrived so did a pair of twins which delighted Megan and Olwen. Ray grumbled that he would have to watch day and night now and when was a man supposed to sleep.

'I never realised how much work there was in the country.' He remarked to Fred who gave a shout of laughter saying 'This isn't even a real farm my boy but it'll keep you quiet until yer mate gets better.' Fred never doubted that Greg would get better; he had great faith in the Health Service had Fred which kept Ray from brooding as they went about their jobs with one eye on the house.

The weather seemed to promise some thunder as it went dark over the hills and became too warm for the time of year. Greg began to have difficulty breathing in the heavy atmosphere. Bronwyn calling in one morning found him sitting alone in the garden beneath an apple tree, beads of perspiration beading his forehead. His breathing laboured his lips slightly blue.

'Good God alive! Man. what are you thinking of? You can't go on like this.' She whirled into the house startling Olwen and Sally who were sitting in the lounge which was cool with open windows.

'What are you thinking of leaving that poor boy out there in that state?' she demanded. 'Haven't you any sense at all?'

'What?' Olwen flared. If you mean Greg, he won't come in. I have been out there with his mother these last two hours. He says there is no air in the house. What are you doing?' Bronwyn was at the phone dialling rapidly. Olwen was suddenly frightened at the look on Bronwyn's face.

'Is he worse? Oh! My God! She turned to run but Bronwyn caught her arm.

'Not worse exactly but he must have oxygen now. Hello is that Doctor Davies? We have a problem here, Greg must have oxygen at once. No he is still the same and he won't go into hospital as you know. Oh! good you will see to that? Thank you. See you soon.' She replaced the receiver. 'That was lucky, he has just finished surgery, he'll fetch a cylinder and be here as soon as possible. Didn't you notice Girl?' she glared at Olwen.

'I didn't think.' Olwen burst into tears. Sally jumped up.' I'll go and fetch him some iced water and bring down one of the fans. He can have it on the terrace.' She left patting Olwen's shoulder as she went.

Olwen dried her eyes. 'I'm sorry Granny, I should have been more careful of him. I know he's very ill, but he won't let me do anything to help him. I am hot and clumsy and he just sends me to rest. I'm overdue by two days. When I went to the clinic they wanted me in as my pressure is up but I daren't leave Greg.'

'Why on earth didn't you ring me yesterday? You know I can help you.'

'I don't know I am just like a zombie, willing the baby to come, frightened for Greg and this weather on top is too much. I can't think straight anymore. My head aches and my back aches all the time. It feels like one big race between Greg and me and the odds are awful'.

'I have only been away two days because I had business to see to. Bless me child, all these around you. Ray, Megan, Greg's parents, all busy helping and doing nothing.'

Within the hour Greg was propped in an armchair by an open window. Doctor Davies had given him an injection, helped Bronwyn to sponge him down with cool water and placed an oxygen mask in his hand which he found wonderful relief. He still refused the idea of a hospital even for a couple of nights.

Bronwyn sent Olwen to shower, made up a bed on the wide couch next to Greg, where she was given a sedative and was soon fast asleep. Bronwyn went to the kitchen where Sally was preparing sandwiches where she accepted a sandwich and a strong cup of tea.

'I am going back home to see to my chickens' she said as John and Ray came in. 'then coming back for the invalids. I shall be on hand tonight.' John sat down beside her.

'We'll take it in turns through the night.' He rubbed his soil covered hands worriedly over his face. 'Sally won't sleep much tonight either.'

'John I am sorry I was a bit harsh this morning and I had a go at you all but it is different for me because I can do something to ease Greg; I should realise that you wouldn't know what to do bar call an ambulance. I didn't mean to upset Sally either. I do apologise Sally.'

'You didn't, I am so glad you are here. Sally is fine with a sick neighbour but no good at all while Greg is ill.'

'I realise I didn't used to be so hard on a patient's relatives. I'm afraid age has made me crotchety.' John had not been a minister for many years without recognising a troubled mind. He took Bronwyn's hand in his earthy one.

'I don't wish= to pry but I must say to you that if you ever wish to talk I can listen and I know when to keep my mouth shut,' he smiled at her. She withdrew her hand slowly.

'Thank you. You are rather like your son or rather he is very like you. I appreciate the offer, one day I might take you up on it. At the moment I think we have enough on our plates. Im only concerned that I didn't upset your wifr by implying she didn't notice her own son's discomfort.'

'You needn't worry. She is too wrapped in her own distress to notice what you said. She is very frightened today.'

'Yes, something is going to happen today. I don't know what. The baby I think and Greg will want to be with her, so we must all be prepared.'

Sally came back into the room looking pale and distraught she smiled abstractly at them both. 'I feel so useless' She murmured. 'I just wish I could do something'

'You could if you will' Bronwyn shot her a keen glance, her strange light eyes; always had an adverse effect on Sally who smiled nervously and looked at John. 'I would be glad to if it would help'

'Would you pack a bag for Greg, I know he must have one already for when he goes in but he will need an overnight if Olwen goes in first.' He will want to go with her but he mustn't travel more than necessary, They will give him a bed should he need it. I have discussed this with Doctor Davies and he agrees with me. Don't you think that is best?' John stood up. 'You will see to that, love won't you?'

'Of course I will. I'm sure Olwen's and the baby's is already to go.'

'I would put them together if I were you. I've a feeling they will need them by tomorrow.'

Ray put his head around the door. I'm seeing to the animals if you want me. Fred is staying on too. Something is going to happen soon I can feel it in my water. Give us a shout if you need me.'

Olwen came through from the lounge.

'Granny, Can you come? I'm having quite a lot of pain suddenly. I woke up with it

'How often are they coming?' Bronwyn was on her feet glancing at the clock.

'I don't know but here comes another one.' She bent over. 'That's about six minutes I think.'

'We'd better get going. Sally would you give Ray a shout please while I fetch her bag.' Greg appeared in the doorway. 'I must get a quick wash, I am coming with you.'

'Are you up you up to it? Bronwyn's going with her, we could go in later.'

'Of course I'm going, I've practically slept all day. I'm fine it's Olwen I'm worried about.'

'What's that noise?' Ray coming in the back door with Megan opened the lounge door. 'It's your bleeper Greg. What are you waiting for? 'He raced to the phone, calling for Greg as he ran.

'What are we going to do?' Sally began to sob. 'It's all happening at once and all of it urgent' John raced up stairs. 'Come on Sally. Grab a few things quickly we're going with him.'

'A helicopter will be here in less than fifteen minutes. Greg old son, I wish you the best of luck.' With a man hug and a tear in his eye Ray grabbed the jeep keys and ran to start the motor. Greg took his wife in his arms.

'I don't want to leave you to go through this alone and I so wanted to see our baby born. But I have to go too. Please God we'll be back together soon. Don't cry Sweetheart. It's not over yet. Take care of yourself and the little one. I will come back I promise'

Olwen struggling to cope with it all hugged and kissed him tears pouring down her face. 'Oh Greg, you must go quickly. I want to be with you too but you mustn't worry about us, just get well as quickly as you can so we can be together for ever. I love you and it is all really wonderful news. We just can't see it yet. She gasped as another contraction grabbed her. Greg kissed her hard on the lips. 'Love you my angel.' See you soon God willing.'

Sobbing in each other's arms they were lost to all around them until Bronwyn took Olwen's arm and led her to the car. John and Sally came downstairs with their overnight things and Greg's holdall just as the sound of the Helicopter came above the trees. 'Megan are you going to be alright on your own? I'm worried about you alone here with Rocky especially at night.' Sally put an arm around the sobbing girl.

'Im okay I'm just worried sick about everyone and can't do anything about any of it. Don't worry Ray will be back as soon as Olwen's settled, before dark anyway.'

'She hugged Greg.' Good luck Greg bring that new heart back safe.' He kissed her.

'Thank you Megan, for all you've done and are doing. Look after Ray for me'

'I will'

The paramedics were at the door after checking Greg over they seated him in a chair and his parents walking behind him tears in their eyes but hope in their hearts, he flew away to the biggest adventure of his life.

Chapter 41

Megan stood a long time in the untidy house lost in the aftermath of sudden departure. Silence filled the room. Hers was the hard part waiting, wondering, hoping praying, listening for a phone call bringing birth or death, new life or bitter end. She sighed hearing Samuel Peeps barking she let him out and fed him before doing the same for Rocky who was moping about wondering where everyone had gone. Shortly afterwards Fred arrived after shutting in the chickens and feeding the horses, seeing her distress he sat with her for a while. As he left he patted her arm.

'Keep cheerful Lass, they need you here for them. They be all emotionally involved and need a strong maid like you at their backs.' They went about their tasks knowing there wouldn't be any news for a long time.

Fred had finished but was talking a long while at the gate with Glen Edwards who had come to see if there was anything he could do. Megan watched them for a while until finally pulling herself together she set about cleaning and tidying. She sat awhile with a cup of tea cooling at her side staring into the darkening shadows of the evening sky. The hill lay in shadow, young lambs calling demanding their dams answer. The soft notes of a wood dove called from the roof of the shed. The scent of wallflowers mingled with the smell of the bonfire left burning in the garden drifted idly through the open window. It was growing colder now but occasionally lightning played about the hills. There was no bright sunset but a black cloud edged in gold lay across the skyline, promise of a storm before morning. Megan sat on until late waiting for Ray, her thoughts swinging like a pendulum between Olwen in the delivery room and Greg quite possibly already on the operating table. Alone in the gathering darkness Megan prayed.

Greg lay in a side ward waiting. He could hardly remember the journey, so elated with the chance of life, so unhappy at leaving Olwen when she needed him most, so worried about both. In pain both mentally and physically he just lay at the end of a very long journey. His parents had been with him until a short while ago only persuaded to leave when the doctors came to examine him. Greg saw Mr McLoughlin arrive with pleasure. The keen grey eyes smiled into his.

'Good to see you Greg. You have worked very hard at staying alive. I said you were a fighter.' After the examination the Consultants had talked outside for a while then MrMcLoughlin had sat for a while asking what Greg had been doing. Gradually he had drawn from him a picture of the past year. He was amazed at the story.

'I am delighted about your wife and baby. It must be a delight for you.' On hearing that the baby was even now on the way, he commiserated at Greg missing the birth.

'That's sod's law at work as usual. I will phone for news for you and keep you posted. You couldn't have helped much anyway. Men only get in the way.' His eyes twinkled sympathetically. True to his word he phoned the hospital; all was well but baby hadn't arrived yet.

Greg lay thinking about Olwen knowing there was a chance that he may never see her again or his child so eagerly awaited. He prayed silently that his little son or daughter wouldn't give Olwen a bad time and all would go well.

'My love my love. If I have to die how I would like to know which it is, not that it matters but I should like to know.' He thought about the farm and how far it had come in the past year. It was practically ready to open, he felt instinctively it was going to be good, it was going to work. It had the right feel to it. Sponsorships had been overwhelming and still coming. Thanks mainly to Bronwyn although everyone had worked hard. He smiled at the thoughts of all the animals, remembering with a pang that he hadn't said a goodbye to Rocky. His eyes filled with tears for his dog, his loved ones and himself. He prayed again that he might pull through.

He felt very sleepy, he wished they would hurry and get on with it. How long could you keep a heart anyway? He shuddered better not o think about that better to think of a clean white machine to replace his old clogged one. His thoughts turned to Patience who now served them well, he and Ray had enjoyed doing up that old Land rover. He could remember how they had shouted and laughed with glee when they found it. He was smiling as he fell asleep.

The orchard was in full bloom, pink and white apple blossom, grass green and deep, thick with spring flowers.

There came the bleating of goats and their kids and surely the squealing of young piglets. Birds were singing so loud it was almost impossible to hear anything else. He felt well and strong. He turned, the sun was hot on his face and looking down on the house it seemed strange. The old part was familiar but the new building had creepers and vines growing up to the roof, stared with small blue flowers. Surely they hadn't grown that quickly? He looked over the wall that divided the garden from the orchard that too was well established. Soft fruit trees loaded waiting to be picked. He could see cabbages and onions in straight rows, flowers planted he hadn't seen before. The sounds of children playing in a stream came to his ears, shouts and laughter, splashing noises. He turned again he saw Ray digging in a bed of shrubs, weeding and tying back roses. The new building nestled into the background as if it had always been there. A window was open in the farmhouse, a towel fluttering from it like a flag. As he stood watching the gate to the orchard was flung open and a small boy of about three years came running towards him.

'Daddy, Daddy I wanted you and you was hiding' Greg caught him, swinging him around high above his head. He heard his merry laugh, feeling the baby hands clutching his hair, looking deep into sparkling green eyes peeping from a riot of red –gold curls. 'I know you' He heard himself shout with laughter. 'I know you.'

Mr Morgan, Greg? I know you have been sleeping already but it's time for your pre-med and you can go back as soon as I give you this injection. There now you will be beautifully relaxed. Off to sleep again with you then we will take you for a little ride. Sister Knowles began to take the brake off his bed moving it away from the wall.

'Sister there's a phone call.' A small dark nurse was hurrying up the ward. Sister Knowles left the bed and went with her to the office. Greg was dozing and almost asleep as she came back.

'Greg, Greg. Can you still hear me?' she shook his shoulder gently.

'Yes' he whispered.

'Listen carefully. A message has just come through from Abergavenny hospital. It's a lovely message for you. Can you still hear me?'

'Yes' He whispered again.

'You have a son Greg. Olwen and Craig send their love. They are both well and your wife said to tell you that she loves you and Craig weighs eight pounds and has red hair.' A smile spread over Greg's face as he slid towards sleep. Sister leant over him to catch his words.

'That's magic' he murmured.

Lightning Source UK Ltd.
Milton Keynes UK
UKOW04f2233241017
311560UK00001B/49/P